Praise for *What Falls Away*

"The red sandstone and gnarled jun̶ ̶ ̶ ̶ ̶ ̶ ̶ ̶ ̶ ̶ ̶ ̶ ̶
Utah have shaped unforgettab̶ ̶ ̶ ̶ ̶ ̶ ̶ ̶ ̶ ̶ ̶ ̶ ̶ ̶ ̶ ̶ ̶ ̶ ̶
Edward Abbey. Now comes ̶
narrator named Cassandra, wh̶ ns of
exiles coming home. Sinewy, mu̶ ̶ ̶ ̶ ̶ ̶ ̶ ̶ ̶ ̶ ̶ ̶ ̶ ̶ mined, as hard
on herself as she is on those arou̶ ̶ ̶ ̶ ̶ ̶ ̶ r, Cassandra brings us a
vision of what family and redemption can and should look like,
if we get real, as real as the desert demands that we be. Outstand-
ing."

—JOANNA BROOKS, author of *Mormonism and White
Supremacy* and *Book of Mormon Girl*

"No contemporary novelist renders the apostates and patriarchy of the American West with more life and depth than Karin
Anderson."

—CHARLIE QUIMBY, author of *Inhabited* and
Monument Road

"Anderson's novel is remarkable. It captures the unfathomable
complexity of a human ecology embedded in a richly envisioned
rural space. She captures how patriarchy, greed, and privileged
institutional abuse can create generations of harm. The novel
unfolds in gracious sympathy for how complicated and complex
navigating matters of faith, betrayal, greed, fundamentalism
and family secrets can be. She powerfully depicts how patterns
of harm and trauma can reverberate through generations. And
how such inheritances can subvert efforts to escape its lifelong
existential heft. Exceptional in every way. This novel's literary
ambitions are completely fulfilled in what will likely become a
classic of Western literature. Don't miss this treasure."

—STEVEN L. PECK, author of *The Scholar of Moab*

"Like her main character, Cassandra, Karin Anderson is a 'she-coyote'—a truth-teller and a trickster—who fearlessly enters the rocky terrain of family, religion, and patriarchy, to bear witness to a nightmarish collection of ages-old outrages born by women. If Cassandra is a priestess who learns to draw images of what family, belonging, and healing might be, then Anderson is a visionary who understands the transformational power of story."

—KAREN AUVINEN, author of *Rough Beauty: Forty Seasons of Mountain Living*

Praise for Karin Anderson

"In powerful prose, Anderson lets a chorus of voices tell their own often surprising, sometimes heartbreaking stories."

—*KIRKUS REVIEWS*

"A narrative extravaganza that ponders the bristled roots of ancestry, unbroken by time or place, and the muddled truths and fallacies of family history that inform who we believe we are. This masterwork flouts expectations."

—*FOREWORD REVIEWS*

"Anderson's keen prose shreds the myths of American history."

—MICHAEL WALSH, author of *The Dirt Riddles*

"Through language rich in metaphor, that is as rhythmic as melodix as a poem, Anderson reveals to her readers that family is more than genetics, home is more than place, and understanding is always fragmented."

—LAURA HAMBLIN, author of *The Eyes of a Flounder*

what falls away

what falls away

a novel

KARIN ANDERSON

TORREY HOUSE PRESS

Salt Lake City • Torrey

First Torrey House Press Edition, August 2023
Copyright © 2023 by Karin Anderson

Published by Torrey House Press
Salt Lake City, Utah
www.torreyhouse.org

International Standard Book Number: 978-1-948814-79-9
E-book ISBN: 978-1-948814-80-5
Library of Congress Control Number: 2022939874

Cover design by Kathleen Metcalf
Interior design by Rachel Buck-Cockayne
Distributed to the trade by Consortium Book Sales and Distribution

Torrey House Press offices in Salt Lake City sit on the homelands of Ute, Goshute, Shoshone, and Paiute nations. Offices in Torrey are on the homelands of Southern Paiute, Ute, and Navajo nations.

God bless the Ground! I shall walk softly there

—Theodore Roethke

Part One

. . .

Return

Chapter 1

S he believes she remembers everything, that she's come to terms with Clearlake Valley, even Big Horn itself.

She might be able to frame it and walk away.

The first shock: miles and acres—and more miles and more acres—of franchise malls, subdivisions, freeway tangles, and Mormon churches like brooding hens every half mile in any direction. Glittering cloned temples on the foothills, gold-plated replicants of the Angel Moroni blowing a long trumpet atop the middle spires.

Cassandra should have expected this. It's not like she's lived in a thirty-six-year time warp. The Midwest, too, has been stockpiling Walmarts and spaghetti overpasses and cheap-housing clusterfucks. She's read about flames and smoke choking each succeeding Great Basin summer. But here, now, turning north on the Ninth East Clearlake exit—the rush of magnitude, incomprehensible change in the fifteen uncanny miles between her and the foot of Big Horn Mountain (recently blackened, gashed with flash flood ravines), where her mother may or may not understand she awaits her daughter's arrival.

Cassandra traces what was once a narrow country road toward town. She strains to picture the precise spot on the old one-lane freeway entrance, once so unkempt and remote that Jane May, just licensed to drive, a class ahead of Cassandra's, had stared with iced-over eyes into the side ditch, all night long with

her head smashed into the windshield. Frigid dawn before someone passed near enough to spot a dead girl in a Volkswagen.

Despite the many lanes, the old route is evident. A mile
north. Left on State. Right on Third East. Thirteen miles north
toward Big Horn Mountain, Big Horn City at its base. As if she
drove the route just last week (as if hundreds of subdivisions and
Mormon churches and supermarkets had sprung up like dry
fungus just yesterday).

Nothing but seismic violence can alter that skyline.

The precise problem with death, she recalls again (and
again), even though she doesn't want to recall Jane May (for
example), is the fact of the body. Maybe pondering those old
lies about resurrection allowed her, early on, to fray the religious
lifeline. The horror of her grandmother's skin, brain and guts,
and bone, and iron-gray hair, awash in a heavy box until the
churning planet sprays the atoms free.

The problem with you, Cassandra (her father's voice butts
into her headspace), *is that you don't learn to stop picturing
things. That doesn't mean your pictures match the truth.*

Well, right? Her father had turned so many of Cassandra's
"problems" into pithy diagnoses, she should have compiled
them into a $2.99 truck-stop parenting manual: *How to Fix Your
Daughter in 10,000 Random Homilies*, by Hal Soelberg, Who Just
Knows Things.

Then again, the problem *is* that she can't stop picturing
things.

She tells her car to text her brother James, who appointed
himself family patriarch after Hal's death. *ETA twenty minutes.*
No reply, but the screen says he's read it.

Flat valley approach, broadened since her childhood. An
upward angle levels into the shallows of long-extinct water. Big
Horn City a round ghost bay at the feet of colliding ranges. Orig-
inally it was accessible, at least by car, only here at the strait. Now
Cassandra is surprised to see a new road, lined with faux Tudors

and ski mansions, straddling the foothills toward the Salt Lake Valley.

Up Main, right, and left, north again facing the fang-tooth jag of Big Horn itself, passing ostensibly pastoral Cemetery Hill, muffling her grandmother and unquiet father. A cousin she never knew, brains blown clean via self-inflicted birdshot. Six Big Horn settler generations. Probably Shoshone and Pai-ute remains as well, older, hopefully far more comfortable where they lie. Higher, at the crown of the hill: pioneer children, lined in rows, commemorated by tiny lambs and sentimental verse:

...too pure for earth, the angel said...

Cholera. What even is cholera? She doesn't really wish to know.

A right curve, again gaining altitude. The city proper sits at five thousand feet. Her parents' place two hundred higher, where jutting foothills crease up from phantom strands. Once they were the outskirt hillbillies, but now her childhood home sits in obeisance to rich foothill estates. Grandma's house gone, her proud little acre bisected by a cul-de-sac of faux-stone monstrosities. Steady rise for one more mile. Grim crank into the driveway.

Her childhood home looks shabby and quaint in contrast to the new-money facades that alter the mountain and valley views from every side. But the yard is neatly trimmed, the roof in good repair. She knows this is Brian's doing.

Early summer, and already smoke in the air. Rumors of sickness and war, as the crisis mongers in this town will reassure one another, are merely God's hand upon the wicked. Nothing to fear in Zion. Ammo to spare.

Hot shimmer kneads unsettled atmosphere above the western hills.

Cassandra sits, windows closed, ignition off.

Sweat drips down the back of her neck, moistens her temples.

The engine ticks like an alarm clock.

Chapter 2

N|o sign of presence. The curtains are closed. Winter doors shut firm behind the summer screens. No one could possibly be inside, shut tight in this heat. Cassandra pictures her mother melted to butter.

She considers pulling the car into the shelter of the carport, but it feels audacious. She is a stranger. She opens the windows and kills the engine, here in the sun. An air-conditioning unit hums ragged, set somewhere behind the west wall. Now she pictures Dorothy encased in Freon ice.

Just. Get this over with.

She opens herself out. Stepping onto hot concrete, Cassandra lifts her face north to the high granite of the Big Horn Range, close and distant and insistent. Snow clings in the shadow lines. She swivels rightward, holding her sight above the insult of grandiose rooftops. Her eye traces the summit lines as they collide with older Wasatch limestone heading another direction entirely. She's told herself—and her people beyond this place— that her first geography is no big deal, that memory is warped in hyperbole. She has likened this return to revisiting a comically diminished first grade classroom.

But it is not so. The up-heave stone magnitude cools her legs behind the knees, softens the small of her back, like a first hit of good tequila.

. . .

She walks toward the house with nothing in her hands. Plenty of time to unpack, but the truer point is that she's not ready to lay objects from one temporal dimension upon the prior. Her lungs sting in the arid smoky air, devoid of the scent or sensation of Minnesota water. She chooses the front over the familial side door, stands at the threshold considering whether to knock. She reaches gingerly to unlatch the screen, holds it ajar with her heel, turns the heavier knob, and calls into the stifling chill. "Mom? James? Brian? Anybody home?"

She steps onto freakish white carpet (did she expect the old green shag?), protected here at the entry by a clear vinyl shield. The room smells like airconditioned fabric freshener.

"Mom—Mother? It's Cassandra. James told you I'm coming, right?"

Cassandra hears faint busy humming from the kitchen.

"Mom? Don't let me startle you. I'm coming around the corner. It's Cassandra. Okay?"

A wizened rendition of her impeccable, impenetrable mother stands at the sink. Even so, unmistakable: the compulsive thrust of Dorothy's shoulder at the scouring pad. A single copper pot in her hand, in the water, already clean—a prop in a teleplay. Soap bubbles cascade over the counter to the laminate floor.

Cassandra steps toward the old woman and leans gently to shut off the faucet.

Dorothy turns her face in Kewpie surprise. "Oh! Hello there! I didn't see you!"

"Mama. The water was about to run over."

Dorothy's expression arrests under a sequence of gaps and blinks, as if she is clicking through a tray of photographic slides.

"Emma? When did you come in?"

"No, Mama. It's Cassandra. I just pulled in a minute ago."

Dorothy's eyes open wide. She steps back for a clearer perspective. Cassandra stands, helpless and frank, as her mother strains to process.

"That's funny. For a minute you looked so much like my sister Emma I thought it was her. But she's dead now." Dorothy reaches for her own face, searching for something. "Isn't that right?"

"I—I think so?"

"Well, you've really come to resemble her. But you're Cassandra. How could I mistake my own daughter?"

Cassandra cannot discern the lucid from the demented.

Dorothy inquires: "How are your classes coming along?"

Okay, demented. Even so, her mother sounds closer to human now than she did in prior life. She's tempered the cutie-pie intonations Cassandra once thought were integral. Slightly. Cassandra shivers as if it were cold, and in fact it is: the air-conditioning has chilled the house to something like sixty.

"Did you bring a warm pair of boots?" Dorothy asks. "You're going to need them."

Cassandra gapes. Dorothy gazes, blank.

Who is this old woman? In what cosmos does she reside? Last time Cassandra saw her mother in the flesh, Dorothy was—what? Forty-nine? Cassandra is now at least ten years older than the woman who pushed a desperately token twenty-dollar bill into Cassandra's coat pocket, just before Cassandra pulled away once and for all. James has furnished no intelligence beyond the self-righteous missive he sent last month, routed through Cassandra's professional website. She hasn't exactly been hiding, but this was his first—his only—effort to make contact in over three decades.

...It is your duty as the daughter of the family to return home to care for our mother. You have no children of your own, which makes it all the more shocking that you would not see caring for a helpless elderly woman as your primary moral responsibility. I am weighed down by Professional Demands and by my Calling

as First Counselor in our Ward. My wife and myself have nearly exhausted our Selves making sure there is someone in the house with her at all times. We have provided meals, helped her bathe, and washed her clothing. The Relief Society has assisted us, as is proper in the Church's design, but our mother must not be reduced in the eyes of the Ward to an object of charity. Brian and his wife do what they can but they continue to farm her family's property and must meet the Water Schedule. You have neglected your duties long enough...

*...blah blah blahblahblah...*such pompous bullshit it barely warrants personal offense. James never did have the courage—or brains—to inhabit himself beyond role play, and Cassandra has long since learned to blunt the impact of his religious theatrics.

Cassandra guesses she might persuade Brian to talk. Human to human. Or his wife. She once knew the girls who grew up to marry Soelberg brothers. They do have names: James married Paige Jenkins, drill mistress of the Big Horn Ramettes as Cassandra recalls her—shrewd beneath a vacuous, immaculate sheen. Brian married Elaine Goddard—a true farm girl and a good match, Cassandra surmises from the filtered distance of hometown traumas. But she'll be religious. Bone-deep and home-churned.

She realizes, and then forgets in a matter of seconds, and then remembers again, that she's buzzing in emotional and temporal shock. Thirty-six years since she's stood in this kitchen, in this town, beneath these mountains, inside (but ever quite beyond) this impenetrable population.

Here.

Decades since she's breathed the same dry (and now artificially chilled) air as her mother, so familiar and so changed there is nothing to do but pick up with the practical tasks of the moment, as if there has been no gap. No breach. No death.

No child. No loss.

Or maybe nothing *but* loss, an unbroken featureless field.

Dorothy, she means.

Dorothy speaks it: "I can't quite place what kind of thing this is. I don't understand—you know—when are we. Now, I mean."

Cassandra reaches with both hands. Dorothy takes them in hers, more childlike than maternal. Cassandra pulls her mother close, shocked by the frail bird bones, and embraces her, awkward but tender. Dorothy sinks into her daughter's form, then startles like a wild kitten and pulls away.

Chapter 3

Cassandra lives in a world of electronic communications. The two sheets of lavender stationery tucked under the vase on the kitchen table are a novelty. She examines the curlicued signature: "Your sister-in-law, Paige J. Soelberg."

She'll probably want to sit down for this.

"Mom, let's settle in for the afternoon. That pot is sparkling clean. Just let me rinse it for you."

"Well, all right. Is something happening today?"

"We'll see. I need to find my bearings. I'm as confused as you are."

Cassandra makes short work of rinsing and drying. She opens the right cabinet door by motion memory and sets the kettle inside. She seats herself at the table next to her mother, who is puzzling over Paige's letter.

"It's upside down, Mom. Here, let me read it to you."

"Well, what beautiful handwriting."

The letter is clearly not written for Dorothy's consumption. Does Paige assume Dorothy can't process the content? Or that she'll forget as quickly as she registers? Cassandra has no idea how her mother's mind works now or doesn't. Then again, she never has. Cassandra has sometimes envied the blackout curtain her mother can drop so blithely between stage and backstage. It requires a strange discipline. The closest she's come to seeing Dorothy's psychic structure collapse on itself was the night Social Services came to collect their pregnant teen hostage. Even then, "collapse" displayed no content beyond cowering anguish.

Maybe, later, that twenty...

In her mother's moral universe, manicured passivity is not just strength, but virtue. Abjection is blood sport.

Cassandra holds Paige's letter but does not yet read. She takes her mother in: pink jogging suit with an embroidered cartoon corsage. White geriatric sneakers over compression stockings. Legs locked together at the knees, ankles angled neatly to the left, as if she's sitting for a photograph. Going nowhere, yet even so, candy-pink lipstick. Haphazard foundation and uneven blush. Eyebrows—god, that eyebrow thing—plucked clean and replaced with pencil, drawn askew. Dorothy's hair is silver, but not far off in tone from the earlier metallic blond—"mostly natural," as Dorothy once liked to describe it, "just a tad enhanced."

The incarnation before Cassandra now is impeccably coiffed and sprayed; Paige or somebody must have taken her to the hairdresser. Or maybe Paige is doing it herself? Didn't she go to beauty school? Cassandra has no idea how to make a woman's hair do that. Whoever's coiffing Dorothy will need to continue coiffing, or Dorothy's going natural.

Cassandra pushes an open-fingered hand through her own shoulder-length hair, exactly between her father's very dark brown and her mother's whatever, now beginning to silver. Dorothy reaches toward her daughter, then pulls her arm back— maybe recalling an old reproach. *Don't touch my hair, Mom! Leave me alone!* Dorothy's sunken eyes and prominent cheekbones, the small sag of her geriatric neck and jowls, make Dorothy oddly beautiful in a way Cassandra has never perceived. Something at the structure. A hint of Irene. A lot of Lander—old Caldwell, as Dorothy always proclaimed, but Cassandra could not read through the cosmetic veneer.

"I know you've been busy," Dorothy tells her daughter now,

who has been absent for thirty-six years—plenty aged herself. "It's so nice to see you. Thank you for coming."

As if Cassandra is—what? A Relief Society visitor? A drop-in neighbor?

Cassandra attends to her sister-in-law's letter:

June 15, 2019
Dear Cassandra,

I hope your long drive from Michigan or where ever went well. I'm sorry I can't be here to greet you but I took the opportunity to put dinner on our own table. For once. I left just after you texted James, so I don't believe Mother Dorothy was alone more than fifteen minutes. If you got here when you said. James says you learned to cook back in the day (haha we're all so old) so I didn't worry about dinner for Dorothy tonight. There's some ~~bolon~~ bologna and cheese in the fridge in case you just want to just make her a sandwich. She likes them just fine, besides she forgets what she ate right after anyhow. I think James will come over tonight or tomorrow to catch you up on things. But he's in the bishopric now, he's very busy with work and church duties but it's so sweet how he makes time for his ageing mother. I hope you can appreciate the sacrifices he's been making to help her out. Brian or somebody from that family usually comes in the early afternoons twice a week or so to make sure the house and the yard are allright. So you will probably see them. The kids and grandkids can't hardly believe you are real but James Jr. and Karla say they remember you a little. They are all very devoted to the gospel so I do hope you can respect that. The grandchildren have not been around very many people who do not believe in The Church. The Relief Society keeps tabs on mother Dorothy so they probably know your coming.

Warm Regards,
Paige J. Soelberg

Cassandra recalls illustrating Goethe—eerily spotting an older version of himself, the old man riding into town as the young one departed.

Cassandra pushes the thermostat up to something above Arctic. She opens the front curtains now that the sun shines through the back. East mountain overwhelms the window, limestone facets lit orange over slate-blue shadow.

She steps out to the front porch to take it in.

James does not appear, nor call. No signal from Brian. Pumping her mother for information yields nothing.

"Mom, how often does family come?"

"Oh, I don't know."

"Mom, are you hungry? What did you have for lunch today?"

Blink. Blink.

"Mom, did you shower today? Want me to run you a bath?"

"Well of course I did. I don't go to church dirty."

"Yeah, but it's Thursday."

"What are you talking about? I taught my Relief Society lesson. It was about living the Word of Wisdom."

"Mom, when does Brian come to mow the lawn? Do you know what day?"

"Sometimes I see boys out there."

Dorothy does release random bits of coherent information from the centrifuge; to Cassandra's relief, her mother is fixed on a manageable evening routine. She leads Cassandra to the Cozy Room, back behind the two-sided fireplace. Cassandra almost expects to see her long-legged, heavy-boned father stretched over the La-Z-Boy, cursing at a ball game. Cassandra has never entered this room without Hal in it. Since she was a child, she's had recurring dreams of walking into the shock of a slathering cur, writhing in a ball of shadow behind the boulder of a man in the leather recliner.

The room seems exorcised, although the absence is as shocking as presence.

Dorothy exclaims, "Just look at all these wonderful movies!"

Sure enough. Rows of videotapes in their cases. An old tube TV on the stand, with a VCR rigged to feed it.

"I allow myself to enjoy one per evening," Dorothy says. "When my work is done and the children are in bed."

There might be two hundred cassettes, lined up in alphabetical order. Her mother says, "This little elephant goes between the ones I've watched and the ones I haven't. It moves a little every night."

As if by magic. The scene deserves respect. Someone has shored up a tender way to soothe a lost old woman into a sense of familiar safety, evening after evening. Who? Paige? Elaine? A grandchild? The sweetness of it almost makes her angry. She does not want to be drawn in. She intends to see this rude existential interruption through, and then she will return to her authentic life. Away from here.

What will mark the end of it? Dorothy's death? Hospice? Some spasmodic reenactment of primal Soelberg drama?

Attend, now, to the beginning.

"So, what is it tonight?" Cassandra asks, scrutinizing the titles. "Let's see: *Flower Drum Song.*"

"Oh, I love that movie!"

"Wow. Are they all musicals?"

"I hope so. I love musicals!"

Ugh. Cassandra scans the titles. "Well, it looks like you're in luck."

Her mother, mooning over 1940s musicals, rerecorded on 1980s magnetic tapes. Somewhere between their productions and reproductions, with room to spare, Cassandra's entire first existence cycles and rewinds within these rooms.

Since then, what?

Little pops of light shimmer in the air. She's finding it hard to fill her lungs. Altitude? Smoke? Freon? Existential shock? She wants a stiff drink. Soon. Good Midwestern whiskey, a gift from her studio friends, still in its little crate, bootlegged over three state lines, awaits in the trunk.

She settles the old woman who was—is—her mother, into the paternal recliner. How many years ago did Dorothy lose her fear of sitting in it? Probably not until she lost her damn mind. How many years ago was Hal's collection of apocalyptic anti-Communist "literature," maybe shelf by shelf, replaced by bright musicals on VCR cassettes? Where did Cleon Skousen, Ezra Taft Benson, Robert Welch, Joseph McCarthy, Bruce R. McConkie go after the evacuation? Probably straight to James's shelves, exacerbated by Glenn Beck, Rush Limbaugh, Cliven Bundy...

"Mom, do you want me to open the window? It's cooling off out there."

"It already feels like winter. Why make it worse?"

"That's because the air-conditioning has been set to the Ice Age. It's June. It's hot outside."

"Do you see my blanket?"

"Here."

"Should we turn on the fireplace?"

"I think we'll be warm enough."

Cassandra tucks fleece around her mother's shoulders. "Do you want to lay the chair back?"

"What?"

"Never mind. Here goes *Flower Drum Song*."

"Oh! Good! I love that movie!"

Cassandra inserts the cassette. She turns the artifactual television on by hand, but finds the remote to FF through the FBI warning, then on through so much blankness that she fears the tape is empty. But then the title appears. The music begins. Dorothy repeats, "Oh, this one? I love this movie!" although she can't wrangle the name of it. Cassandra sticks around for the opening because the watercolor graphics are lovely. She guesses, just before the credits confirm, that it's the work of Dong Kingman.

It feels like a small strange grace.

She leaves her mother wrapped and enraptured. "I'll keep checking on you, okay? I'm going to unpack."

"Where have you been?"

"Oh, Mom. So many places. But here I am, now."

The sun is falling behind the foothills. Cassandra opens the sliding kitchen door and steps out to the back deck. The old house, trendy in the early 1970s, has its odd charms. Once there were twenty acres of apple and peach trees, fed by a channeled stream behind the sandbar ridge. Beyond, against the foothills, Caleb Brown (lean and dry as jerky) worked a penurious farm with his wife and strange-eyed daughters. Caleb shook his shovel, and sometimes a shotgun, at Cassandra and her brothers when they played at the headgate. "Don't you truck with the flow. That water don't belong to you."

As if their wet cutoff jeans were cheating his corn. He'd cross the fence to patrol, hours early, prowling the line before every water turn, suspicious and unfriendly even to Hal, who could sometimes chat with him in the conspiratorial tones of the old hill families. Caleb's nineteenth-century sons came home once in a while, bringing their wives (*all their wives*, Matthew would smirk), and they'd set up camp in the fields. Somber children would swarm the green shaded yard around the vertical adobe house, but none strayed from the property. They called themselves Mormon but held their own services, and when they went somewhere it never was any destination in Big Horn. They passed through, staring directly forward in the truck or the antique Oldsmobile, until they got beyond the eyes of their fellow citizens, on to wherever they found kin and providence.

No doubt the Brown family is long gone from Big Horn. She can't see behind the ridge, but houses sprawl on up the hillside beyond, where Caleb's barbed wire and horned cattle ran. Bland-hued houses, blank rooflines, closed windows, the ominous thrum of air conditioners. White vinyl fences with elaborate gates. Not many trees. Scrub oak scrubbed out. Ancestral poplars, locusts, and Scotch pines have succumbed to the hissing of half-acre lawns.

Above the toxified grass, between stuccoed walls and vinyl borders: already drying hills, rough gray-green against the peachening sky.

Chapter 4

Dorothy is asleep in Hal's chair; Cassandra comes in to check just as Mei Li begins to sing how much she's going to like it here.

Lucky Mei Li.

Cassandra's old bedroom awaits like a dimensional cavern. She will not open that door.

She walks out to her car. You'd think the neighbors would be out; it's eight o'clock and cooling. The light is blue and orange at the same time, vibrant, casting lavender shadows. The graphing summits hover.

Maybe everyone forgets where they live if they keep living here. Maybe at this intensity, where land and altitude and backward and forward eons rush the eye at every turn, damage and beauty must by necessity deaden the senses. Cassandra can only absorb a supercharged glance at a time. Intermittence the only way to take it in.

She opens the trunk; what furies release? She is relieved yet displeased that her arranged and insulated belongings lie as she packed them. She eases the big bubble-wrapped computer screen into the house. Sets it on the kitchen table for lack of a better option, half-expecting some heedless adolescent brother to plop himself on top of whatever she lays on the sofa. She returns to the car for the pad and stylus, the extra hard drive and sorted cords, the paper pads, and charcoal, and pigments. The sable brushes wrapped in soft linen.

Art emerges from meaningful spaces, a revered professor, long ago, insisted. Cassandra took it to heart. How, here, will she learn—relearn—to make?

The clothing can wait. Her books, but for a chosen few, sit vigilant with wasting and wasted Sam, whom she peculiarly loves, in her house in a faraway place. In St. Paul—named for the fanatic saint who, mid-wickedness, met an angel who blinded him at the crossroads.

Cassandra knows his kind.

Where, in her father's house, can these objects hold their resonance? How long must they abide? She chooses the sewing room, once Matthew's—Matilda's—bedroom, beside Cassandra's.

No. Nothing within these walls was ever hers.

And yet the patriarch is long dead. Likely everyone but Cassandra has absorbed this fact. By now this is Dorothy's house, as much as the bewildered remnant of a woman can inhabit it.

Matthew's room became a sewing room after Matthew moved downstairs to boy-world with the brothers, the year Cassandra turned eight and he was already ten. Still she remembers the comfort of his early nearness. She opens the door. The sewing machine sits abandoned. The closet, once filled with Matthew's toys and clothing, then with well-intentioned fabric, patterns, and thread, is mostly empty. In fact the whole house is sparse and gutted, as if everything useful or memorable has been appropriated, taken somewhere else, purged. A thin coating of useful or semi-nostalgic objects, like props in a play, left to appease an old woman's waning sense of the familiar.

Not Dorothy's house, then. No one's home.

However, here on the west wall: a framed faded print. A choo choo engine with a friendly face—as if no one dares, or cares, to remove a modest shrine to Matthew's passion. In Matthew's early handwriting, blue crayon, on the protective glass: *CHRANE*.

Cassandra searches the house. In the musty wood-paneled basement she finds a big-enough computer desk, an archaic CPU still perched upon it. She lifts the awkward metal box to the floor, slides it into the gutted game closet, and pushes the desk upside down up the (still shag) carpeted stairway. She considers taking the sewing machine to the basement but decides to leave it for now. It's getting late. She has been traveling a very long time. She establishes the desk under the image of the choo choo chrane.

She checks on Dorothy. Her head leans awkwardly to the side, lit by bluish flickering light. Mouth slack. Cassandra pushes the recliner flat. She pads her mother's head on either side with cheap plush pillows. Dorothy's features fall to the bone in the new position. Cassandra flattens a palm on her mother's chest.

"Mother," she whispers. "Dorothy, are you with me?"

Small air.

Cassandra arranges production supplies—paper pads, tubes of acrylic paint and watercolor, wrapped brushes, a collapsible easel—on the floor of her lost brother's bedroom. She can work for several weeks on the computer, but the concrete reassurance of "art stuff" seems suddenly crucial. She returns once more to the car for her duffel   mostly shirts and jeans. She's not going anywhere fancy. Across the street, an old man putters in his open garage. He glances in her direction and waves, unsmiling. It's creepy to wonder if she knows him.

Just up the street, preening but dated homes—the "rich" neighborhood built up around the stolid rural domiciles her Primary friends went home to. No doubt the old stratifications have been complicated and realigned.

But not in her mind. Up there, crowning the curve, hidden by Dry Creek cottonwoods, pulsing like uranium: them.

The chlorinated pool.

The sperm.

Cassandra gazes into the landscaped trees.

She slams the trunk, retreating into what shelter this house of dementia can offer.

She wonders whether to disturb her mother's sleep. She turns off the TV, emitting electronic light but no image. She pushes the button to unstrain the clicking cassette.

"Mom, let's get you to bed. Do you need to go to the bathroom? Do you need any help?"

Awakened less by her daughter's voice than by silence and dark, Dorothy opens her eyes. "What do you mean, do I need help? I'm a grown woman. What are you doing here this time of night?"

Cassandra stands back. Dorothy struggles to pull herself up from the recliner. Cassandra leans down to release the lever, pitching the old woman toward the television. Cassandra responds with a full-body block, rather athletic. Dorothy accepts the offered hand, perplexed.

And now Cassandra's mother is asleep on the king-sized poster bed, a tiny mound under a quilt pieced together by her own mother, Irene—a woman so dissimilar to Dorothy that Cassandra has never managed to portray them together, to render them visible within the same composition.

Chapter 5

Maybe it's stripped and transformed like Matthew's, or possibly fluffed and awaiting improdigal return. Regardless, Cassandra has no intention of encountering her old bedroom. Ever. She attempts to sleep on the harsh polyester sofa in the living room.

Toward morning she dreams that her mother's sewing machine in Matthew's bedroom is a tiny green tractor—the kind her father used, gruffly teaching his spawn to clutch and steer, berating them up and down the orchard rows as he sprayed Malathion. She recalls the groaning driveshaft, visible through a small rectangle cut out of the floorboard, spinning as the gears found purchase. *That thing won't stop for a pant leg or even a leg, you know. Pull you down relentless as the devil. You better remember that.*

The tiny tractor lures her down an unfamiliar hallway. In the anti logic of dream, she's surprised she's never noticed this angled wing of her childhood home. Mindless as a housefly, the tractor crawls the stairs to a split-level floor, an Escher trick. The dim space glows milky green like a superball. Wrapped furniture; mounds of discarded linens and amorphous clothing; outlandish gardening tools lined along a rail; taped cardboard boxes with runic labels. A wall of drawers and cabinets stuffed with enigmatic accumulations extends too high and deep to make spatial sense.

The tractor creeps forward, disappearing behind a shrouded easel and into a foggy portal. Cassandra reaches to uncover the image on the canvas but musky atmosphere closes in. She stands arrested in the mist.

She awakens on the harsh fabric of her mother's sofa. She stares around the dark room, sensing that she's still dreaming, then wishing she were.

She paces the small distance to the window. She draws the unnaturally heavy curtain. In the moonlight, Cassandra reviews: two weeks ago, she opened a first-ever email from her brother James, read desperation and maybe something like human grief in the imperious diction, and packed for a long drive back to Big Horn, Utah.

Why, after thirty-six years, did she consent? Simply, it was time—whatever that might mean. Can she work from here? How long? She can't measure. What about her studio, her acquired family, her friends, Sam—steady but waning as the summer rises. She pictures him on the back porch, head clouded in THC smoke, savoring the warmth. She cannot allow herself to ponder. Are these questions of relation? Love? Such words are uncomfortable. She has lived behind glass, and she favors it. Because of what happened here, decades ago, in the jagged terrain of humiliation.

Chapter 6

In the morning, Cassandra gathers the pillow and blankets and pushes them into Matthew's bedroom. Inside the room with the chrane, she will call him Matthew. Beyond this house, she will respect the name Matilda, since that's who fled to the mountain in their mother's long Sunday coat.

Cassandra had so little time to absorb the particulars, back when there was no language at all to help or hinder comprehension. Did her sibling alternate between personalities, or was Matilda the sole truth of Matthew? Both forms were, truly, the same person. One name was not encompassing enough. He called himself Matthew, clear as clean sky, because that's who he was. And she was Matilda when Matilda answered her name. They did not speak separately of one another, did not seem all that distinct, except Matilda was, for a Soelberg, witty and sociable. Elegant, as Dorothy wished herself to be. Matilda had a way with language, lively and expressive. She dropped fragments of Grandma Irene's French poems, sounding more *française* than Grandma ever did. Matilda gestured with graceful hands. She made warm, knowing eye contact. She'd look puzzled—resigned but a little hurt (very old hurt)—when she was mistaken for a man.

What did Matthew/Matilda know and refuse to know? Who, in this tight-jawed family, in this cagey, incessant town, knows either, or some, or all of them?

. . .

Dorothy is sitting up in bed as if expecting someone, but she can't pinpoint whom.

Certainly not Cassandra.

"How nice to see you," Dorothy hedges. "Where are we now?"

"Mom, I'm Cassandra. Your daughter. We're here in your bedroom. It's morning. Let's get you dressed. I'll make breakfast."

Cassandra opens the curtains.

Dorothy squints in the light. "Cassandra got herself pregnant and went away."

Dorothy kneads the quilt with arthritic fingers. Her daughter's reappearance must have lapped all night at the shores of memory.

Women here speak in eruptions. Even (especially?) the senile ones.

Cassandra is washed in a reflex of rage, an urge to slap the old woman's cheek bright red. Dorothy's tongue licks along her upper teeth, then juts out and retreats, reptilian. Her eyes gaze nowhere, opaque. Cassandra parks herself on the foot of the bed to calm herself. She recalls the twenty-dollar bill, a talisman.

Even so: "Well, I can't see how the girl could have gotten *herself* pregnant. Any guess who helped her with that?"

Dorothy sighs, burdened and confidential. "You know, Matthew's been having trouble in school. I don't know what's got into him. He's a very smart boy. There's no real harm in him."

Cassandra sits attentive, awaiting more, but her mother has expended the night's accumulation. Cassandra calms herself to address the vacuum: "What do you want for breakfast, Mom? I'll make whatever you like."

"Well, I don't mind."

Okay then. Not much to choose from. Oatmeal. Cassandra sets the boil, then rummages through the freezer compartment.

Frozen berries, a wrinkled bag of hard pebbles. She warms them in the bubbling porridge. Sets a steaming bowl, topped with milk, before the old woman.

"So beautiful," Dorothy murmurs, as if it were a bouquet.

Cassandra retreats to the bathroom. She finds a clean wash-cloth, wets it a little with warm water, and returns to wipe something like tears from her mother's cheeks. She dips the spoon into the oatmeal, blowing it cooler. "Here. This will taste good. You'll feel better."

Dorothy opens her mouth like a baby bird. Cassandra withdraws her hand in surprise. "Here, Mom. You can feed yourself, can't you? You ate the sandwich last night, all gone. You used this very same spoon for tomato soup."

Dorothy closes her lips, then thrusts her chin forward, quivering. She opens her mouth again.

I'm not really the touchy-feely kind, Dorothy used to say. *There's something to be said for respecting personal space.* In fact, she'd said it so often it was a quality of her, like the enhanced platinum hair. The plucked and repainted eyebrows, the layered cosmetics (is this how Cassandra learned to layer pigments?). Long ruffled sleeves, polyester pantsuits, girdle and full slip, lift-up bra and pantyhose under dresses and skirts—all layered over the "second skin" of her temple garments. All of it, armor. Against what, exactly? Against everything, by the time Cassandra was old enough to consider the question.

Cassandra thinks she has not been so literally close to her mother—the body, the mouth, hunger, the dank scent of her now-geriatric breath—since their positions were reversed. Since Cassandra herself opened her infant mouth, somehow expecting she would be nourished. It's difficult and unsettling. Familiar bodies are the most mysterious.

Will this evolve into a story of family discovery? Self-revelation? Reconciliation?

No. It will simply finish, and Cassandra will depart again.

Cassandra lifts the spoon to Dorothy's tongue. Taken by warm texture, Dorothy closes her eyes and swallows.

Spoon by proffered spoon, sensual, her mother eats it all.

Cassandra wipes Dorothy's mouth. Warding off a shudder, she rinses the pot, bowl, and spoon, setting them on the rack to dry. She pulls the floor-length curtain open, then the sliding glass door. The morning air, come down from the canyons, wafts in through the screen. Mother and daughter—aging, carnal female bodies—sit together quiet, gazing over the rooftops toward the western hills.

Chapter 7

G randma Caldwell was having herself a flag crisis.

"Horrid things," Irene said. "They look all grand and regal for a week or two in June and then they spend the rest of the year clogging the soil against everything else. Tubers all wrapped around each other like sea monsters under there. Stuff of nightmares."

She handed Cassandra the hoe. "I'm going for a shovel. I'll be right back."

Cassandra considered the bed, spiked with upright green spears. Wilting petals on tall rigid stalks.

"Wait," she said when her grandmother returned, grim and newly weaponed. "These big purple flowers? You're taking them out? You've never not had these here."

"Well, time for a change. I'm sick of them. Colonizers is what they are. *Fleur-de-lis.* Whatever the heck *lis* means, they're not Frenching up my garden anymore."

"Well, what does *flurda* mean?"

"*Fleur.* Flower. *De.* Of. *Lis*: Who knows? Maybe some town in the provinces. Like here. Or maybe one of those Louis kings."

Grandma might have bobbed up against five-three in her prime, but now in her eighties she barely reached Cassandra's shoulder. Cassandra herself was five-six, she knew, because they'd measured for scoliosis in PE before school let out, and her jeans fit the same now as then. Maybe she was done growing.

Grandma studied French literature for a couple of years before her folks made her quit college to get married, back in a time Cassandra could not imagine.

"How's that for impractical?" she'd say. "All it did is allow me to mutter a little Proust. Tend a garden like Voltaire. But it keeps my mind occupied. It's an ugly-pretty language. Much choking. Like these flags."

When no one was listening but Cassandra, she'd add, "If you're lucky, you'll get to go off to college and learn something every bit as useless. Gratuitous knowledge is one of life's great gifts. Do not forfeit any opportunity."

Cassandra often wondered why her grandmother didn't talk like everyone else. It wasn't the accent; Grandma's French words were formed within an incorrigible Utah throat. But the words Grandma knew and used—English or French—as casually as if they were everyday tableware? Long after she'd left Utah for good, it occurred to Cassandra that the question should be reversed: Why *didn't* everyone talk like that, there in the ample home valley? Why didn't awakening to slopes of descending light (imperial yellow in summer, mercury blue in winter), reclining to the sound of crickets, the loud silence of stars, the knowledge of fawns in the fields and languid yellow cougars in the high forests, poeticize the tongues of people who affixed every meaning to this place?

Cassandra's mother's language was a singsong assemblage of homilies and self-soothing maxims, trite affirmations and pious slogans—even though Dorothy had grown up in Grandma's house, saturated with books, drenched in Grandma's words and ways of seeing. Repressing all that must have required superhuman commitment. That kind of voice control—lilting and chipper, unnaturally pitched as if she were ever addressing puppies—requires marathon vigilance. Her mother's sister Emma practiced some variation of it, and their cousins, too. Irene was the family anomaly. Among Irene's daughters, convention became a perverse strain of rebellion. After Lander's death, religion a weapon of passive rebuke.

"Your mother was a pure wild thing when she was small," Grandma had told her. "A passionate imagination, sincere and soaring emotion. Life just got her afraid of all the wrong things. I thought after Lander died we'd all find release, maybe a new way to be as a family, but she and Emma doubled down. I guess Lander's dissatisfaction with me made them eager to prove they could be irresistible wives. Made them hungry for masculine approval."

Cassandra blinked in the insect-punctuated atmosphere. Her parents, before they were her parents, made no sense. Grandma poked at Cassandra's shoulder. "Listen. I'm not saying your father was a bad choice. He has his qualities. But you know there's not a relenting bone in him. I've come to terms with it. Seems Dorothy got the clarity she wanted."

What clarity did her mother want, Cassandra wishes she'd asked. Something about keeping a man in thrall (sex education ala Dorothy Caldwell Soelberg: "My mother greeted my father in her dirty garden clothes. What did she expect? A man wants an ornament on his arm."). So many questions she has, now, for a guide who can no longer answer. Maybe she never could. Cassandra can't measure the woman she needs now more than ever, the woman she's come to resemble, at least if Cassandra squints from a certain angle in the mirror.

Grandma pointed at the hoe in Cassandra's hand. "You intend to employ that thing? Or are you just going to stand and gape?"

Grandma—all five feet of her—went at it with the shovel. The ground was unyielding as concrete. "All right. Bring the hose over here. Let's soak them out. Toss them into the wheelbarrow and we'll dump them at the bare patch by the far fence. They want to root there, we'll let them rise in their brief glory."

Cassandra stanced up to hack. Iris tubers looked like malformed feet of monstrous birds. Or like something intestinal, tubes and tentacles twisting around themselves, saturated in thick mud.

"You'd never know they make beautiful flowers."

"Well, beauty does very often emerge from ugly. Doesn't fix the ugly, and it might not last long, but even so."

"What will you plant here now?"

"Annuals. Every year, something I've never tried. The old pioneer women planted irises because that's what they had, at least from their former lives, which they never quite let go of. I'll concede, an iris is a gorgeous thing for its spell. It was a practical choice too. Plant them once and they come back every year. Whole lot of dutiful fleur-de-lis waving about in June, because everybody has to display a respectable European yard. Everybody my age, anyhow."

Grandma rubbed a sunburnt cheek, streaking mud like war paint. "Kind of depletes the magic of them, though, how they were socially required. Plenty of other dutiful perennials we can count on. This bed's going rogue."

"What will you plant first?"

"Zinnias. Zinnias are living kaleidoscopes. Zinnias are egregious. We still have time to bring them to bloom, if we put them in soon."

Chapter 8

A week now with Dorothy. Evening approaches. No sign from the brothers. Damned if Cassandra will call them.

Children pedal past the house. Used to be sting-rays. Now, mountain bikes. The asphalt is too rough for skateboards, and there are still no sidewalks on this transitional neck. Grove Street has always been about escorting people to another spot. Four-wheelers and lawn mowers and other motorous sounds cut through the drone of air conditioners.

She'd like to take a long walk, but she's not braced for human encounter. She'll have to go out at some point. A gentle hike along the base of the north mountain, maybe—but where does the trail pick up now, among the subdivisions? She does not wish to encounter fences or request permission. She does not want to disturb her blood pressure. Or, for that matter, get shot.

The refrigerator needs stocking. Her reassuring coffee stash won't hold out long. They sell coffee here, don't they? It's 2019 even in Clearlake Valley, is it not?

Fresh cream yes please. But she'll have to go out to find it.

Well, shit.

She paces like a prisoner. She searches the cupboards for improvisations. Not much. Downstairs in the storeroom, bottled goods from ten years ago and beyond, contents floating like disarticulated specimens. Canned corn and beans dated for the

1990s. Rice and flour—and weevil—in ten-gallon bins. Packets of spaghetti mix, mostly salt and MSG—probably perched there among the boxes of Hamburger Helper since she was in high school. The ancient chest freezer is so furred with ice she can barely open it—and now it will not close again.

This house, this family: entropic. The chasm has been collapsing behind their every step since whatever forever means to white people in this overrun place. Ever since their misfit Scandinavian ancestors got themselves banished from fanatical old-world families for embracing a magic golden book, excavated—one way or another—from a New York hillside. She marvels, again, how her entire existence owes itself to the phantasmagoric visions of a horny nineteenth-century child.

Maybe too simplistic, she hears her grandmother say.

Then again maybe not.

This town this state these bewildered anachronistic people this city greened up with stolen water and emerald glasses. This family the woman upstairs this meat in the freezer. Cassandra will disassemble this museum of delusional plenitude at some point; the imperative will certainly overtake her. She retreats upstairs to the remains of a functional kitchen. Soft white bread in a bag. Flat squares of processed cheese. Margarine in the butter compartment.

Dorothy eats perfectly well by herself, so long as she can pick it up with her hands. She's even okay with a spoon and fork toward the end of the day. Mornings confuse her most. She appears to enjoy the hydroponic tomato slice Cassandra has softened into the melted cheese. Cassandra watches her mother eat, bite by slightly lascivious bite. None of the self-demeaning guilt of the perpetually dieting 1970s wife and mother. So there's that.

Looks to be a fairly easy procession toward bedtime. Dorothy loves a warm bath and can manage most of it on her own. Toothbrushing, soft pajamas, the movie chair—

Dorothy nearly pitches the last of her sandwich at the sound of the doorbell. Cassandra registers, then panics. The doorbell rings again, followed by a vigorous knock. Mother and daughter gawp toward the entrance, which, like a horror shot, swings open by itself. A manicured hand waves from the gap, followed in quick succession by a youngish woman's portrait-ready head and shoulders, a baby carrier with a baby in it, the rest of the maternal body, and yet another Insta-Mom, final arm attached to a sudden toddler.

"Sister Soelberg? Are you here? Ministering sisters? Here to see if you need anything?"

Women here pitch their more amiable sentences like questions, an upward flip at the end.

Dorothy's head bobs like a wind-up toy. Baby Mama coos from the doorway. "Oh, hellooo, sweet lady! We thought we'd just come in so you didn't have to come all the way to the door?"

The cooing stops short, as the source perceives another presence in the house. "Oh! My goodness! You already have company? We didn't mean to startle you."

Dorothy looks confused but delighted, perking up at the sensation of attention. "Oh, hello there," she says, but that's all she's got. She puts one hand on the tabletop, the other on the chair back, struggling to stand. Cassandra stoops to hoist, then guides her mother to a living room chair as the church ladies await, curious. The little boy, decked out in tiny sweats and a camo T-shirt, gelled whitewall haircut, leans into his mother's leg. The infant, adorned with instructive female signifiers (including a flowered pink—what? Is that a turban?) is asleep, rosebud lips in a pucker.

So many children here. Cassandra used to babysit everyone's kids. Neighbors started calling the year she turned twelve. Every night that she could be persuaded (not difficult—a good reason to leave the house), another family—five, six, eight children at a time. Tired parents so relieved to escape a while, they'd stay out until three or four in the morning, trusting an insubstantial and criminally untrained teenager to make dinner, change diapers, settle squalls and soothe bedtime fears, stand down rowdy boys just a little bit younger than herself, and often bigger.

She liked children back then—not in a clamoring way but as what she assumed was a simple feminine fact. Now she knows better: a uterus does not a natural mother make. Look around. But Cassandra was good with kids; she had a "knack," her father would say. She'd been flattered by his recognition then, although now it strikes her as a little pimpish. Even so, she liked the money she earned, liked buying her own school clothes, experimental makeup—and, eventually, tubes of watercolor and oil pigments, canvas and opulent fiber papers from Priddy's Office Supply, down in Clearlake. A sensuous awakening.

She's nearly forgotten all that, until just now. At least she's forgotten to think about it. Now children agitate her. She doesn't get close.

Unhappily, Cassandra invites the women to sit, which they would have done anyway. The baby moves her tiny lips but slumbers on. The toddler stands in the center of the room, wobbling in miniaturized basketball shoes. His mother calls to him. He slobbers and gapes.

"So..." says Baby Mama, expecting clarification. Mormons do not account for themselves on home turf, Cassandra recalls. These women view themselves as the legitimate presence in Dorothy's living room.

Cassandra will wait them out.

A foray from Toddler Mommy: "Sister Soelberg, it's good to see you have company tonight?"

Dorothy lights up. "Oh yes! Isn't it wonderful?"

Aaaand lights out.

Toddler sways on the absurd white carpet, balance expended. Down he goes, onto his diapered butt. His mother reaches for him. "Jantzen! Come to Mommy," but he tucks and rolls, wails a half minute, runs snot, and pulls himself up again. His mother extracts a wet wipe from an elaborate diaper bag to scrub at an invisible slime spot on the carpet.

"Oh for heaven's sake," Cassandra says. "Let him muck things up a little. He can't unwhite that carpet no matter how hard he tries."

The women have no reply; this is not a cue they recognize.

All eyes default toward the (admittedly cute) wobbling boy.

"Just look at that little fella," Dorothy says, probably recalling Cassandra's brothers. "Well, aren't you something?"

Jantzen steadies himself, reviews the mechanics of ambulation, then suddenly arcs and chugs toward Cassandra.

"Jantzen!" his mother says, uncertain whether she should get up and pursue. "Come here right now!"

The kid plants his wet face into Cassandra's thigh. Contact raises her hands in a reflexive truce.

"Jantzen! Oh my goodness, I'm so sorry about that! Jantzen, come here!" the mother says, rising.

"Isn't he cute," Dorothy says. Then, maybe to Cassandra: "Is this your child?"

Cassandra stands, lifting the hot, dense little body upward, gentle but urgent. He leans into her shoulder. For a moment his wide eyes in hers. Long lashes. Milky breath.

She meets the mother halfway. "Here you go."

"I'm so sorry."

"Don't be. He's a cute little guy."

"But your pants—"

"Made to be washed."

"I would have left him at home with my husband, but he's late from work and—"

This woman will not stop apologizing?

"Here, why don't you talk to my mother. Visitors make her

39

happy. I think I have something to entertain little—uh—Jantzen. I'll be back."

Relieved to surrender Dorothy to the do-gooders, Cassandra disappears into the kitchen to rummage. She catches phrases and snippets, more discernible by rhythm and pitch than intelligible words. *...without a shadow of a doubt, Sister Soelberg... righteous families can be together forever? if they will only...overcome our trials and temptations with earnest prayer?...when the prophet speaks?...*Okay, that's enough. Cassandra ups the ruckus, pawing through the gadget drawer, extracting a keychain of plastic measuring spoons. She drops a level to dig up nesting containers and a rubber scraper.

She returns to assess: her mother, rapt but uncomprehending. A writhing over-pinked infant about to awaken. Two young women reciting faith-promoting aphorisms, straining to curb their curiosity over the alien presence in Sister Soelberg's house. A toddler, drawn to the figure who approaches with curious objects.

The mamas go silent as Cassandra seats herself on the floor. She fans a tantalizing array in front of Jantzen. The child's fascination compels them, too. His dimpled hand answers the bursts of intention in his busy sputtering brain: he picks up the measuring spoons, gives them a shake, drops them into a bowl. He puts a small bowl into a larger one. He sits back to consider. He picks up the scraper, pumps it up and down. Taps the floor, which prompts a torrent of rhythmic chatter.

"You certainly have a way with children," one mother says.

The other: "Did...did I hear you call Sister Soelberg your mother?"

Dorothy cues in. "Oh, no. She's not my mother. My mother is—oh my. It's on the tip of my tongue. Emma, what's our mother's name?"

Cassandra: "Your mother. My grandmother. Irene Caldwell."

"What's that? Is my mother here?"

Confused silence, but for the nesting and de-nesting of plastic bowls. Happy toddler jabber. The pink-turbaned baby busts out a wail. Dorothy says, "For heaven's sake, what a racket. Somebody ought to take care of that child."

The church ladies stand up, eager to exit.

"Well, um—Emma? It's nice to meet you. I didn't even know Sister Soelberg had a—daughter? Are you in town for a while? Let us know if there's anything we can do for her while you're here?"

"I thought my sister-in-law would have notified the ward."

Now they really are perplexed.

"Sister Soel—you mean Paige?"

"Yes."

"Maybe she was planning on introducing you in Relief Society?"

"Probably not."

The baby writhes and cries in her chair, pitching up to full scream.

"Somebody needs to make that baby quit that awful noise," Dorothy snaps.

"I'm sorry," Cassandra says. "My mother isn't—herself, as I'm sure you know. Babies are entitled to make all the noise they want."

The little boy's mother cocks her head, as if Cassandra has cast a spell. The mother scoops him up. He's crying now too, and wrenching himself toward Cassandra, urgently mistaking her for someone familiar.

"I don't know why he likes you so much," his mother says, a little hard, no upward pitch. "I'm sure my husband can keep him next time."

Cassandra resists the instinct to reach for him, angered by the urge. "I don't know why I attract kids. And dogs and cats, for that matter. My friends laugh that I must give off some kind of scent."

Nobody finds this reassuring, or amusing.

Nobody seems up to sorting. That old, uncanny sensation: speaking a language that makes no sense to anyone. This is her grandmother Irene's fault, Cassandra soothes herself, and feels ruefully better.

"Well, okay. Bye Jantzen," she says, and the boy takes a chittering breath, assembling the significance. Something clicks. He pumps his waving hand up and down.

She makes sense to him, at least. "Bye-bye," he chirps like a baby bird.

Chapter 9

A nother long, strange night. The polyester couch has become unbearable.

Cassandra sits up. She goes to the front window. Her fingers glow in dead sweet moonlight.

She takes up the pillow and steps quietly toward the hallway. She stands at the corridor, recalling her childhood terror of devils and spirits, scriptural formulas for discernment, rituals of casting out. The hushed and lurid tales of Satan and his malevolent servants, lavishly embellished by full-grown adults— parents, teachers, camp leaders, secretaries, nurses, neighbors— rained down upon petrified children.

Everyone but her grandma Irene. "Frightened sheep trying to frighten lambs," she scoffed. "Don't get suckered into that."

This, after a particularly zealous Primary lesson. "Speaking and thinking about evil spirits attracts them to you," her teacher had warned. "They'll do anything to lure you to their side. The Millennium is nigh. Satan is desperate to corrupt the young warriors of the Latter Days. Ten demons—sometimes more—are assigned to tempt every precious Mormon child, every hour and every day in these end-times. You must always be vigilant. He that endureth to the end shall be exalted."

Grandma notwithstanding, nine-year-old Cassandra had lain awake night after night under a rosebud coverlet, there in that very room at the end of the hall on the right, across from the firmly shut door of the master bedroom, desperately trying not to think about evil spirits.

Now the tulle and floral room of her childhood pulses with some other malevolence, but still. Maybe an actual bed awaits within, something better than the sofa. She collects her nerves. She steps past Matthew's room, reaches beyond for a knob she has not turned since the last night she ever stood in her father's presence.

Her hand, possessed by its own refusal, jerks back. Drops limp at her side. Her fingers flex. The cheap veneer is an aesthetic abomination. She could punch through it like paper, but it might as well be a dimensional wall.

"Devil you know—" she murmurs as she turns ninety degrees to the master bedroom. If she would have ever—*ever*—tried to enter her parents' room at this time of night as a frightened nine-year-old, well...she can't quite imagine. Something like a medieval vision of God's power: the visceral image of Hal Soelberg, splayed huge and snoring on the king-sized bed behind another flimsy unbreachable hollow-core door. Her mother in curlers, spiraled like a lapdog in the negative space. Angry, abrupt rebuke.

Dorothy can't fall asleep unless she's shut in tight, but Cassandra cracks the door once her mother drops into dreamland. She peers in, now. Dorothy is a molehill on a dim king-sized plain.

Cassandra reels and retreats to the living room floor, softening it as she can with the blanket she brought from her own house. No need for cover. The night is very warm but the air, at least, is authentic with the scent of sage and high stone rolling down mountain flanks.

She longs for her own good bed, in a city coursing with water, where the ground never threatens to shake. She yearns for the luxury of pure private nakedness. She wants to make breakfast for a sleepy, happy, gently damaged sometimes-lover.

Dorothy bites toast, demure in the bright morning light. Cassandra has set up her coffee maker on a little table out on the deck, beyond the sliding doors. She's not hiding it. She just doesn't want something so precious, so comforting, to lose its bright energy in a stifled space. She takes what pleasure she can by slipping out into the morning shade of the west-side balcony. She sits on a folding lawn chair, sips the coffee black for want of cream, and braces for another bungling meander of a day.

Matthew's room remains cluttered and disorganized. Cassandra is quite sure she won't get to that today. And now the goddamned doorbell. Dorothy flings her toast. Cassandra spills a little coffee on her jeans.

"What's going on?" Dorothy squawks. "Who's coming in here?"

"It's okay, Mom. I'll go see." She half expects the door to open itself again—seems the way of things.

Cassandra tarries at the entry, hoping she has only imagined the sound.

A gentle knock. Cassandra commits. A plumpish, very neat mid-fortyish woman stands on the porch, face forward but politely distanced.

"Can I help you?" Cassandra asks, uninviting.

"Cassandra Soelberg? I can see the family resemblance."

Cassandra clamps, then attempts to relax, her anxious jaw. Her fingers flex of their own accord. "I guess you know my folks."

The woman wears unobtrusive wire-rimmed glasses. She's dressed in spring-green slacks and a short-sleeved cashmere sweater. Low-heeled pumps. Her lightly graying hair is trimmed short in a pleasant no-fuss sort of way, complemented with modest clip-on pearl earrings. Real pearls.

Her gaze is direct. Voice too. "I know most of your family, at least by sight. I know your mother best, and your brother James and his family. I wish they would have told me you were coming. I would have made sure you received a better welcome."

Cassandra and the not-off-putting woman maintain eye contact through the screen. Cassandra is wearing torn jeans, and a T-shirt layered under a collared work blouse. No bra. Slippered feet.

She locates her manners. "Would you like to come in? My mother loves company."

"I'm always glad to see your mother, but I came to introduce myself to you."

Cassandra opens the door. "Dorothy is managing breakfast pretty well this morning. Why don't we go in and sit at the table with her? She doesn't follow, but she likes the sensation of conversation."

"That sounds perfect."

Dorothy looks up from her toast as they seat themselves. Cassandra wipes jam from the corners of her mother's mouth.

Dorothy takes stock of the women at her table. "Well, here we all are. Isn't this nice?"

"It sure is," the visitor says. "Sister Soelberg, I came to meet your daughter Cassandra. Nobody told me she's come home to be with you. You must be so happy she's here."

Dorothy's expression, such as it is, goes blank. She brushes crumbs from the table beside her saucer. She lifts the juice glass to her lips, sips nothing, sets it down.

"She doesn't exactly understand who I am," Cassandra explains—which, come to think of it, has always been true. "I think she knows it's me, in a way, when we're here alone, when she doesn't have to try to account. When we're just sort of existing in the same space, she talks to me as if I've been here all along. She gets pretty talkative, in fact. But when she needs a name, she calls me Emma. Her sister's name."

Cassandra considers this. She truly can't decide whether her mother is calculating or clueless. For so long, they were the same thing. Maybe they still are, in senile exacerbation.

Dorothy nibbles her toast. Her eyes are fixed on nothing in particular just beyond Cassandra's left shoulder. The kitchen sink.

"Well, let's just let her imagine she's in a regular state of good company, then," the apparently familiar woman says. "It's a good chance to talk to you, if you're willing."

Cassandra grants the woman a frank, expectant stare. The kind that capable women give one another in the world beyond the oblique feminine politesse of a place rutted in congregational relations. The woman rises to it. She smiles, warm and seemingly authentic.

"I'm Toni. Toni Fuller. I'm the Relief Society president of your mother's ward."

Cassandra resists leaping to snark, as this woman presents as human. "Okay," she says. "I know how much this all means to my mom. At least to the person she was. I'm happy to welcome you, and the—what did they call themselves last night? I thought they were visiting teachers. But they called it something else."

"You were right, though. New name, same thing. Mostly."

"Well, I'll make sure they're always welcome to visit Dorothy. They seemed a little unstrung last night."

Toni laughs. "They're just young. Over their heads with kids and—I shouldn't say this, but—rich, childish husbands. Money doesn't exactly make their lives easier. Young couples these days have a lot of unrealistic expectations to live up to. They're trying. I don't envy them, even though I guess we're supposed to."

Cassandra squints. Toni Fuller herself does not look remotely poor.

"Where do you live?" Cassandra asks. "I guess I mean, where are the ward boundaries now?"

Toni raises her eyebrows. "I know what you're asking. I live up past the Crease," she says, meaning the point where the tiered valley floor folds sharply up into mountain slope. The new rich streets. No pretending otherwise. "In fact, my husband is a BYU business professor. We're not un-implicated."

"How much of this ward lives above the Crease?"

"Quite a lot. It makes for an interesting economic divide. I know this might sound flippant, but I don't mean it to be. The people in this ward have their particular trials. Money is a mixed blessing at best, but I can't say I don't benefit from my husband's venture capital convictions. And those young wives—their husbands work out there at the Point, all that tech and startup stuff out there. Lots of money flying around, but also lots of people living over their heads, emotionally and financially, even while they blog about their beautiful lives. But—something tells me you can read the complications without my help."

Toni appears to be anticipating actual conversation.

Cassandra blinks. "Do you mind if I pour another cup of coffee? I like to sit on the porch and enjoy something sinful while Mom works on her toast. But it got—"

"Interrupted? I'm so sorry. Please. Brew up a new kettle. I'm sure that one's gone bitter."

"What?"

"My parents were jack Mormons. I grew up with the smell of coffee in the morning. It's one of my favorite sensations in the whole world."

"I don't have any cream." Cassandra sounds petulant, even to herself. "I've been too messed up by all this to gather my nerve for the grocery store. But it still tastes good. It's kept me from running."

"So far," Toni says. "This can't be easy. Please let us help in any way we can. I promise we won't try to reconvert you. I'll make sure that doesn't happen, at least from any angle I can influence."

Somebody has informed the Relief Society president, at

some point, that Dorothy Soelberg's absent daughter has gone to apostasy.

Dorothy pipes up. "You're going to miss the bus, I'm afraid."

Cassandra goes out to conjure fresh coffee, leaving Toni to answer Dorothy's non sequiturs. She takes her time getting the grind just right. She scoops four tablespoons into the filter, pours fresh water into the well, and pushes the light-up button. She waits for the low rumble of first heat.

Dorothy is burbling on about the cold winter weather. Her arrested sense of season can't catch on, even in the pitching morning heat. Cassandra will have to capitulate to air-conditioning within an hour—not so much to cool her mother down as to simply appease her convictions.

"Yup. Pretty cold out there," Cassandra says, gratifying coffee in hand. It occurs to her that drinking hot coffee as she anticipates heat is its own contradiction.

"Sit, again," Toni requests.

Cassandra complies. Anywhere else, she would immediately like a woman like Toni. Here, every instinct is tempered in mistrust.

Cassandra says, "So, how do you know my name? The girls last night went away believing my name was Emma."

Toni laughs. "Yes. That's what they called you when they talked to me. They were pretty bewildered."

Cassandra sips.

Toni says, "I called your brother."

Cassandra sips.

Toni continues. "He should have told me weeks ago that you were coming. I knew he had a sister—that your mother had a daughter who left Big Horn a long time ago. I know your brother Brian, too, a little, but he and his wife keep more to themselves than—"

Cassandra laughs. "—than James and Paige? I'm not surprised to hear that."

"Well, James makes more noise but he isn't exactly forth-coming. I imagine you know that. He's more public—you know he's the first counselor, right?"

"Yes. I've been informed several times."

"And Paige does her part as a supportive and sociable wife. I admire it. But they hold their cards close, if you know what I mean."

Cassandra's tongue burns. "Yeah. I do."

"I'm just saying this to explain why I had no idea you had come home to take care of your mother until Kylie and Michelle—the ministering sisters, I mean the visiting teachers in older terms—talked to me last night."

"Does anyone else know?"

"No one I can speak for. Do you want it to stay secret—I mean, private? Can I talk about you, make you the contact person, that is, and assign families to bring in dinner once or twice a week? Send people over to give you a break? You know, your mother really has been competent—lucid, I mean, and seemed like herself—until just a few months ago. Things changed, it seems, just as the cold weather was ending. When the roads cleared. I think it took everyone a while to realize how bad it had gotten."

Toni stops, gauging her listener. "Maybe you know this already."

"No. Not a lot of communication in my family. At least not that I'm privy to."

"She seems more settled into the house, now, but for a while she was getting into her car and then—well, who knows what she intended, but she'd get lost, pull into the wrong driveway, walk into other people's houses. Nobody minded, of course, but James was mortified, and everyone was worried about her safety.

"The point is, it wouldn't be any trouble to assign dinner twice a week, and make sure someone shows up a couple of mornings a week to let you get out and stock up on groceries, or just breathe a little, you know? Caretaking is a taxing occupation."

Cassandra's first impulse: *Hell no.* Let these people in and they'll go crazy with an opportunity to reconvert. Or gape and tell stories. Why do these people need so much reassurance that their doctrines are irresistible?

Then: get real. Credit where credit's due: Mormons rule the bring dinner-and-help-out-on-a-schedule game. She's been rehearsing to herself, barely but necessarily convinced: let good things be good. Take people one by one. Try.

Toni raises an eyebrow. "I don't know if this is the right thing to say, but—well, I get the sense that your brother, and sister-in-law, have reached capacity."

Cassandra considers this. Everything here so familiar, readable. So unintelligible and foreign. "Of course they have."

"I think they've done the best they can."

"Yes."

As far as James understands things, Cassandra is certain, his sister took the easy route—cut and ran while he stayed home to shoulder the family responsibility—the "leadership" he's always craved as his right while resenting his special burden. Right now, this is simply a thing she knows about him. The emotion is mere math—a simple matter of moving quantities.

God, she doesn't want to fight anyone in this place. Feel anything. Swim in a pool that only flips her back into the same processed water, lap after lap after lap after exhausting pointless lap.

"I'm not looking to hide. I'm way past accounting for anything I've ever done or been in this town. Whoever I am to people here is a scarecrow I don't want to contend with. I'm here for Dorothy, because James wrote to me and said she's more or less lost her mind and she needs live-in care, and they've had it. And yes, I am her daughter.

"But I'm not happy to be here. I planned on never coming back. And whenever this—whatever it is—is over, I'm returning to my life and my house and the people I call mine and I intend to go forward. I learned a long time ago that my origin cannot be my home."

Cassandra has no idea what Toni Fuller knows, or thinks she understands. As Relief Society president, she must have some access to institutional records. Clearly she knows that Cassandra does not claim the faith, has made no effort to consort with Latter-day Saints.

In this world, apostasy isn't just some choice to walk away. It's—the ultimate, hideous affront. The red telephone. What has James told Toni? What's Paige's rendition? Who waits in the wings, eager to blurt hometown tales?

Toni lays both elbows on the table and leans toward Cassandra, about to speak. But Dorothy gets there first: "I've always loved the smell of coffee. Makes me feel like I'm somewhere exotic."

Toni and Cassandra swivel toward the old woman.

Come to think of it, Toni probably sees Cassandra as an old woman as well. Which is strange because Cassandra can't figure out how old she is in this place. Mostly, a very tired sixteen.

"Me too." Toni smiles. "The smell of coffee always feels like a little getaway, doesn't it, Sister Soelberg?"

"Daddy, at the veteran's hospital. We sat with that lady."

"What the hell?" Cassandra says, and then corrects herself. "I mean, what the—"

"—hell," Toni finishes. "Right? She's been this way, you know. Little things remind her of something. You'll probably be able to make more sense of her random talk than the rest of us."

"He died when she was fourteen," Cassandra says. "Crazed horse, in a lightning storm. He wasn't even riding it. It just came running out of the dark. Hit him like…justice."

"Do you have any more of that toast?" Dorothy asks Toni.

"I sure do." Toni stands up and drops two slices into the toaster. "Coming right up, Lady Dorothy."

Dorothy giggles.

Toni turns back to face Cassandra. "Justice? Sounds like some history there. I might come from some of the same kinds of people." She picks up the butter knife, regards the toaster, lays the knife down again. "Does she like jelly?"

"She likes toast, period."

"Let's slather it on. Why fix what ain't broke. I came here to make sure I get this right with *you.*"

Toni sets buttered, jellied toast onto Dorothy's plate, then turns full attention to Cassandra. "Help me confirm. You're no secret but you don't want publicity. I'll make it very clear that Dorothy here is the ward project, not you. And you could use a break once in a while. I can help make that happen. Did I get any of that wrong?"

Cassandra considers. She almost wants this Toni Fuller, this realistic and unexcitable Relief Society president, to get it wrong. Cassandra wishes to be indignant and solitary in a town she resents, abetted by useful stereotypes.

However. "Thank you. This is very kind."

"Can I ask you a more personal question?" Toni inquires, and then, when she sees Cassandra stiffen: "Not terribly personal. Just—more sociable than the mission at hand."

Cassandra nods.

Toni says, "I've heard from people here and there, over the years, that you're an artist. The real thing."

Cassandra drops her taut shoulders. Eases her jaw. Her ears are ringing, as they do when she's feeling stress, which currently is all the time. "I guess so—whatever the 'real thing' means. I make a living at it. I care about it—"

She pauses. She watches Toni Fuller for signs of distraction, for dutiful but shallow chat, for something like *I sure wish I could live a wonderful creative life like yours, but I have responsibilities.*

"—a lot," Cassandra finishes. "Maybe it's all I know how to care about."

"Well, you cared enough to come back. That speaks volumes."

"None coherent."

"You've been in Minneapolis?"

"St. Paul."

"I love that area. My son was a missionary out there. We flew out to pick him up when he was finished. We spent a week to let him show us the sights."

Cassandra pictures the conspicuous Mormon boys in white shirts, their neckties and bright scrubbed faces as they ride through the streets of a city that shelters her from what they represent. "I see them ride by sometimes on their bikes," she offers. "I think how far from home they must feel."

Toni Fuller stands, and circles around the table. She puts her hands gently on Dorothy's frail shoulders. Dorothy tilts her face upward like a child, pats Toni's diamond-ringed hand. Toni says, "You're kind to think of them that way. My son struggled the whole two years. Came home and fell into a deep depression. He hasn't been the same. At all."

"How long has he been home?"

"Almost a year. You know, Bishop White is all about the healing wonders of missionary work for young men. It's kind of his special cause. He tells mission stories every chance he gets, and as bishop he gets plenty. He says he had a powerful revelation on his mission in Florida that changed him forever. Converted hundreds, by his telling. That's all fine, I guess, but not every man is made like him. Not every mission experience—"

"What did you say?"

Toni stops short. "I'm sorry. I didn't mean to go on and on—"

Cassandra backs toward the glass. "No. Who?"

"My son? I'm sorry. Here I told you I wouldn't go on about religion and then I start gushing about my missionary son—"

"Bishop? Who?"

Toni emits a sharp laugh, not rude but nervous. "I forgot

that you already know people in this town. I mean Bishop White. Allan White. Your brother James is first counselor. Brandon Jensen is Second Counselor, but he's young and just moved here with his wife and kids a few years ago, so—"

"Allan White?"

Toni stops speaking entirely, perceiving something she does not understand.

Cassandra glances toward her mother, who is licking her lips, engrossed in smoothing a paper napkin.

No wonder James and Paige have been evasive—if communicating almost nothing at all, ever, even in the throes of maternal geriatric crisis, is the definition of not-evasive. Dorothy must have become one hell of a pain in the ass for them to summon Cassandra home. They must be counting on Cassandra's isolation, or, short of that, her sense of shame.

Cassandra drops into blank. Everything feels compressed. She steadies herself for the second cyclone wall.

Toni Fuller stands across the table, blanched. "I'm sorry. It's clear I said something wrong. I'm so sorry."

Cassandra says, "It's nice to meet you. I appreciate all you do for my mother. I just—I just don't—"

The window above the sink spins like a pinwheel. The bottom of Cassandra's skull feels like sponge. Her knees buckle; she sits down hard on a dining chair—hard enough to hurt. Hard enough to make her gasp. She suppresses a nauseous heave.

Dorothy—*Dorothy*—tunes in, most improbable: "Cassandra, are you all right? What's the matter with you?"

Toni says, "I—I don't want to just leave when I've clearly put you in a bad place. Help me understand the best thing I can do—"

Cassandra hears herself make a request. "Do you think, maybe…I mean, do you have just a few minutes to sit here with my mother? I think I need to take a short walk. I haven't really been out of the house since I got here."

"Of course. Please. I can be here for the next hour. I can even call in reinforcements."

"No, that's not necessary. Just, maybe, twenty minutes."

"Go."

She reels out the sliding door to the deck. Rattles down the stairs to the basement level and lurches, for lack of direction, toward Hal's tool shed. The shimmer of her father's form sets her on another trajectory, forced along an impostor's high privacy fence to the south corner. A hard left turn launches her upward toward the street. In a strange vein of clarity amid the spin, she recalls a parade of animals as she ascends: ducks in the runoff pond, now sealed and capped. Pet sheep, rough mountain ponies from Grandpa Soelberg's place, stray cats, pheasants in the brush, a succession of mongrel dogs, each cloying and, as much as her family was capable, beloved.

A vivid projection of Matthew, joyful, arms full of orchard kittens.

She's at the street. North, the Crease, the big city headgate, the rolling estates of rich comers and old-school strivers. The spectral infernal charismatic ruthless Whites between her and the granite loom of Big Horn Mountain. East, houses and cul-de-sacs obscuring the irrigation routes that once snaked below the steep upward shove of Box Elder.

South, the broadening valley, stretching three towns and twenty miles to the algae-ridden water of a ravaged lake. Beyond, one colonized range after another and another and another, each a distinguishable but unnameable shade of blue in the shimmering haze.

She stands in a mirage rising from unnatural heat, the edge of asphalt.

Her crazy mother and a disconcerted visitor await her return.

From here, the small house looks harmless.

From here, the small house pumps like a malicious heart.

...

Later, evening: Toni Fuller stands once more on the front porch.

"I won't come in. I brought you something."

Cassandra steps out to the porch.

A little paper sack, tied with a yellow ribbon. Inside, a chilled carton of lush cream.

"Toni, this is so kind. I'm sorry—"

"No. I stepped somewhere I shouldn't have. Please forgive me."

Cassandra draws her gaze upward to the high canyons, green amid the burns. She pictures the descent down the other side, the encircled hanging valley. The sapphire reservoir at the drain point.

"I left this place in 1984. I've spent my life since telling myself that none of it matters. I'm working very hard to make it true. But—"

She tapers.

Toni: "I'm not a therapist. Right here I'm not even a Relief Society president. I don't have many people to talk to who don't hold me to that role. You hardly know me. You owe me no explanation. At all."

A kid next door, maybe fourteen, dribbles a basketball, as he always does this time of day. He will persist until he's called to supper. Clearly he dreams of stardom and grace.

A young man and woman, egregiously Aryan, fit as supermodels, dressed in matching sweats, push a deluxe baby stroller between them as they jog by.

It's still too early—and hot—for the sound of crickets.

"Bearer of cream," Cassandra says. "That is a lovely role."

"Big Horn kid, forever here and not," Toni replies. "An impossible role."

Chapter 10

She awakens, wrapped in a soft blanket on the mattress she laid out on the covered deck, just below her mother's window. The solution. Why did it take so long?

The air is cool and only a little smoky.

Early trill of a canyon wren.

She sits in the lawn chair outside the open sliding door to watch the west hills illuminate, tips to base. She sips coffee with rich cream. Dorothy is at the table, engrossed in meticulous nothing. This must be something like caring for a compliant but incapable child—largely eventless, perpetually consuming. Slow, low-grade frustration.

There's something about air with no water in it—a sensation of lift, body half helium.

Cassandra holds an early, sun-drenched memory—so primal she might be recalling a vivid early dream. Must be a ward picnic, or maybe the annual Big Horn City celebration. Yes. Snippets of parade: homemade floats, bright crepe paper flowers pushed into chicken wire. Children in pioneer costumes—all "big kids" in the memory, so she must be only three or four years old. "Cowboys" and face-painted "Indians" on decorated ponies and sting-ray bikes. Candy raining down at her feet. Late-summer greenery in the park, peaches and pears and raspberries, sheet cakes and fruit pies laid out for sale in makeshift stands.

Cassandra's visual recall levels with the display tables: cakes receding on a horizon until her father's hands wrap fully around her ribcage and he lifts her up in one swift dappled arc, setting her on his shoulders. Suddenly a giant's view: confections, people, balloons. Leafy branches framing gray-green mountains, high granite, blinding sky.

Infused: the luxury of water. She knows from later experience that her brothers were further on, big enough to romp in the showers streaming from hydrants and hoses. Big enough to take their turns launching water balloons from homemade catapults, to jitter in the dunking box awaiting a true softball aim.

But here in the recessed quiet and shade of the city hall courtyard, a multitude of small children and smiling watchful parents. An estuary of plastic kiddie pools, glinting metal feed troughs, clean-rinsed washtubs, all filled kid-ankle-deep with snowmelt water siphoned from the open ditch. Her small friends from Grove Street and Sunday School, kids she knows and doesn't, blond and brown and sorrel mops, ponytails, buzz cuts, little sunhats, underwear, bright shorts and shirts with cars, flowers, butterflies, or no shirts at all. Pure joy of hot sun, cold limbs, breathless splash, the smell of wet green lawn, walled in by parental legs like solicitous trees. Mommy and Daddy hands reaching to steady toddler bodies, dipping and un-dipping hesitators and daredevils alike.

She senses, most striking now, the sweet pure joy of the young parents, the unstrained levitation of love and protection. A community of bedazzled mothers and fathers, Eden before the many falls to come, the tensions and pressures and fatigues, the alien world encroaching.

The wonder of this childhood illusion: perfect safety. Timeless love. A mirage of order and early sensuous joy. And in the center of the memory, in the very eye of this exuberant scene of sunlit water: a radiant boy. Was it Allan? Has she transposed the phantom of her own lost child over the memory of another? The father, or son? Ecstasy in tiny blue shorts, wet curls lengthened to his darling shoulders, dripping with melted mountain snow. Miyazaki legs. Wide, wondering high-blue eyes. He stands in a tiny pool, alone in exuberant thrall, vital in the embrace of an ample planet. A Primary children's song pours from his throat, his choirboy voice pure as a meadowlark's:

I'm small I know but wherever I go
the grass grows greener still.
Singing, singing all the way!
Give away, oh give away!
Singing, singing all the way!
Give, oh, give, away!

Chapter 11

Evening. Dorothy in the Cozy Room, tucked under fleece, euphoric as she watches *Here Comes the Groom*. Cassandra on the lawn chair on the deck, watching the sun set over what was once her father's orchard. Local fables long marked the low dividing hill as an "Indian graveyard." Was it? When did her brothers sell? Even if they sold early on, the profit must have been hefty. Where did it go? The house, here, is stripped and fossilized. Is there nothing left for Dorothy? Is it spent? Stashed? Maybe Dorothy should be living happy and oblivious in a cushy old folks' home, surrounded by people her age, sopping up milk and soup with buttered toast, watching TV from a soft overstuffed chair, exclaiming with her friends over the musical numbers and bright Technicolor motion.

Maybe not.

Hal told Cassandra the day she left for college that she would not inherit any part of his "estate." Irene's college legacy was more than she deserved, and since her brothers and cousins received only "pittances" in comparison, Hal would have to make it up to them.

"I guess you'd better find a way to make an art degree pay the rent. Unless you manage to find a competent husband. You've shot your chances here."

Again with the mixed legacy. She *has* made her art degree pay the rent, and more. The education was luxurious but not

61

gratuitous, despite her grandmother's sentimental passion for pointless knowledge. Hal's cynicism has kept his daughter grounded as an artist: it's a lucky (*say it: blessed*) gift, yet also a hard-earned ticket to bread and sometimes butter. His voice is too deeply ingrained to let her wallow in oversaturated art school theories of transcendence, elite discernments, hypersensitive aesthetics. Funny, though, how much all that artistic bullshit actually sounded like her father's religion. All that chosenness. The capital of special suffering, the preoccupations of purity, the degradations of living amongst the madding crowd.

Hal's tool shed sits in the back corner, better preserved than the house itself. She guesses the power saws, the sprayers and hoses, the compressor, the hammers and wrenches and meticulously arranged screwdrivers and boxes of nails, washers, screws, and bolts have been dispersed between the extant brothers.

And the guns.

The door is latched and padlocked. Another portal she will not open.

This morning Cassandra remembers everything as if from a movie seat, her body only eyes and ears. Her father's jerking gestures, hinged at the elbow. The foil glint of flocked wallpaper behind him. The pitch of his voice, somewhere between hellfire preacher and sonorous councilman. His voice percussing the orchard quiet. The chronic choke of disappointment.

She had been direly afraid of him. Even now her nerves jerk at the echo of his voice—once it intrudes, her brain loops him on tireless, warping repeat.

He never hit her—not even the night he'd made her strip, eyed her up and down like a piece of livestock, confirmed his suspicions, and dismissed her forever from whatever had once passed as love and approval. Not even then. In fact, beyond the one bright memory of the kiddie pools, she had no memory at all of him ever—*ever*—touching her. He had hit her brothers plenty, but he laughed and chattered and romped among them, too. The four of them, wild horses, inseparable. Her brothers had each been physical, lean and muscular even as children. Hal took them fishing and riding in summer, deer hunting in the fall. In winter they cut ice on the reservoirs, hauled up lake trout and cisco, grilled them onshore over a roaring fire. They slept in pungent bedrolls under October stars. For all the violence, or maybe because of it, they were father and brothers. A warrior band. Goddamned Vikings, reduced to livid desert Mormons. Indignation of the once-persecuted, nothing coming at them now but prophecy.

In her father's world of useful things, a daughter was a whet-stone: *Look at that. Even your sister can do it. What's wrong with you, pussy?*

Come here, Cassandra. Show this fool James how to tie a square knot.

You'd look cuter than Cassandra in a little pink dress. Get a haircut before I make you wear a pinafore, you little faggot.

Thus Hal had taken care to teach his daughter a profitable range of masculine skills, country-girl style. In those moments, he was patient, almost tender—but she'd learned it was only one point in a cycle. How to hold a framing hammer, down at the base, letting it swing to impact. At his parents' place, out in the desert, Hal showed her the gentlest way to slide a bit into a horse's mouth—all trust, no fight. When she was fourteen he'd sent her out to East Field on the red Massey Ferguson to rake hay—at least until Wyatt McDaniel called Hal to say he'd been watching from the north acre. *The girl rolls the rows too tight, ya know.*

Were she a boy, Wyatt would have called from across the fence: "You're rolling that hay too tight! Ease up a little so it can dry apace!" But because she was a girl, this was the confirmation Wyatt was looking for. No use instructing a female. And no matter what paternal opinions might ever have sprouted in Hal on his own time, other men's declarations put a quick end to them. *Something awfully fragile in your father's picture of himself,* her grandmother said once, in a crucial season. *He needs other men to approve. It's just a thing to know about him, not a thing to try and fix. Some things you have to understand as the simple facts of family relations.*

Even so, for Hal, every skill his daughter mastered ignited a moment of flickering joy. A smile of paternal pride, ingenuous pleasure. Cassandra couldn't not crave it. Because he expected nothing from her, anything she delivered was a disconcerting surprise. His sons, from whom he demanded proof of Everything, could never rise to his unconveyable standards.

Whatever the effect upon Cassandra as a child, it did accumulate into unusual grown-up competence, the antithesis of his attraction to Dorothy. Cassandra's house in St. Paul is largely restored because she understands everyday tools and machines. Now with the internet as education, she finds confidence to make plumbing repairs, to rewire a lousy breaker, to take down a wall or frame a new window. It doesn't require masculine strength so much as masculine know-how, in her world passed from father to son but sometimes cue-balled against a convenient daughter.

As she approached puberty: *Go help your mother now. A girl looks unfeminine with a hammer in her hand. Don't get carried away with this.*

Hal was a skilled and careful craftsman, probably the source of her artistic hand. She'd surprised her professors by taking up the welding torch in a sculpture class, by helping her classmates corner canvas framing with the studio's chop saw. Hal: *Too bad you're not a boy. A lot of unnecessary talent you got there.* He was most tender at this stage, patiently building evidence, accumulating a case for pitting her brothers against the foreboding feminine.

James, oldest, high-strung and insecure, caught the worst of the verbal abuse. Cassandra imagines their father's voice continues to shout even now in James's unhappy head: *You damn fool! Check your mirror! Watch the rear! How many times do I have to say it? Turn the wheel the same direction you want the back of the trailer to go!*

Slam. Trailer bumper bent around the gatepost. James proclaiming his chronic innocence. *Something in my eye! You said left, not right! You told me wrong! The gear slipped! Stupid truck! Dammit, you pathetic crybaby! Get out of that cab! Let this little girl show you how it's done! Cassandra, take the wheel!*

Brian, second, solid and impassive, transformed into an automaton. He took the tools from his father's hands, proceeded through the motions, succeeded or failed, absorbed the abuse, and walked away.

Hal was compelled to chase him down.

Don't you know how to speak, boy? Answer me when I'm talking to you! You need me to slap some sense into you? Haven't you got a single question? You can't learn what you don't ask.

Hard slap, upside the head. Brian's fixed gaze, hard angular jaw.

Slap. Hard slap. Shove. Brian on the hard gravel, bloody palms.

You gonna make me take off my belt? Well, you're the one begging for it—

Matthew, youngest boy, two years older than Cassandra. Smart and quick, easy grin. Sly as hell. That tumbling curly hair. Waited and watched, let their father exhaust himself on Brian, made himself look busy and angelic for the denouement.

The denouement, a jab in every direction: *How is it I got myself four daughters, not one! Cassandra's the toughest of all of you whiners.*

The long-arc denouement: Matthew—Matilda—lost among the teeming chemical homeless somewhere in Los Angeles. Or by now, Cassandra hopes, just somewhere, unlost at least to himself. She wonders whether the superhuman street campers, the incorrigible wanderers, the underpass denizens congregating or hoofing it in heat and rain and blizzard, are the genetic inheritors of Indigenous travelers and mountain men, fierce wily conduits of anachronistic human capacities in a post-natural landscape.

She carries a twenty in her pocket each time she walks in the city, making sure she hands it off to some ghost, or another, of Matilda.

Matilda was the only sibling Cassandra had communicated with for decades. An email, every so often, from some public computer, somewhere. Sometimes he'd signed his name "Matthew." More often, over time, "Matilda." The sporadic, incoherent requests for money had become sparser every season. Now Cassandra does not know whether Matilda is alive or dead. She has no idea which parts were cause, which were effect, or which were simply unaccountable cosmic tangles.

All of them. All of it.

Their mother is well beyond knowing much at all, at least in real time.

Yet Dorothy is, on this day, in a sunny mood, and she knows her own daughter.

"Good morning, Cassandra," she says from the kitchen, buttering her own toast. "Are you ready for your big test today?"

"I certainly hope so," Cassandra replies. No irony here.

Chapter 12

The fact of her femininity was, as early as she remembers existing, a crucial one. So crucial it required perpetual proof and demonstration. As far as she can make sense of it, the proof had no purpose in and of itself. The point was to demonstrate that other people in the family had effective dicks. Maybe especially: Matthew.

"Your mother wanted a girl," Hal liked to remind her. "She wanted a daughter so bad she took the risk of having another child, even after a difficult pregnancy with Matthew. The doctor told her it would be dangerous. Sure enough, she spent the last two months in bed, useless to everyone but you. You'd better show some gratitude."

Did she, though? Did Dorothy really want a daughter? Doesn't seem to Cassandra that she'd fulfilled any species of longing in her mother at all, ever. Dorothy was radiant in the presence of men—particularly when she was the only "female"—as her father usually referred to girls and women. Cassandra was, somehow, despite herself, competition.

Alone with her daughter, Dorothy was brusque and instructive. Cassandra learned early that women spoke straightest when no man was present. On first-grade school shopping: *Always pick vertical stripes, so you don't look fatter than you actually are.*

Pink and red look garish together. Blue and light blue are soothing and compelling.

Keep your knees together. Forge the habit now and you'll never be caught looking coarse. I wish my mother had emphasized this sooner.

Dorothy, yanking a fine-tooth comb through Cassandra's little-girl hair: *Stop your crying. Crying makes you ugly.*

A peculiar disgust—barely contained contempt—on her mother's face in the mirror as she rolled pin curls in a rote pattern on her daughter's head. *I can just send the boys to bed, but I have to spend half the night making a girl presentable* (Cassandra's straight, fine yellow hair. Matthew's tumbling curling puppy-brown locks…).

Now Cassandra can better trace the contours. Her mother's work was all intervention, a perpetual vigilance against the revulsion and wrath of the man she married. Maybe of men in general. And when Cassandra stands in the right places (not many of those), she can make herself see her father as a constitutionally hurt and damaged man (was there any other kind, in that place and time?), so anxious to prove his legitimacy it overrode every softening impulse.

For all the many memorable images she carries in her mind, she knows nothing at all about her father's people, taut shrub-desert Mormons, big-boned and pollen-eyed, shut-mouthed, suspicious, good with horses.

Why did Hal despise "unfeminine" women even more than he despised the "feminine" ones? She's not sure he hated women, but he was obsessed with their behavior. It occurs to her now that he felt sorry for them for having to be what they were. Yet even so, they had to be women. It wasn't his fault. God required it. The urgent, necessary, tenuous order of things.

As far as Cassandra can reassemble her, Hal's mother, Velma, was little more than a farmhand. Shapeless, plain, and plain worn out. She lived in a small house—almost a cabin—on the east edge of the family "ranch"—a few hundred unattended cattle, some alfalfa struggling under inadequate sprinkler pipe, the Great Salt Lake shimmering like a taunt along the northeast horizon. Her garden alongside the house was a matter of subsistence, no joy in it. She wore a cotton frock and a full-coverage apron, Oxfords with rolled-down socks. Green Wellingtons when the mud rose.

"Tell me your name again, honey," she always said to Cassandra. Every damned visit—which, to be fair, happened once a year at most.

Did Hal love his mother? He spoke gently to her. He stood near her, stormy and protective, when his father was present.

He never spoke of her.

Cassandra suspects her father was raised fundamentalist, which helps her see his life beyond it as an act of guilty self-liberation. Which affiliation? Maybe none. A thousand sects out there in those visionary hills. A new wave of fiery purists every generation. Did old Grandpa Soelberg fancy himself a prophet?

Were they polygamists? The scattered but congregated housing—trailers, cabins, a couple of rundown farmhouses, a distant bunkhouse—women and kids, "aunts" and "grandmothers" and "cousins" present but obscure, murmuring talk of angels dark and light, low reprimands, homilies, incantations and insider epithets...those old Soelbergs must have seen painted Dorothy as a whore of Babylon. Hal loved her modern trappings, as much as he could love anything or anyone at all. In that sense, Hal and Dorothy's marriage was a romance. So much seemed to depend on Dorothy's "classy" presentation, up-to-date and beyond reproach. As far as she can tell, Cassandra slept every night of her childhood in the misery of hair curlers, every Sunday beyond eleven years old compressed into nylon pantyhose, every hunting season stuck in the house watching "doe party" musicals with her mother, every youth activity night producing evidence of future wifeliness, because Dorothy's project was to prove to Hal, demonstration by demonstration, that the daughter she'd produced was no regeneration of Velma Soelberg.

Or of Irene Caldwell, for that matter. Why, in Hal's philosophy, would any woman don a man's work clothes by choice? What kind of woman revels—*thrives*—with a hoe in her hands? To him it must have seemed plain retrograde. Irene, not her Barbie daughter Dorothy, was the unnatural feminine aberration. That he'd rescued his wife and all future female progeny from wearing coveralls, from casing dirt under broken fingernails, from their coarse "masculine" voices or useless, mercenary feminist fantasies, smug language ill-got from "so-called intellectuals"—all of it, to him, marked the hard-earned virtue of a righteous man. Why any woman within the sphere of his bounty would transgress was beyond him.

A memory, unaddressed: Cassandra, nearly eight. October air, cold and warm in colliding currents. This day, her grandmother made a rare visit; Irene and Dorothy and Cassandra—and daughterless Aunt Emma, whose sons were on the mountain—spent the day peeling apples, cutting and mashing, cooking them down by the bushel into fragrant winter preserves. The house smelled of cinnamon and vinegar—apple butter in clean jelly jars, applesauce and chunky pie filling sealed in hot Mason glass. Dorothy, for all her trappings, never cottoned to the feminine crafts of her pioneer ancestry; in this ritual absence of the men and boys, off to the deer hunt, Irene and Emma arrived to assist. To be generational women together in warm kitchen conversation.

Cassandra had never seen her mother in this way. Among her mother and sister, Dorothy was hearty and brash. She was irreverent, witty, ratcheting up a family talent for mimicking voices and gestures, reenacting local gossip, old Big Horn jokes spiked with digressions and annotations. Sometimes the women in the kitchen got laughing so hard they lost their breath; once, Aunt Emma had to sit on the floor, weak, tears running down her cheeks, and laughed even harder when Cassandra said, "I don't get it."

Cassandra did not want this day to end. She could hardly bear to go to bed, to lose the bright vivid hours. The departing women stood on the porch in the gusting wind, pointing out the bonfires, orange star beacons high on the dark mountain slopes. "Up there at the Sinks," Irene gestured. "See, Cassandra? Way up there to the right, just before the ranges come to corner—you can see the flicker. Your dad and your brothers, uncles, and cousins are right up there. Keep watching. It comes and goes."

"That was Daddy's hunting spot," Emma said.

"And his father's, too," Dorothy added. "Caldwell men have been bringing deer down from the Sinks since they came to this valley. Everyone knows it's reserved at deer season. It's hard to get to, closed in among the cliffs. We used to go up there on the horses—all of us, when we were kids, while the weather was still warm and dry. We camped and climbed the rocks. Mama cooked over the fire, just like the old pioneer grandmas. Everyone pitched in to clean out the old shepherd's cabin for the autumn hunt."

Little Cassandra could hardly make sense of this. Her mother? Prim Aunt Emma? Up there in the rocks and high pines? It seemed a fairy tale, and she yearned to enter.

The next day, her mother was restless and moody. She spent most of the day in satin pajamas, often taking to the bed, curlered hair protected under a silk scarf. Cassandra made her own dinner—chicken noodle soup from a can. She carefully poured a mug for Dorothy, only spilling a little. She carried the soup to the bedroom, mincing steps.

"I don't want it. Close the door, please."

At twilight, Cassandra put herself to bed.

Her brothers awakened her. Darkness, inside and outside, made her believe she was dreaming.

"Come see! It's a big one!"

Out she trailed, barefoot on the frost, in her white flannel nightgown. The horses were tied at the fence, shifting and nickering in starlight. Her father and uncles were in a fine mood, big cousins jostling and jovial. Two bucks still slung over saddles. The biggest, a six-point, lay on its side on the lawn, dead-eyed, breathtaking muscular beauty. A well-cut slash ran the length of the gut.

"Dad bagged it. Long shot, straight to the chest. Here. Want to see inside?"

She tried to back away, but James stood behind her, blocking retreat.

Brian said, "Matthew wasn't afraid. He learned how to gut them, up there." He gestured toward the Sinks. The high granite glowed vaguely, answering the slender moon. She thought of the animals cowering in their dens, hiding in the groves as hunters slept among their rifles.

She stole a glance toward Matthew, who answered with a gremlin grimace.

James: "Just take a peek. It's all clean now. You can see the ribs. The red meat is pretty."

Cassandra leaned down, then, morbidly curious, fell to her hands and knees. She crawled forward, cautious. James leaned over her to pull the top side high, exposing the cavity. "Go on in. It's like a little room. Just your size."

"You can hide in there. Jump out and surprise Mom when she comes to see."

No!

"Come on. It's no big deal. We've all done it. First hunt, you have to go in and come out, like getting born again. Born to the wild."

Cassandra was incredulous, but her brothers' faces curved around her, nodding. She was the center of their rare and smiling attention. They wanted her to be one of them!

"C'mon, Cass. Are you scared?"

Cass? No one had ever called her that. "Cass" sounded cool and sleek. She knew their mother would not approve.

"Matthew wasn't afraid."

Matthew's expression neither contradicted nor confirmed.

"You can do it," Brian said. "It's scary, but so is nature. It's not all pretty trees and flowers, you know? It's a kind of special trial. Like Jonah in the whale."

Once, later—after she came home from college—she asked him. "What were you thinking? I was seven. It was dark and cold. I was in my nightgown. All those boys, just standing there, watching."

Brian's veiled green eyes, wide open but blinking, rhythmic, met hers a moment, then dropped in shame. "I don't know. Stupid things happen on the mountain. It gets weird up there. I guess we hadn't shook it off."

Then, looking at the sky: "I'm sorry."

Cassandra took a breath and crawled in. The meat was cold and strangely fragrant. White cartilage gleamed in dull stripes.

James dropped the cut and set his foot on the carcass. She could hear him, muffled but clear.

"Matthew, go get Mom. Make her come out and see."

The white flannel of her nightgown soaked through at the contact points. Arms pinned under the compression, she kicked at the walls, threw her head back against the hard spine.

She could not interpret the muffled screaming sound, could not pinpoint the source in her own throat. No words in it. Guttural, pitching, raw, unchildlike. She could hear masculine voices, even laughter, outside the layers of bone, meat, hide, fur. She believed her father would deliver her, but she was not released.

Her mother's garish wail opened the gash. The big boys laughed, then stopped and backed away. Brian's strong hands pulled her out. His canvas coat flaps wrapped around her. His breathing flannel chest, his pounding heart.

"Get away from her, now," he said—quiet, almost indiscernible, but everyone shrank back into the darkness. The men at the periphery, including Hal—the grown men who had not intervened—got busy with tack and canvas.

"Matthew," Brian barked, "go run a bath."

"I had her all ready for Sunday morning!" Dorothy wailed, unable to address the actual horror at hand. "Now I'll have to start over. She'll probably catch cold. Me too. You're just making more work for me with shenanigans like this!"

"Go inside, Mama," Brian said. "Quit your fussing. She's not going to church tomorrow. I'll put her to bed."

He sat on the floor, outside the bathroom, waited out the warm water and his sister's muffled, frightened sobs. He wrapped her in a blanket when she emerged—wrapped it right over the towel. He set her up on the counter and blew her hair dry. Brushed it smooth, gentle.

"Your hair is pretty," he murmured. "Mama ought to leave it alone."

He lifted her down to the floor. "Go put on some clean pajamas. Get under the covers. I'll come settle you in."

He sent Hal and Dorothy—and James and Matthew—off to church in the morning.

He sat with Cassandra in the late-autumn sun—chilly air, warm sideways light—in the backyard, the edge of Hal's poisoned orchard, as she slept on the quilt he'd spread for her.

Part Two

. . .

Reconstruct

Chapter 13

A dvanced Art at Clearlake High School was a fancy title for a class long established as a time killer. Qualifying was a matter of racking up antecedents: Introduction to Art and Intermediate Art, both of which could be taken sophomore year. The beautiful thing about Advanced Art, according to the stoners who sat in a far corner and ranked heavy metal bands, was that it extended over two periods, and you could take it over and over, each semester with a negotiated "emphasis," reserving dependable shelter and time for zoning out.

Jocks liked the class for the same reasons, but they sat up front and made more noise. Girls attracted to one group or the other sat at the peripheries, laughing when it made them look pretty.

Plus, it was okay to play music, sometimes a source of contention but too much of a privilege to squall about. Heavy metal some days, pop on others. Disco, never.

The actual art nerds milled about and managed to produce "art" in the marginal spaces. The 1977-78 school year art nerds: Lane MacClurg, a cheerful hefty guy with a yellow bowl haircut and a talent for graphics; Deborah Swain, an unaccountably personable cheerleader who drew cute cartoon animals; Ansel Portland, not a talker until his hands were engaged in wet spinning clay; Cassandra Soelberg, undeveloped as a human being, yet beyond her own comprehension an unerring visual conduit: object to setting to photographic brain to hand to line to paper. "How do you do that?" she'd been asked, as if she were performing magic tricks, since before she started elementary school. She drew pictures to entertain children she babysat. Orangutans. Kitty cats. Ponies. Spaceships. The children themselves.

"I don't know," she'd answer, ingenuous. She still didn't know, any more than she knew why her head grew hair or her body made blood. How do some people know, as soon as they hear it, how to make music? How does calculus ignite a particular peculiar mind?

The high school art teacher, Mr. Judd, asked no such questions. For him, natural artists were tacit bureaucratic currency. A possible stoner himself, he held down a fairly pleasant job—leisure-ish time in a sheltered classroom he'd inhabited like a grubby fox for twenty years at least. He seemed content amid the semi-busy clutter, spoke in a level unstrained tone when anyone asked a question—of any sort—and mostly sat at or on his desk, gazing toward, if not through, the enclosed patch of featureless lawn beyond the south window wall.

Even the "worst" kids were trouble-free in the art room; Judd had the temperament and good sense not to antagonize large itchy groiny human beings near the finish line of K-12 incarceration. There were two rules. Judd never spelled them out but everyone understood:

1) The talented kids must cover for everyone else—that is, the "true artists" were to convince the principal and school board that Art Was Happening at Clearlake High School, by actually making stuff.

2) The Advanced Art students—the whole motley crew, no one excused—must produce a grand mural for the junior prom, every spring—colored chalk and/or powdered tempera and/or colored Magic Marker on taped-together butcher paper, stretching across the north wall of the deluxe boys' basketball gym.

Nobody complained. The vice principal himself, usually seen returning truants to class, officially excused every Advanced Art student from every class period for a whole week before the prom. The basketball team was banished to the "old gym," a separate building semi-preserved on the original school site, across the track and football field where the old high school once stood.

Cassandra knew her job. Everybody knew Cassandra's job. Alignment of the minor stars over the course of this one week made her the most important person at Clearlake High, whether she wished to be or not. Possibly this made her feel proud, or wanted, or identified, or *something*, but now, trying to recall it, Cassandra is mostly struck by her younger self as simply obedient, accepting a remarkable talent as precisely what it was. Is: something she did not request but nevertheless received—more or less on the same plane as everything else, good or bad, beautiful or tragic, that ever chanced her way.

She does not recall, as a child, ever really wanting anything. She never thought to wish her father kinder or her mother less opaque. She accepted the facts of her brothers—superior in age and gender—at face value. She understood the planet as defined by rough mountains, dispensing sparse water to corresponding valleys at the caprice of an abstemious master. She went to church because she was required to. Because it was True. Women were equal to men in the eyes of the Lord but sidewise that is, women who helped men be important were blessed by that importance.

Some girls had incidental talents designed to serve a larger purpose, like the kingdom of God, or the junior prom. The world was a self-enclosed system of logic. A job chart. Cassandra's first job of prom week was to produce a thumbnail sketch based on her classmates' input. She taped three pieces of scratch paper together to resemble the proportions of the butcher paper to come. The burnouts were already assembling the real thing on the floor, guided by Brent McMillan, an underappreciated metal shop senior who understood the importance of a straight edge. Joey Johnson had rolled a scrap-filled tube the size of a trombone; the guys couldn't agree whether it was more entertaining as a giant joint or enormous dick.

Consulting the theme song was visually worrisome. "I Go Crazy" prompted all kinds of images the principal would not approve of.

"Well," Sandra pointed out. "There's, you know, eyes."

"That could get kind of gross."

"You could draw a guy looking into his girlfriend's eyes. And then, you know, we can just make romantic stuff."

"It could be raining, like, you know, tears."

"But it can't be too sad. We could put a huge rainbow over the whole scene."

"Or one in the background, at the focal point," said Lane. "Then everything can sort of lead toward the rainbow."

The jocks were fooling around with a stray practice ball, trying to hit the shooter's square on a drawn-up standard. The ball kept bouncing onto the laid-out butcher paper, triggering pepper sprays of *fuck you*s and *knock it off, assholes.* Mr. Judd said, "Okay, you guys. Get over there where Cassandra is and help plan the mural. Now."

The basketball boys orbited around one another in an atomic buzz, emanating a collective funky metallic scent. The butcher paper guys approached in sultry smoke. Various groupie girls threaded in, floral and perfume-ish. Everyone milled in a loose donut formation, leaning toward Cassandra, sitting on the floor.

"'I Go Crazy.' Who came up with that lame-ass song?" somebody said. "It's about a breakup."

"Shoulda been 'Do Ya Think I'm Sexy.'"

"Nooo. That one song—" Kendra Price said. She started to sing. "…and sometimes when we touch / the honesty's too much…"

"Oh, hell no," a third of the crowd shut her down.

Allan White, spinning the basketball on his middle finger, sang in a pretty effective falsetto: "Party! Party! Party! / Let me party with you! / I know what I'm trying to do / I'm trying to get it on with you..."

"What even is that song?" Deborah asked.

"I dunno. Some Black dude named Bunny."

"That's some ni—I mean, negro music. We ain't—"

"Don't say it, Brandon," Mr. Judd cut in. "We don't talk like that here" (although they did).

"Besides, Paul Davis is a negro. I mean Black. Whatever."

"No he isn't. Haven't you seen the record? He has blond hair."

"How about 'Hopelessly Devoted to You.'"

"Eeeuw."

"'Come Sail Away.'"

"Look, the song's already been chosen," Mr. Judd reminded them. "The junior class voted. Our job is to make a mural, not pick a song. It doesn't have to match all that much. Just do a hokey romantic thing that everyone will get all sentimental about. So, what are we going to put on it?"

Cassandra sketched out a vague background landscape on the typing paper: Gently rolling foothills receding into peakier mountains. A gap in the skyline in the upper half, crowned by a beckoning rainbow.

"Okay," she said. "Is it snowy, or is it more like Hawaii?"

"Hawaii." Unanimous.

Cassandra added some palm trees, and up-close tropical-seeming flowers in the foreground.

"You can ski on the high mountains in Hawaii. Put a little bit of snow on the peaks."

"So, there could be something like a pavilion, you know, where people are dancing."

Cassandra summoned memories of anything resembling a

pavilion, then sketched out the shape of the Clearlake Alfalfa Days merry-go-round, assembled in the town park every summer.

"Maybe it should have a grass roof," someone offered.

"Yeah, like a tiki hut."

Cassandra obliged.

"Okay, now it needs, like, a guy looking into his girlfriend's eyes. Maybe kissing in front of the sunset."

"They broke up, remember?"

"Well, he could be remembering back."

"There could be a band—like an old-fashioned big band for the dancers."

"No, a rock band."

"Wouldn't it need ukuleles or something?"

"Make another guy looking all jealous."

"I could put in some animals," Deborah offered. "What kind of animals live in Hawaii?"

"I don't know. Monkeys? Put in some ocean, and then Deborah can draw some dolphins and stuff."

Cassandra put down her pencil, overwhelmed. "Okay, give me a few minutes. I have to think about how to get it all in."

"Go," Mr. Judd commanded. "Everybody, get that paper rolled out and put together. Deborah, why don't you sketch some preliminary sea animals. And Hawaii has lots of birds, and sea turtles and stuff. Probably fancy lizards. Somebody go check out an encyclopedia. *H* for Hawaii. Maybe *P* for Polynesia. Tell the librarian I'll make sure it gets back. See what you can come up with. Lane, you can help sketch out ideas for details. Help Cassandra figure out where everything goes. And make sure you get 'Clearlake High Junior Prom 1978' somewhere that shows up in all the photographs."

Mr. Judd took a long stare at Ansel, the ceramics kid. "You," he said. "How are you going to contribute, here?"

"I can't draw. I have to feel what I make."

"Yeah, we know. You like to put your hands in wet, dark—"

"Knock it off, Brandon," Mr. Judd interrupted. "Okay, Ansel. Help Brent measure and tape the butcher paper. And then I want you to go talk to the Pep Club advisor about the design of the whole gym. They'll be coming in two days from now to get rolling with the crepe paper and shit—I mean, stuff. They've got paper lanterns, I think. Think you can make them look good with the mural? Maybe some stenciling or something. Three-dimensional enough for you?"

Ansel's lank dark hair, impossible to feather in an appropriate 1970s-guy fashion, dropped over his face in dismay. "Yeah, I think so. But I have to talk to the Pep Club?"

Mr. Judd said, "No, not the Pep Club. The Pep Club *advisor.* Miss Pirelli is probably in the girls' gym right now. How about... you three there..." he pointed at Kendra, Lisa B., and Dawnene, "...go with Ansel so he doesn't have to face the dragon lady alone. See what they've got planned so far. Let's try to figure out in advance what we'll have to fix once they've put their tacky little ideas all over the room."

Mr. Judd was a uniter—so good at his job, Cassandra sees now, he was undetectable. He didn't hate kids. Whoever he was on his own time, it was nothing to prove to sixteen-year-olds. He had the good sense to understand he wasn't training up artists so much as potential human beings who could come up with ideas, however outlandish, and troubleshoot. Jocks, artists, stoners, and groupies murmured together in common cause.

"Go!" said Mr. Judd. "If you don't have a specific assignment, figure out where you can help. I'd better see everyone busy on something every minute for the next four days. Then we'll see what happens on the day *of,* all right? Cassandra will start on the big sketch by tomorrow and you can all follow her along with the colors. Right, Cassandra?"

"Um. Yeah."

"That means, Cassandra's the one in charge. Do it exactly the way she tells you. Everyone! Hustle!"

...

Maybe the light show called the internet has eclipsed the attraction people used to feel watching Cassandra draw and paint. But then again, even now she shoos spectators away from her easel, from the emerging figures on a scratch pad, from the compulsion to narrate, comment, anticipate the effects of her stylus on an electronic screen. She doesn't really mind watchers; the weird magic of composition often surprises and fascinates her, too. After all these years, it's a simply good thing she takes pleasure in giving. Mostly.

But now, back in Clearlake Valley, amid the vestiges of a world she fled long ago, memory returns the source of her unease, the low-grade terror that accompanies any display of creative production. Once she believed she could pinpoint a precise moment, the single small turn or event that expelled her, spun her away from what she must now frankly confess was the root of selfness, passion, purpose in making: a landscape so stark and beautiful, so unlike any "scenic" place she's inhabited in her life beyond, so entirely *home*, she could not at sixteen recognize it as a thing to be named, or held, or removed from her.

She's told herself it was the night of the prom, the garishness of a stupid life in a stupid time. A beam of headlights over geological forms millions of years older than her religion allowed them to be. An imperceptible perturbance above pure cold mountain water, however channeled and abused, below stars and the primordial violence of the skyline. But that night was just one stroke of an absurd progression, now infinite regression.

What point on that timeline could have dislodged a single stone? What might have been made beyond an invisible mother? Some man, features, blood and sinew, a telling overkill of DNA, a story irrelevant to hers beyond first fluid and float? Children of his own, formed up from this mineral this water these doctrines this massive yet inconsequential cosmic fuck-up. On this planet, yet all these small immeasurable decades a phantom.

Unless he was hit by a car at seven, or drank himself to death at a freshman frat party, or got shot by a crazed coworker, or languished after chemotherapy, he walks the planet, idly entertaining the mysteries of the double helix, a living, breathing body stewed up in a ludicrous prom week concatenation.

A man exists, somewhere, because teenaged Cassandra Soelberg removed her pantyhose above a dark mountain reservoir. That "father," this "mother," spring 1978 in the Clearlake basketball gym, about to collide beyond a week of grubbing about in image and myth, chalk and powder paint, mating rites, religious phantasm, and whatever passed in a midcentury anti-communist bougie Caucasian Mormon town as secondary education.

Allan White was a charismatic boy, and beautiful—integral grace arcing into luminous prime. Made from an otherworldly beautiful family, shallow and socially vicious as they were. Classical marble or Renaissance oil could have rendered him timeless—the slender waist of a kouros, broad yet boyish shoulders. Tender pink lips contradicted the sharp line of his jaw, vulnerable but inscrutable.

She'd always taken him for granted, something like a brother—familiar and foreign, buzzing at the edges of her time at church and school, riding his sting-ray, then his raucous enduro past her house on the way to his. Milling about, grabbing at things, kicking dirt, making fart noises with his older brothers and hers. Garrulous, curious, impulsive, opportunistically sociable, apparently devoid of self-doubt.

Allan White was pretty good at anything he put a hand to. Football, for his father's sake. Easy with a basketball if it bounced in his direction. A consistent Little League hitter. The men in the neighborhood went slack-jawed describing his natural aim with a deer rifle, his casual accuracy picking off cans with a pistol.

He liked to sing—or, he simply sang, spontaneous, his warbling notes a product of the body like spit or wavy hair, or cum. Once Cassandra heard the Mutual boys jostling into the church after (yet another) outdoor activity. The girls were (yet again) consigned to the church kitchen, this time learning how to make dinner rolls, which the boys had returned to sample. Allan White's choirboy soprano whippeted over and through the racket like a fly line. She realized how Allan's exuberant scats had been part of the soundtrack of her whole communal life—his pure, effortless pitch had buoyed every Primary song. It turned a gear in Cassandra's emerging aesthetic consciousness, a grounding insight. Liminal communal memories define family and "kin."

What does this mean for children sent away? Is this her way of setting her child free?

A professor had once offered a Roethke poem as a text to illustrate: *Of those so close beside me, which are you?* She couldn't draw it; every rendering reduced it to literality. A revelation: words and images are mutually untranslatable. *What falls away is always, and is near.* She'd decamped to Frost: *The woods are lovely, dark and deep*—a manageable rendering of a pony and falling snow.

Is this kind of thinking a gift from Allan White? This boy she barely knew yet has known forever, a man she cannot comprehend nor extricate. Impossible to render. Here he is, forever forward and back, the boy who sang his way through the world he took from her in one brutal mindless thrust.

He was good at things, a quick study. He was enrolled in Advanced Art because he was not inclined to exert himself. Even so, he could render idiosyncratic and appealing responses to Judd's assignments: a still life with, say, car parts, or a five-gallon glass jar in the window light. A cartoon parody of any teacher who deserved (or not) a heady shot of mortification. He liked word games, puzzles with numbers—Cassandra could almost see his mimetic mind play them out as he muttered, repeated, riffed.

...

Once the basketball had been confiscated, once the stoners had played out the roach jokes and gathered around somebody's portable record player as if it were a campfire, after describing his hot date from another town in confidential and conciliatory tones to every girl in the class except Deborah Swain, who was a cheerleader with a jealous and muscular boyfriend, Allan White fixated on the (temporarily) most interesting person in the room: the enigmatically talented art-girl with a graphite stick in her hand.

The swath of blank white butcher paper was assembled—fifty feet long, twelve high minus masking tape overlap—and spread out to await the apparition of Art. Mr. Judd had forbidden any hand but Cassandra's for blocking. Now that she could see the whole "canvas," it wasn't hard to section off parts and relations: the sunset AND rainbow, the up-close gazing couple, the jealous lover, the semi-distant tiki pavilion, enough ocean for Deborah's underwater animal scene. Ukulele crooners on the beach. A heavy metal band, placed to look like they were playing into the actual speakers on the night of the dance. She left space in the tropical sky for Lane's lettering, a design he was perfecting at Mr. Judd's temporary desk in the corner.

Allan's role today was commentator: sportscaster and color man at once. "You guys, look. She's got the mountains going, see? I don't know if we'll need snow on them. I mean, it's Hawaii, right? Okay, yeah. That's actually working. You could put some little skiers up there. Make one doing a helicopter!

"Okay, I see what you're doing. The tiki hut, right? Okay, but how many people do you really want to draw in there? I mean, we only have a week. Maybe you could cover some of it up with trees or something to make it easier.

"Is that what palm trees look like? I mean, I've been to Hawaii lots of times and I really don't think—mmm, yeah. I see now. Those flowers are nice. Are you gonna put that other boyfriend in there? Where does he go?"

"Allan! Give the artist some space!" Mr. Judd called from the far side of the gym, where he'd set up a lawn chair (was he reading *National Lampoon*, or has Cassandra placed one in his hands after the fact?). Allan backed off a little, but he'd attracted a crowd. By the time Cassandra had progressed to the outline of a rock band, every student in the class was leaning in to watch.

Mr. Judd ambled over. "Nice," he said. "You're going to outdo yourself from last year. Okay everyone, here's how it goes. Cassandra sketches out the forms today. Tomorrow, she'll go back on each section and give it definition with a marker. Basically, folks, it works like a giant coloring book. You all go in and fill it with paint. No slop. I mean it. Cassandra and Lane and Deborah will touch it all up with chalk highlights after we get the thing in passable shape. I want three or four of you on, say, a ten-foot segment."

"We get the rock band," Brent said on behalf of the stoners.

"That's fair," Judd affirmed. "Kendra, Dawnene, Lisa B., are you working with Deborah on the ocean scene?"

"Yeah but we want to have some other animals in the flowers and trees and stuff, too."

"Work that out with Deborah and Cassandra. Fine by me. Follow your lights, people. Git 'er done."

On Tuesday Cassandra went to the details, which confused the totality.

"Okay, I put the rainbow back there to mark the vanishing point," she said to Mr. Judd. "But the mural is so wide I don't know how to make it the focal point, too. I don't get how to guide everything all the way over."

Mr. Judd, extra disheveled as if he'd gotten out of bed and come directly to the gym, stood beside her to assess. He smelled faintly like a laundry basket. "We're at a bit of a disadvantage because it's on the floor," he said. "Skews the view angle. But if we mount it up on the wall we'll have all that brick texturing the fill-in. So you'll have to—you know—keep leaning over it, thinking through accidental foreshortening, right? Draw from the top sometimes. Upside down will help you think compositionally."

He pushed his slender fingers backward, combing through colorless hair. Cassandra imagined her teacher might look almost sexy on a backyard patio, firing up a grill. Sitting on a log in the canyon, under the pines, slow-roasting a marshmallow-padded stick. Was he married? Did he have children? Was he from here, or somewhere distant? No family photos on his desk. No reference to anyone, anything, beyond the low-grade clutter and chaos of his stop-time classroom.

"Hey, burnouts!" he called. "Bring us a ladder, okay?"

The ladder squeaked across the Varathane.

"Climb up there, Cassandra. Give it a big-picture stare. Sure, the rainbow can be the focal point. But you can also think it through in other ways. Medieval muralists—tapestry makers, for example—thought about their composition as more of a pattern than a realistic look-out-the-window thing? You could make a sort of triptych—a main scene with complementary wings. Or imagine it as a sort of panel sequence, a little like a comic book, you know?

"A long stretch of butcher paper with a mob's random visual ideas isn't an ideal fit for Renaissance perspective. You have to consider the facts of cheap paper and lousy paint, plus an amateur crew. Plus low lighting at the prom and a whole lot more putzes than just us, in various states of mind, milling around it at different points. Tweak your plans every time you hit a plateau. Work with the thing you're making. You don't just think once. At this point we get faithful to the outcome, not the conception."

He trailed off. For Judd, that was a hell of an expenditure—a phenomenon not lost on Allan White, cocking his head from the threshold of the locker room where he'd been chatting up an eager Kendra Price.

"Wow, Judd. I didn't know we were taking a philosophy class. We should get extra credit."

"Shut up, Allan," Mr. Judd snapped, which took everyone by surprise. "I'm talking to the class genius here. Anyone else benefits, chalk it up to your sparkly socialized education."

"Socialism is evil," Kendra piped up, grabbing at Allan White's forearm. "This is America."

"Socialism has this very season blessed us with a roll of butcher paper and all those plastic jars of color in compact powder form," Judd intoned. "Praise the bounty, oh ye eager scholars who clamor for wisdom."

"Whoa," Brent muttered.

"What even are we talking about?" said Joey.

"My dad sponsored the football uniforms this year," Allan expounded. "That's what we call free enterprise. Give smart people the freedom to get rich and stuff trickles down to the untalented. Capitalism works on natural principles like that."

Scripture, as it had been trained to do, leaped to the wall of Cassandra's visual mind in a lettered blaze: *The natural man is an enemy to God.*

What did these things mean?

Maybe because she stood on the ladder at that moment, the scene congealed just above human height, perfectly composed: the grating fluorescence of the hanging fixtures softened by an upper rim of translucent plexiglass. The clutter of snacks and paintbrushes, book bags and jackets, discarded paper, rolls of sawdust-colored masking tape. Shoes lined up on the floor against the coaches' office wall. Children in aching beautiful grown-up bodies for all the zits and sweat and baby fat and family flaws, sheltered in the minimal efficacy of institutional space—about to return to unknowable homes, fraught families, foreclosed yet mystifying futures.

92

Chapter 14

Wednesday, all bodies were variously sprawled on the floor. Mr. Judd led a color tutorial, so much as powdered tempera would allow. Water was emerging on the mural in a uniform blue. Four standardized shades of green allowed the island to "pop" and "recede" in dimensional increments. A cluster of floral hues, premixed, sat ready for vegetal and aquatic elaboration. Grays and browns for the creatures Deborah had tucked in the foliage.

It did seem that Cassandra's rendering was in a process of annihilation. Careless and earnest hands alike slopped down gobs of cheap hue.

"It's going to be fine." Mr. Judd leaned sideways to murmur toward Cassandra's right ear. "It's a high school project. Think toward the future."

They stood and watched, everyone engrossed and leaning in together, assessing, de-cliqued.

"Your deep design is strong. But it's only a harbinger. They'll get it all filled in, you can give it a hard stare and build from there. Intention, accident, judicious response."

"You talk like my grandma."

"Really? Some grandma."

"I think she's crazy."

"There's another world out there, you know. Someday, high

school will feel like a drunken dream. A *bateau ivre.* Don't decide too quick what's crazy."

"Haha. I'm too young to drink."

"That's not what I mean. Don't run home and tell your folks I suggested anything of the kind."

"Maybe my grandma."

He stepped away. "Maybe."

Chapter 15

She stands in the home bathroom where she once mulled the budding of her breasts. Pebbles, fixed but slippery under the skin. The guilt of touching.

She had feared they were tumors, and the pain of pressure had convinced her.

Dark laminate cabinet under a Formica counter. Chipped white sink, fixtures oxidized after decades of running hard water. Mirrored glass affixed directly to the wall. The claustrophobic space has been repainted with a roller, maybe more than once, without masking. Latex slops against mirror, tile, frosted glass, ceiling and mopboard.

Updating has only reiterated the unease of a claustrophobic enclosure made for evacuation, body after body, five decades and counting. Every formation of family flesh: shower after shower, soap after soap after shampoo, towel, detergent, refolded, restacked, reabsorbed. Water piped from mountain springs, heated in a rusted tank, sputtering up and out and down the pipes.

She stands as James, Brian, Matthew, examining themselves: the dropping sacks. The lengthening shafts. Grin. Smirk. Scowl. The broadening shoulders. Fine fur. She can envision each one so clear he might as well be standing beside her. She can picture them—she could still draw them—at thirteen, sixteen, nineteen.

And yet she can barely perceive herself. Only in parts,

fetishized: at fourteen (late), the small swell beneath each aureole.

The alarming patch of hair, somehow more obscene than smooth nakedness.

The widening hips. Swelling and receding abdomen. Aftermath.

No consistent face in the mirror. Sometimes the wide eyes of a child. Sometimes the hooded gaze of a wary adolescent. Lips glossed, bleeding, chapped, waxed. Braces—another burdensome investment in a daughter's future—tearing the soft inside pink of her mouth. Boys look better rugged (troubling, Cassandra was sure, to Matilda, now discernible, eyes clouded and perplexed).

Matilda, however, must have seen herself—complete and immitigable behind the obfuscations. Cassandra ponders the one figure she cannot capture on canvas, paper, or screen although it stands before her, moves when she moves. She unbuttons her shirt. She rolls her shoulders backward, dropping the draped cotton to the floor.

If she looks in the mirror for Irene, her grandmother lends the form a certain definition.

She unclasps the bra, shakes it off. Until this very month, Cassandra has never seen her mother's breasts. Dorothy's are still full, very round, stretched by gravity but pink and vital at the focal points. Their brazen presence, erect in the cool air beyond the bubble bath as Cassandra towels Dorothy dry. A vertical purple line bisects her stomach—a Caesarian scar? God. Would Dorothy have revealed this to her only daughter, ever, had Cassandra kept to the righteous path, returned to produce unforbidden children? Would mother and daughter have leaned toward one another, answering the intimate instinct to murmur together, to swap uterine anecdotes, laugh over indignities, quickenings, pain?

Did her father love her mother's body? Did he thrill to see

her whole, or was it all fumbling rush for access? Either way it must have been a process, considering the armored layers—scarf and sweater, buttoned blouse, cross-your-heart bra. Belted skirt. Elastic-waist half-slip, girdle, pantyhose. Her mother's attire a drag queen's but for the final layer—the "second skin," worn for "protection": filmy Mormon underwear, capped sleeves, scooped neck, thigh-length coverage, appropriated Masonic signs.

Did Dorothy love her own body, underneath all that? Was it the covering or the uncovering that excited them enough to conjure three tightly wound sons and a sinful daughter? Did she revel in the hard vision of him?

These, in the mirror, are not her mother's boobs. Are they Irene's? No. Tiny Irene had some mighty big tits—Cassandra had watched them strain against work shirts, move like marmots under a nightgown. Velma's? Too worn and shapeless to guess.

Did Dorothy nurse her babies? Cassandra can't imagine it, but then again, nothing that led to the need for her mother to nourish a baby is imaginable.

Hardly a trace of pregnancy, labor, or delivery here, in the mirror. A stretch mark below the navel, a whitened slash lined with fine red. She feels the hardening of the doctor's jubilant "husband stitch," explained in birthing class as a way of preserving the pleasure of a man who "likes a tight fit" (also, of preserving an illusion for a man who liked to believe he was first and only, yes? She had been instructed to return home, speak vaguely of a fictitious educational "trip," proceed as if nothing sexual, reproductive, maternal, or horrific had ever happened). Her breasts (these breasts, but how?) stretched to breaking with milk, unattended, leaking on the plane ride home. Layers of sweaters, a winter coat from the box of abandoned clothing, soaked through. No acknowledgment, no advice. No help.

She'd walked down the terminal with her book bag against her chest. Her father, grim at the base of the escalator. No greeting. No gesture.

She raises her arms, leaning toward the mirror. She cups her breasts in her hands. She lifts and drops. She considers the cradling hips.

The stunning evacuation.

Chapter 16

Cassandra called her mother for permission to stay late and work on the mural. Mr. Judd told everyone else to go home, to be ready for finishing and mounting tomorrow. He consulted with Miss Pirelli and the Pep Club lunging at the doorway, raring to slather the gym with crepe streamers, fabric flowers, and paper lanterns. They had a mirror ball, which, Mr. Judd insisted, could not be hung until the mural was complete. No, the mural could not be moved this afternoon. Yes, tomorrow. No, not in the morning. After school.

Dorothy told Cassandra to call her grandmother. If Irene could pick her up, Cassandra could stay until dinnertime.

Grandma Irene said, "Of course."

Cassandra worked on amid the shrieks and chatter of thirty girls with high ponytails and excellent posture, perfectly groomed even in their matching sweats and practice T-shirts. They strolled over in little groups to discuss the mural.

"That's really good. Do you take art lessons?"

"Um. Mr. Judd's class, I guess."

"Wow, you're so talented."

"Thanks?"

"You should add some more roses."

"Darn. Too late."

"Are you even going to the prom? Do you have a boyfriend? Because my cousin—"

"No."

"He thinks you're cute, but he's scared of your brothers."

That almost made her happy. "What? Really?"

"Do you think they'd get mad?"

"I don't know what they'd think."

End of conversation.

Cassandra wondered idly whether Miss Pirelli, hawkeyed, hungry-looking, liked her job. *Explain your answer.* She stood up to assess. Mr. Judd had been right, of course: the wild application of color had emerged into perceptible patterns and relational shapes—not quite the original vision but alluring in its possibilities, at least for a high school mural on butcher paper, painted with wet powder.

"Palimpsest," Judd had pronounced. "An image laid over an image over an image over an image. Sentences written on the same sheet of paper, between and then across and then in diagonal over other sentences. Palimpsest is three-dimensional. It recedes and comes forward in layers, inciting the viewer's imagination. It heightens the pleasure of composition, incorporates the gestures of process, preserves intimations of other trajectories."

Cassandra: "What?"

"Yes. What," Cassandra mutters at this moment, stylus poised, allusion to paper glowing opaque on the tablet in her lap. Dorothy, in her accustomed upholstered living room chair, is engrossed in unwinding tight, neat balls of crochet yarn from the basket, reorganizing them into sloppy puddles of color on the white carpet.

"It's about time I put all this to order," Dorothy keeps announcing.

"Me too."

Cassandra lowers her hand to the translucent surface. The implement hovers, then falters, then quickens and finds its pace.

...

As promised, Irene was waiting under the Big Horn Rams marquee at 6:45. The expanse of darkening spring-blue sky diminished the car to matchbox proportions. Most of the snow had melted, leaving the grass spongy but trekkable, so Cassandra ignored the squared walkways and cut a tight curve from the south-facing gymnasium doors, west across the main entrance sidewalk, and then semi-rightward to reach Irene's boaty Dodge Dart, white paint extra stark under neon. The driver inside was a bobbing whiff.

"Hi Grandma," Cassandra said, opening the shotgun door to drop her bag on a fifty-pound sack of chicken feed in the back. She slid into the passenger seat. "Thanks for coming to get me."

"Well, you know I'm happy to spend a few minutes with my granddaughter."

Cassandra did know.

"How's the masterpiece?"

Cassandra smiled. "Fine. Almost done."

Grandma craned her neck to back out, pumping the accelerator and brake at the same time, two-footed as if she were working a clutch. She wrenched the manual steering around. The car barely heeled.

"Want me to drive, Grandma?"

"Hell no. I've done my time with teenagers behind the wheel. Awful, all of you. Besides, it's a horrid car. Dangerous."

Irene stopped backing, kind of, to let a pickup blaze by, heading north. Inspired, she put the car in drive, turned the wheel hand over hand and gunned it, truing the lane after a couple of hard corrections. Cassandra gripped the armrest.

"Whew! Here we go," said Irene.

"Uh-huh."

"Do you have a date to the prom? I keep forgetting to ask."

"No."

"What's wrong with these boys? You're the most beautiful girl in the valley."

Cassandra rolled her eyes.

Irene: "Do you want to go?"

Cassandra: "I don't know. Kind of. Not really."

"Which?"

"Kind of."

"I don't want you getting all enamored of some Big Horn dickhead, you hear me? You can have a little fun, but you don't want to marry one. Is there someone you favor?"

Cassandra considered. Irene interrupted.

"All those pretty shoulders. Tight little hips. So cute."

"Grandma!"

"You've got an eye for beauty. I like taking a gander, too. All that flowing hair, boys these days. They look like little Vikings. But don't be fooled. Not a lot of brains left to go around. This gene pool is like the Great Salt Lake. No outlet. You don't want to marry a brine shrimp."

Irene was driving the back road, a twisting no-shoulder lane that ran along the mountain's base, east of the straight-shot Big Horn highway. Dark was descending, rendering cattle and sheep, and spindly country horses, into shadows along the fence lines. Cassandra guessed they were traveling twenty, twenty-five miles over the speed limit, whatever it was. No signs, which might be why Grandma favored this route.

"Girls have been taught in this valley, generation by generation, to sink their talons into the first pimpled boy looks at her cock-eyed. Locked and loaded by sixteen."

"Nobody looks at me cock-eyed."

"You're a smart girl, Cassandra, but your intelligence lags on this topic. You'd better savvy up. Plenty of looking going on, cock-eyed and—" Grandma pumped her left foot on the brake pedal, skidding and then stopping hard, middle of the road. "Forgot to turn on my headlights." Grandma reached to the dashboard, flipped the switch. A good-sized Angus steer, black in the daytime but blacker in April twilight, stood directly in front of the car, white-eyed and offended.

"Not like it would have made much difference. Look at that mindless beast. Bred for idiocy." Grandma laid on the horn.

The steer floated a little left, a little right, not far enough in either direction to open the route. "I'm tempted to draw an analogy," Grandma admonished.

Cassandra considered the switching tail. The insolent ambling hips.

"You know, even the bright ones—" Grandma trailed off.

The animal found direction, an oblique rightward path, fixed on the Taylors' ragged spring lawn. Grandma hit the gas, cleared the hill, and dropped into Big Horn proper.

"I'm sorry," she said, not referring to the near-miss of an Angus steer. "I didn't mean to go on about mating rites. Seems no one can look at a perfectly marvelous sixteen-year-old girl and hold forth on anything else."

"You're the only person who thinks I'm marvelous, Grandma."

Irene braked, this time easy and incremental, pulling alongside the edge of Main Street Park.

"Step out of this car a minute."

Cassandra opened herself out, then hopped across the puddled sidewalk. The grass smelled like melting snow and dirt and early forage. Grandma had already begun the sermon as she released her seatbelt, fumbled with the glitchy handle, opened the laborious door to circle around to the ample city lawn. Cassandra tuned in mid-sentence.

"...you want to question marvelous? You don't trust my judgment? Look at the sky! This very sky, same sky as every poet, every artist, every astronomer and philosopher ever put their eyes upon. It's yours too, you know. Perfectly marvelous!"

Grandma strode, small but substantial enough to push

twilight air like water as she advanced. Cassandra braced for impact.

She sees her still.

"Cassandra! Behold the ancient hills and mountains! The rocky peaks, the cold coursing waters! Marvelous! Every creature of the field! The fawns in the brush! Pikas of the high tundra! Coyotes singing from the clifftops! Perfectly marvelous!

"Breathe in the night spring air, the earth returning to life, seeds and bulbs stirring in their beds. Blessed ground, Cassandra! Only this blue. Wasatch Blue! Perfect! Marvelous!

"You came from nowhere! From nothing but the molecules of this untenable planet. If I'm the only person who can see how perfectly marvelous you are, then I suppose I'm the only person who can see anything at all! Marvelous doesn't mean perfect. Marvelous means a strange and blazing thing that causes us to gape and grope in its blinding path, beckoning us to lean after it. Marvelous calls us to live on the earth, amidst the wreckage, above the mundane hours that tick on toward tomorrow and tomorrow and tomorrow, toward that stifling heaven of a poor prophet's wet dream.

"How is it you were made, Cassandra? How many incidents and disasters, passions and surrenders, missteps, detours, delays, decisions, sleights of hand, nonce encounters, trepidations of the spheres, starry alignments did it take to grant us this moment together, here? How, Cassandra, how perfectly unlikely? Someday, without time passing, yet so much passing, you'll stand here again, an old woman like your grandmother. You will regather all the bright illusions of time. You'll see what a sweet small moment you've had to imagine you exist."

She stands here now on the overwatered lawn of Main Street Park, an aging woman. All of it here. All of it gone. Irene become Cassandra. Cassandra, Irene. The mountain slopes await combustion. A nation froths after a madman with cartoon hair. This population, committed to apocalypse.

Future and past, the stench of black smoke.

But this small moment, the skyline. Moonlight.

Headlight beams swept across the scrub oak, lit the front lawn and brightened the windows as Grandma churned the car into Cassandra's family's driveway.

"What was that?" Irene asked.

"Somebody coming across the yard," Cassandra answered. "Maybe it's—"

Allan. It was Allan White. His sudden face appeared in Cassandra's window. He opened her door.

"Hi," he said, grinning. "I almost beat you here."

"Was it a race?" Irene queried.

Allan pushed his head in, pungent. "Oh hi, Sister Caldwell. I called your house. I mean Cassandra's house." He pulled his head back out, took a couple of steps backward, upped the volume. "I talked to your dad. He said you'd be here any minute."

In fact the very figure of Hal stood at the window, peering out like Goody Cloyse.

Cassandra turned her head toward her grandmother.

"I don't like that boy," Irene muttered. "I don't like that family."

"He's in my art class," Cassandra said. "Maybe he wants to talk about the mural."

"I'll bet he does."

Allan White offered his hand, gallant, to usher Cassandra out of the car.

She took it, and he pulled her toward him. He stepped back to look her over.

"Once you get that paint and chalk out of your hair, you know…"

But it wasn't her hair he was appraising.

She said, "I need to go in. My dad is strict about dinner time."

"Don't worry about it. Your dad said you can stay out and talk to me."

"He did?"

"Yeah." Allan glanced toward the front window, lifting a few fingers as a friendly signal for the man behind the curtain. "So. I had a date to the prom. This girl in Salt Lake. Our families are friends. Both our dads are lawyers."

Irene revved the engine. "Shut that door. Let me back out."

Cassandra ducked her head in. "I'm sorry, Grandma. I—"

"I don't like him."

"I know."

"Your dad sure does." Irene's hand lay on the blue leatherette bench seat, but her pointing finger jerked toward Hal's form.

"Yeah."

"You. Be careful."

"I will. Don't worry."

"I will."

Cassandra startled at Allan White's hand, pressed flat against her back. "Bye, Grandma," she said, standing up.

Irene reversed, pumping the brakes and hitting the gas. The Dart stopped with a hard jolt, then lurched forward. The tires squealed a bit, meaning to leave a stern impression.

"Hot rod Grandma!" Allan grinned. "Look at her go."

He made a little Earth, Wind and Fire spin, stopping with a suave pointing hand as he faced Cassandra.

"So," he continued. "Suddenly she's all mad about something, or she's sick or whatever. I'm pretty tired of her anyway. I've been watching you in the gym all week. You're hotter than you let on, you know."

"Huh?"

"Will you go to the prom with me? I mean, I'm all set to go with a tux and stuff, and I have reservations at House of Steaks with some of the guys on the football team, so it's all set up and it's just a waste if I don't go."

He drifted. Then, "And, of course, I really do think you're hot and I'd, you know, like to get to know you better, now that we're, you know, older."

Did sixteen-year-old Cassandra want this? Was there a germ of self that hoped this was the beginning of a passionate romance, the story she'd tell her children all breathless as they tanned by the pool behind their fancy gated house, waiting for their loving and fun-loving father to come home from his important churching and announce the next exciting family trip to Disney World?

Yes. No use pretending otherwise.

"So?"

The porch light came on.

"Sure. Yeah. Okay," Cassandra answered, flush.

"Cool. I'll pick you up at, like five o'clock."

Sure. Yeah. Okay.

Chapter 17

"You need to be nice to that boy," her father said. "He comes from a good family."

Cassandra bit her lip.

"Don't do that."

"Don't do what?"

"Stop maiming your face. Why do you bite yourself? Keep your teeth in your mouth."

"What?"

"You're a pretty girl when you give it a little effort. But you remind me of my sister. Plenty of the guys my age wanted to ask her out, but her manner put them off. Clifford Mayne said to me once, 'You know, Leanne just has this way of shrugging me off, like—*I don't need you.*' You're the same way, Cassandra. Boys need a little encouragement. Plenty of girls would be thrilled to be asked out by that boy. Plenty of girls would jump at the chance to show it."

Cassandra's mother appeared brightly but cautiously from wherever she'd been listening.

"Really, honey, it's just a matter of smiling a little more. Boys your age aren't as confident as they might seem. They're always looking for those little signs of encouragement."

"Not *too* encouraging," her father said. "You don't want him to think you're loose."

"Well, that's right," Dorothy said. "Just be natural. Let that sunny personality shine."

"A little makeup wouldn't hurt. Look at your mother. Middle of the afternoon, hair curled, face on. Your mother is a true lady, morning to night."

"Dad, I know."

"Do you? What is it you know, Cassandra? Tell me."

Cassandra went blank.

Her mother gestured, encouraging.

"Um. I know Mom's a true lady?"

Her father grunted. "Are you asking me a question? Or are you telling me something you actually understand? What's the point of all this?"

Cassandra spoke carefully. "The point is, I should act like a lady."

"Speak up!"

"I should be nice to Allan White. I should be...I should need more."

Later, he stood at the bathroom doorway as Cassandra brushed her teeth.

She spat and rinsed. Stood up straight. Kept her teeth in her mouth.

He smelled like soap-cleaned hands and faint metal. A recent shave. His shoulders spanned nearly from one side of the doorframe to the other. His coarse, oil-combed hair almost brushed the lintel. He stayed put but leaned against one side, folding his arms in front of himself, and crossed one leg in front of the other.

And then he told her the most tender, self-revealing story he'd ever shared. In fact, the only. Ever. A skeevy prom date made him go all Daddy-Daughter on her.

"You know, my first date with your mother was junior prom.

I was seventeen. I went to high school way out west of Tooele, hardly a school at all. Almost everyone there was related somehow. It was hard to—well, compete. For a date. I didn't like any of those girls anyway. I was a starry-eyed kid. I wanted to find my princess.

"I had cousins out here—down in Clearlake City, not Big Horn, but both towns went to school together, like now. Then, Big Horn was almost as small a town as where I came from, but it was closer to things. Bussed to a big school. The girls seemed so sophisticated, so worldly, they scared me a little.

"My cousin Boyd had a crush on your aunt Emma. Dorothy and Emma were well-known as the prettiest sisters around. Boyd hung around with their brothers and cousins. They were good hunters, took it serious, and now it mattered to put meat in the freezer. Lander hadn't been dead long and Joel had just gone off to the air force, but Jimmy was working down at the IFA and Paul of course was still in school."

Minimally signifying names for Cassandra. Vivid characters for Hal.

Her father ran a hand, careful, down the thigh of his trousers. For a guy who worked in grease all day, Hal was fastidious about his appearance. His features—hawk nose, flattened cheekbones, once-sensuous lower lip over badly-formed teeth—were in this uncharacteristic moment unstrained. Cassandra caught a flicker of the boy he was—earnest, slender as a tree, yearning for purchase.

"The whole family was grieving and worried. Irene had gone down to the Training School, gotten a job working with the retards—the retarded people, I mean. Dorothy and Emma worked at the bakery down on Main Street, walked home after their shifts because their mother was still at work. I know Irene had to work, but it was a hardship for all of them. Irene thought a little too much of herself once she started making her own money. Coming home to an empty house while she was gone changed them all. It's not something I wish for you, or your husband and children. Marry well and you can be the kind of wife and mother God intends a woman to be."

Was that all? Cassandra lingers there, in the memory, straining for more.

Did he say, "I want a man to love you as much as I love your mother."

Did he say, "But you have to do your part well, all the time. It's not easy for a man to settle with just one woman, once and for all. It's not the eternal order of things."

She can't remember. In fact, she can't quite recall very much at all between that touching little moment of paternal confidence and Allan's decision to leave the prom early.

Does she recall the careful steps she took to prepare for his arrival, or is she assembling a montage of getting ready for church, Sunday after Sunday?

Did she know the difference between a Sunday suit and a rented silk tuxedo?

She recalls the clear plastic clamshell box in his hand, the pink carnation, her mother's fawning assistance as he struggled with the long pin. Her father, stepping out at the last moment, reciting appropriate guidelines, expressing warm trust.

A quick resentful drive back up to his parents' house. Older brothers smooching like apes from the edge of the yard. The lawyer and the pale nervous mother in the entry. Rehearsed greetings and admonitions.

A photographer.

Dinner at the House of Steaks. A few kids she knew: Kendra Price, from Cassandra and Allan's ward, unhappy with her date from another school. Deborah Swain and her boyfriend since seventh grade. Others she knew by name, from classes.

So much meat.

. . .

At the school: faculty chaperones, charged with containing a rite of passage designed to incite and forbid; Mr. Judd rolling his eyes at Miss Pirelli; gushing compliments and critiques over the mural, lit up and surrounded by crepe, tawdry and amateur but also bright and striking. At one point, the principal summoned Cassandra to the wall, told Allan to wait just a minute while she posed in front of the tiki hut with him and the vice principal. He called Allan over, said there should be a picture of the artist with her date.

Allan waved him off, surly. He took Cassandra by the hand and drew her back toward the scorch of younger bodies.

A few dances, which, for white kids in 1978, consisted of minimally swaying torsos, no footwork whatsoever, and, so much as the chaperones neglected to peer into the dark, the perennial slow-grind bear hug. Processed pink lemonade. Tiny paper cups offering sacraments of peanuts and butter mints. Mini cold-cut sandwiches.

"Let's blow this Primary party," Allan whispered. His voice was strained and hoarse, his neck tendoned. "This sucks."

"Are you okay?"

He took her hand. "Say goodbye to your little friends," he said, pulling her through the crowd, high-fiving groupies as they progressed.

The sterile fluorescence of the high school hallway reminded her how overwrought this frenzy was. She knew there were kids in there who, like their parents, truly saw this as the night of their lives, the Genesis story to tell their children and grandchildren, corny photographs and dried corsages as cherished props. On Monday, how many promise rings would shine on manicured hands, gleaming in the murk of the algebra room? How many sudden missionary haircuts parsed from Van Halen shags, how many vacuous promises to wait out a two-year eternity? Variations of her mother's breathless tales, reified year after year after decade after generation at Clearlake High School, home of the Big Horn Rams.

Allan's hand was slick but firm. She thought to pull hers away, wave it dry in the sudden night air, but his long fingers were tight at her wrist. He drew Cassandra through the morass of cars, clear in his purpose even as he nodded, pretend contrite, toward Officer Finlayson lounging against the grill of the Clearlake City Cop Camaro, specially detailed to impress high school students.

"Loser fuck," Allan muttered as they passed out of audible range. "Couldn't score in high school. Now he thinks he's impressing the ladies. What a pathetic wad."

Did she quell an intimation? Maybe she hadn't been genuinely stupid. She'd heard plenty of stories, but interpretation, at her age, was obscure. Ted Bundy molesting and re-molesting dismembered "girls" in the mountains—these very mountains. In church, and sometimes school: "Girls, you must understand. A young man's sex drive is a powerful force. Just a glimpse of a young woman's body, in the wrong ways, can drive him into an uncontrollable frenzy. You are the guardian of morality, the very fortress of chastity. When you dress or act provocatively, when you allow things to go too far, you are responsible for unleashing urges a healthy young man simply cannot control…"

Murky local perverts; shadowy men in the hills; maniacs on the news; creepy fathers and handsy stepfathers. One thing she has come to know: people in her home valley mean what they say. She alone was responsible when the warnings hardened into parts. She alone was responsible for the night her lifeline was cut like a tramway cable.

Chapter 18

Even now it is so. Why, yet again, attempt to understand? Yes, she knows the word for this. What more does it clarify? What does it repair?

She stands above the reservoir, a lifetime beyond the fact, at the scene. In the valley beyond: family, childhood friends, teachers, church leaders. Every source of wisdom she was provided. No wisdom. Grandmother silenced. North Fork, here, above the city-to-city route, a twisting high-altitude road toward the wilderness line. The other side of hometown summits, reversed but recognizable forms. Asphalt parking, once hard dirt, at the east end where ground drops abruptly toward the water.

Tonight, as Dorothy watches her next videocassette under Relief Society vigilance, true stars up here, above the smoke. Glimmers of campfires up on the Flats. No visible remnants of snow now, in late-drought July.

Winter had lingered in prom-time spring, snow stained along the shore, extending into frigid water. Moon spotlighted the glassy surface when clouds divided. Squaw Peak a pyramid, rising behind the canyon cleave.

She has feared the scenery would show itself complicit. But here it is, terrible only in its ownness and anti-time. What happened here is only hers. Not even his, anymore. Whatever that veiled mind has retained or purged is as disinterested as the water itself.

She hears the surge of the spillway at the dam, a hundred yards distant.

Allan chattered like a happy child as the canyon twisted upward. His hands fluttered and leaped against the wheel, animating colliding, half-formed stories.

"Once I was up here with my brothers, because we were scouting deer before the hunt. We only brought .22s, just dinking around. Will comes up over a ridge back behind Crystal Pond and he sees this huge—and I mean humongous—bull moose down in the stream, just chewing up moss fast as he can pull it up. We snuck closer when it had its head in the water. When it came up we all shot in the air at the same time, dropped boulders down the face, scared the living shit outta that thing. He came up out of the water, tripping all over the rocks, shot straight up the other side limping like a motherfucker..."

Other things. A cute story about his little niece. Her first words.

Breaking his arm on a tote gote when he was ten (remember when his arm was in a sling at church? You don't *remember* that?).

More on the brothers (assholes! but funny as hell!).

Something about his dad (always something about his dad) (a lawyer, prosecutor in fact, nobody gets away with jack shit when he comes after them). Some things about his mother (never comes out of her room except for church, all dressed up like everything's perfectly normal). His two sisters (one a bitch. The other a wannabe).

The Second Coming and proper preparations for the end-times, entailing underground bunkers and much ammunition.

A point-by-point breakdown of the quadratic equation. His intention to major in math, because soon everyone would have a computer in their home, just like they had refrigerators, and programmers were the ones going to get rich.

He was enjoying his pontifications so much he nearly missed the left turn onto North Fork, but he swung hard, fishtailing, and hit the gas again, upward. The road pitched and curved along the streambed but kept northward until the long spillway slide appeared to the right. Sharp rise. Sudden shine of half-frozen water. Wide curve around the shoreline.

Allan parked the pointy orange car with its headlights shining over the reservoir, front tires edged close to a small but effective plummet.

Cassandra caught her breath, overwhelmed by a thousand monochrome tints.

"Like we're hovering," she said—her first verbal contribution since the canyon's mouth. "Thirty feet up."

She peered across the line of illumination, toward the headlight-tipped pines on the far shore. The reservoir was small but very deep. In summer her brother Brian could swim the width—she'd watched him butterfly the very line of Allan's headlights, water nearly as cold in high summer as it was now, partly iced.

"I'd say forty," Allan said. And then, under his breath, almost subconscious: "*Hovering. Hoverrrrring. Hover...ing...*"

His eyes flickered in the dashboard light as he blinked. "It's pretty. And we have it all to ourselves for a while. We'd better take advantage."

He reached a hand to her shoulder and squeezed. Her adrenalin jumped, surprising her more than the hand itself.

"What do you mean?" Voice disembodied.

He said, "I just mean it's pretty and we have it to ourselves. You're still wearing your coat. Let's get out and get a better look."

She'd been here so many times—day and night, sun, thunder, and ice. Swimming and sledding. Tonight it frightened her but she couldn't pinpoint why. Sure, the Sunday School warnings about being alone with a "young man," unsupervised, might be *hoverrrr-ring* in her mind, but, really? Allan sat within a desk or two in every alphabetical school seating chart since kindergarten. He was just a guy who'd asked her to the prom, last minute, after the sexy Salt Lake cheerleader called in sick. A convenience date.

"Okay," she said. "I'm wearing the wrong things for it, though."

Or right, depending on the plotline. The detestable pressure of nylon pantyhose, waist to toe. Silkened jersey dress exacerbating the breeze, inviting ruin on sharp gravel. High platform sandals.

He giggled. "It's okay. I'll hold on to you. Let's just get out and stand under the stars. Get a better look at the mountains."

She reached, instinctive, to open her door. Forgot this was prom night.

"Huh-uh uh!" Allan said, reaching across, brushing her chest to grab the offending hand. "Ladies wait for the gentleman to open the door."

Did all that wrist-grabbing frighten or even offend her? Yes, she was frightened, but so encompassed by fear there was no contrasting sensation to distinguish it. Fear of being cut off from her family for time and all eternity if she committed a defining sin. Fear of being hacked into parts, buried only to be unburied in some sick play of reanimation like the girls up there at Granite Flats, in plain sight of where she and Allan stood. Fear that she would not be considered beautiful enough to be in danger of being hacked into parts. Fear of her father, waiting at home for her account, probably composing an interrogation about her treatment of this fine young man from a fine family.

Fear of her mother. Fear for her mother? Fear of becoming her mother.

All of it added up to blank compliance, so when her date grabbed her wrist, hard, for the third time that night, she blushed in shame for her breach of femininity.

"Oh. Yeah. Sorry."

"I'll come around," he said. He touched her glued-in-place

hair, ran a finger down her cheek, and made a gallant show of stepping out. She heard his wing-toed shoes crunch icy dirt around the back of the car, then a loud thump on the roof, and his face was in the window, leering. He made a long moaning sound, and then broke into hysterical laughter.

"Thump-drag! Thump-drag!" he hollered through the glass. Every teenager in Utah—hell, probably America—knew that campfire slasher tale. She only flinched a little. Good thing she had brothers.

He howled like a werewolf as he opened her door.

"Come into the night, m'lady," he grinned, offering his tuxedoed elbow.

Did she hesitate? Beyond this gesture, the scene plays and replays like a movie reel, footage unspooling to its scripted climax.

She took his arm. She bumped her head stepping out of the low-slung car, miscalculating trajectory between platform soles and the force of his pull. She firmed up her ankles, but the ground was unsteady and she had to lean into him. Pleased, he picked her up in a dramatic sweep and carried her to the drop-off edge. He set her down gently, helped her find footing, and then stood decently, even tenderly, beside her.

For a few very cold minutes they stayed like that, breathing the clean night air. Cassandra relaxed even as she shivered, absorbing the impact of dark water mirroring skyline and sky, canny home landscape, a cautious but burgeoning wonder of standing beside a beautiful masculine human being—no longer, at least in the moment, the dope who'd filled so many desks beside hers, leaned back in his folding chair against the painted cinderblock walls of Sunday School classrooms, another oblivious snot-flicker among her rough brothers. The contours of a grown man. Young and strong, broad shoulders stretching the seams of his movie-star jacket.

He turned his face toward moonlight to meet her gaze. He

looked happy, eyes ice-colored as the clouds. Then, a stiffening, almost a shudder.

"You're right," he said. "These are the stupidest clothes ever. I'm going to get rid of this dumb jacket. Watch."

He stepped back, stancing like Travolta. "No, really. *Watch!*"

"Okay, I'm watching."

"Ah! Ah! Ah! Ahhhhh staying *aliiiiii—ii–ive!*" he sang in a high falsetto. He thrust his hips forward, then back, and at the next forward he ripped off his jacket, strutting, grinning, cute if he'd been a fourth grader but now heady in his newly sinuous limbs, muscled by football practice and surging testosterone.

The absurdity of the ruffled linen shirt and silk bowtie, garish in the bright moonlight, muting beneath the movement of clouds.

Allan said, again, "Watch this!"

He yanked the jacket under the nape, like a principal grasping a truant kid by the collar. Like a helpless dog. Allan picked up a softball-sized rock, wrapped it in the gabardine, folded the bottom upward, and tied the arms. He swung the whole package above his head, hips in disco thrust, and then slung the whole bundle in the air, arcing toward the water. Time stalled as the tuxedo-wrapped stone dropped, as paper-thin ice cracked and collapsed, and the night-blue silk was swallowed.

Cassandra pulled her own long Sunday coat a little tighter. "Didn't you rent that jacket from Durfee's?"

"Ha ha yep. Special order. The most expensive one. They can dive for it." He looked pleased, as if he'd jettisoned a bag of trash. Cleaned his bedroom. "My dad will pay for it. I'll tell him it got stolen. You won't tell, will you?"

Cassandra pictured herself dropping by the White residence, knocking on the door, asking to speak to the lawyer. It almost made her laugh out loud. "No."

"Good. Now, you," he said.

She stepped back, perplexed. He grinned. "Not *you*, silly. I mean your turn to offer a sacrifice to the reservoir god. How about those shoes?"

"My mom would kill me. She took me special to buy them for the prom."

"My dad's gonna tear me up for losing the jacket," he said. "I can't be the only one in trouble. You gotta play."

The wind picked up, enough to push the water in smooth arced lines toward the earthwork dam, the rectangle of black nothing where the reservoir sucked itself back into a rushing downhill stream.

"Hurry," he said. "It's getting cold."

The reservoir god would not value anything she had to offer. No sacrifice but harsh veneer.

"Turn around, then," she said. He turned his face toward the high slopes.

"I mean it," she said.

"I won't look!"

She made fast work of it: slipped off the bulky sandals, reached under her skirt to her waist, peeled nylon downward and off. Viscera. She stood, barefoot, disconcerted but relieved in the mountain dark, hose crumpled in her hand, prom sandals on the cutting gravel. She felt at once returned to earth and transported beyond anything at all, ever, familiar. Here, with this other person, made of what she was made of, beneath these intermittent stars. Familiar slopes flattened to a single plane of contrast against the sky.

"Okay," she said, and Allan turned, still fully dressed but for the jacket. Buttoned and bow-tied, ruffled, long and lean, eyes glinting like alien stardust. Wavy gold-streaked hair almost black in the dark.

"Yee-HAW!" he whooped. "Good choice! Let's throw 'em in!"

He scoured the ground, then bent down to pick up stones. Packed them in rough snowballs.

"Man, that hurts. Okay, open up," he said.

"Um. What?"

He grabbed at the unnatural mass in her hand. "Have to give it weight."

She extended her arm. He took the hose and opened them at the top like a Halloween candy sack. "Hold it like this," he said. "Wide open. Higher."

He stuffed the snowballs down into the feet, pushing up against her a little, nudging, engrossed. "Okay. Stand back."

She stepped backwards, gingerly.

He whirled the stockings like nunchucks. David with a sling. Reared back and let fly. The assemblage took on a weird life of its own, a deranged and entropic albatross suddenly finding trajectory. Now too dark to follow. A half second longer and they heard it strike thin ice. A shimmer of breakage like a submerging chime.

Biting wind.

Allan laughed like a cartoon hyena. From a distance, she imagined, he might sound like a screaming woman. Maybe that occurred to him too, because he cut it short and peered into darkness.

Cassandra did manage to register this moment as one of the weirdest of her life thus far. She'd stood at the North Fork Reservoir shore a hundred times, skipping rocks, dragging inner tubes and kayaks, wearing far less than she was wearing now, splashing and laughing in summer sunlight. Toboggans and snowballs among the many children she'd grown up with—girls and boys together—many of them now perspiring in the boys' gym-turned-ballroom, silhouetted against Cassandra's overwrought mural. Driving these canyon roads, picking hideaways, or righteously returning home for photos and kitchen snacks.

Allan turned away from the vision of cracked ice and deep water. His face was blank but focused. He said to Cassandra, "I can't believe you just took off your *nylons*. On a *date*."

He stepped closer. "Are you even wearing underwear?"

She stepped back, brain buzzing static, forgetting that she was barefoot, the ground painful. She glanced over her shoulder, gauging the distance to the car.

Ten feet.

What safety could it offer?

"Allan," she bleated.

He reached for her, caught her arm. "Whoa there. Don't fall. Let me help you."

He moved very fast, lifting her in a muffling bear hug, moving her upright but backwards, pressing her against the car. "Feel this?" he said. "What do you think this is?"

He took her wrist, tight, and pressed her hand against him.

She wasn't certain what it was. Because she was sixteen, and in her family's fashion, sheltered. She thought, blurry, that he'd pushed something into his pants.

"You *enticed* me." He moved her hand up and down, pressed it tight against the iron rod. "This is what you did."

Her brain a stone wrapped in hard ice.

"Kiss me. It's the least you can do. You're really beautiful, you know? I've been watching. You've changed. You stayed flat as a board while all the other girls were getting tits but now look at you. Like, overnight."

She remembers every word, crystalline. She doesn't have to stand at the reservoir decades later to replay it, line by line. But standing here now she remembers the sharp scent of wind coming off the night water, the contours of metal and glass against her back. The taste of prom punch and cheap mustard and cold cuts still coating his tongue.

What did she say? The only voice she heard was Allan's. Answers and protests and rebukes crowded the space in her mind, yes, but in the voices of teachers and parents and sometimes brothers, perforating the high back of her brain among girls' cryptic comments at school (*there are so many things you can do without ever having sex! You can keep him wanting it all night!*), in the bathrooms at church, whispering in the back seats of carpool parents' sedans. Voices and visions within and without. But Cassandra herself? A vacant balloon in the shape of a girl with big new tits.

Did she speak? The sensation at the mouth, a moving tongue but as in a dream.

Why can't she speak it?

the distance between what he and she knew at the time

the practiced moves

the confidence

It was over before she could formulate a weak argument, let alone fight to the virtuous death. Chink of the belt buckle hitting the ground. Hand snaking up her thighs, pulling downward in one smooth motion. Shocking pain of the first thrust, and the five or six after. He held his hand tight, bruising, over her mouth.

Come on, bitch, just go with it. You know what you started. Now I'm gonna give you what you asked for...

It occurred to her later that the lines must have come from a bad porn script. His tone almost tender, and then he was finished: thrilled, then blank, then shocked and defensive in a single motion of retreat. Then cold and commanding. He stood back, breathing hard.

He said, "Pull yourself together." Decently turned his back.

Cassandra retrieved her underwear, a gray blob like a shriveled brain at her feet. She stumbled toward the drop-edge in search of her sandals, afraid to leave them, to explain the loss. She bent to pick them up. Her feet felt nothing.

"Here, let me get the door for you."

In the low-slung seat, she buttoned her coat. He strode around to the driver's door and settled in behind the wheel. He turned the key. They watched a pair of headlights snake up the narrow road in their direction. Another, and then another.

"Dance must be over," Allan said.

"Must be."

"Look, Cassandra. This was our first time. Of course it was awkward. We'll get better as we go, don't you think?"

She couldn't lift her head. His voice produced a strange hollow resonance at the edges. He sounded further away than right beside her. He put his hand on her knee, firm but gentle. Then they were in her parents' driveway. She reached to open her door.

"Haven't you learned yet?" he said. "Let me come to you."

But he made no move. "I know we just committed a sin, but, really, what's so terrible about it? It's just a natural thing, right? I think Heavenly Father understands that our hearts are in the right place. I think he'll forgive you for enticing me. He'll forgive me, too, for acting on the urges he implanted in my body. Don't ruin this, Cassandra. I feel so close to you right now."

She struggled to speak. It seemed she was sinking, folding into herself as if she were breathing gas in the dentist's chair.

"Please. I want to go to bed."

"Fine." He opened his door, took his time walking around to hers. "Put your shoes on. Your folks won't notice the nylons unless you make some big deal of it."

At the porch, he whispered, "Remember. Stay quiet about this."

And then her own father opened the door, her mother behind him.

"Right at midnight, just as we asked," Hal said, smiling.

"Did you have fun, kids?" Dorothy inquired.

"You've raised a fine daughter, Brother Soelberg."

"That we have. Thank you for bringing her home safely to us."

"It was an honor. Good night, Sister Soelberg. See you at church."

Cassandra heard her father's questions, untranslatable, as she was somehow transported down the hallway. She closed her bedroom door. Slept in her polluted dress, waking every hour in shock and pain. Too frightened to creep down the hall to hot water and aspirin.

Chapter 19

Cassandra considers: how narrow the passage. Had he found the courage or shame to claim or confess. Had he been forced to propose. Had he been kinder (she needed so little to be grateful), had he made the line between coaxing and coercion just a bit more ambiguous. Had their fathers chosen to negotiate (what was it, between them? Something groveling and cruel). She was made, generation by generation, of such rehabilitations. She may have gone along, convinced herself it was just a rough start to a fulfilling life, reserved the chapel, sent the invitations.

She could have squeezed herself into a concealing dress, said *I do* in an empty chapel or her parents' living room, or his. She might have publicly promised to repent, inspiring a tearful congregation with a temple wedding after a year of dutiful penitence.

Maybe, had her grandmother lived beyond the crisis, Cassandra would have had reason to stay. She might have raised her son, and more sons. Daughters.

What cost, what grace?

Who would they have become?

Oath makers. Secret keepers.

After the reservoir, Allan told Cassandra that since she wasn't a virgin anymore, "we can have sex any time we want to."

"It's cut-and-dry. You're a virgin or you're not. We'll repent of all of it, all at the same time. It's a year no matter how many times we've done it."

Two months, a little more, of *any time we want to.* In Allan's car. Between the muffled velvet curtains of the red church stage. Under the junior high bleachers. Up the canyon. Bang, bang, bang, bang. Cassandra could hardly walk. She couldn't think. She stopped making words. She did not draw.

Bang Bang Bang.

"This is our secret, Cassandra. It's going to be all holy and stuff but right now, you need to keep your mouth shut."

Once, he picked her up, all shiny clean in a polo shirt and neatly pressed chinos. He came to the door, spoke to her father, promised to have her back by ten. In the car, he handed her a magazine bookmarked with paperclips. "Look those over. That's what I want to do. Figure it out before we get up the canyon."

She opened the pages.

"You look just like her," he said, poking at the centerfold. "You don't know how beautiful you are. Why don't you act like it for a change?"

After sex on a picnic table, up the canyon, near the stake lodge: "You know, if you ever go to Europe, don't fall for any hotel that says they serve a 'continental breakfast.' All it is, is a pastry and coffee. Total rip-off."

That was the last time.

Chapter 20

"I want you to stay away from that boy," Grandma said, shaking a trowel.

Too late.

"I don't like to intervene," Grandma continued. "You're a big girl and you have to try things. But it's clear he's been given far too much rope. Not enough chain."

Cassandra struggled to keep her voice steady. Invested but casual.

"I don't know what you mean."

"You know very well what I mean." Grandma dropped to the ground, fierce, going for bindweed.

But Cassandra did not know at all what her grandmother meant. Adults—even her beloved straight-talking grandmother—had a way of believing that children in newly adult bodies could read a minefield without so much as a hand-scrawled map. With a sequence of gestures. The task of growing up in Big Horn was to navigate the darkest hazards telepathically.

Cassandra had been told since she was twelve years old that sex outside of marriage was a sin. Spelled out in red letters: *the sin next to murder*. Promiscuous women were ruined goods. Chewed gum. Foul water, disgusting to men who desired a pure and exclusive wife.

By twelve she knew from school, church, and even her high-strung mother that a penis entered a vagina, and thus babies were made, either as broadcast punishment for the unmarried or gracious blessings for the temple-married.

But this was all she knew. First, the minimal physical and starkest moral facts. Now the harried force of entry and thrust. This was the sum of what she could bring, at sixteen, to *You know what I mean.*

The questions she could not form among her grandmother's vegetal vines: The engorged urgency, the astonishing size. The lightning pain of unreadiness. The blood fury of his desire. The irrelevance of her. Her words, her protests and attempts at negotiation, her fear. The cellar of his garrulous impenetrable mind.

The broken link between her eye and hand.

She believed this loss was the result of her heinous sin, this sin she had been warned against since her first sense of being, weighing her down, shutting down her intellect like a popping electrical surge. It stopped her hand on the drawing page, dreadfully blank. Skyline, tree line, fence line, shoulder line, water line—undecipherable, incoherent. Vision, meaning, pattern and shape turned to vapor. Hand erratic. The Holy Ghost, that nudging, gentle guide, that channel of cosmic insight, was punishing her.

"Grandma," she choked. "Please..."

Irene, trowel in one hand, rogue geranium in the other, shuddered as if she'd heard a dark spirit. She turned, head and shoulders, toward Cassandra, even as her feet remained planted. A small spiraling tree.

"Is he...are you... "

Cassandra cried out, a sharp animal sound. Her skull prickled at the base, her vision gray at the borders. Suffusion of nausea and fear.

Down she went.

August morning light. Her grandmother sat in a chair at the foot of the bed. Cassandra had slept through the night, here in

Grandma's composed and quiet house. She saw that her grand-mother had not slept at all.

Cassandra's father would be angry she had not come home. "He won't," Grandma said. "I called last night and told them I needed someone in the house with me. Said I wasn't feeling well."

She looked toward the open door, the still-dark hallway, then back to her granddaughter. "And it was the truth. I wasn't." This room had for a little season been her mother's. That is, it had been the nursery. Each child slept here until old enough to join the siblings upstairs. After the babies were grown, this had become a sick room. Sometimes a grandchild's sleeping place, but Cassandra had not slept in this bed since she was nine years old.

"What happened?"

"You passed out on the lawn."

"How did I get in here?"

"You came to and walked in with me. You were sick in the bathroom. I put you to bed."

Cassandra strained to recall. Between standing at the edge of the garden and waking up, nothing. Not even a memory of sleep.

The doorway to Grandma's room was open, kitty-corner. Cassandra had entered but always with trepidation. Her mother's father had slept in there, on that bed, with his wife, a young woman who was now somehow her grandmother. His side of the closet, once filled with wool and tailored linen. Silk ties. *He was a dresser, my daddy*, Cassandra's mother liked to say, breathless like a debutante.

Whatever artifacts Grandma guarded, tangible or ethereal, resided in that room. Even now Cassandra dreams about that house, its alcoves. High shelves. Cellar stairs. Recesses. No segment of Irene's house was forbidden space, yet, in her dreams, Cassandra can't cross the threshold.

...

Cassandra sat up. Her head spun. Her voice had something sticky in it. "Grandma, something is wrong."

"Yes. Very wrong. We need to make a plan."

"I've done something terrible. My dad's going to kill me. My brothers will know. My mom—"

Cassandra tried to stand. It took her grandmother's stern and frightened voice to inform her that the snarling sound in the room was coming from her own throat.

"Cassandra! Calm down! Please. Right now we have a little time to get rational. We mustn't let it slip from us."

Cassandra quieted. She felt the back of her head, heavy, pulling her downward.

"Lie back," Grandma said. "Count slowly and breathe. You need fresh air."

She cranked the squeaky pane wider. "This is not the end of the world. It's only a disaster. People survive disasters. They find their lives. We just need to get you there."

"I can repent. I'll talk to the bishop. I'll do whatever I need to. I can't go to the celestial kingdom now, I know, but maybe terrestrial. You can come where I am. You can come visit me there. I don't care about anyone else. I'll figure out how to live a good life with him—"

Grandma cut her off, sharp. "Cassandra! What in the hell are you thinking?"

"I know it's the sin next to murder, but people who do it can repent and go to the temple, right? If they're really sorry, if they repent for a year? And never sin that way again?"

"Cassandra! This is not the time to be overcome by fairytales! This is real life! Tune out that lunacy and let's get rational about the next few months. And then the next several decades."

"What?"

"I wouldn't go to that hideous Mormon heaven even if I believed in it. And I certainly do not. You've seen the pictures. Who could live there?"

"Grandma, what?"

"I stopped capitulating to that bullshit decades ago. Why do you think your folks don't want you spending time with me? They don't like me talking to you like this. So, let's not. Not right now. Let's talk about the real crisis, because it's barreling toward us."

"Grandma, what?"

"What do you mean, *what*? Stop making that silly noise."

Silence.

"Here's what, my beautiful granddaughter. I think you're pregnant. We need to get you away from here, and fast."

Part Three

. . .

Represent

Chapter 21

I n college, the beginning of her life on the other side, she began to perceive the contours of another knowledge.

Halting. Chary.

Some of her professors reminded her of religious zealots, which was, at least, a familiar dynamic. She knew how to tune out idiosyncratic rants and passionate intensities. Religion was surprisingly good preparation for college. Let the minutes go by; enter desultory rooms of thought and memory, bolt a few doors. Come back when the tone shifts. Carry it home for perusal.

She was hungry. Each professor had something to teach her—even the bad ones. One professor's obsession with line quality. Another's insistence on graphite gradations, drilled and practiced like musical scales. A painter's passion for transitional hues.

Color charts. Lino cuts. Literality. Abstraction. Emblematics. Negative space.

After a few overtaxing reactions to class critiques, it occurred to her that she did not have to admire or even like her teachers. Not even her classmates, although she was beginning to trust sensations of camaraderie. Unlike religion, she did not have to admire what they admired, believe what they believed, or paint what they painted. She could simply take what they had to give, however obscure, and assemble as she chose.

For a while that was the whole job of college, and it felt like shelter. Her private preoccupations were an advantage: class-work was an exquisite distraction. Drawing and painting were skills, progressions with no finish line.

"You do realize you have a prodigious talent," Professor Linhardt said, after class, from somewhere behind her in the studio. Cassandra registered the statement only as much as she absorbed so many of her professors' words—enough to consider whether it was instruction or a bonus comment. Cassandra kept walking, bracing for the shock of Cache Valley winter wind.

"Cassandra. Miss Soelberg. I am speaking to you. Do you have a few minutes?"

She did not turn, but the professor's callout signaled other students to file out fast. Cassandra stood, a stone in a stream.

Professor Linhardt was the kind of woman Cassandra had been taught to fear. Earn credit and get out. Cassandra knew the words her father would use, so well that she fought to keep them from leaping to mind every time the professor entered the studio: *Hard* (devoid of makeup, not prone to social smiling). *Unfeminine* (the professor, although beautiful in a way that would have agitated Hal, sometimes wore jeans and boots to class, particularly on the coldest days but sometimes just because that's what she put on. Sometimes Cassandra spotted Professor Linhardt walking to campus from somewhere north, cutting through the cemetery. She leaned into it, a long stride). *Arrogant* (she spoke as if she already knew things).

Classmates speculated that Professor Linhardt was a lesbian, but Cassandra would have vaguely suspected it anyway. What else would account for a grown woman like this? Her very black hair was long—well below her shoulders, sometimes tied back with string, sometimes dropping loose. Cassandra did not know any adult woman, in real life, who did not cut and perm her hair. Linhardt wore artistic rings on both hands, none clearly matrimonial. She wore set stones around her neck but kept them under her shirt when she was in class.

Cassandra read Professor Linhardt's demeanor as cold; she did not chat in studio time or in the halls when she saw her students, although she acknowledged them by name in passing. She rarely veered off the subject at hand. She spoke directly from memory, walking among the easels and light tables as she articulated her thoughts, summoned quotations and philosophies, recited poetry. Her lectures were meticulous, her critiques were disquieting; she seemed to perceive intention and evolution. She emphasized revision over error.

Cassandra's urgent work ethic was camouflage—consistent attendance and on-time production kept her invisible. And yet here she was, the only student still in the studio, hailed by the most enigmatic professor in the art department.

She did not want to be seen.

But Cassandra turned, startled to see that Professor Linhardt had walked across the room. She was right there.

"Well, do you?"

Cassandra said, "Do I what?"

"Do you have a few minutes to talk? We can stay here. No classes in this room until evening."

Evening. Grandma would have used that word.

"Okay."

The professor raised her eyebrows. "Am I making you uncomfortable? Is this all right? I only want to talk about your work."

Cassandra gathered herself. "No. Yeah. I mean, you aren't making me uncomfortable. I'm okay. Sure."

"Well then, have a seat. Why don't you pull your drawings from the cabinet. Let's take a look." The professor's voice was underlaid with a kindness that, horribly, produced tears in

Cassandra as she walked. She stood at the cubbies, breathing blood and salt into composure. She opened the wide flat drawer, inhaled the scent of good paper, and carried the stack back for tribunal.

She laid down the drawings with care. She wasn't certain she wanted to look at them together, as they might reveal something she did not intend.

"Okay," Professor Linhardt said. "Give me a few minutes to look them over. You do the same. Try to bring a new eye to what you believe you've produced. Then we can just talk about them. Easy."

Linhardt took her time. Drawing by drawing. There must have been twenty-five or thirty. The professor's absorption gradually calmed the student.

"Come around. Sit by me. Look."

Cassandra did.

"Look at the whole surface," Dr. Linhardt instructed. "Pay attention to visual and thematic relations. It's a bit outdated to tell you to consider content as well as form, but even so I think it's worth the effort. Think about what you're working to convey. Even abstraction bears meaning, although I think you're hiding too much behind it. Some of my colleagues might tell you something else, of course. Make sure you listen to them as well."

Cassandra was surprised. Professor talk had seemed random, idiosyncratic. Classes, separate islands. Linhardt spoke with a certain fervor, but there was no malice or competition in it. What was she after? Cassandra leaned in. The lines on the paper—*her* lines—seemed suddenly exotic. Sinuous and unfamiliar. She'd believed she was drawing objects. People. Scenery.

"What you've been producing is *lines*," Linhardt said. "You can't lose sight of that. Yes, they create illusions. They fool people into believing they're seeing the object you're drawing, but it's not the thing at all. Not the person. Not the canyon. Not the cloud. Not the toy monkey dropped into the jar for a class drawing exercise. This—" she shook a page of cylinder exercises "—is a record of graphite moving across dry pulp. A conscious event. The motion produces its own meanings, to a point."

...you think you're something great?...too frivolous for someone like you...you think you're special enough to be an artist...a talent can become a dangerous distraction from your true purposes, a temptation...

"So, Cassandra, why do you do this?"

She wasn't prepared for a question. Only a talking-to. "Um. Why?"

"I'm asking *you*."

"I don't know what you want me to say."

"I'm asking you a question. It doesn't need a final answer. Just what makes sense to you right now." Professor Linhardt's hand hovered over the drawings, as if she were blessing them. "You're more prolific than any student I've known in a decade. You draw and you draw. You paint and paint and then paint more while the rest of us are struggling for a starting point."

Professor Linhardt lifted a few exercise drawings from the top of the stack. "Let's take a look at this one, for example," she said. She lifted bottom corners on the remaining pile until she found what she was looking for. "Are they in order?" she asked.

"No order."

"All right then," she said, extricating a feral cat and laying it on top of sinuous sloping canyon lines, student huddles in the Fine Arts stairwells, abstract delineations of her brothers, sometimes Hal and Dorothy, her grandmother's vegetation. Ponies in the winter fields. Ducks on the water.

Children, half present, inchoate, immanent. She kept them generic beyond their little definitions.

"What do you have to say about this one?"

"Well, it's a cat," Cassandra said. "It wails from a tree outside my window sometimes." She lifted her eyes for the first time. "No. Wait. It's not a cat. It's graphite lines on dry pulp, calling to mind the idea of a cat."

Linhardt smiled. "Magritte, yes? *Ceci n'est pas une pipe.*"

"Oh! Finally I understand that weird painting!" Cassandra laughed out loud, which felt rude, and she stopped.

Linhardt paused. Cassandra took a deep breath. "My grandma...she had some books in French. I used to look at that pipe. I could not figure out why it wasn't a pipe."

"Did your grandma speak French?"

"Well, sort of."

Linhardt seemed surprised. "Can you draw her? Three lines only."

One: stance. Two: tilt of her head. Three: spade.

"Okay." Linhardt smiled. "What did you do?"

Cassandra reached for the words. "Well, maybe—something like, a drawing is a way of marking something that's..."

The professor waited.

"...that's not here. But it was."

"Sure. It's one way of holding to something lost. Is that why you draw? Can't you remember this cat, this grandmother, without recording it on paper? Let's go to the easy one. What's so important to you about reproducing this cat?"

"I don't know. I had to draw something. It was an assignment. I picked a cat."

"*A* cat? Or *this* cat?"

"This one."

"What makes it this one?"

"What do you mean?"

"I mean, there are millions of cats in the world. People who look at *your* drawing of *this* cat are going to say, 'That's a cat.' But then, somebody might look closer and see something they've never seen, or never brought to mind. What do you think that might be, in this image?"

Cassandra pulled it closer.

"Point to it," Linhardt commanded. "Point to the graphite line that shows me this cat, this time."

The graphite cat peered over his peaked shoulder from the graphite branches of a stunted graphite cottonwood tree. Cassandra ran her finger above the curve of the spine, its languid descent into tail.

"Yes," Linhardt said. "What a casual motherfucker. You nailed him. Think why."

The shock of it—not the language, although novel in its innocuousness, so much as her professor's admiration—hit Cassandra like clean wind.

"Here's the thing, Cassandra. This world produces plenty of talented artists. We're not special, no matter how we natter in class about 'true art.' We're no more tuned in to the grand meanings of the universe than people who have good ears for music, or a gift for working wood, or baking bread, or teaching first graders to read."

Professor Linhardt paused, her planed forehead refracting the north window light. She stood partway, pushing backward to angle her chair and face Cassandra more directly. Her motions were curving lines, but curtailed, as if she reached from a partially opened door.

Cassandra wrapped her arms around herself, locking her ankles under her chair. Linhardt reached toward her but did not touch.

"You don't have to listen to this extra rant if you don't want to," she said. "This isn't on the syllabus."

Cassandra lifted her chin. "I want to."

Both were silent.

Cassandra said, "Please. I want to hear."

"Okay. You have to help. Participation is a virtue."

Cassandra smiled. "Yes." And then, "Well, sometimes."

"So, answer my initial question. You don't have to unload

anything personal. Just think about what informs your need to put lines on the paper. Your gift is formidable, do you understand? Plenty of people can render a cat, or a child, or a barn or a tree. But what you're doing here—it's prodigious. It keeps going. You fill the whole page, even when the composition is spare. Your proportional instincts make everything here into *drawings*, well beyond their subject matter."

Cassandra glanced nervously toward the stack on the table. Considered the spiraling embryonic lines on paper back in her room, down the hill, under the mattress. Not drawings. Only subject matter.

She did not know how to stop making them. Did not know how to dispose of them.

Linhardt chose her words slowly. "If that's all you want from all this—to be a freakishly gifted visual processor—you'll be amply rewarded. You don't even need to finish this degree. There's a mechanistic quality to inborn capacities like yours, set so deep in the nervous system you can't shake it if you try."

This brought the flush, the leap of tears. Cassandra was mortified. She stood up, backed away. "I'm not leaving," she said. "I just need space for a minute. I'm so sorry."

"You have no reason to be sorry," Linhardt said. "Is this enough?"

Enough communication?

Enough reason to move her hand in response to her voracious unappeasable eye?

Enough college talk?

What?

She did not realize she'd uttered out loud. Maybe she hadn't. She said, "I did shake it, once. I couldn't draw for more than a year. Now that my hand moves on the paper again, it's different. I'm afraid it will leave me. And sometimes I'm even more afraid that it won't."

"What's different?"

"All of it. The way I feel when I'm drawing. The way I draw. I think I drew pictures when I was a little kid the same way I ate cereal. I liked it but I didn't think about it."

"Don't you like it anymore?"

"I do. I'm afraid it will be—"

Cassandra stopped. Linhardt waited.

"You're afraid it will be..."

"...taken away."

"*Taken?* Who could possibly take it away from you? It's yours. It's a living thing. It's in you. Congenital." Linhardt took charcoal from her apron pocket. She walked toward her own desk, pulling blank newsprint from the supply shelf. "Look. How about we both draw while we talk? Would that be easier?"

"Yes."

"So, one more time: Why do you *want* to do this? Why do you make images?"

Cassandra opened her own scratch pad. She closed her eyes. Fought the apparition of the child.

Flags.

"My grandma," she said.

Long stalks. Standing spears. Churning tubular roots. Overwrought bonneted blooms implicit above the paper boundary.

"She went to college for a while. She meant to get her teacher's license. Her family didn't approve of college in the first place, and she said she made it worse because she wouldn't stop taking classes in French literature."

Linhardt laughed. "I have to say, I wasn't expecting *that.* Where did she go to college?"

"She said it was some podunk joint in Idaho, but there were committed teachers on the faculty, especially one who made her all passionate about poetry. She had a scholarship—I think because she won a spelling bee—but it took her away from the dairy. Help was money. Her dad was so angry that she'd been wasting all that time and money on dirty atheist frippery he made her come home and get married in the middle of a semester. She hardly ever talked about that part to anyone. Except me, I guess."

"What did she say about it, though, to you?"

A sudden light-drenched vision: July heat. Frigid ankle-deep water submerging the lawn, shimmering lines between the vegetable garden rows. Towering lace-leafed honey locust above snowmelt saturation. Her grandmother's sudden turn, perceiving her presence. Overalls tucked into muddy farm-store rubber galoshes. Wet bill of the shovel lifting as she waves.

Cassandra's hand moved in answer.

"She said I needed to take any chance I got to go to college, and to study something exquisite. And—she said this was most important—useless.

"And she talked in poetry. She liked French poems, and some American ones, and haikus. Sometimes she'd make one up and tell it to me when I was with her."

Big Horn skyline stretched behind Irene's busy organic form: long grade rising from the left. A disturbance of once-molten knobs. A sharper lift, a plummeting notch and recovery, sudden pyramid pitch toward hard summer sky. Rolling peaks and a flattened knife ridge beyond, a gut-stopping drop-off on the other side. Brian and Matthew hiked the whole distance with her when she was ten: kids at precipice, legs dangling over plummet, shapes seared into her eyes.

Professor Linhardt said, "I grew up in Quebec. I speak French, but it's not the Paris French your grandmother probably learned."

Cassandra smiled. "I don't think she made any of the sounds right. She said she spoke 'redneck FranSACE.' But she read French books. Slower than English ones, but she could make sense of them. She said if she could have done it right, she might not have come back, never gotten married, never had children.

She would have quit religion and gone off to Paris or Martinique or Vietnam—"

Cassandra caught herself, suddenly registering Dr. Linhardt's disclosure. "I'm sorry. I just went right on talking. I'm so sorry."

Cassandra put down the pencil. Maybe for the first time in her life, she saw nothing. Not because there was nothing to see, but because something had not yet arrived. Nothing in the way but distance. She looked at a new sheet of paper. Raised the line that meant horizon. "Why did you come to Utah? From Quebec?"

Linhardt laughed, maybe some bitterness in it, but not unkind. "If you grow up in Quebec, then Logan, Utah, is going to seem exotic, right? The grand American West."

Cassandra winced, waiting for the eastern dismissal.

"You know yourself—I've seen your images—this part of the world is beautiful and strange. The bare geology—my god."

Cassandra squinted toward the ladder-steep Wellsville range, even though the studio wall obscured it.

Linhardt said, "And, I have a good job. Not always exquisite, but not always useless. A tenure track position in a field I care about. Do you have any idea how lucky that is? I don't know whether the young women I teach here understand what's at stake."

"All…all by yourself? Is your family—"

"No family. Not here. Not, um, exactly. I married here, but we're divorced. Still friends, but he went on to California."

"Oh."

"Is your grandmother happy with your field of study?"

"She died, almost four years ago. But, yeah. I think she'd be proud. She left me money. For this. Only reason I'm here."

"Only? Your parents must be proud of a daughter with a gift like yours."

The professor's question made no sense to her. To consider whether parents might be proud of a thing like this.

"Well, no. Not really. But since Grandma said this is the only way I get the money, they let me come. Seemed to them like—"

Cassandra tore the top page off the newsprint pad. She made tiny strokes.

Small, dispersed. Mindless. Strokes.

"Like what?"

"Like, the best solution."

"Are you a problem?"

"Yes."

Professor Linhardt stood again. "I'll be back in a minute," she said. "Please, stay until I return."

The studio darkened, and illuminated, and darkened again as storm clouds passed across the north-facing clerestory windows, and apparently the dropping winter sun. A few students walked in, quiet, settling in early to complete work for their next class. The north-light atmosphere either depressing or reverent.

When Professor Linhardt returned, she said, "Maybe you should change color. See what happens."

She set a slender box of red Prismacolor pencils near Cassandra's hand.

"You know," she said, almost murmuring, "it's a gift to render exactly what we see. Cézanne said Monet was 'only an eye—but god, what an eye.'"

Linhardt gestured toward the table. "Art people love to throw that kind of stuff around. And sometimes such talk is valuable. Monet's eye was only Monet's. But Heidegger says we bring objects—that is, what we can perceive beyond our walled-in selves—into being by engaging with them. By *seeing* them. Exchanging something with what is not us. That's something different than just being an eye."

That sounded almost religious to Cassandra. Then, not at all. A howling sacrilege. It was the end of doctrine. *Finis.*

Chapter 22

One good thing about Big Horn's rather malignant growth is that she can wander beyond her mother's neighborhood without running into people from her past. Couldn't duck class for fifteen minutes, back in the day, without some officious spy calling her parents. Now she paddles through a population of eerily familiar but unacquainted clones. Nearly everyone resembles a cousin, or somebody's mother or father, or a former bishop or teacher or sobered-up cowboy uncle. A few are marked by family traits so distinct she senses she's in a time warp. Even the comers look like everyone else, but healthier, unnaturally luminous.

While the sameness stirs something unhappy in her, it provides a sense of anonymity. For a few weeks, even in the heat, Cassandra works the camouflage. She wears long trousers when she leaves the house. She wears shirts with sleeves to cover her shoulders, inviting assumptions that she's covering Mormon underwear rather than tattoos.

So it's a jolt to hear a woman calling her name at the four-way Food Town.

"Cassandra!" Paige calls from the far end of the freezer aisle. "Good to see you out and about! How's our sweet Dorothy today?"

As if this were an incidental sister-in-law encounter a week since. Cassandra does not wish to converse across the distance, but Paige, who sports the same layered bouffant she perfected in high school, makes no move to come closer.

"Oh, you know," Cassandra replies, voice half-raised. "Cheerful. She's craving ice cream."

"What's that?" Paige warbles.

Cassandra cups her hands like a megaphone and hollers, "Ice cream!" and Paige bends her mouth upward, pained, rolling her cart out of view.

Five minutes later, ice cream softening against bananas and bagged lettuce, a reunion at the check stand. Cassandra concedes to herself that she is not passing in the least. Her silvering hair drops down her back in a lengthening braid. Whatever she does for her face does not qualify in this town as cosmetics. Paige, wife of Cassandra's eight-years-older brother but only three years older than Cassandra, is dyed, coiffed, and manicured, smoothly compressed into a cream-yellow blouse and black boutique jeans with embroidered pockets. Her lacquered toes peek from silver lamé sandals.

Cassandra says, "Oh, hello again."

Paige is high school vivacious. "Oh hello again! Fancy meeting you here!" and then, flummoxed by proximity: "Looks like you only have a few things. You go first so you can get that ice cream back to Mother Dorothy."

Even so, a line. They'll have to wait.

It appears that Paige knows everyone in the store. "Oh helloooo Megan," she says to a mid-thirtyish woman, next line over. Baby propped in the child seat. Toddler in the cart with the groceries. Two more, standing. Boy and girl.

The young mother named Megan looks startled, but gears in. "Oh, hi, Sister Soelberg. How are you?" which startles Cassandra. Sister Soelberg is her mother, not the Pep Club drill mistress who married James while Cassandra was "away."

"We're doing well! Look at those darling children! Growing up so fast! How old are they now?"

The line is not moving. The kid at the register does not know the entry number for Napa cabbage. Nor does anyone, which is why the electronic voice above them pleads, "Produce to Register Four, please. Produce to Register Four." Cassandra makes a mental note to avoid purchasing anything exotic at the four-way Food Town.

The kids huddled around their mother's cart look a little wan. The bald baby wears a headband with an enormous bow spanning the top of her head, like a radioactive butterfly. The boys—even the toddler—are shaved up the sides, topped with mowed gelled mops combed stiffly sideways. Cassandra wonders whether they are supposed to look like white supremacists or if it's coincidence. The "big" sister, donned in floral leggings and jelly shoes, gazes frankly at her and everyone else. Cassandra gives her a pinky wave, which the child returns, expressionless. Cassandra is relieved that Paige's attention has veered away from her, but she feels for Megan, anxiously engaged in processing the entourage through the grocery line without disaster.

Cassandra glances at her phone, but chooses to save the St. Paul messages for quiet pleasure later on. A guitar clip. Go Sam. The overhead voice once again summons Produce. Produce does not appear.

"Cassandra?" a woman's voice bellows, not overhead but from back behind Paige, who is still chatting up the peasants.

This time, louder: "Cassandra Soelberg? Holy heck, is that really you?"

Taking a cue from the little girl, Cassandra turns a neutral face into the gale.

"All cashiers to the registers," the creepy overhead voice commands, nearly drowned out by the hefty, sexy woman exclaiming, "Holy cow! You've barely aged since high school! I'd recognize you anywhere! Where have you been all this time?"

Cassandra reels through her visual catalog, slowing and then stopping on the image of Andraya Parkington—or, rather,

Andraya's mother, with updates. Right here, beaming among the slicked-up corporate wives and festooned children, a true old-town vision. Cassandra delivers a smile, and then, firming up, "Andraya? Am I right? Wow, it really has been a long time. It's so good to see you!"

Paige quits chumming to cast an actual hook, swiveling to assess Andraya's heavy mascara and emerald eye shadow. Graded foundation shades, not quite blended. Maroon lipstick lined in an unsettling liver hue. Skunkish roots stripe a chestnut-brown home color—a new box in Andraya's cart. Massive concentric hoops stretch her double-pierced lobes.

Paige turns back to fix an expression on Cassandra, blinking as if she has a mote in her eye, clearly attempting a signal. Cassandra guesses it's something like *this is not the kind of person we chat with in the grocery line* but reminds herself she does not know this woman beyond outdated impressions. The only keys to interpreting Paige's inner life include sartorial impact and the knowledge that this woman has been married to—well, *James*—longer than the time Cassandra knew her own brother before being put on a flight to hell.

"Yessss!" Andraya gushes. "How *are* you? How's your mother? I heard she's a bit—"

Paige yanks the line. "A bit what, Andraya? What have you heard?"

"Oh, hello, Paige," Andraya grins, wicked. "Haha! Didn't even see you there! Distracted by the Cassandra sighting, I guess. You here together?"

"No."

"Mother Dorothy is doing very well," Paige declares. "We've been combining forces as a family for many years—" she shoots Cassandra a signifying glare "—to care for her in her heart-breaking decline. Cassandra has finally returned from her gratifying artistic career to grace us with her assistance. In this late hour."

Andraya throws her head back like a tango queen, gracing the crowd with a raucous laugh. "Well, good for you, Cassandra! Your mama lives in her own special lala land, just like mine? And pretty much everyone else's?"

"Not my mother—" Paige begins, but Cassandra leans around her to answer Andraya: "Dorothy woke up at three o'clock this morning to tell me Hal was riding down the mountain with a barrel of hard cider."

"Cassandra!" Paige protests, and Cassandra reminds herself that she answers to no one here—not anymore—until the boy at the cash register says, *Next, please!* and she leaps toward the conveyor like a busted truant.

Ice cream drips from the carton as she lifts it from the cart. She looks at the kid who didn't know Napa cabbage, about to say, "Do you know the entry number for melted ice cream?" but a man's arm reaches from behind to take it from her hand. She turns. He hands her a hard-frozen replacement.

He's wearing a maroon—not red—baseball cap. She looks a little closer: not a trucker's hat—a true baseball bill. His eyes are obscure behind half-darkened transition lenses. Expensive.

"All good," he murmurs. "That was a long wait."

She does not want to bond over this. "Um. Okay? Thanks," she says, sensing Paige's interest. She hears a little *woohoo* from Andraya's direction. Mom and kids next line over are bagging up, eager to exit.

The man stands near the loading zone as Cassandra blinks in the sunlight, scanning the lot for her car before recalling she drove her mother's ruby Cougar. She registers his presence, a good fifteen feet away but attending. Late thirties? He's youthful, so it's hard to guess without staring. His hair brushes his well-cut shoulders. Looks like the kind of guy who comes to climb cliffs in the canyon. Pocketed shorts and hiking sandals testify.

"Would you allow me to talk with you sometime?" he asks, without moving closer.

No one in Clearlake Valley speaks with this diction. Professors at the universities, maybe.

"Do you need money? Run out of gas? I have a few bucks change if you want it."

"No. Don't need money. I have a job. And a full tank. I'm actually working right now."

Cassandra snorts. "I'm almost sixty years old. Are you a gigolo?"

He smiles, orthodontic white teeth. His glasses have darkened completely, but the eyes behind the lenses flicker in the flashbulb sunlight. Something arresting about him. Her heart clutches, obnoxious.

"Wait. Who are you? What do you want?"

He looks like he might scoff and run, but, instead: "Can I come closer? I don't want to seem pushy. I'm a writer. Journalist. Sometimes I get lucky with a feature assignment and I get to travel. I've never been in Utah. Not even the West. I just want to talk to someone who can help me find my bearings."

"I've got this goddamn ice cream, remember? Can't melt another carton. My crazy mother awaits."

"Can I walk you to your car?"

"My mother's car. I want you to understand that I do not own a Mercury Cougar sedan. I drive it sometimes to keep the battery charged."

"I like that color."

"Nevertheless."

At the car: "Credentials? Who do you write for?"

"This time, *New York Times Magazine*. I pitched a proposal. They went for it."

"Show me something? Help me trust you."

"Like, press ID? Or, I don't know—I have plenty of junk in my car over there. Stuff from not here."

"Sure. Press."

"I'll still have to go back to my car," he says. He points it out, two rows over. Nevada plates. "It's a rental. Look, here's my driver license." He pulls his wallet from a back pocket, holds it up for her to see: the word *Massachusetts* clearly shows from the pocket. He attempts to thumb it out, but Cassandra says, "Okay, fine. I'm not a cop."

He puts the wallet back.

She says, "What's your name?"

"Matthew. Matt. DeLuca. You can look me up. Plenty of stuff online. I'm on staff for the *Boston Globe*, and I've done some short features for other magazines but it's not my regular. A few smaller pieces for *New York Times*, but this one they went for, and they gave me money to travel, so…here I am."

He lifts his eyes to the summits. "Lost and confused. This place is surprisingly claustrophobic. Not exactly the wide-open spaces I have been caused to expect. Feels like those mountains are about to drop down on us."

Cassandra gestures west. "Drive thirty minutes that way. You'll get more wide-open spaces than you can take in."

Then: "Why do you want to talk to *me*?"

"Quite a dynamic there in the checkout line. Sounds like you've been away for a while. Like you used to come from here. Where do you live in your real life? Your—what did that woman say—your *artistic* life?"

"You can't 'used to come' from someplace. You always come from that place, like it or not. But, now, St. Paul. I'm an artist. Illustrator. Where did you grow up?"

"Amherst."

"Speaking of claustrophobic. Nothing but goddamn forest. Can't see thirty feet in any direction."

She stands back to take him in. He gazes back, apparently guileless, but what does she know? The broken-glass glitter of his eyes, behind the expensive glasses.

"Do you have family?"

"My partner and I have been together for seven years. No

kids. My dad's in New Hampshire. My mother finished her degree at Amherst and never left. Works at the college."

"Did they shut you up in prose?"

"What?"

"Nothing. My name is Cassandra, as you'll recall from the recent saga. Cassandra Soelberg. I need to take ice cream home to my mother. If you're really hanging around this delightful community, I guess I'll see you. Might be nice to talk to someone from the real world."

He gestures toward skyline granite. "That isn't real?"

"No. Movie set. Collapsible."

She opens the red car door, sets the groceries in the passenger seat. "DeLuca, huh? You don't look Italian."

"Adopted."

"What?"

"My dad's Italian. My mother is Irish. I don't resemble either one." He delivers a strange expression, as if he realizes he's been speaking the language wrong. "Adopted," he repeats.

She freezes, then erupts. "Fuck you. Get away from me, you sick troll."

He steps back.

"Who put you up to this?" she shouts.

She scrabbles for the keys in her bag. She shuts the door and turns the ignition. She does not hear or see his response, but she is certain he's got sense to leap out of the way. She yanks the car into reverse and squeals the curve.

Chapter 23

She drives home in her mother's ruby time machine.

Dorothy is still in her soft living room chair. Cassandra moves past her quickly, heading for the freezer. She thanks the nice Relief Society volunteer for "tending" and sends her home.

"Ice cream, Mama! Let me put it back in the cold for just a few minutes, and I'll scoop some for you."

She sets the ice cream in the freezer compartment.

She arranges produce, bread, milk, and cream on the refrigerator shelves, then retraces the path toward her mother. Dorothy is hunched over, motionless—eyes fixed on something in her hand.

"Mom? Are you okay?"

"What should we do with this?"

"What have you got there?"

A fine thread of drool stretches from Dorothy's lower lip into her cupped palm. The cup runneth over.

"Oh, Mama. Just a minute."

Cassandra wets a hand towel from the bathroom rack. She wraps Dorothy's hand, soaking up the pool of spit.

"Stay right here. I'll come back with a clean washcloth."

She rinses the towel under hot water, wrings it as well as she can. Her own wrists have lost strength, forcing her to recall that she's not so far behind her mother. She hangs the towel over the shower rod, warms a washcloth under the tap, squeezes, and returns to Dorothy, who now slouches in an unladylike pose, butt forward, shoulders pressed against the chair back.

"Oh no. Mom. What's that smell?"

Hot geriatric urine spreads into the plush fitted cushion. Dorothy, wide-eyed, holds her hands in the air, away from her own wet clothing.

"I don't know. An awful thing."

Cassandra forces her reflexes and guts to relax. She breathes through her mouth, light. She does not have the iron constitution of a nurse but she can reason herself into functionality. Nasty as it is, a chair saturated with an old woman's piss is somehow less heave-inducing than a cupped palm of saliva.

"Stay right there, just a minute. I'll come back with towels."

Dorothy begins to cry. Cassandra speaks softly. "It's okay, Dorothy. We can take care of this. Don't try to stand until I'm back to help you."

She runs for it. She throws the towels on the racks into a laundry basket and reverses back out to Dorothy in a single motion.

"Here Mom. Look. This is not a disaster. It's just a little mistake. You'll see."

"It will be a disaster if Father comes home to this!"

Cassandra attempts an awkward full-body lean over her mother, reaching under the arms and stancing for lift. "You're going to have to help me, Mom, as much as you can. Pull yourself up as much as you can manage."

Dorothy does not help at all. She blubbers like a child. Cassandra remembers to lift from her legs—difficult, considering her back is humped like a dog's, but suddenly Dorothy is upright. Mother and daughter are soaked—Dorothy in back, Cassandra along the shirtsleeves, at the knees and thighs of her jeans. The chair is stained and redolent.

"Can you stand by yourself, Mom? We'll lose the wet clothes

right here. I'll wrap you up in this extra-big towel and we'll get you in the shower."

Dorothy stands meek. Cassandra spreads a towel on the floor and Dorothy steps onto it by instinct. Cassandra pulls at her mother's cream-colored terry pants then peels the filmy, knee-length temple undergarment from the wet reddening skin. "Okay, step out, all right?"

Dorothy puts ginger fingertips to the Caesarian scar and begins to cry again.

"Come on, Dorothy. You can do this. Just step to the right. Or left. Or forward."

Her mother steps, contrite. Cassandra drops the wet fabrics into the basket, wiping her hands dry on her own shirttails. She unzips her mother's fun sporty jacket. It drops to the covered floor. Dorothy attempts to help with the tedious buttons on the blouse, which keeps her engrossed until Cassandra catches up. She gently swats her mother's hand away. Dorothy erupts in a disturbing giggle. The blouse falls.

Cassandra turns her mother around, resisting an impatient yank, deploying the fine motor skills required to unclasp the armored bra. Dorothy's breasts expand in release. The Masonic signs sewed into the religious garment stretch taut, in front, against the pressure of new-sprung flesh.

"Okay. Almost there," Cassandra urges, straining to keep the copious bodily requirements of religion at a distance from this distasteful task. "Last layer. It's icky, so let's get it over with."

Upward, over Dorothy's half-raised arms, wetting her increasingly naturalized hair—which, Cassandra has noted in less distracting moments, is quite beautiful brushed smooth. Dorothy hasn't noticed, which means she's forgetting to scrutinize—or recognize—her reflection.

They're more saturated now than when they began. Deep animal odor.

"Let's get you to the shower."

"I get dizzy in the shower."

"Okay, let's run the tub. But let me wash you down first."

Something switches in Dorothy's mind. Time folds back on itself. "We'll have to clean this all up before he gets home, or it will be the garden hose for you."

Cassandra steps back for that one. "What? Who?" "Don't think you'll be spared because you're a girl. He has no patience with bedwetting. Don't you remember how it went with James? The other ones, too, but for them it only took once."

"How would I remember? I'm the youngest."

"That's no excuse. I'll help you hide it this time, but I can't protect you from your own behavior forever. He doesn't look away. He sees more than you understand. He does pay attention."

"Mom, what in the world are you talking about?"

"Some things are a father's job. How many times has he told us that? Don't make him demonstrate."

Would it be wise to interpret any of this? Do uncanny emissions ever clarify anything? Once, in the thrall of late-century feel-good feminism, Cassandra imagined she ought to excavate some revelatory key to her mother's ways of knowing—to illuminate some essential feminine kinship to whoever—whatever—coursed beneath the shellac of *Fascinating Womanhood*.

Now? Maybe not. What about James, and bedwetting, and the garden hose? In a way, she understands perfectly. Hal standing in her room, blocking the closed door, commanding his body-grown daughter to strip, bluntly assessing her angry swollen breasts, skin tightening over her abdomen, the stark functional truths of her wide hips and stout pioneer thighs. The humiliation unbearable, searing—but (to his credit?) his interest exclusively dutiful.

His daughter's harrowed segments a matter of evidence. Like every other familial duty, performed by necessity, a list of unpleasant tasks carried out with gritted teeth. Violence, power, authority a heavy yoke he'd been trained to accept like a congenital defect. His love for Dorothy was founded on her willingness to do her job: look, sound, and act like a woman without complaining, or usurping. He felt sorry for women, in his way: they'd been assigned an absurd role in the cosmos. He did his job as a man, however unpleasant. He was grateful to Dorothy for doing hers, propping her up as noble exception to the kind of woman he despised, which was most of them. Complainers. Harpies. Bitches. Feminists gumming things, thwarting masculine duty. God, an unyielding father, assigned the roles before creation itself.

James? How young? How old? Also stripped naked, out in the yard—the front? That's where the hose connected. Howling. Redundant. Public. A self-reinforcing cycle of noncontrol.

Did the man stare down his naked wife in the same way? What a honeymoon: a checklist of proprieties, necessary proofs, the burdens of masculine charge. How far did this go back, how deep, this *mise en abîme*, this room of reflections encasing her panicked mother: nakedness, emissions, mortifications, violence, protection, control?

How were they all captured?

Now Dorothy is safe in the bath, with a fizzing ball of floral salts shooting color and foam. Blissful, oblivious. Cassandra returns to the reeking room. She opens the front door, fixes the screen so she can push the whole chair out. She gives it a kick from behind, making it roll sluggish down the concrete steps. She returns with the basket of laundry and sets it on the lawn. Circles back to give the upholstered chair a hard heel shove onto the lawn.

She turns on the hose, turns the nozzle to "jet," and proceeds to assault the plush.

Chapter 24

"Cassandra, wake up."

Her mother's voice, in a tone Cassandra did not recognize.

"Cassandra, please. Wake up."

The strange sleep, half-dreaming voices in the house, quiet deliberate motions, fell away. Clock radio: 1:47. She sat up.

Her mother signaled hush, reaching to wrap her hand around Cassandra's upper arm, squeezing. "Don't speak yet. I have just a minute to talk to you alone."

Her mother's directness, stripped of her practiced wheedling lilt. The synaptic friction of deep neural response. Her body's answer. And then, the child's: A flutter. A flickering roll, unambiguous.

As if Dorothy had summoned the quickening, an otherworldly minute, gray rabbit light. Mother, daughter, and another.

An other. Time and place surreal.

And the rest, in such rapid sequence, past and present and loss and replacement and silence and roaring simultaneous:

"This is not my idea," Dorothy whispered. "I need you to understand. This is not what I want. I have been pleading for hours. I have no choice. My mother—"

Cassandra came back to time and place, into the room that was never hers although they'd placed her in it, in the body that belonged to the men who defined it, the women who policed it, the tethered butterfly in the inner space of it.

A full moon moving motionless at traveling speed.

"My *mother*," Dorothy said again. "Your grandma—"

"No! No no no no no—"

"—a stroke. She's alive, but she's very ill. She can't speak. The ambulance has already come. They'll make her as comfortable as they can at the hospital."

"Can I see her? Can we go now?"

"Cassandra—"

"I'll get dressed. I can drive." She reached for the lamp switch. "Even if we can't see her yet, we can be there. She'll know we're there, waiting—"

"Cassandra! Please! There's more."

In the light, she could see that her clothes were laid out for her on the chair, at the curlicued hutch. Her mother's honeymoon suitcase, latched and demure. Cassandra's open school bag, already packed with her Triple Combination scriptures from seminary and her mother's favorite book of poems—*Beginnings*.

A stir of presences beyond the bedroom.

An internal leap of terror.

"Mom? What's going on?"

"You're going somewhere. You're starting to show. Your father won't have it—"

A sudden forceful knock. Mother and daughter started like fugitives. Hal stood, supernaturally large, in the open doorway.

Dorothy emitted a small wail. Cassandra could make no sound.

"Shut it down, Dorothy! We don't need the neighbors in on this. You and your crazy mother have drawn this out to the brink of disaster. Cassandra, you can come quietly or I'll carry you—and that thing you've cooked up—out like the trash you've become. You've done more than enough damage to this family. Get up! It's time to go."

Some memories alter with time. Some words descend into gist, some images diffuse into mist. She dreams this moment in horrific transmutations: a thirty-foot stick man, scribbling flies fattening the figure in shifting proportions, screaming down at her tiny form, her hands clumsy like a toddler's. Her father, brothers, congregation standing at the doorway, a multitude shouting shame: Cassandra bewildered at the cause until she raises her arms, bleeding stumps at the wrists. Allan White, flickering between young and decrepit, mummified and blooming—mittened with a flannel puppet of himself, reaching lascivious to yank her out of bed as her father diverts his gaze.

She stood as if pulled upward by animating strings. Her father held sentry position at the threshold, only lowering his eyes to the green carpet as his daughter disrobed, pulling on underwear and miserably capturing her swollen breasts into inadequate cups. As if he hadn't already made her strip and show herself, stark and defenseless.

She fit herself into her roomiest jeans, unbuttonable. She did not know this body. She did not know this room, this home, this mother cowering and nearly invisible on the alien bed. She did not know this humanoid swimming in her intimate guts. But brusque and intractable as he had always been, and terrifying as he was in this moment, she knew this father, and she knew the God who made him. The concrete floor, the iron ceiling.

Hurry up.

She groped through her closet for adequate cover. Soft fabric at her palm: Matthew's flannel shirt—the one he lent her at the campfire, a ward dinner up the canyon. A rush of gratitude as she buttoned it over her swelling stomach. Even washed, the shirt smelled faintly of smoke and Matthew.

A rotund man in a lurid polyester suit stood in the hallway, gesturing like a fun-house nightmare. He made no sound, but he put a finger to his lips as he grasped Cassandra's arm above the elbow, tight. The front door opened of its own malicious accord, and Cassandra was ushered outside. More ghouls—dark figures flanking a sedan in the dim driveway, at least two others at the curb.

Where were her brothers? Oblivious? Colluding?

"It's all right, Cassandra," the lurid man who held her arm whispered. "This might seem strange, but these people are all invested in your well-being. They're good people who work with the church. Just stay quiet and get in the car, and you'll see there won't be any trouble."

Cassandra looked back to see her father's form filling the doorway. No signal. No motion. The man beside her smelled like sweat and cheap soap. His fingers were fat and powerful, clamped like a crescent wrench around her biceps. Why didn't she scream? Why did she not call out? How is it she didn't collapse, or faint, or die?

He opened the rear passenger door and planted her in the seat. He closed the door gently, ensuring minimal sound. A man's shape sat in the driver's seat, hands on the wheel. Keys ready to turn.

A woman's voice from the seat beside hers, cold syrup. "Hello, Cassandra. It's so nice to meet you. We understand your situation and we've made preparations for you to live safely and quietly elsewhere during your pregnancy. I know this seems scary right now, but I assure you, you are in good hands. Many people are acting together for your benefit. We're doing all we can to make something good come from a sinful act. This is your first step onto the path of redemption."

The key turned. The car started with a quiet purr. The driver kept the headlights off as he backed out and angled into forward.

At the end of the street, the stop sign at the southward turn, a sudden form at her window. A palm at the glass.

Matthew.

Chapter 25

E very square yard of Big Horn is stratified with past seasons and scenes. Cassandra used to assume that other people recalled their lives in similar ways, but maybe not. Her studio friend Pauline has always insisted that her Minnesota childhood is by now a fairly agreeable blur of winter mukluks, summer lakes, corn on the cob, and potato casseroles. Cassandra's own mother always said that her only clear memory of Big Horn childhood, at least before her father's sudden death on the crossroads, was the arrival of irrigation water at the Whetstone headgate.

Now, though, in the throes of dementia, trapdoors open and stories fly up. Especially in the car. Dorothy spills anecdotes from the shotgun seat. She's chatty, almost witty. Doesn't matter what's covered over by subdivisions—she sees the old orchards. No matter the strip mall or the new charter school effacing former corn and alfalfa fields. Dorothy is a dimensional tour guide.

"That's where Daddy's truck broke down and we had to haul it home with the draft team. So much for modern technology! Ha ha!"

"That's where the penny candy store used to be. I could make a Sugar Daddy last all day if I was careful."

"Eeuw. Mom."

"Sometimes the ward would rent movies from the studios because there wasn't a theatre up here in Big Horn. We'd all come to watch them at the cultural hall at the old stone church that used to be right there by the fountain. Sometimes even a double feature—only time our parents let us stay out past eleven o'clock. At least without sneaking. *What Ever Happened to Baby Jane?* Ha ha!"

"That's where Sally Murdock's beauty parlor used to be, before she got lupus and couldn't control her hands anymore. She gave Emma and me perms one day—worked us both at the same time. She was good. Had customers all day, every day. The bishop had to tell her to shut down on Sundays, said she had the freedom to break the commandments if she wanted to on her own time, but providing temptation for others was another thing.

"We'd just finished our perms once, and they looked pretty, so we walked home. Right there at the intersection, Billy Packard kind of slowed his dad's pickup at the corner but he didn't look close enough. Bunch of his pals in the bed. Dale Potter standing up behind the cab, everybody else sitting on the rails. Three or four dogs with them, barking. Billy didn't see Karl and Mable Wilcox coming up in his blind spot until too late. Hit the gas to get up ahead of Karl's big clunker, sideswiped it instead. Big boys and dogs went flying everywhere. German shepherd arced right over the cab, came down with a horrible thud right at our feet. I don't know if it was dead in the air or killed by landing. I'll never forget the sound of that dog's skull cracking against the sidewalk—"

"Mom! My god! That's awful!"

"Don't speak the Lord's name in vain! What if Daddy heard you say that?"

"I'm Cassandra, Mom. Emma's not here."

"Oh. She must be home already. She saw that dog splatter at our feet and just bolted. Had to dodge truck parts and moaning bodies in the street. She never had any tolerance for carnage, you know."

Did Dorothy? Come to think of it, she'd been pretty cool and businesslike when her kids came home gushing blood. "Stop your crying." Butterfly tape.

Cassandra has heard tales of this disaster, of course. Nearly every kid in town had an uncle or somebody in the crash, and a rendition of their own. Three dead teenagers. One with a head injury that changed him for life; Cassandra recalls him, an ageless man in a work shirt, one eye turned up toward the ceiling, carrying a bucket and towel to wipe the lunch tables after children made a run for the playground. Everyone in Big Horn knew this story. But her mother, born and raised in Big Horn, never mentioned it until she lost control of her mind.

"See that house, kind of tucked back behind the others? Made of stone? Prichetts lived there. All daughters. They took care of a grandfather—Sister Prichett's father, so his name was something else. I don't know what. Old coot pretended he was crazy, like he didn't know what was going on, but he had an army chest filled with girlie magazines and pornographic postcards. There were some very unusual objects from his service in all those Oriental places, people said. Must have put sick ideas into his mind. Turns out he was going into the girls' rooms every night, picking out one or two and doing nasty things with them. Maybe they were asleep. Maybe they just didn't want to get hurt, or they didn't know what else to do but get it over with. Maybe they even enjoyed it—who knows?"

"Mother! How can you say that?"

"Well, things were different back then."

"I doubt it."

"My cousins in Montana said, females don't have to go out and milk cows in subzero dark every morning. Didn't have to pick up calves in the freezing March wind. Least they could do was offer a little heat when the boys came in."

"*Females?*"

"But I never liked that kind of thing. I married Hal because he didn't, either."

Cassandra grips the steering wheel.

Her mother enjoys getting out. It occurs to Cassandra to ask a question. "So, what happened to the Prichetts? I never heard that name in Big Horn."

"Who?"

"The Prichett girls, and their grandfather. In that house back there. The army trunk with the pictures."

"I don't know what you're talking about."

"The rapist grandfather!"

"Oh, I don't know if we can go so far as to call him a rapist."

"What would *you* call him?"

"Who?"

Another mile.

"What do you mean, Hal didn't like that kind of thing?"

Not like she expects an answer.

Chapter 26

Dorothy's kitchen still has a landline. It's not the telephone Cassandra recalls from the 1970s, but it's connected at the same spot on the wall, face height, near the pantry door. Cassandra and her brothers used to stretch the spiral cord into the pantry over the stairs, fitting themselves among soup cans and boxed mac and cheese. Now the sleeker, cordless anachronism on the wall is ringing. Cassandra expects a brother or brother's wife, maybe a chirping "ministering teacher" from the ward. But the voice on the line throws her back into a weirder framework.

"Cassandra! Honey! I took a wild guess that your old number still works and sure enough! It's you! I knew it! My mother still has her landline, too!"

"Are you there, at your mom's house?"

"No. I'm in my driveway. Looking for a duck."

"Why?"

"She just likes to get out. Like you I guess."

"Well, they got me back in now."

Even if she hadn't seen Andraya in the grocery store, Cassandra would have recognized her on the line. Unlike the body, the voice was unchanged: hearty, exuberantly conspiratorial. Andraya came on way too strong in elementary school—and junior high, and high school until Cassandra had been abducted by Church People and lost track. Andraya comes on way too strong now, over the brick of a handset.

Cassandra smiles. For real.

"It's really good to hear your voice. Sorry we were so rudely interrupted at the grocery store."

"Interrupted? Hardly! I saw you talking to that good-looking guy and got out of the way. One hundred percent support, sister! Us girls got to back each other up for setsy times! We're not getting any younger, right? You're looking great, by the way. Like I said, you've hardly changed since—" Andraya peters out, then, predictably, relocates her confidence "—since you freaking disappeared before senior year. And you didn't miss a thing, by the way. You were so smart to get out of here."

Cassandra has known Andraya as long as she's known anyone beyond her parents' household. Andraya comes from a giant family, all girls until the last, a boy named Eleventh. Everyone inquired after Twelfth so often he became a de facto presence, bug-eyed and overbitten like his hypothetical parents, ten sisters, and brother. In reality Jerald Parkington refused to tempt fate after he'd gotten his boy. How Andraya's father—or mother, for that matter—had put the brakes on reproduction remained a topic of local speculation.

Vocal pitch made for the most striking distinction among the Parkington siblings. Andraya—along with Sariah, JoAnn, and Jeraldine—inherited their mother's baritone guffaw, her disconcerting sensual voice. Shauna, Marsia, Bethany, Pauletta, Catherine, Sadie, and Eleventh picked up their father's high nasal whine. If you heard them without seeing them, you might not imagine the two camps were related.

Hearing Andraya's lusty tones on the landline, here in this moment, lifts Cassandra into a mild euphoria—the sensation of a world before the fall. Embodied belonging, a child's conviction of cosmic plenitude.

Apparently, Andraya has not lost her enviable talent for living on the planet as-is. Not naïve, not inclined to second-guess. Wry and blunt since they were Sunday School Sunbeams. The first thing Cassandra remembers Andraya saying to her: "Troy's our nursery friend but sometimes he has poop on his shoes. Tawnie is not our nursery friend because she bites. You can be my nursery friend if you don't bite. And we should always check our shoes."

Deal.

Andraya's curiosity now is lasered on the man in the grocery store. "So, you gonna tell me about that guy? Are you married? Divorced? I heard you went away to be a lesbian. Well, that's *one* thing I heard. Did you? I also heard you got pregnant. I also heard you're a bigtime artist somewhere, too good to come home to Hicktown."

"Wow. That's a lot to answer."

"Well right? But it's been—what—forty years or something? You know we have a high school reunion coming up, don't you? You left before senior year, so it's been more than forty since I've run into you. Have you even been back? Did you come home for your dad's funeral?"

"No."

"That was an easy one. So what's with that guy who was looking so damn interested in you a couple days ago?"

"Just some person. He's from Boston or somewhere. Talks to strangers."

"It didn't look like he's from here. But then again he kind of looks like—"

"So, how's your life, Andraya? What's been going on with *you* for the past forty years?"

"Oh, you know. Pretty much what you'd expect. Did you know me and Dean Hansen got married?"

"Really? Dean Hansen? When did that happen?"

"Summer after high school. You know how it is. Barely notice some skinny guy all through the first part of your life, then you're married to him and making babies. Then you're pushing sixty and got a house full of grandkids coming and going. Am I right?"

Cassandra blinks toward the west window. Glass door. Whatever.

"Uh, yeah. I guess?"

That Parkington bellow. "Don't sound like it went that way for you though. You went for adventure, didn't you?"

Out the window: beige houses, asphalt rooflines. The broken uniformities confound her eye, hungry for distinctions. She needs the scene to yield.

"Haha, sure. Adventure."

"Well let's catch up! Let's do lunch! Is your mom okay if you leave her for an hour or two? Maybe Sister Paige Marie Jenkins Pep Club Soelberg can sit with her for an afternoon without damaging her manicure?"

Cassandra laughs out loud. "The Relief Society is on call. How about Thursday?"

"I'll take a long lunch break. I work at the new charter school there by the bank. Putting in some summer hours. Twelve? There's that fancy new pizza place down at the corners. I'll just walk over."

"I'll be there. Good to hear from you, Andraya. Truly."

"*Truly.* You always talked funny. It's gotten worse."

"'Thursday. Twelve o'clock. Fancy pizza place at the corners."

"Yeah, well, it might not be fancy to *you.*"

Chapter 27

"It's pretty fancy," she tells Andraya, who is already waiting in the foyer. "Nothing like this when I lived here. Not even close."

"Haha the Marshalet, am I right? Marsha did make good onion rings."

"That was it, at least in Big Horn. What—Hi Spot down in Clearlake."

"Haha the Fly Spot. The jack Mormons were lucky. They had the Brigadier all to themselves down there. Rest of us had to hide up the canyon. Which is also plenty crowded now. Did you know you have to pay a fee to the Forest Service just to go up there and have a picnic anymore?"

The canyon. The reservoir. "Mmm. Yeah. I went up there." Cassandra brings herself back to the moment. "Now look at all this. Franchise paradise. Two big grocery stores. So many churches. Temples. How spiritual."

"I'll bet you hardly recognized this place."

"Still don't."

"Well, in plenty ways it ain't changed much."

An earnest young woman approaches, dressed in something resembling Italian peasantry. She's slight, pale, not Italian-looking at all, hometown pretty. "Table for two, ready for you. Oh, hi, Sister Hansen."

The girl gives Cassandra a puzzled stare, then looks politely away. Andraya grins. "Well hi, Dani. This what you're up to, now you graduated?"

Dani seems to take this as commendation. "I got this job last spring. Been working here all summer."

"Tips any good?"

"Sometimes, if they aren't from here. People here say—"

"Haha I KNOW what they say. I was a waitress in Provo when I was your age. 'The Lord only asks ten percent, and you want fifteen?' Make sure you get our table and I'll bet this lady here will do right by you. She comes from the big city. She probably thinks along the lines of twenty, twenty-five."

Dani flushes and turns toward the dining room. Cassandra, head down, and Andraya greeting just about everyone as they proceed, follow the girl between crowded tables to a booth against the wall.

"I'll be right back to take your order," Dani says, addressing the woman she calls Sister Hansen. "Do you want sparkling water, or regular?"

Cassandra: "Regular."

Andraya: "Got any of that classy lemonade? We're having ourselves an occasion."

"Do you want it in a carafe?"

"A *carafe*. Yes! That's a word worthy of a Soelberg. Put some raspberries in it, all right?"

Dani makes a run for it.

"Cute kid, ain't she?" Andraya says.

"Uh-huh."

"All of them like that. A little closed up out there in the hollow but friendly once they warm up. Only family hasn't sold the old farmland. Must be sitting on a few million dollars' worth of dirt, but they don't mind."

"What?"

"All that Goddard land. Probably the ghost of old chinless Nephi comes every night to—"

"Andraya, *what*?"

"Don't you know who that girl is?"

From the safety of the wall booth, Cassandra sits up straighter. Surveys the room. Every patron looks eerily familiar. And everyone an uncanny stranger. Her pulse congeals. The smell of the wood-fired oven suddenly makes her queasy. She pictures the black mouth, the unbearable heat, the sweating cooks with their long paddles, tending to flames.

"Here's your lemonade," Dani says, setting it on the table.

Cassandra sees the girl's hands place two glasses of ice, gentle, between them. She flexes her own, under the table.

"Are you ready to order?"

"Not quite. I'm sorry."

"I'll give you a minute."

Andraya says, "Cassandra, stop staring at the table."

She looks up. Andraya's face is alarmingly close to hers.

"Cassandra, you really don't know, do you? That's Brian's girl."

Cassandra says nothing. Andraya checks her mental calendar and corrects: "Wait. Brian Jr.'s. She's your brother's granddaughter. Can't you see it?"

"I—I'll have to look closer."

"She don't know you either. Does she."

"I don't know. I don't have a guess what they've told their children. We haven't been in touch. I just got a message on my website from James a couple of months ago, telling me it was my job to come home and take care of Dorothy."

"Hellfries, girlfriend. I had no idea it was like this. I live in another ward since way back. I've been getting on with my own screwups. Your people ain't real talkers anyhow. I guess I didn't think it was great between you all, but—"

"Well, 'not great' isn't a fraction of it."

Andraya swallows lemonade, nearly coughs it up, and chugs more.

Cassandra lifts her eyes right, and up, toward the giant picture window, mostly framing strip mall signs and storefronts but including a high glimpse of Tank Canyon's tireless rupture of King's Point. Her right hand squeezes into itself, wishing to grasp a pencil.

The girl returns. "Have I given you enough time?"

"More than enough," Andraya says, in a gentle tone Cassandra does not recognize as Parkington at all. "I like that personal-size pizza with pepperoni on it. And let's have one of them big salads with the salty olives in it, to share. *Cassandra*—" she enunciates the name as if for a foreign tourist "—you probably want one of them things with artichokes or gold leaf or whatever."

Cassandra smiles wanly at her friend, but can't meet the eyes of the girl who awaits her order. "I'd like the Margherita," she says. She tilts her head so Dani can hear. "Plenty of fresh basil, I hope?"

"It comes from my grandpa's farm. My cousin brings it here first thing every morning, just picked. Oregano, too."

There's a surprise. No one in her family could have identified any herb beyond maybe chives (or one of those godawful MSG spaghetti packets) when she was a part of them. She hails from a salt-and-pepper, meat-and-potatoes clan.

"Wow." She manages to look up, now perceiving her brother's cleft chin, much softened but unmistakable. She stops quick tears. "That's amazing," she says, sensing red emotion splotching her neck. "I can't wait to try it."

Dani: "You won't be disappointed."

Andraya: "Well aren't you just the little family ambassador?"

Dani smiles, shy but more relaxed, and turns toward the kitchen.

Andraya's eyebrows follow the girl, then return to stake the conversation at hand. "She has no idea who you are. Where in the world have you been, Cassandra?"

Cassandra's face is in her faux-linen napkin.

"Are you okay? Do you want to leave? It's okay if we need to."

Cassandra takes in a heavy whiff of hot oregano-scented air.
"Are people looking at us?"

Andraya takes a gander. "Nope. No more than usual small-town spy-ops."

"Am I walking around with a sign on my back? You spotted me first thing at the grocery store."

"Well, we been friends a long time. You look like your mother, actually, without the gewgaw fluffery she always went out for. I pay closer attention than most people. Worked at the high school in Clearlake all them years I was raising my kids. School secretary, but they don't call it that anymore. It let me keep track of my own spawns a little closer when they were at that hard stage. You'd be surprised at how oversensitive mine turned out. You know how me and Dean are.

"So while I was at it I sort of kept track of everyone else's kids, too. Now I work at the charter school over there because it's closer. I can just walk over. It's all given me an eye for family resemblances, and I seen a lot of people grow up here—old families, like our folks, but plenty of comer types, too. Gad, there's a lot of money come in here. Or at least people who act like they got money."

Cassandra shows her teeth.

Andraya says, "Yeah, and I'd of known that cat fang thing you do, wherever I might of run into you."

"I sort of want to stay incognito."

"Well, that'll depend on who you run into, won't it. Haven't seen you out on the street much, so as long as you hunker down in Hal and Dorothy's 1972 time warp up there, you oughta be fine. But that looks to be miserable after too long."

Yes.

"So, guess you'll have to make a choice to get out and face the music, some point. Last I saw her, maybe at Christmas, Dorothy was pretty scrambled time-wise—kept mooning with my mother about wedding plans. Even so, she don't look like she's going down in a physical way for a while yet. I seen a lot of old folks—mostly women—like her, sucked down to the barb wire that holds them together, but still strung tight enough to stand the posts. You know what I mean?"

"Yeah. Strange though. Remember how my grandma Caldwell went down so quick? She was six years younger than Mom is now."

"I sure do. That was an awful thing. But most of them Gundersons got a way of living to a hundred or two, unless they have a stroke, I guess. You know that. Irene was one of them on her mother's side, wasn't she? I think my grandpa and her was some kind of cousins."

"God. We're all fucking related, somehow or another. No wonder everyone here looks like someone I ought to know."

Andraya sits back to squint this out. "You ain't Mormon no more, I guess."

"Oh, Andraya, sorry. Sometimes I forget. Everyone I know now talks like this. I'm really sorry."

Andraya leans close. "Hell. I'm not nearly as churchy as I pretend. It's just around here, that kind of talk stands out. Plenty of *hell shit damn* still when we're out around the campfire. Course we all learned the F-word in high school. Plenty of the kids like it because they like that hip-hop stuff on the Instagram or whatever. It's probably good for them. But saying the Lord's name in vain's gonna wipe out any incognito you're shooting for."

Andraya taps the convexity of her spoon against the table. "You ain't gone big-city Communist on us, though. Have you?"

"What?"

"Just because I don't do much church anymore, don't mean I've lost my values. We got elections coming up. Socialism at the door."

"Really?"

"Haha just kidding. Wanted to see your face when I said that."

And here's Dani, thank god. Sweet as a strawberry, shareable salad in hand. "Here you go! The pizza will be out in just a few minutes."

Andraya says, "Dang it, that looks good. Did that lettuce come from your grandpa's place, too?"

"No, it's cheaper to bring it up from California. But the beets, see? And the green onions. Wax peppers. Garlic from somewhere else."

"Do you help on the farm?" Cassandra asks in a passably natural tone. "I thought it was all alfalfa and corn around here."

"We all do. At least until we get other jobs, like this. My grandpa changed the crops once he and Grandma took over the old place. A few at a time. He likes to try things."

"How many is all of you?" Andraya prompts. "I may of lost track."

Dani stands to calculate. "Well, there's five of us—" she begins.

"Five Brian Jr. and Julayne kids, you mean."

"Uh-huh."

"And you're the middle, right?"

"Yeah. Lander and Hal are oldest."

Andraya keeps after her. "Then—"

"Then Holden and Marianne."

"And?"

Dani looks a little overwhelmed. "Well, my dad's brothers and sisters and their kids."

Andraya throws down. "Bet you can't name them all."

"Sure I can. Uncle Jessie and Uncle Jonah. Uncle Brantley. Aunt Sarah, Aunt Emma, Aunt Cassie."

"Aunt *Cassie*?" Andraya bellows.

"Well, Cassandra, but everyone calls her Cassie. She's youngest. She has these really cute kids. They almost stopped at two, but she's pregnant again."

Cassandra feels herself falling into a centrifuge.

Andraya is revving. "Yep. You guys raise more than green onions out there, dontcha. 'Utah's Best Crop,' right? How many kids between 'em all? How many cousins you got?"

"Well there's us, and then fourteen cousins so far, so nineteen, but I don't got time to give you all the names. You know them, anyway. You're just giving me a hard time."

"Good girl! Way to keep track of your people, Miss Lisa Danielle Soelberg! Family's a good thing to hold onto. Mostly. Course it's got problems. When's that pizza done?"

Dani rolls her eyes. She stands, pondering, and then comes around. "Any minute. Enjoy your salad. Do you want more lemonade?"

"We sure do, honey."

Cassandra has taken in as much as she can.

The pizza comes.

The basil is a sensuous distraction. How did a Soelberg come up with this?

Andraya: "Give me the fast story. I promise to keep it on the down low."

Cassandra cannot answer.

Andraya waits her out.

"Do you remember," Cassandra says, "the first conversation we ever had? It was in the nursery, in church."

"I don't know. Remind me. We've had a lot of conversations since we were two."

"You said we could be friends as long as I didn't bite. Or have poop on my shoes."

That elicits a snort. "Well, by then I'd already been bitten a lot. And stepped in poop. And it has happened since."

Cassandra says, "I don't care if we step in shit, but don't bite. Please."

Andraya sits very straight. Her hair, rolled into a rollicking messy bun, is thick and compelling. Her earrings are truck-stop dreamcatchers, complete with dangling feathers. "Looking for collateral?"

"No. That's not what I mean—"

"Well, tit for tat. I'll go first: Dean and I both know he lusts after men. He married me as cover, more or less, and five kids make us look like regular boring people from Big Horn. So far, far as I can tell, he gets by on releasing his frustrations in front of the computer. We both guard the door from opposite sides. I don't know what he does at the annual conference in Vegas, and I don't ask. Maybe there's some hunting shenanigans. I'm thinking there's a few other men in this town know his secret, but they got their own to protect."

Cassandra reaches a hand to cover her friend's. Andraya holds it still a moment, methodical, then pulls away.

"Also, we say the youngest is ours, but really she's only mine. I got so angry and horny and resentful one year, when I went to some training conference for the school I just said screw it. I let loose and had one hell of a week. Chicago. Some bald potbelly small-town vice principal from who knows where is the dad, and hellfries, was he up for some fun. We both went home after, never even caught each other's full names and as far as I know he has no idea he's got a daughter in Utah. Never will, believe me. Dean figured he owed me, and the pregnancy was good for appearances. He likes kids all right. He's no perv. He's a decent man, sticks to his responsibilities. He ain't mean, which you know yourself is saying something. Sometimes he's funny and he's good at fixing things."

Cassandra gapes.

Andraya says, "Want me to keep going?"

"No. Well—yeah, of course I have questions. I want to hear more. But I'll answer yours. Fair is fair. The fast story—"

She falters.

Andraya leans in. "Let's have it."

"I got pregnant the spring of our junior year."

Andraya lifts one side of her mouth.

Cassandra works to compose.

"That's it? You got pregnant?"

"My grandma was getting ready to take me down to an old family place, down past Navajo Lake, to give me time to decide what to do. About motherhood, I mean."

Andraya says, "That's about the time she died though, huh."

Cassandra sits herself out. Starts up again. "Same night she had the stroke, my dad went berserk. He was livid about the pregnancy. Or at least that the pregnancy didn't get me married off. Said from the first revelation I'd shamed him and the rest of my family past repair. He really couldn't deal with it, and underneath it all I think he'd been hoping I'd get forced into a marriage that made him—you know—"

"Richer?"

"Yeah. At least connected to richer. Something like that."

"You was always scared of him. He made everyone nervous. The kind of guy always about to blow, even though he never did, least not that I know of. At least not in public. Until he—I guess—did he die natural? Seemed pretty, you know—self-inflicted."

"I don't know. Official story is heart attack, but it seems there was blood. Pitched forward in the tool shed, they said. I didn't come home anymore, after a point. I'd finished trying to know anything at all by then."

"Hate to say dark things about our own people, right? But, yeah."

"The very same night—maybe the very hour—my grandma had a stroke, Hal called LDS Social Services, or some two-bit contractors, and they came out like a SWAT team. Maybe they were already on call. Who knows? My mother woke me up, had a suitcase packed. Dad was waiting outside the door, got impatient, came in and told me to get up and on with it. Next thing I know I'm in Washington, somewhere outside of Seattle but I never got off the property so who knows, and I spent the whole pregnancy living with this self-righteous cough-syrup couple and a bunch of other knocked-up girls.

"They sent me off to have the baby in some building somewhere once I was in labor. I didn't see him. They took him out of me, turned their backs, and carried him away. I heard him cry in another room for maybe half an hour while they forgot about me, cleaned him up, and then suddenly they put me under. I woke up in a hospital room, the social worker was there, and then I was back on a plane headed for Salt Lake."

Andraya looks aghast. "No baby..."

"No."

A swallow of water.

"I went to college on my grandma's will, Utah State. It was a good thing. I came back a few times, thinking I could pick up something like a life. I was home the night Matthew ran off into the mountains. Dad went out of his mind, telling me that my mortal sin had screwed Matthew up, made him over-sympathize with me and want to be a woman. Whatever."

"Oh, hell. Every kid in town knew Matthew thought he was a girl. My cousins said he was the best woodsman in the mountains come deer hunt. Best rider, best shot, toughest hiker, didn't care how cold and wet he got, just kept going like Bigfoot. None of them cared what he wore at night in his sleeping bag."

Cassandra is stunned. "They all knew it, that far back?"

"That's what they said. Way back. It was—you know. *Matthew*. Nobody but Hal Soelberg got worked up about it. Nose pickers, bed wetters, tiny dicks, boys who wear their sister's nightgowns...what's really all that strange when you're a kid?"

Dani appears at the table, looking jumpy about another grilling. "Did you save room for dessert?"

Cassandra looks up, maybe too wild-eyed.

Andraya answers, "How about some of that chocolate cake

you know Dean likes so much. Bring me an extra piece to take home to him, okay?" and Dani hightails for the kitchen.

Andraya raises her eyebrows, expectant.

Cassandra: "Well, I stayed in touch with Matthew—actually Matilda—for quite a while after I left home for good. She's disappeared now, though. Doesn't answer my emails. I sent money when she told me where to address it, but last few years it's gone unclaimed."

"I'm really sorry, Cassandra."

"So, now I live in Minnesota, sometimes with people, sometimes not. You remember Sam Young from Clearlake? Band kid? He's tending my house. Ran into him in Minneapolis a long time ago—he really followed through on the musician thing. He was playing sax at some art opening. He says he's never coming back here. Ever. But it's something, you know, to have Clearlake Valley in common."

"Are you a thing? I mean you and Sam."

"Not a thing this town would recognize. And he's got cancer. In remission, but he's not going back for treatment when it returns. We just do okay in the same house, in spells. We both like our own lives, and sometimes they fit together."

"Is that rumor about you being a—mmm—big-time artist true? All you artistic types made a run for it, one way or another."

"I don't know what 'big-time' is supposed to mean. I kind of found my lane, illustrating rare editions and single-run literary…" She peters off.

Andraya loses the thread at the work talk. "I don't really know what you're talking about, but I'm not surprised. You were crazy talented. But I have a question."

"Lay it on me."

Andraya opens her mouth, but speaks instead to Dani, who has brought cake. She lights up the electronic pad mounted on the edge of the table and awaiting a credit card.

No drinks make a cheap date. Cassandra finds her wallet.

Andraya is undistracted. "Who's the father?"

Surely everyone within shooting range must be able to guess. The windows of his stupid orange penis car had been transparent enough. Prom photos were probably somewhere, stashed in a box under somebody's bed, maybe even in the closet of the bedroom she refuses to enter. Both families had leaned in; both sets of parents must have haggled through heated encounters. Nothing is ever private in a small Mormon town.

"You can probably guess."

"Yeah, I can. And you weren't the only recipient of the golden seed. There might be a few of his, um, descendants flung to the wind—and that's besides the ones who trooped to church with him and the actual wife once he figured inheritance was better than—well, whatever he thought was true romance."

"What do you mean?"

"He just went a little further out there than most, although there seems to be a sort of club, you know? He lost a couple of little kids early on. Wife dealt with it one way. He did in others. You can imagine, I'm sure, if you think about it a while."

Cassandra strains at that one. "Not sure I can."

Andraya, born to be a universal mother, and clearly a good one, leans to cup Cassandra's shoulder. "You took off, just like you should have. A couple of the accidental mamas made a little noise up front. Did you know Eleventh went to law school? He's a source of fascinating information, let me tell you. Them girls shut up fast, though, once they got served a subpoena. But the man finds his ways, even now. Something weird about him."

Think now, freak out later.

"Why does everyone worship him as bishop?"

"Scared people like a man who thinks a lot of himself. Why do you think this town is overrun with MAGA flags?"

"What's everyone scared of lately?"

"End of the world. Secret pedo communists. Not having enough money or respect. Men in lipstick. Belligerent spawn. Same shit they scared us with in school. All come back, just looks a little different with the internet."

"How many kids came to church with—? And, who? Who married him?"

"Kendra. Price."

"Kendra? From our Sunday School class?"

"That exact Kendra. You want to see what your life could have been like? Watch close. But right there, sign that iPad, see? Isn't that modern, right here in Big Horn? I have to get back to work. You have to get back to crazy Dorothy."

"Jesus Christ. This is all too much."

"Well, whoever figures any of this shit out, right? We're just chugging through the lives that happen to us. I got more questions and it looks to me you'll be sticking around a while. So, rain check, chickie."

Cassandra scrawls her name, hits the highest tip on the screen, adds more, and stands up. "Yeah. Right now I just feel like I can't come up from the nightmares."

Even so, she feels pretty good. Stronger. Clear-minded. She can discern the contours of that lost seventeen-year-old as someone beyond her: she looks like Dani. A child, over her head, granted nothing. Punished beyond comprehension. Cassandra feels a novel rush of compassion for that girl.

Chapter 28

The one event that never glitches in Dorothy's mind: evening VHS musical in the Cozy Room.

The perpetual glitch: Dorothy has lost track of the seasons. It is always "cold out there," largely because Dorothy has a way of pushing the thermostat in the wrong direction, making it cold *in here*. Then she flips the switch on the gas fireplace. "Isn't it remarkable? In these times you can just turn the fire on when you're cold. No matches, no kindling. Just turn it on, like a light."

"What is it tonight? Let's see," Cassandra says. Dorothy is settled in the La-Z-Boy, snug under light fleece. Cassandra knows by now her mother won't move from the chair once the movie has begun. Pajamas on. Teeth brushed. "Hmm. *I'll See You in My Dreams*. Doris Day."

"Oh, I love that movie!" Dorothy exclaims on cue.

Cassandra pushes the video in, skips the dead space, and hits "play" at the opening credits.

"Oh, this music just sends me," Dorothy sighs.

Does her mother remember every—or any—one of these films? Does she follow the plots, or is it all conditioned response? It doesn't matter. Cassandra leaves Dorothy to her bliss, switching the fireplace off as she passes into the living room, heading for the thermostat. She turns the air conditioner, which she has already pushed up to seventy-five, off. She walks through the house to open every window to the cooling air. The national smoke is skipping Big Horn tonight. Breezes drifting north.

Leaning over the sink to the kitchen window, Cassandra hears the side screen door creak open. She jumps to as the knob turns and the door flings wide open, just as it always did when her father entered. And for a good ten seconds, the very man stands before her—aged but still tall and heavy-boned, lips puckered by a stiff-set jaw. A white dress shirt, an authoritarian tie. Eyes veiled but appraising.

He smolders in the entry, possibly awaiting a vampire cue.

"Oh. James. Wow. You startled me. You look so much like Dad."

Her brother scowls, then steps into the kitchen proper. He is, in fact, taller than Hal was, by a good three inches, and their father had been well over six feet.

The effigy speaks. "If you intend to make contact with our descendants, I must ask you to go through the proper channels."

Cassandra catches herself just before dropping into the abyss of 1978. "What the hell did you just say to me?"

"Cursing will not advance your cause, Cassandra."

"I have no cause, James. But if I ever pursue one, you won't be the damn magistrate. And I'll make a wild guess there's not a Soelberg living in this century wants you telling them who they'll talk to."

He steps closer, becoming bigger, but just as she recalls, his imagination is expended after the first volley. He must have been rehearsing that line since whenever he'd caught wind of yesterday's pizzeria encounter. Cassandra hears the grind of molars. His hands tremble with frustrated energy. His football shoulders rise and fall as he breathes. Will he strike? Is that the kind of thing he does? Does he hurt Paige? Has he thrown a kid, or two or three, down on hot Utah dirt? Stripped a little pisser and turned on the hose?

What might he possibly do now—to his long-distant sister? Clearly, he can keep sputtering. He certainly enjoys displaying his stature. He stances up to look more commanding, opens his lungs to deepen his squirrely voice.

"I say in the name of the Lord that ye must not defile the faith of this righteous family."

Cassandra expects more, but apparently James has spent his vocabulary. "Did you just say *ye* to me?"

James opens his mouth, then shuts it.

Grind, grind.

Glare.

"You. *You*, okay?"

"James! I'm your sister. I don't hear from you in decades, and suddenly you send me a letter asking—no, commanding—me to come home and take care of our mother. I leave my home, my studio, my profession, my—my *life*, James—behind and drive thirteen hundred miles to a place I remember as hell. I don't see anyone in the family except Mom, who isn't Mom anymore, for weeks after I show up to do my *duty*, as you put it, and now you're here to cuss me out for being visible? Are you serious?"

James stands like a butt-hurt ten-year-old. The deep church voice evacuates. The old country whine whistles in. "Cassandra, I just want whatever dark spirits that might be troubling you to leave—to leave you, and the rest of us, to our better aims."

This man is fast approaching seventy years old. Brother and sister are, at this reunion, decades older than Cassandra recalls either of their intact parents. And yet, here they are, spouting Dark Age superstitions, snippeting folk incantations. Primal rage leaps in her. The retorts, the rejoinders.

"James, this isn't how I talk anymore. I don't consort with devils, and if you really think I do, why would you ask me to come back to take care of our mother?"

To her first people, it makes no sense to be wrong, because

they are by definition the only right people in the first place. There's no template for reversal.

He does the best he can. "I didn't say you consort with evil spirits. I never said that! You're probably a good person. It's just that we've all been trying to raise our families in the gospel. In fact you seemed like such a good person to Brian Jr.'s girl that it might have made her doubt what we've been trying to—what we're all trying to teach the next generation. It's not like it used to be. There's the internet, you know, and all that social media bringing in influences and—"

"So, I'm dangerous to impressionable young Soelbergs because I seem like a good person? You're afraid that the kids will be led astray by my—what? Goodness?"

James ponders the paradox. "Yes. I'm afraid so. I hadn't thought about it that way until Brian Jr. told me how Dani came home all confused, a little mad, even, that you weren't anything like—" He stops, flummoxed.

Cassandra says, "Like what? Like you told her I was?"

"We've never told them you were a bad person. We just, um, haven't told them anything. How do you tell a story like that to children?"

"You just let them picture the Wicked Witch of the East, out there riding a broom in the wind."

"No—"

"Do you want me to play the part? Want me to give every Soelberg kid in this city a scare?"

"That's not what I'm saying to you! I don't judge you, I just—"

"The hell you don't, James."

"We merely want our children and grandchildren to under-stand that they can only achieve the highest kingdom of heaven by remaining true to the only true and living gospel upon the face of the earth. And you have betrayed that gospel. Every-one knows that, if they know us at all in this town. I've seen the records myself. Between you and Matthew—"

"Matilda."

"—you've stained our family reputation, and because of your stubbornness you have paid a price that we don't want our children to have to pay. Wickedness—no matter how you package it, no matter how you try to justify your apostasy with your protests of victimhood—never was happiness. We want our children and grandchildren to be happy in eternal life. It's easy, at their age, to mistake temporary mortal pleasure for genuine happiness in the godly sense."

Tonight her brain will replay his words on a repeating loop. His pompous diction will crowd the silence and awaken her. His bingo barrel of stock phrases.

...your protests of victimhood...

Nothing here will ever be resolved.

Detour is the only way forward. "James. Did you come to see Mom? She's back watching her musical thing. She'll be happy to see you."

He hesitates, wide-eyed and bewildered like the awkward adolescent brother she recalls. He regains himself to stride through the house. Cassandra follows. Dorothy is tucked in and glazed, but she startles like a busted wife when she sees James's face hovering over hers.

"Oh, my goodness! What are you doing home so early? Cassandra, help me get up. Dinner's almost on. Just give me a minute."

"Mom, it's me, James. Don't get up. I ate dinner before I came. Just here to see how you're getting along."

Dorothy finds what bearings she has. "Oh, James! You caught me watching my nightly movie. Emma here set it all up for me. What an indulgence. Is it still cold outside?"

"No, Mom. It's still hot. It's not quite September. Hasn't Cassandra been taking you out? Have you even had dinner?"

"What? I don't know. I'm watching my favorite musical. What's the name of it again?"

"I can't remember," Cassandra answers, turning to the fat screen. "Is that man in *blackface*?"

They all stare at the flickering scene.

"Wait. Is that *Doris Day* in blackface?"

"Oh, now you're politically correct," James says. "Come home after all these years with that bull crap. You have no call to judge your mother."

"I'm not judging our mother. I'm staring at Doris Day, singing in blackface."

"Doris Day! I love Doris Day!"

Blackface Doris Day finishes "Toot Toot Tootsie, Goodbye."

"I just love that song!" Dorothy says, and her oldest and youngest offspring step out, leaving her to it.

"She likes the windows closed," James mutters, feeling the scented breeze. "It just wastes air-conditioning when they're open."

"The air-conditioning is off. What's wrong with outside air? You don't have to sleep here."

"She doesn't feel safe unless the windows are closed. I'd think you could relearn her needs and habits."

"Can you stop?"

"Can *you*? You've always caused contention. Dad used to say there wasn't a compliant cell in you."

That surprises her. "What? How could he say that? I was so scared of that man, I spent my whole childhood beating him to his own orders."

"How did you end up pregnant, then? Why did you take Grandma Caldwell's money when you knew he disapproved? Why did you appease Matthew's unnatural delusions? Why did you cut and run rather than repent in accordance with your calling as a wife and mother? Why couldn't you shut your mouth and take responsibility for your own condition? How could you break our mother's heart? She lost a mother and a daughter on the very same night. She lost a son to his perverse obsessions.

She lost a grandchild because it was conceived and delivered in unrepentant sin. And then, after all that, she lost the love of her life, too soon and sudden. You wouldn't even come home to give her comfort in this tragedy."

Cassandra is speechless.

James shimmers in righteousness.

Cassandra speaks as if from a remote-control room. "Who are your children?"

"What?"

"How many children do you have? How many grandchildren?"

"Four. Children."

"Do they live in Big Horn? Tell me their names."

"Three of them do. Jimmy. Howard, after Paige's father. Alicia."

"The other one?"

"Laura. She's—not here."

"Where did she go?"

"She married a dentist. Lives somewhere on the coast."

"California?"

"Yes."

"Do they come home?"

"Some of them. Laura, not—lately."

"Do you love them?"

"Of course I do. But you don't understand how difficult it is to be a parent, seeing as how—"

"Seeing as how I conceived and delivered my son—my *son*—Hal and Dorothy's grandchild—in sin? I am also a parent, James."

"You know what I mean."

"My son is, as far as any of us can know, alive on this planet. He probably resembles his cousins—the very ones you've named. He might be good with tools, the way his grandfather was. Maybe he's tall, like your sons must be."

"Well, Cassan—"

"He might have a deep sense of womanness in him, like his uncle Matilda."

"Cassandra! This is why—"

"He may love tulle and chiffon as much as his grandma Dorothy, who for all her grief would never rise to claim him. Maybe he likes his hands in the dirt. Maybe he plants flowers and tomatoes in his garden every spring. He may have children of his own, people we'd somehow recognize. I did not forfeit this child, James. I did not forfeit yours. I was *sent away*. I was taken from my bed in the middle of the night. Where were you that night? Safe in your bed with your pregnant wife. My child was taken from me, and now he is lost to all of us."

"Well, why—"

"Well? Why? Conjure up any self-soothing stories you want, James. But don't you ever refer to the human being who walks around with your children's DNA—don't you ever refer to my son as 'it.'"

His face drops into humanness, jaw slack and eyes wide. He reaches to remove his tie, unbuttons the collar at the top. "It's still so hot," he says. "I wonder if it will ever end."

Cassandra bites her lip. Brings her hand up to stop the quick blood.

"I mean," he says, "just that it's a long summer. I'm not talking about global warming." He runs a huge hand through his thick dark hair, barely graying. "Laura—" he says.

"No. I'm your sister Cassandra."

"I mean, I was going to say something about her."

"Okay. Say it."

"She married a dentist. A woman. Dentist."

"Oh."

He looks like he'll cry. "She was my favorite. My little girl. Loved me, loved doing things with me, going places—"

"Was?"

"I just—she doesn't come home. Like you."

"Will you allow it?"

"Paige won't."

"Have you met this…dentist?"

"Yes. She's pretty. They're both so pretty, I don't understand—"

Cassandra laughs. "Why beautiful women would be attracted to each other?"

"That's not funny. The thing is, every time one of the kids—or grandkids—goes wrong, they say it's because of you."

"They don't even know me. I don't know them."

"But they imagine you. They say you got out of this place. They think you found some wonderful life out in the world."

His face: Rigid, collapsed. Soft, vulnerable; hard.

Cassandra murmurs, "How many do we have to lose? Call your daughter. Speak her wife's name, like a human being. Invite them home."

He re-knots his tie.

She says, "Help me get Mom to the bedroom before you go. She'll be sound asleep in the recliner. I think the movie is over."

They skirt around the fireplace to the Cozy Room. Dorothy snores in the chair.

"I've got this," says James. He leans down to pick Dorothy up, lifting at the back of her neck and knees like a baby. Dorothy tucks her head into his chest. Cassandra beats them to the bedroom to open the bedsheets. James lays their mother down, pulls the covers up.

"'Night, Mama," he says.

"Who made Dad's cave into a movie room?"

"I did. Bought them all for fifty bucks at a garage sale."

"Holy…did you put them all in alphabetical order on the shelves?"

"Of course I did. Do you think I'm stupid?"

"No. That's not—not at all what I meant."

He purses his lips.
She says, careful, "Good night, James."
He turns his broad back and slips into the night.

Part Four

. . .

Revise

Chapter 29

D ays at the "home" were both over-regimented and form-less, a grid stamped over entropy. It was as if no one—not the social workers, not the Grunfeldts, not the church people, and certainly not the girls in question—could grasp the right metaphor. Was this a charity house? Juvie? Charm school? A medical clinic?

Were these "unwed mothers" paper-doll morals of the story? Emblems of sin? Crock pots? Used cars? ABC gum? One way or another they took up space, required nourishment, took their infernal time yielding the prize—the hot little bundles that God had chosen sluts to make and saints to take.

Cassandra recalls it in fragments of suspended time, exac-erbated by measurements impossible to intuit: the "fetus" was at "seventeen weeks." "Gestation" was 280 days, measured from the first day of her last period, which made no sense at all. How had the practitioner made that calculation when the uteral body in question had no idea? Her cycle had not been regular; her not quite seventeen-year-old body had not been allotted enough time to establish patterns. She hadn't been bleeding for much more than a year. As Allan White had so gleefully observed, her "tits" had come late and sudden, and to her unaccustomed eye, incomprehensibly large. A cadre of Sunday School boys had been paying close attention, far more rapt than Cassandra.

She can think it through now, but she tries to avoid it. She is that girl but also she never was. She was denied language and time to learn to inhabit herself—an unfamiliar body—and once the textbook facts of gestation had taken hold, the doctrinal facts of embryo-cum-fetus-cum-Spirit-Child-of-God (not *yours*, Handmaiden) transformed her into casing. The unfortunate and distracting personal presence of the girls (the *ladies? Sisters? Mothers?* Sullied daughters of God? Young women with names, effaced by scriptural pseudonyms?), the literal volume of breathing, sweating, hungry and excreting bodies, was the inconvenient problem at hand.

First day after the flight:

A "Personal Priesthood Interview" with Elder Grunfeldt, the loquacious, disheveled retired businessman ("Technology, you know, contract work. Boeing. Neither here nor there, not germane to the issues at hand, just mentioning…") who owned the place, technically with his wife.

A tour of the Grunfeldt "home," somehow grandiose and depressingly shabby at once, guided by Sister Grunfeldt (her husband called her "Mother"), a Nancy Reagan knock-off who made it "crystal clear" that temporary residents of the home were not to cross into the front rooms of the house "under any circumstance," and certainly not to allow themselves to be seen in the front yard "under any circumstance," let alone leave the property unattended "under any circumstance."

A tutorial on bedmaking, personal hygiene, and prenatal nutrition, with emphasis on returning home attractive enough to deny everything.

A rundown of "dorm rules": no unauthorized whispering / refer to self and others by scriptural names only / do not divulge personal histories / no bickering / no reading unapproved books or magazines / television and radio forbidden except as approved group activity / comport self as an exemplary young Latter-day

Saint woman at all times / no political discussions / under no circumstance whatsoever cross the line into the front portion of the home / under no circumstances leave the premises unescorted / etc. /.../ etc. /...

A preview of the weekday routine: awaken at six o'clock for thirty-minute scripture study / seven thirty "family prayer" and breakfast in the ladies' dining room / GED study courses for residents still in high school / lunch and cleanup / homemaking lessons / dinner and cleanup / leisure time with occasional group activities / evening scripture study / lights out by nine o'clock, no murmuring, no conspiring, no gossiping, no giggling / etc. /.../ etc.

A trip, escorted by a no-nonsense social worker, to the "clinic" a half mile away for a feet-in-stirrups exam, performed by a commendably thorough obstetrician, who reported his "findings" to the social worker as if the speculum (a tool, and a term, Cassandra only understood much later, in a college anatomy class) had merely opened itself, of its own accord, into an instructive cadaver.

As promised, dinner with six other "unwed mothers" with assigned scriptural names, plus Brother and Sister Grunfeldt and a frowning woman, possibly an auditor. Free time staring in shock out the window, the view oppressed by evergreens.

The first of many nights of garish anti-sleep.

Naturally, it was Brother Grunfeldt who came up with the aptest, and therefore most disturbing, analogy for the entire absurdity. Brother Grunfeldt lived for his hour (plus) of glory—unhinged flights of fancy as he taught the Gospel Doctrine class every Sunday morning at nine.

"Your residence here, sisters, is much like serving time in spirit prison, where the unbaptized are held after mortality until the Second Coming."

The man paused for profundity, lips compressed into an anal

pout. He made a perceptible humming noise as he scanned the room—seven uncomfortable pregnant bodies.

"Can anyone here tell us more about the plan of salvation, and the part spirit prison plays in the grand picture?"

Rebecca/Cassandra gazed toward the skylight. Martha/Lori Ann studied a chipped fingernail. Rhoda/Johnetta (her actual name a parental portmanteau) looked as if she might pipe up, causing Sariah/Colleen, Eve/Sammi, and Rachel/Trudy and another girl, about to deliver and disappear, to lean helpfully in her direction, prompting Brother Grunfeldt to call on her.

"Rhoda, help us calibrate our scriptural knowledge. Erecting a solid platform from which we can fix our common perspective can help us all move forward together in light and knowledge."

Being addressed by the wrong name had a way of slowing anyone's response time. And Grunfeldt's rhetoric always threw Johnetta.

"Huh?" she managed, after several extra beats.

The pedant was happy to rephrase. "Well, to put it in simpler terms—within a layman's purview—truth becomes apparent when we stand together in holy places. I'm asking us to erect a holy place on which to stand, from which to look beyond—"

Lori Ann cut to the chase. "Okay, from where we stand, or let's say sit pregnant in this pathetic allegory, we are to comprehend that we are unworthy to live among the Saints of the Latter Days until the day of judgment, which in this case is the day after we have our babies. And even then it's a maybe."

"Martha! Were you called upon to speak?"

Lori Ann rolled her eyes. Cassandra put a hand to her mouth, trying not to laugh. She'd never heard anyone, especially a "female," talk the way Lori Ann talked. Brother Grunfeldt belched words like thesaurus confetti, enamored of his unctuous voice. Lori Ann was an unnerving production of echoes.

That, or she was silent, encased within her pallid skin and lank tall frame, preoccupied. Cassandra pictured the child inside

Lori Ann as a ropey little Russian doll, not tucked and rolled in a ball of fluid so much as contoured within the whole shape of the mother, a small hand in a larger glove. Lori Ann was well along in her pregnancy—nearing her seventh month. The bulge of the child was distinct but integral; unlike the rest of them, she carried it with a heedless, linear stride. Cassandra was, despite her shock and self-pity and abysmal rage, fascinated and perplexed by Lori Ann.

Lori Ann had a strange effect on Brother Grunfeldt, too. He rose to the bait every time she cast, unhinged by his compulsion to patronize and explain.

"I must ask you sisters once again to raise your hands before you interject," he said. "However, Sister Martha in this case is correct, to a point. You have all, in a manner of speaking, *died* to your former lives. You have been absented from familiar environs and now reside in a temporary dimension of separation. If you choose wisely, your separation is temporary. Like the spirits of the dead who pass on without the saving ordinances of the true gospel, you are not in a place of damnation, but neither are you in a state of salvation. Like the unbaptized dead, you are in a condition of waiting.

"Now, while the actual dead will remain in spirit prison until the great day of judgment, learning what they must know in order to accept the gospel through vicarious baptism and endowments, you all await your personal day of release when—when—"

Lori Ann's hand rose just before she said, "—when the baby interjects."

"Sister Martha! What have I told you?"

"Raise my hand before I interject."

"You know that's not what I mean!"

Cassandra burst out laughing. Johnetta asked for the definition of *interject*, and Colleen said, "So, being pregnant is like being dead? That makes sense. My mother said I'm dead to her."

Johnetta muttered, "It feels like we're dead. Can't go anywhere, can't see or be seen, closed up in a freaking crypt."

This part was just like high school. Frustrated teacher, cap-
tive children in adult bodies, sham relations, vestigial relations
of authority. Brother Grunfeldt was heating up. Literally. His
face was a study in mottled pink, set off by an overlong red tie
(Cassandra recalled her mother's color cautions) and, despite
the expensive fabric, an ill-fitting, oddly revealing executive
suit stretched slick over an ample matronly ass. His speech was
a melee of pedantry, whine, and fed-up fury, punctuated by a
rasping reach for breath as his heart rate climbed. Cassandra
wondered idly whether they'd be witness to a coronary event, or
maybe just as traumatizing, a resonant zipping fart.

Also, she was distracted by stomachs—her own and the
others'. And Grunfeldt's for that matter. At twenty-five weeks,
her condition was obscurable if she wore a loose blouse. "You
have excellent reproductive hips," the practitioner said. "You're
keeping it all deep in the recess so far." Evocative references to
an actual developing child were rare; the program was averse to
naming what it was farming. At least to the barns.

Her skin was too sensitive. Her Sunday dress chafed at the
breasts and shoulders. Bra straps felt like a punishing harness,
and the goddamned pantyhose, a size up from her usual, felt like
they would cut her in half.

"We have a strict dress code here," Sister Grunfeldt had iter-
ated on the first day and every day since. "We don't use our condition to justify a sloppy, unfeminine appearance."

"How can we possibly look unfeminine while we're pregnant?" Lori Ann had inquired.

"You'll be going back home to do it the right way next time,"
Sister Grunfeldt snapped. "Just take a look at the young mothers who think they already have a husband in the bag. You can't
afford to look like that. You'll need to get back in and compete."

Brother Grunfeldt's "lesson" was heating up as well. Once he got going there was nothing to do but endure, and every miserable girl in her plastic seat knew it.

"The difference is, souls in spirit prison await final judgment and possible reunion with family members who have accepted the truths taught between death and resurrection. You ladies, on the other hand, were taught the gospel from your birth. This is a special home reserved for Latter-day Saint young women. You have all been baptized and you received the gift of the Holy Ghost at confirmation under the hands of worthy priesthood holders. The spirits in spirit prison did not have this opportunity in their mortal lives, and so they are granted the chance to accept the saving principles performed for them vicariously in the holy temple.

"Do you see what I'm driving at, here? Now, I want someone besides Martha to answer. You are all in a position of moral peril, and your ability to navigate the technical aspects of the restored gospel matters more than you might now imagine."

Trudy was leaning forward over the enormous ball of her thirty-two-week stomach, breathing ragged and tuned in to something so far beyond the gospel map she seemed otherworldly. Cassandra suppressed a prescient shiver, hoping to slip under Grunfeldt's radar, but no luck.

"Rebecca!" he barked, and Cassandra said, "Help your fellow—uh—your sisters in—"

"—sin," Lori Ann furnished.

"Martha! Stop it now! I'm trying to guide you!"

Lori Ann: "And we are abject in our gratitude."

"Rebecca! Rise to the occasion here! No one leaves this classroom until we've completed this crucial point of instruction."

By the time she re-registered her fake name, Cassandra had lost track of the finer points. "What was the question again?"

"Let me make it plain: Why are all of you, young Latter-day Saint women sent to earth as the finest, strongest, most valiant of all Heavenly Father's daughters in the pre-earth life, saved for the last days of tribulation, actually in greater peril at this point than the dead who await salvation in spirit prison?"

Inklings of rejoinder flickered through Cassandra's mind, but she considered her fellow inmates. Trudy was pallid and shivering, sweating at the roots of her limp hair. Johnetta and Lori Ann had both reached an uneasy ecstasy of oblivion, each in her own fashion. Sammi and Colleen and the about-to-deliver-and-therefore-vanish girl sat red-faced in their hard chairs, hands on stomachs, fighting tears.

"We're in greater peril," Cassandra said, "because we were raised in the true gospel to begin with. And we're still alive, and can commit heinous sins of the body, which we have done. We know better than the people—the dead people—held in spirit prison, who are hearing the gospel for the first time. Their sins are ignorant. We are more responsible because we know how grievous is the sin of premarital sex."

Each miserable girl looked up in gratitude, hoping Cassandra had put an end to the endlessness. Each ducked her head again when Brother Grunfeldt took a thick-throated gulp to continue.

"Well, that's precisely correct. You must have been paying attention in seminary and Sunday School. Now, I don't mean to cast aspersions on anyone's personal character. We are all sinners in the eyes of the Lord. But it is imperative that we answer to every jot and tittle of celestial law, and so there's no way to sugarcoat this: you are here, in this place, awaiting release because you have committed the second-gravest sin, the sin next to murder.

"This is no time for levity. Your path to salvation is treacherous and narrow, and it is in no way assured. When you stand at the edge of a cliff, a single misstep can send you plunging toward destruction. Because you accepted the gospel before you sinned, you have placed yourselves in a unique category in the eyes of the Lord: you may be cast into outer darkness, reduced to the merest thread of your identity, cut off eternally from the presence of God, from the kinship of faithful family."

(The reservoir in cold spring moonlight. Barefoot, mincing, fearful of ice in black water. Once, a science teacher made an offhand comment that had irrevocably altered Cassandra's eye: "Stars," he said, "are mapped by astronomers as if they lie on a flat field. That's a mere convenience, a method of representation. The truth, of course, is that when we look into the night sky we are seeing astral bodies of every size, shape, composition, and quality in endless, inconceivable depth.")

Depth beyond depth beyond depth. Outer darkness somewhere beyond, where no light exists.

The girl about to deliver, a wild-eyed mouth breather, whispered, "What about—the baby?"

Grunfeldt lit up. "That's a good question, Sister…Sister… your child does not bear your sins. As the second article of faith says, 'We believe that men will be punished for their own sins, and not for Adam's transgression.' Even so, is it wise to raise up a child in the location of sin?

"Raising your child—a child without sin, but who was conceived in sin—as an unwed mother would mean that child will be ever in the shadow of your sin, thwarting your journey to full repentance and forgiveness. What loving mother—no matter how depleted by the wages of sin—would ever wish to do such a thing to an innocent child, especially when there are worthy married couples who yearn to raise that child in an environment of material and spiritual safety?

"Sacrifice, ladies, is only an act of giving up one thing for something better. If you follow through on your commitments here, your sins will be erased so entirely that you will never need to refer to your error again. You may go on to lives of fulfilling wifehood and motherhood—contingent, of course, on keeping this detour a closed subject. Always remember: do not speak of this time, or this conception, to anyone, especially your future husband and children. Your vow here to remain silent about your—about this—about the whole—"

"Crime against the universe," Lori Ann furnished.

Grunfeldt looked like he wanted to rip Lori Ann out of her seat, maybe slam her against a wall, but he soldiered on: "The—issue—will belong to another eternal family, sealed for time and eternity in the temple of the Lord. Do not go forward intending to disrupt Heavenly Father's solution to this perversion of your divine power to bring children to this earth in the Latter Days."

Cassandra's visual mind has a way of arresting terrible scenes into ineradicable photographs. She does not draw them, but sometimes she draws from them. This one: Autumn sunlight diffused through evergreens, almost a stifled scent as it stammers through the frosted glass. The cheap chair-desks arranged in an erratic half circle, in a parlor made over to allude to a classroom.

Madonna-whores extracted from home and family, names effaced, so forlorn they are nearly indistinguishable. Johnetta from somewhere in Idaho, a farm kid, freckled and pudgy with baby fat, frizzy hair erratic in the northwest humidity. Even over her Sunday clothes, she wears her high school FFA jacket. A patch bearing the name of her hometown has been removed.

Colleen from California, Orange County, who arrived small, fit, and tan but becomes paler and more amorphous by the day. Sammi and Trudy, for the time being inseparable, hailing from twin desert towns in Colorado and Utah. Sammi so generic in her European features, her narrow bony shoulders and wide childbearing hips, Cassandra now sees her as ethnically remarkable. Trudy's dark glossed hair, and something about the angles of her striking face, suggest Indigenous ancestry—but Trudy makes no move to confirm this, even (especially) when Brother Grunfeldt waxes eloquent on the fallen state of "the Lamanites," a people he dearly loves because he cherishes the Book of Mormon.

Lori Ann, a long white salamander.

Cassandra, invisible to herself, except her growing stomach.

The young women were forbidden to speak of homes, families, memories, but in loosely supervised hours they murmured their own names, and the names of the people they loved. What they imagined they were. What they had lost and what they had fled, where they might go and to whom.

"Fuck this," Lori Ann exploded. "Who the hell do you think you are?"

As if Lori Ann had delivered an incantation, Trudy screamed and pitched off her constricting seat, hard to the worn parquet floor. She clenched into a ball, opened and flailed.

"Mother!" Brother Grunfeldt hollered, paralyzed but for his wattled throat. "Mother! Come quick! Call the nurse! Help! Somebody help!"

Trudy sucked in a protracted rasping stream of air, and then another, without exhaling. Lori Ann said, "Sammi, go get her blanket. Run. And bring that pillow she loves."

Sammi bolted. Lori Ann dropped to her knees on the floor beside Trudy. A shock of warm relief shot through Cassandra's own body at the sight of Lori Ann's palm touching Trudy's forehead. Cassandra feels the aftershocks of that sensation even now, her grounding access to surreal memory. She thinks it must be the first time she saw grown women touch in something like love: Trudy, wrenched into her own stratosphere, reached reflexively for Lori Ann's face, found smooth heat, and calmed. Lori Ann leaned to kiss Trudy's cheek. Colleen and Johnetta, and the girl who should have been in labor (and was, within a day), leaned forward, compelled.

"Grunfeldt!" Lori Ann barked, turning her head toward the arrested fool. "Move your ass and get help! Where's the nurse? Get her now!" And the man ran, heavy but fast.

...

"This is it, Trudy," Lori Ann said, body and voice transformed by the object of her address. "Come through this last trial and you'll be out of hell. Pain doesn't mean a thing now. This pain has come to set you free."

Lori Ann removed Trudy's awkward Sunday shoes, then reached up her skirt to peel the running maternity hose from her muscular legs.

"Hold her head," Lori Ann ordered. Johnetta obeyed. Lori Ann smoothed Trudy's dress over trembling thighs and knees. "It's just us, Trudy. We're all in it. It's all right now."

Trudy looked as if she would speak, but her mouth produced an otherworldly wail, strong at first, then tapering, then rising again. A trickle of clear fluid wet the floor, and then a stunning course of thick red blood—so much of it Cassandra could not believe there could be any left in the body. Trudy in Lori Ann's arms; Colleen pressed against the wall, heaving; due-date girl curled up on the rug, crying. Nobody praying. Cassandra running for towels, nearly colliding with the nurse coming up the stairs; Sammi on her knees, holding Trudy's hand.

Paramedics. A stretcher coming up the stairs, then going down again with Trudy, twitching and unconscious, upon it.

Silence. Blood expanding like a spring reservoir on the parquet floor.

Social Services. Nametag: LaDonna.

"Ladies, you'll need to retreat to your rooms for the afternoon."

"This isn't how it's supposed to happen, is it," Colleen quavered.

"Everything that happens is supposed to happen. But no, this is not regular. You don't have to be afraid it will happen this way to you."

Lori Ann: "What did you say?"

LaDonna: "I said, don't let this unfortunate event make you

fearful about your own deliveries. What you just witnessed is very rare."

"Unfortunate event? What we just witnessed? Do you mean Trudy, and Trudy's blood here on the floor? Do you mean Trudy's baby?"

"That's enough from you," LaDonna snapped. "All of you, go to your rooms. Now."

All of them did, most of them to wait in wordless horror, Lori Ann to pack a small bag, retrieve a wad of cash from under her mattress, and stride out the front door.

Another arrested image: Tall Lori Ann, in the distance frail, receding into suburban greenery. Thin as a scarecrow, stomach a basketball. Then, a single languid brushstroke. Then, gone.

Chapter 30

Never since has she been able to sleep on her back.
The distributed weight of a muscled body, a hard black hole in the shape of a man, will not let her awaken. The weight of a medicine ball, pressing her organs to the circumference of muscle and bone. Slippery gag of a newt's wriggling hand, reaching upward in her throat.

An eyeless, water-filled membrane: the shape of a grown man emerging from between her legs. Teratomas: incisors sprouting from shoulders, nipples on foreheads, fingers waving on necks, one blue eye blinking, blank, on the back of a hairy hand.

When she sleeps on her back she cannot awaken, and when she turns, she awakens fetal, inert, nerves uprooted from the spine.

Chapter 31

S he can sit on the couch and sketch with the stylus in the September morning light. She's sticking to a task list of small contract gigs, postponing work that requires presence. Today, cover art for a slim anthology; despite the trendy press, the poetry is weightless yet ham-handed. She can indulge in pretentious abstractions to answer the vapid content.

Dorothy sits in an overstuffed living room chair, crochet hook and bright yarn in her lap. Cassandra started a line for her an hour ago. Dorothy keeps admiring it as if she's really getting something done. She seems content to sit with another human being.

Midafternoon, up to stretch and consider her mother's nourishment, Cassandra sees a car parked in front of the house, partially obscured behind the silver maple. A man sits in the driver's seat.

The man from the grocery store, in fact. He's let his beard grow. His hair is longer, too, under the baseball cap. Is he smoking? If the guy means to be inconspicuous, he's failing fast.

She cranes her neck.

He waves, attempting to catch her eye.

She shuts the curtain. "Mom, how's the scarf coming along?" she asks.

Dorothy says, "Oh, just fine. I love the colors."

"Want a drink of water? A soda?"

"Do we have Tab?"

"Tab? Do they even make that anymore?"

"What?"

Cassandra thinks she'll check online. Tab delivery. Uh-huh. She stands again to peer through the curtains. Son of a bitch is still out there. In fact he's leaning against the hood of his rental car, this time Oregon. He stares up at the Big Horn summit line, smoking what the studio interns call a douche flute.

Perfect. Douche. She's had time to think. She's spent a lifetime—somebody's lifetime—envisioning a chance meeting with the human being her body produced. Blood nerves skin DNA leaping to claim. Her eyes have assessed thousands of children— could be him, could be his friends. Might sit near him in school. She's watched the ways boys grow, ungainly and disproportionate, into contoured men—shins like stilts, ears and noses outpacing chins, clothesline shoulders unwieldy. She's kept an eye out for men who resemble her brothers, who resemble her prom date, strained to calm her heart at the hope for mutual recognition.

She's tricked herself so many times, in so many self-battering ways, she's had to get a grip. DeLuca took her off guard in a vulnerable moment. She was just returned, shocked by home geographies, but she's disabused herself of one more notion of relation.

That doesn't mean he's not pissing her off. She's going out there. She twists her ponytail into a topknot, slips her feet into the hiking sandals she keeps at the doorway, and steps out hollering. "What the hell are you about, here? What do you want from me?"

"Hold on!" he shouts, raising his hands as if she were pointing a gun. "I just want to talk! I'll stand right here. I'll go if you tell me to and I won't come back. But hear me out."

She stops on the grass. He sucks in a long fruity hit.

"Really? You're smoking candy?"

"I know it's disgusting. I can't explain. I need to keep my hands busy. I need habits."

"Like stalking older women in front of their crazy mothers' houses?"

"No. That's not a habit. It's a brand-new vice, which is probably why I'm smoking teen toxins."

She's close enough to fan vapor with her hands.

He says, "Maybe it's better than tobacco?"

"Or not?"

"I know."

They square themselves north, instinct, to stare at the mountains between outbursts.

"Do you know the names of them?"

"Mostly. That's Big Horn, obviously. Royal Peak, the rounded one, to the right. Little jags bookending them, Gog and Magog, because this place likes to be biblical even when they haven't done the reading. The granite massif they ride on bisects the Wasatch Range, which runs longer. Tail of Rockies. Granite just hove up and crashed through—something hot and angry boiling under them. See the tilt at the shove points? All that wrench?"

"It's all tilt. What do you mean, wrench?"

"Once you see the motion, you see the mountain. Better, at least."

"It's all too much."

"The smooth-faced Wasatch peak, there—the one with the WPA terracing—that's called Bookman."

"Why did they do that?"

"Holds the slope after a fire when the water comes back. See that long gash further down? Looks like a gutted whale? That wasn't there when I lived here. It's burned and slid."

He seizes his opportunity. "When did you live here?"

"Forty years ago, more or less. Depends on how we're measuring. Came back, on and off, until 1983, '84. Then, not."

He treads softly. He does not seem dangerous, and he clearly isn't stupid. Cassandra can admit she's hungry for grown-up, undemented, nonreligious conversation. "Don't worry, I won't bolt. I'm sorry about the parking lot. You didn't deserve that."

"I might have. Kind of sprang up on you."

"You were entirely forthcoming." She peers toward the doorway. Is Dorothy standing behind the screen? If she steps out, she'll tumble. "Look, my mother's in there alone. She's not stable in any sense of the word. I'm not ready to ask you in. It's weird in there. It's not my home. It would feel like inviting somebody into my unconscious mind. Which, no."

He laughs. "No, of course not. I mean yes, I know what you mean. I think. Can I talk to you somewhere else, maybe, sometime soon?"

"Let's bring her out here. She likes the backyard, when I can get her there. Chairs and stuff, under the trees."

"Really? My god, thank you. I've been here almost a month. I can't seem to break through to any real content. I even sat down in the park and let a couple of missionaries give me a lesson, but damn—"

"So you're a masochist?"

"No. Well, maybe when it's fun. That wasn't fun. I couldn't get them off topic no matter what I tried. There's a big difference between reading about Mormons and—I don't know—trying to hang around with them."

Cassandra laughs a little too much. "Wow. I've been way too boxed in since I've been here. I'll have to be careful not to unload on the first cub reporter who sits in a car outside my mother's house."

"Journalist." His motions are nervous but graceful.

She can only allow herself to look at him peripherally. He

takes another puff of sickly-sweet smoke. "Let me know if I come on too, well, eager. I really hope you'll unload a little."

"Why are you trying to write about Mormons? Always the same old shit."

"What do you mean?"

"Everybody thinks they're explaining the Mormons for the first time. Even the Mormons."

She sees the knob turn. "Okay, that's Dorothy. She's coming out, and she'll fall. See that side door, there under the carport? Wait for us, and I'll bring her out there. We can ease her down the stairs to the backyard."

Dorothy's head pokes out. "Emma?"

"Mom! Wait there! I'm coming to help!"

The door swings wider. Cassandra runs to intercept.

The weather is nice at eighty degrees, a real break. The sun isn't exactly hurtling toward the hilly horizon, but it's easing downward. The apple trees dapple the light.

Dorothy loves handsome young men. Maybe she just loves the word *handsome*. She's settled on the chaise lounge in a rather languid pose, sipping canned lemonade. She probably believes she's competing here with her pretty sister Emma.

Cassandra and DeLuca sit on cheap plastic Adirondacks, likely displaced from some descendants' or neighbors' yard and set here as an allusion to homey-ness. Who has sat out here for pleasure or conversation in decades? No kin she'd recognize.

"Okay, let's talk while she's preoccupied," Cassandra says, composing her mother against the old trunk, the fattening rose and green apples, the pelty cinereous slopes above the rooflines. "You're a reporter from Boston. You're on commission. You're here to penetrate the Mormon mind. What's your story?"

She's not ready to fully take him in. She's repressed the magical thinking, mostly. A therapist friend told her once that the search for something never had, yet direly lost, is a necessary incorporation of grief. How could it be exorcised? The only "solution" is to accept it, acknowledge it, and always carry an antidote.

Dismal, but helpful. She does not want a needle shoved into her heart.

DeLuca leans forward in the awkward chair. He's tall enough to look graceful in it, to put his elbows on his knees without shimmying forward in the low-slung seat. Cassandra, on the other hand, feels like Alice after the Eat Me pill.

"Do you mean, what's the story I'm trying to write? I'm not here to rediscover the Mormons, exactly but...like, what? My personal history?"

"They're probably connected in some way, right?"

"Well, yeah."

"Well, shoot. How about starting with how you found my—I mean my mother's—house? Clearly you've been grubbing about."

He grunts at that one. "'Grubbing.' That's a nice word for it. I've done so much internet time, you know? I've been to the university library, the special collections—"

"Which university?"

"Both. BYU. University of Utah."

"Hmm."

"Very different vibes. And I've driven up through the mountains, out to the deserts, taken pictures of places, read weird histories, chatted with tourists and locals. I don't know if I'm being stonewalled or if people just don't understand what I'm trying to understand any better than I do."

He runs a hand through his truly pretty hair, two-toned brown, yellowish. He takes a drag off the sugar cig. "I talked to a server at the pizza joint yesterday. I think she looks like you but everyone here sort of looks alike. But she told me she's your— what? Niece? I mean, I didn't ask about you specifically. She brought you up, and I made the connection. She seemed a little nervous, like she might be betraying something. She said she doesn't know you personally, but you were the only person she could think of who might—you know—"

"Spill my guts?"

"She just said she doesn't imagine you think the same way as 'everyone else,' as she put it. She said what I already sort of knew—that you've been gone a long time, and come back."

"It's easy to assume that everyone in a place like this thinks like everyone else."

"Do they?"

"No. Yes. I don't know. I mean, look close, listen, and people surprise you with their funny distinctions. Then again, they'll shock you with their sameness. Is it that different anywhere else? I just don't know other places in quite the same way as this one. I don't live in the same kind of snow dome in St. Paul. Feels more, I don't know, pointillist out there."

He takes off his sunglasses and squints at the smudges. He's keeping his head down. She's still taking him in from oblique angles. Sees but won't look. But—

He wipes the lenses with his shirttail and puts them on again. "I don't know," he says. "I'm at the point here where everything feels so alien I wonder if I'm speaking a Martian language. My points of reference have slipped. People send implicit messages over my head. They use words I don't understand. They have weird accents. It's like they're all in on some big secret and they keep it by smudging the vowels. And the landscape is just—I don't know. Another planet. Fucking *Dune*."

Cassandra is pleased to feel a little defensive. A vestige of loyalty? Home solidarity? "Well, if you came here to write about whatever is here to write about, you'll have to lean in a little harder, yeah?"

"That's what I'm doing. I think. That's why I'm showing up on your street like a stalker, isn't it?"

"Not my street. Remember? Not my house. Not my white carpet. And, come on. *Dune?* That's a few hours south, drama queen."

"And also. So many kids!"

Cassandra looks to her mother, who has fallen asleep on the chaise. Drooling a little. Cassandra takes a swipe with her bare fingers, wipes them on her jeans, and then says, "Okay, DeLuca. This time I won't panic. Give me the elevator pitch. I'll try to help."

"Really?"

"Yes."

"All right," he says. "It's a little longer than that."

"The lady's asleep. She'll snore, but don't get distracted."

It's clear he recalls Cassandra's explosion in the grocery store parking lot. He forays in trepidation. "I'm definitely here as a feature writer, but it's got something to do with some, ummm, personal questions."

He holds up his hands, as if to push air in her direction, or to put up a small shield. "I don't mean I'm asking *you* personal questions. I mean personal to me. Like I said, I have an Italian name, but I'm not Italian—"

Cassandra gathers herself in an attempt to look at the man directly. His hair curls a few inches below the bottom of his baseball cap. The structure of his face holds the aviators perfectly in place. His lips are rosy, old-school pretty.

She looks away. "Right," she says. "I remember. And you aren't Irish, like your mother, because you're adopted."

"Right. Which is the part of the story that made you curse me and run over my toes last time I saw you, so now I'm very afraid of you."

"Did I? Run over your toes? I thought you'd get out of the way."

"Almost."

"Sorry. I'll explain in a minute, maybe. Go on."

"This was more than forty years ago. I mean the adoption. So the records are sealed, old-school, and I could push it in some ways but I'm not really sure I want to—you know—find my actual biological parents. I'm not yearning for that kind of self-discovery. I'm fine with my upbringing and I like my mom and dad. They got divorced when I was four, and they both live interesting lives and they worked together to give me a happy childhood. But I want to understand a more general phenomenon, maybe just because I'm a journalist and I happen to be situated to tell a sort of out-there story. Like—something like—what are we in relation to a place that made us, even if it didn't really make us? A paid trip to the Wild West sounded pretty cool at one point. I've traveled all along the East Coast, New England, to other continents, but I've never been west of the Mississippi, here in the US."

Cassandra sits tense in the arid altitude. She situates herself into an intellectual corner. She reminds herself how prone the human brain is to constructing coincidence, spawning scenarios. She's not afraid that this man might turn out to be her son. She's hoped too many times to hope anymore. But she is afraid that her stupid exhausted heart will pitch a frenzy even so, and then plummet to prickling black, and stay there. She will berate herself, around and around and around all night and beyond for imagining a scene she still, after all these years, so many delusions and disappointments, cannot purge.

It's like cursing herself for bleeding every month. For graying hair. For needing air. Pointless energy. Senseless, calorie-burning grief.

She pushes her mind to the surface, forcing herself to engage. She knows how it's done.

She gives Matthew DeLuca her sternest rendition of a matriarchal glare. "Okay. Why Big Horn, Utah, Mr. New England? There's a punch line coming, I suppose."

"Well, turns out one of the reasons I've never come West is

that neither of my parents will come within two states' distance of Utah."

This makes plenty of sense to Cassandra. "Did they come from here?"

"No. But I did. Probably."

"If the adoption was all closed and secret, how would they have known that? How do you know that?"

"It was facilitated through LDS Social Services. My folks converted to Mormonism on a funny lark when they first married. I don't understand it all and they both turn into clams when I bring it up. Any of it. I get the sense they were pretty wild. And young. Did a lot of drugs, my dad got kicked out of college, got into a little trouble with the law. My mom—I don't know. She's a nurse practitioner now, but she got the degree after they hit bottom and steadied up.

"They actually had a baby. A girl. My father told me this story one time. My mother has never revealed any of this to me. I didn't even know the baby's name until I started poking around in my own records. Sally Jean. She was learning to crawl, use her hands. Irish red hair. Somehow put a rusted safety pin in her mouth—you know, it probably fell on the floor, just under a couch or a bed. The latch was weak, the thing opened up, gave her a deep scratch along the back of her throat and embedded in her tongue. Wouldn't have been that bad, probably. She seemed fine, just a freakish little mishap. The ER doctor said she'd be okay, but a couple days later it was clear some deep infection had set in. They realized they'd slept through a whole night without having to get up to feed the baby, and—"

"Oh, god," Cassandra interrupts. "Let's give that a minute."

A couple of magpies settle on Hal's shed, twenty-five feet away, attentive as eavesdroppers. Dorothy jerks, probably dreaming, but maybe about to wake. Cassandra remains troubled by questions of comprehension—of what her mother takes in, and how, and where it goes and what it mixes with. Sometimes she suspects that her mother understands everything plainly, that her thoughts are urgent—that dementia is a strain of aphasia.

Because sometimes, even now, her mother blurts out the most coherent—and efficient—comments Cassandra has ever heard from a woman who has spent her adult life playing stupid and coy. Has Dorothy somehow heard, and understood, this story of a lost baby girl? Where is *Dorothy's* lost daughter, in Dorothy's mind? Where is the grandchild she forfeited for the sake of threshold family status, marital appeasement?

The old woman twitches on the chaise beneath the apple tree.

DeLuca is currently less affected by the distant story of origin than Cassandra is. Old to him, but a shock to her, even as she resists.

She veers. "It's strange, you know, to call you by my lost brother's name."

DeLuca looks surprised. "We didn't get to any of that, last time we didn't converse."

"Matthew." Cassandra turns her head toward her mother, watching for stir.

None. She won't sleep tonight, though, if this goes on much longer. She'll get herself up and make toast for spectral thousands.

"I'll tell you that story another time. This one is yours."

"Okay." He thinks a moment, composing. "I don't want to take all your time. I'll jam through the rest and then, hopefully, please, maybe—you'll allow me to keep in touch with you."

"It looks promising. You're a stranger in a strange land. And you can spin a good story."

He's going there. "So, after a lot of falling apart, and after trying to rise to something like a normal heterosexual suburban life in the 1970s—this is in Michigan, by the way—they open the door to a couple of clean-cut Mormon kids and I guess it just seemed like community and salvation, and support for chemical abstinence, and they went for it. And the priest or whatever promised them that they would be rewarded with another go at having children, and they tried and tried but one or the other, or both, had dried up on that front.

"I don't know. Maybe grief and absurdity can savage a body's capacity to reproduce. Or maybe they needed drugs and rock and roll to rev up the bonding juice, and they'd gone straight. Whatever. No pregnancy. The Mormons got busy fulfilling their own prophecy and hooked my folks up with the omnipotent but ineffable LDS adoption agency in Salt Lake City, made it a whole congregational project, and somehow I shot pretty quick through the pipeline from wherever the hell I got conceived, and born, and processed—directly into the unready arms of Frank and Carlene DeLuca in Ann Arbor, Michigan."

He takes a swipe at his forehead with a paper napkin, then blows his nose. His face is flushed. His hand shakes with a small tremor. "Okay if I light this thing up?"

Dorothy sits up, wide awake, fixed on the young man in the lawn chair. The sun is low enough to place them all in apple tree, and subdivision, shadow.

Cassandra is paralyzed.

Dorothy says, "My daughter had a baby boy. We couldn't keep him, you know."

Cassandra's brain repeats the word.

We?

WE?

DeLuca takes off his hat. He glances at Cassandra. Scratches his head, derailed. Wherever this story was going for him has gone to spiral. "Come again?"

"Conceived in sin," Dorothy replies to a tree trunk. "We couldn't risk our family reputation. Hal wouldn't hear of it."

DeLuca turns to Cassandra. "What's that she's saying?"

For this man, perched on the far bank of bewilderment and broken links, Cassandra collects herself. "Why," she asks, "are you in this obscure, fucked-up, insignificant, admittedly beautiful but criminally pretentious Mormon town, poking around at such heavy questions, Matthew DeLuca?"

Now he sounds like he's confessing a crime. "I took a genetic thing a couple of years ago. Wanted to understand some health history. Maybe I wanted more. I don't know. Seems all my DNA whistles through a twentieth-century bottleneck right here in Big Horn, Utah—a place I'd never heard of and certainly wouldn't have put on my bucket list except for—well, you know. This."

For some reason Cassandra finds her mother the most compelling character in this colored blur, although it does register, in the back of her mind, that she may be shielding herself from the more vivid curiosities the man between them represents.

"I have," DeLuca states, "a lot of very close relatives here, or spawned here." He blinks, and reiterates: "A lot."

Dorothy says, "I told him. I tried, you know. Blood is blood. Kin is kin. Everybody knows they all come different ways. What family can't name half a dozen got folded in, or sent away, only half-secret?"

"Mom. What?"

DeLuca grins. "Right, Miss Dorothy? I've got some hard stats to back them anecdotes."

Dorothy giggles. "Well, I don't know about that."

DeLuca turns to Cassandra. "So. Ummmmm. Personal question: Do you happen to have any—"

"Sisters? I do not."

He molds his spine to the back of the vinyl chair, shrinking to give her space. Neither dares ask the next question.

The air cools like slim grace.

"Is your mother lost in the delusions of dementia?"

"Usually. But, strangely, not in this significant moment. We've both been through this too many times, haven't we?"

"Is this why that girl told me to come talk to you?"

"I don't know. How much did you explain to her?"

"Not much of what I just told you."

"I don't know how much she knows about me. I think they've been told I'm a villain because I'm an apostate. It's hard to overstate what a big deal that is. By their lights I should have repented and come back to the welcoming fold. And I don't get the sense that anyone talks about the—"

"—sinful conception?"

Dorothy says, "You mean the baby."

DeLuca: "Yeah. The baby."

Cassandra: "My son. Who is now a man, somewhere on the planet, healthy I hope. About your age."

"Could it really be this ridiculously coincidental?"

"No. You can't imagine how many times I've fallen for that, wishing for—that's just cheap social-issue novel bullshit. Oprah theatrics. Or maybe you can. Makes people like us hope for a smaller, neater world where stories make sense and converge. Makes us hope until we're too hurt and tired to think in rational ways."

"Wow. Mind if I put that quote in the file?"

"That's the kind of thing you're looking for?"

"It's better than I've gotten from anyone else here in Brigadoon."

Dorothy tunes back in. "*Brigadoon*? Is it movie time?"

"It is, Mom. We'll go in and get you settled. Just a few more minutes, all right?"

"What a day this has been! What a rare mood I'm in—" Dorothy warbles.

"Why it's almost like being in love," DeLuca sings with her. He stands to offer his hand.

Dorothy rises to a creaky pirouette: "There's a smile on my

face / for the whole human race / why it's almost like being in love…"

"What the hell, DeLuca! Quit that, now."

"My grandma loved musicals. Every time I got left at her house. Charms the socks off the old ladies."

"Yuck. Old ladies should keep their socks on."

"We're postponing the question."

Cassandra can't assemble the syntax. Her lungs hurt. Maybe she wants this to stop. "Whole lot of illicit procreation goes on in these here hills, you know. Don't let those dry slopes fool you. Fertility busting out all over."

He glances east, and upward. Swivels slowly, counterclockwise, taking in the north range, too. Turns far enough to face Cassandra. "Your lovely mother is getting tired. She has a movie to watch. Should I come back another time? I don't know how much we can—you know, accomplish in one sit-down."

He helps Dorothy resettle in the chaise.

Cassandra blurts, "Let's get this over with. What day were you born?"

"October 14, 1978. I think I was born somewhere near Seattle, but the genetics point toward conception right here in this valley. This weird-ass town, in fact."

She's in a white room, cold. Flat on her back. Naked (why? The nurse says this is how it's done, but now she knows better). Legs splayed, feet in stirrups. Grim figures above her, scrutinizing everything but her face. Touching, palpating, probing. People she'll never meet wait in the room beyond to inform some happy couple of miraculous news—to make a second delivery.

The shocking, comfortless, grueling pain. No mitigation. A full day, and minimally apparent night, in the small casement window beyond the fluorescent glare.

A man's voice above and behind her, out of sight. The doctor? God? The incorporated sound of her own self-loathing?

Remember this pain, so you'll think twice before trivializing the divine powers of procreation ever again. Take comfort in the knowledge that his child is pure and blameless...

White gives way to dull gray. The room is empty. Her body evacuated. An infant wails from another room, behind the wall, but the sound trails away. She's still stripped, but covered with a thin hospital sheet.

A syringe. Nonexistence. Return.

Thought we'd lost you there. You've lost quite a bit of blood. Let's see if you can answer some questions. What's your name?

Cassandra.

Who's the president of the United States?

Richard Nixon? No, wait. Jimmy Carter.

Yes, sad to say it, but Carter it is. Thanks to him, that perfect, beautiful child could have been aborted—

What beautiful child? Whence the perfect, beautiful child?

The wonderful thing is, you'll always have this cherished memory of the child's birthday. Tell us what year this is.

Nineteen seventy-eight.

Good girl. Looks like you're back among the living. What's the date?

What was—the baby?

A healthy boy. He's going to have a wonderful life, with a real family that loves him. He'll be raised the gospel, prepared for eternal life. We're almost finished here. See if you can remember the date. A date to remember all your life—

Cassandra hoists herself from the low-slung chair. DeLuca rises to face her.

She says, flat, "I'm not your mother."

He steps backward. Sits down hard on the grass.

She remembers the girl from another town—the one who got "sick" and broke a date lined up by lawyer fathers for the Big Horn junior prom. Is she the one? Cassandra has not, until now, given that woman a careful thought. Perhaps she should have. Andraya said there were others. Maybe she ought to send DeLuca to talk to Eleventh.

"Take off those glasses," Cassandra says, barely audible. "Come here. Let me take a good look at you."

He approaches crying. Slate-blue eyes. That singing voice. Now that she dares take it in, she can trace the precise junction of lean jaw to graceful neck. She puts a finger to it. The surprising cupid pink of the upper lip, the wide furrow of the (she sees her Anatomy for Artists professor, poking a pointer at a projected human face) *philtrum*.

(Such a beautiful family!)

(If you would have played your cards right...)

"My son was born that next January. You're three months older than him."

She could say many strange things, but thought burns to cinder before she can compose.

"I'll make a very good guess he's your half-brother."

He parts his lips to swallow the news, too hard. He coughs cherry smoke.

When the lungs clear, she says, "At least we know who your father is. Unmistakable. Unless it's one of his brothers, I guess."

They stand.

"We'll talk again, when we've—"

"Recovered?"

"How in the world would we do that?"

"Talk? Or do you mean recover? I'll walk your mother to the house."

Cassandra stands, back to the sunset, watching their erratic progress across the lawn, then strides to meet them at the stairway. "Good night, young man," she murmurs.

"Are you him?" Dorothy inquires. "Have you come back?"

"Who do you mean, Mama?"

"Matthew. He must be so cold."

"Good night, Dorothy," this Matthew says, tender.

And: "Good night, Cassandra, mother of my somewhere brother. Can we—"

"Yes. I think. Let's give it a few days."

"Yes."

"Walk on up the street a quarter mile. Get a feel for the neighborhood. Look to the right."

He gets in the Oregon car. Drives south, away.

She can't make herself call. He sends an email to say he's gone back to Boston for a while. Can he send questions? He's drafting. He wants to come back / he does not want to come back.

He'll text when he returns, if she'll allow it.

Chapter 32

The lawn kids are back. Either the same ones, or clones. The driver is skinny and mop-haired, looks barely old enough to be licensed. Same old truck, pulling a two-wheeled trailer made from the cut-off bed of an even older truck. The riding mower, just coming down the ramp beneath a confident middle schooler, and an arsenal of power trimmers are very much up to date.

Like last time, the boys get on with the job. No glances toward the house. Big boy signals little brother to cut the mower engine. They gesture and squint in the sunlight. The little guy shifts from foot to foot as Lanky lays out the strategy.

"Mom. Come to the window. Do you know those boys out there?"

Dorothy peers out. "Well, James and Matthew, of course. Why are they home already? Is school out?"

The hem of Dorothy's housecoat is caught in the waistband of her underwear, exposing the sag of Dorothy's adult-diapered butt beneath the filmy fabric. A streamer of toilet paper runs like a long tail as she strides toward the door to quiz the yard boys.

"Mom! Hold on! Let me fix something!" Cassandra grabs at tissue and fabric. Dorothy opens the door, calling, "Is school out already, boys?" as Cassandra reaches in for the last of the paper. She re-drapes the pastel pink hemline with the door wide open.

The kids look up, startled. They wave, and the younger one calls, "Hi, Grandma Great! Just here to mow the lawn!"

"That's not Matthew. He called you Grandma Great. Is he one of Brian's?"

"I suppose so," Dorothy answers. The old woman assesses her own evidence, then erupts: "I just sent you off on the bus! Are you skipping your classes? What has your father told you?"

No wonder the boys avoid communion.

"Come over here," Dorothy commands. Big boy grins, whacks his brother lightly upside the head. Middle schooler rolls his eyes. His eyes flash river green as they approach. He's freckled, and he's missing a lower tooth behind a scar that underlines his lower lip.

The up-close bodies confuse Dorothy into silence. Her face has gone stupid and blank.

The freckled boy says, "Grandma Great, we don't start school until next week. Grandpa Brian sent us to do your yard."

Dorothy grants him a petulant glare.

The big boy speaks up. "We won't take long. Your place will be spiffed up in no time. Want to come out and watch? I'll get the lawn chairs. You can sit under the locust tree with—um—"

"Aunt Cassandra," little brother furnishes, pleased to demonstrate he's in the know.

Cassandra jumps at the address, shocked that this means something to her.

Why have they all kept themselves away?

"Who are *you*?" she queries the kid. "I don't believe we've been introduced."

"He's the Brother of Jared," his brother says. "So, guess what his name is."

Cassandra blinks herself through a quirky mnemonic of scriptural characters. "Really? No way—"

"Mahonrimoriancumr."

"No. My name is Charlie," the kid retorts. "Quit it."

Cassandra can't help but laugh at the Book of Mormon joke. She says, "How about those lawn chairs, Charlie? I'll get Grandma Great a sunhat while your brother—right?—gets her settled under the tree. She needs some entertainment."

Charlie says, "But my brother really is Jared. This one, anyhow."

"How many you got?"

"Three."

"How did you know my name?"

"Our cousin Dani told us."

"And, Grandpa," Jared adds.

Jared smooths his tumultuous hair under a baseball cap, pulling the unorthodox length out the back opening. He rubs his eyes, also green, but flecked with brown and red-rimmed in the late-summer pollen. "Sorry. I'm not wearing my contacts," he says. "Grandpa Soelberg says you used to look just like Dani though."

"Who do I look like now, do you think?"

"I can't see very well without my glasses. Or contacts. I'd have to get—"

"—closer? Maybe we'll get around to that."

"You don't look like anybody," Charlie says. "Not really."

Cassandra laughs. "I don't look like Grandma Great, here? She's my mother, you know. I don't look like my brother Brian?"

"Well, you're a—" Charlie stops himself, confused.

"A what?"

"A lady. Grandpa is just this old guy."

"Charlie, go get those chairs," Jared urges. "Grandma Great can't just keep standing there. Here, let me help her down the steps."

"I'll go get her big hat. I have lemonade. Want some?"

"Yes, please."

Dorothy, still gummed in confusion, seems content to sit in

shade, pleased to sport a romantically broad-brimmed hat with a ribbon tied under her chin. Cassandra realizes part of Charlie's perplexity is rooted in his mysterious lady relative's attire: she's wearing a smocked sundress, sleeveless. Even were her shoulders appropriately covered, the hem is probably short enough for a polite Mormon boy to discern that she doesn't wear the knee-length temple garments required of grown-ups in the world he understands.

Jared's curiosity is waxing, now he's retrieved his glasses from the truck. "Is that a tattoo?" he asks, trying not to show the wrong kind of interest in a woman's calves. "I can't hardly believe you're my grandpa's sister."

"It's a line from a French poem. Your great, *great* grandmother Irene Caldwell—your grandpa's and my grandma—taught me the whole poem when I was younger than Charlie."

"What does it say?" Charlie leans low to examine the letters. "Oh! There's a pony, too."

"Charlie!" Jared says. "Don't be rude."

Are these regular Mormon kids? There's something otherworldly about them. They don't look like the jersey-donned, ear-budded boys that preen at the fast-food joints, down at the corners. These two are wide-eyed and Mayberry polite.

"It's okay," Cassandra says. "It's a carousel pony. The poem is about getting sort of drunk with joy on a stupid merry-go-round ride, even though it's just a cheap thrill, and even though there are bad guys—pickpockets—waiting on the sides to wreck the fun."

Jared: "There's a poem about that?"

Charlie: "Better than the dumb poem I had to memorize for church."

Jared: "Will you read it to us?"

Cassandra laughs. "What, the church poem?"

"No! The one on your—I mean, the French one."

"I know. I'm kidding. I might still remember the whole

thing, but the tattoo says: *C'est étonnant comme ça vous soûle / D'aller ainsi dans ce cirque bête...*"

Both boys, reconstitutions of Irene Caldwell, are captivated.

"What does it mean, though?" Charlie whispers.

"Something like, 'It's astonishing how drunk it makes you, to just ride along in this beastly circus...'"

Dorothy sips lemonade, propping her hat for better effect. She emits a ladylike belch.

Jared looks astonished, either by old lady burps or banished aunt poetry. His eyes avert, zigzagging upward as they trace the trail to Big Horn summit. Cassandra is astonished, too. These visions, so many years hers and in her memory alone, are Jared's. The true link, beyond the genetics.

Cassandra asks if he's learning a language in school.

"No."

Charlie: "We're homeschooled."

"You are?"

"All of us. I mean, all the cousins."

"What cousins?"

"Soelbergs."

"James's family, too?"

"No. Us. Grandpa and Grandma. Brian. Elaine. So, Goddards."

"Who's your teacher?"

"Our mom. Some of the other mom and dads, sometimes."

"Who's your mother?"

"Janice. Janice Hastings Soelberg. Our dad is Lander. She comes from out past Tooele, like the Soelbergs. She went to college."

Cassandra takes in the facts, but hardly knows what to think.

Then again, she knows exactly what to think.

Jared takes off his cap. He shoots Cassandra a nervous side-eye and shakes himself like a mostly-grown puppy.

Cap back on.

"Let's mow this beastly lawn, buddy. Hop to."

The mower fires up, and Charlie mounts, stretching to clutch. The pungent stench of two-stroke oil burns out of the pole trimmer in Jared's strong hands. The scent of cut greenery beneath. Dorothy draws in the exhaust like nicotine. Cassandra half expects her to say, *I just love the smell of napalm in the morning.*

Chapter 33

Another pickup pulls up. Settles in the driveway. A gray-haired man steps out—a wiry guy in work clothes.

And then, completely, he's Brian.

Cassandra tries not to drink diesel air as the exhaust settles. The boys glance toward their grandfather, but also hunker down to demonstrate industry.

Brian's green eyes flicker as he blinks against the afternoon sunlight. He strides toward Dorothy and Cassandra. "Mama, how you doing?" he asks, bending to kiss Dorothy's cheek. "What a nice hat you got there."

"Oh, thank you! Emma lent me hers."

"Is that right? Good of her."

He straightens to full height. He never reached six feet like James or Matthew, but the bulk of muscle on his shoulders and chest made him the most visually formidable. Although diminished—even leaner than he was in his twenties—dense strength animates his flannel work shirt and faded jeans.

He smells of diesel and dirt, a glaze of sweat, soap, and alfalfa clover.

His torso follows the swivel of his head. His hands go to his back pockets.

He speaks gently, just loud enough to exceed the buzzing trimmer in Jared's hands. "Cassandra."

She laughs out loud, strange voiced, an eruption of uncanny joy. But no words come.

He grins like a kid. He looks about to cry. He scouts for an extra chair, then plants his butt on the grass. He stands back up. He whistles through his fingers at the boys, signaling them to cut the noise.

The silence is confounding. For a few moments, only the deafening muffle of the timeless massif beyond them.

"Guys!" he calls. "Come sit a minute."

The boys approach their grandfather. She attends to the way they watch him—Brian, the whipping boy—a body (and soul, whatever that is) that absorbed blow after blow, strike after strike after strike. She discerns nothing of boy-Brian's bone-deep rage in his grandsons' eyes. No bracing, no cowering as they come.

Maybe the fortunes of battle have favored Brian. Hrothgar of Heorot, friends and kinsmen flocked among his ranks.

Oh, be true.

Brian, the brother who drew her out and up from the carcass of a gutted buck, ran hot water in the tub, wrapped her clean and warm. Combed her hair, sat vigil as she slept in their father's poisoned orchard. Stepped out into winter night, strode into the storm, searched the high slopes and canyon nooks on foot for another, fled in their mother's Sunday coat.

"We talked to her, Grandpa," Charlie says. "She's nice."

Jared stands in his work boots, absorbing evidence.

"She's more than nice," Brian says. "She's my baby sister."

Dorothy pulls herself forward, up from the back of her chair.

Cassandra: "I'm reasonably nice. And I am his sister. All these years. Why have you taken so long to come? I've been here since the beginning of summer."

Brian stands back. His physique softens like clay even as his features harden. His eyes are yellowed and opaque until he lifts them to sky. The blue turns them green. He prepares his lips and tongue to form a few simple words. "Because I am ashamed. I did not know if I would be welcome to you."

Jared murmurs, "Charlie, go get Grandpa a lawn chair," and Charlie makes a run for it. Jared drops onto the grass like a stringless marionette. He pulls a tuft of grass to blow it from his fingers toward the Big Horn summit. He sprawls face upward, pulling his hat over his eyes.

"Stand up with me, boy," Brian urges him. "I want you to hear this, and you need to know I'm speaking for all of us. You'll need to speak it again among your brothers and sisters. Cousins. Your mom and dad. Everyone."

Jared rises. Charlie arrives with the chair, but drops it to join his grandfather and big brother.

"What's going on here?" Dorothy demands, straining to lift herself from her seat. Cassandra reaches to assist. All of them stand together in conference, heads leaning in. It feels like a prayer circle, in fact, which nearly causes Cassandra to retreat. But she holds. Brian says, "Jared, Charlie. This lady here is your family, and I'm sorry you haven't known that. To our damnable discredit, we caused her to leave us, and then we let you grow up—all of you—without comprehending your kinship."

Cassandra strains to feel something, but she's standing unsteady in a heady mirage of home and residual summer heat, of cut grass and male sweat and old-lady cologne. She'll do well enough forestalling a swoon. Will Brian go on? She's probably heard him say more in the last fifteen minutes than the first two decades of life in his presence.

"She's my sister. I should never have let her go."

Dorothy leans into Jared, who eases her back into a chair.

"I failed two siblings. I've failed my sister," Brian laments.

"My sister is Emma," Dorothy pipes up, sensing she's not getting enough attention.

"Yes, she is, Mama," Brian says. "But this is Cassandra, not

Emma. Your daughter is Cassandra, named for Dad's pioneer grandmother, who crossed the ocean and prairies, and Rocky Mountains, to come to Utah. Came to make us a home. All of us."

"*Cassandra* means, 'to shine for men,'" Dorothy recites from some available mental mailbox.

Charlie snorts. "What the heck?"

"It means to *outshine* men," Brian corrects. "I looked it up, kind of accidentally, a long time ago, once when I—" He stopped short.

"When you what?" Cassandra asks.

Brian's eyes are green again. Clear and vivid as they meet hers. "When I was trying to look you up, a few years ago. When I found your artist—what is it? Website. Boys, your aunt Cassandra was born with a miraculous eye, and a magic hand. You wouldn't believe it unless you saw it yourself. She's painted these mountains, a million ways. Shows you how to see them."

"You should let us use the internet, then," Jared says.

"That's up to your folks. How old are you now?"

"Sixteen."

Charlie is undistracted. "Maybe *Cassandra* means 'artist'?"

Cassandra laughs. "No. It means that no man will ever believe what I say, no matter how true it is."

"That's a Greek story," says Jared. "I read a book of myths. Mom said it was okay as long as I remember the stories aren't true. Not like scripture."

"See what I mean?" Cassandra says, and Brian shoots her a glance, and then a grin, and Jared laughs, happy to catch the joke.

"Wait." Cassandra turns toward Jared. "What? You don't have the internet? Don't you use it at school?"

"Homeschool, remember? Yeah, we have the homeschool kind. Mom says we can do what we want when we turn eighteen, once we've been trained up in the ways that we should go, but then I'm supposed to go on a mission, and…" He trails off.

"How does that—" She stops herself. "Never mind. Sounds like you like to read."

"Not me," says Charlie.

Jared: "Yes. I do."

Cassandra suspects Brian will cut this conversation short. Clearly these kids answer to an encompassing home philosophy. But, after a patient silence, he says, "You boys have any questions for Aunt Cassandra?"

Charlie scratches his skinny dirty neck. "Are you a Mormon?"

She waits for a signal from Brian, which he does not provide.

"No. But I used to be. I understand your family's beliefs. I think."

Jared: "Why aren't you now?"

"I just—hmm. I took another path, I guess."

"Do you believe in God?"

"Well." She punches Brian's rock-hard arm, seeking permission.

He raises his eyebrows, then lifts one side of his face the same way he did when he was Charlie's age. "I told them they could ask you questions. You ought to answer."

"Okay then. No. But I believe in working hard to be good people while we're alive. That's something I learned here in Big Horn, when I was a child, and that idea hasn't left me."

Charlie says, "I've never known anyone who wasn't Mormon. I thought it would be worse."

Cassandra laughs. "You hardly know me. It might get worse."

Brian: "I already told you, she's the best of us. Don't let anyone tell you different. In most ways, you already know her."

Jared frowns. "We don't, though, Grandpa. And if Mom and Dad and Grandma were here, we wouldn't even get to talk like this. I've lived my whole life without knowing her. I don't know where she's been, or where she lives. I hear some things, always just before everyone goes quiet. You and Uncle James and even

Grandma Great before she got—before she started to forget everything—and Grandma Elaine and Aunt Paige, even people at church sometimes. All of you know her, and we don't, because nobody lets us. And here you're telling us that she's got this magic eye and she's the best of everybody and here she is right in front of us, and we *don't* know her. Would you all do that to one of us? Just pretend we were never even here, not real anymore?"

Jared gestures toward the mountains. He stands, lean and breathlessly young, bewildered. Sixteen. Her own age when she was taken in the night, drawn away from all she knew and loved and knew how to see. Brian reaches toward Jared, and for a moment Cassandra fears he'll strike. Because, here, in her memory, men hit boys when men are in the wrong.

Brian cups his palm on his grandson's shoulder and draws him closer. "Jared. This is what I'm trying to tell you. Never. Never, ever again. The shame I feel, here with my sister, so many terrible years. Never again. None of you, no matter what."

Jared straightens and steps away. He's taller than Brian. His features, his tall build—Hal's. His stance, his gestures, his expression, (his glorious hair),—nothing like Hal. Hal stiffened into nailed scrap wood. Jared, slope and water.

He addresses Cassandra: "And there are others."

"Our brother Matthew. Your grandpa did everything he could to find him, to bring him home. Brian was nearly lost himself. They found him hypothermic, freezing, all the way up—" She gestures.

"I know. The Sinks. That's why he's missing a finger."

Cassandra yanks her head in surprise. Brian holds up his left hand, grinning, ring finger shortened to the middle knuckle. The pinkie looks a little off as well.

"What the f—I mean, what the heck, Brian."

"Forgot my gloves. Took a while to make a fire."

Silence.

She reaches toward Dorothy, who appears to be listening.

Dorothy takes her daughter's hand, shakes it as if she were meeting a stranger, and unclasps. She checks the bow under her chin. Maybe all this woman should have possibly done, after some point, is forget.

Jared isn't finished. "Aunt Cassandra."

"Yes."

"My grandma says you had a baby."

She will not show these children tears. She tightens her jaw, the way Brian taught her to, whether he knew it or not. She flattens her tone. "I did."

"Was it a boy? Or girl?"

"Boy."

"What happened to him?"

"I don't know."

"How old is he?"

"Forty-one."

"Our dad is forty," Charlie says. "He's—"

Jared: "Do you think we can find him?"

"He might not want us to."

"Maybe he'll find us."

Dorothy is up and doddering toward the driveway. She leans a bit to the left, which might cause her to walk a mile-wide circumference were she unobstructed. She seems attracted to Brian's black pickup.

"Mama," he says. "Want to go for a ride?"

"Why yes, I'd like that."

"Come on, Cassandra. I'll show you the farm. Jared, you and Charlie see this job done. Then head on home. Get some ice cream on the way."

He hands Charlie a couple of tens, then strides toward Dorothy, swooping her up like a Southern bride to carry her to the truck. He opens the door and lifts her in. "Slide over now, Mama. Cassandra's getting in beside you."

He stands ready to lift Cassandra as well.

"Are you serious? Get out of my way," she says. "I'm way younger than you, Superman."

"Always did have to do it yourself."

"Dad said I'd never attract a husband because of it."

"And here you are. Never scored a one. All those Big Horn blowhards to choose from, back in the day, and you scared 'em off like the ugly badgers they are."

"Well—"

"—well, nothing." He circles around the driver's door and hoists up. "Wait," he says. "Maybe you did score a husband. How would I know? Did you get married, after you left?"

"Mmm. No. But I've been…"

"Well, isn't this an adventure?" Dorothy exults.

"Ain't it though?" Brian eases the truck into reverse. "Here we go."

Chapter 34

The old Goddard farm, tucked among the western hills, sits arrested in time. Irrigated green flats morph along elk-toned slopes blobbed with scrub oak. Big Horn's massive vertical cliffs, plummeting off the blade-sharp summit line, are clearly visible. From here, the whole range, green gray above the dry hills, patched with high hemlock forests and chartreuse aspen groves, reveals its surge-by-surge depth. One subterranean magma heave after another.

"Holy crap, Brian. Who's in on this?"

"Why must you be crude?" Dorothy admonishes.

"Crap? Really, Mom?"

"Elaine's got a brother on up the hollow, mostly keeps to himself. Hermity, but works with us on water management. Comes down for picking. Then it's us. Elaine and me, and the kids and their kids. We bought the old man out just before he died—at least the house and barns. Elaine's brothers and sisters mostly went west, out past Riverton—" he shoots her a sideways glance, over the crown of Dorothy's hat "—and further west…"

Cassandra lifts her eyebrows. "How much further?"

"Well, out past the lake. Out toward Ely. Callao. A few out where Dad's folks come from."

"Oh."

"These old families have a lot of land, even if there ain't much water. It's just that here—you know, along the Front—most of it's just too pricey to preserve in big tracts like this. As you can see, we're surrounded by sellouts."

"So, how much land are you still working here?"

"A little over two hundred acres. Half of it's family trust, out at the edges. A few of the more, uh, modern Goddards are itching to sell."

"How much money would that even be? What's keeping them from getting their way?"

"Aw, you know. Old man Goddard."

"He's still alive?"

"Might as well be. Clutched himself into every last Goddard brain. And hide. We got time to catch up. Let's get Mama out. I sure hope that's her farting, not you."

"Not you?"

"You'd of already flown out of the cab if it was."

Dorothy exudes a new countenance in the farmish atmosphere, straining forward against the measured pace of the son and daughter on either side. "Is Daddy home?"

Brian: "Not the one you're thinking of."

Dorothy: "My, he's a handsome man. And such a sharp dresser."

Cassandra: *And such an enthusiastic un-dresser.*

"What?"

Nothing.

Horses along the fence. Brown cowboy ponies. An aging roan mare. A tall black gelding with a humped Roman nose and white forehead star.

"Think you can still ride?" Brian asks.

"Would you take me?"

"I'll come soon. Look up there. The leaves are turning up the Divide."

"I haven't been in a saddle since...before everything."

"Like riding a bike. You'll be crying all week after, though."

"Guess it will make me sit still and get some work done."

"That's a funny kind of work you do."

"Well, it's definitely work. I might leave a pay stub in a vase on Hal Soelberg's grave before I'm through."

"Hope it rolls him right over. Where do those paychecks come from, though? Do you just make stuff and sell it?"

"Haha, maybe a long time ago. I did sell stuff on the sidewalks in Minneapolis after I left home. Aspiring to be Lee Godie, I guess."

"Who?"

Cassandra smiles. "Just this street woman who fingered people on the New York streets to buy her art."

"Maybe Matt—Matilda—" Brian stammered. "In Los Angeles. Maybe she's—what's her name?"

"Lee Godie. I hope so. That's a good image."

Small children frolic in the fenced yard. Two sit-up babies flap their arms in a playpen under a gracious honey locust.

"Grandpa!" the runners holler, trending Brian-ward. The two fastest wrap pink sunburned arms around his legs. Brian leaves Dorothy to Cassandra, then scoops up the little girl, Amish-looking with long yellow braids, despite the shorts and T-shirt. He sets her on his shoulders. Straight-up Americana.

"This place could be some kind of heartwarming family movie set. Do you know all their names, or are they props?"

"Sure I do. But they'll tell you themselves, every time you ask. Ain't that right, Sally Brown?" he teased, tugging a scratched bare foot.

"Grandpa! My name is Rebecca!"

Cassandra freezes. Her name at the unwed mothers' home. The break in rhythm makes Dorothy, stepping ahead, stub a toe on the flagstone path. Cassandra catches her before she trips.

"What are we doing here? Who lets these children run wild?" Dorothy complains.

Brian pays no mind. "Rebecca! What a pretty name for a pretty girl!"

"*My* name is Jack," says the boy holding his grandpa's left hand. He wants in on the praise.

"Also a pretty name!"

"Grandpa! It's not pretty! It's good-looking!"

"Get along now!" Dorothy says, brushing her hand to keep small humans at bay. "Who's your mama? Go on!"

"You know who these ladies are?" Brian asks the kids.

"Grandma Great!" they chime.

"And? Who's this nice one, holding Grandma Great up straight like the queen she aspires to be?" He sets Rebecca down to join her—what? Siblings? Cousins?

The children circle to scrutinize.

Rebecca: "A…customer?"

"Nope."

Cassandra holds her mother back, then takes in alfalfa-scented air and commits. She puts her free arm akimbo and squints like an inspector, assessing each child—four of them, not counting the playpen droolers. The little mob gazes back in unison.

"My name is Cassandra. I'm your aunt Cassandra."

Jack and Rebecca, maybe twins, are perplexed.

Jack says, "Are you teasing us?"

Rebecca: "Cassandra is our mama."

A smaller girl pipes up. She sounds like a cartoon poppet. "You not Aunt Cassambwa."

Brian gets down on his haunches. The children await the punch line.

"This is the first Aunt Cassandra," he tells them.

Dorothy blurts, "Cassandra? She's not here. Cassandra went off and had—"

"Mom!" Brian says, voiced edged hard enough to make the children shrink back a little. "Cassandra is right here!

Your daughter, holding your arm, right here, plain as day. Tell Grandma Great, kids. Who do you see right here in front of you, real as real?"

"The first…" Jack begins.

"Aunt Cassandra," Rebecca enunciates.

"Your mama," Brian declares, "is the next Cassandra. Named after this one. This Cassandra is my sister. Your mother Cassandra is my daughter. I named her that, when she was a baby, because I loved my sister."

The children find this impressive. Jack's hair is buzzed neat, accentuating his stick-out ears. The front door opens behind them. A graceful pioneer-ish grandmother steps out, shaded under the stoop. She takes time to absorb the scene before her. The smallest girl wheels and runs like a Shetland filly.

The littlest boy pees in his tiny jeans. He looks down at himself, then up toward his grandpa, sheepish.

Brian says, "Cassandra, you remember my wife, Elaine, right?"

"Of course. She was just ahead of me in school." Cassandra speaks directly to Elaine: "You were always kind. You and your sister."

Brian says, "Maybe you two can set Mama inside, or out here, you know. Sip some ice water. I got a little mess to take care of. Back in a minute."

He swoops the little guy up with one arm and carries him off like a muddy pup. "Got to stop leaking like that, big boy! Let's get these clothes off. It's still hot enough, you can run through the sprinklers. Don't that sound fun?"

Chapter 35

Sitting here in an approximation of 1940s Big Horn tumbles small gems in Dorothy's brain. "Do you think he'll come home tonight?" she asks.

"Who do you mean?" Elaine responds from the rocking chair on Dorothy's right.

"Who is it we're waiting for?" Cassandra asks from the left, eyes on the serrated skyline.

"Daddy, of course."

"Oh. Isn't he home already?"

Dorothy offers a confidential snort.

The children shout from the side of the house, weaving through the glitter of a fan sprinkler Brian has set beside a long row of raspberries. They appear and disappear, shrieking as they chase the water. *Manneken Pis* has shed his clothing entirely, dripping joy as he mimics the older kids.

"They're really cute," Cassandra says to Elaine.

Dorothy: "That one needs his britches on."

"Looks to me like that one needs to be buck nekked." Cassandra laughs, and Elaine looks caught between positions.

"Not sure Brian isn't rewarding him for having another accident. He's super excited about his big boy Ninja Turtle underwear. So excited that he keeps peeing in them."

"How old is he?"

"Almost three. He's a piece of work, that one."

"What's his name?"

Elaine looks surprised, then remembers. "Oh. I forget. That's very strange. Of course. You don't know them."

Jack tears around the corner of the house, shirtless, ears blooming like a monkey's. "Grandma, watch. I can do a cart-wheel. Almost."

"Can Grandma Great watch, too? And Aunt Cassandra?"

"Yep." Jack gives it a pretty good shot, but he's unsatisfied. "No, wait. Lemme do it again."

Rebecca appears, down to underwear and a green T-shirt, to coach her brother.

"Are they twins?" Cassandra asks.

Rebecca calls out the answer. "No. I'm oldest."

Jack: "But sometimes we're the same age."

Elaine explains. "Our daughter—Cassandra—had a hard time getting pregnant. They were married a good five years, kept trying, then just tried to stop thinking about it, at least as much as they could. Then, out of the blue, she realized she was four months along. Just hadn't let herself believe it. So, after Rebecca was born, maybe they thought it wouldn't happen again for a long time, or ever, and—well, they were wrong. Jack came just eleven months after. Now he's five. No more pregnancies, no real effort to stop anything, but now all of a sudden she's expecting again. So, who knows? Pregnancy is a funny thing."

"Ain't it though," Cassandra murmurs, and Elaine looks startled.

"I'm...Cassandra, I'm not used to..."

"Neither am I. This is all strange."

"What's so strange about it?" Dorothy blurts. "He's a busy man. Sometimes he works into the night."

"Yeah, okay, Mom."

"What?"

"Where's *your* mother, Dorothy?" Cassandra asks. "What does she do on the nights Lander stays out late?"

"Well, you know as well as I do. She's out there in the garden again. What man wants to come home to a woman with dirt under her nails? I know Hal certainly does not."

Neither Dorothy's daughter nor daughter-in-law wants to tangle with that.

"Wow," Cassandra says. "Is this what she goes to every time she comes here?"

"She hasn't been here in quite a long time. We usually come to her anymore." Elaine thinks a minute, still adjusting to the reappearance of a long-vanished member of her husband's family. She's lived a long, engrossing life since the night Matilda—and Cassandra—departed.

"Brian kept his distance until Hal died. He's better with his mother—your mom—now that she's tipped into dementia. She just couldn't stop herself from justifying everything that happened. Wanted Brian to say Hal did everything right, that it couldn't be helped, that Matthew had fallen into abomination, and you were—" Elaine stops, glancing toward Dorothy, who gazes into the hot milk-blue sky, expended.

"I was what?" Cassandra asks, not certain she wants to be fully caught up on the plot. Elaine doesn't look like she's all that willing to furnish. Appears to be an exhausting subject.

"'Ungrateful' was her standby word."

Cassandra grimaces. "Fair enough. I'm sure she had other descriptions."

"You know how it is. You grew up here."

"Yes."

The scenery before them is the stuff of myth. Arid Eden. The peaks above them shimmer, fading in and out of clarity in small clouds and muted light. The evergreen forests, tucked into high recesses, show nearly black against the gray of the north range, even darker against the tiered browns to the east. Radiant ochre patches among the quaking aspens. The scrub oak is beginning its transformation to flame-orange and red, stippling down toward the gray-green sage of the fat, sensuous foothills that wrap old Goddard's farm.

"What are you growing here? Your folks raised alfalfa, didn't they? Corn?"

"Yes. Lucerne. We kept a few cattle. Sold eggs, and raspberries. My grandpa planted an apple orchard up there, around the bend."

"Now I remember. You and your sisters ran that little produce stand while the rest of us were—I don't know. Babysitting. Jaywalking. Sunbathing."

Elaine provides a short, bitter laugh.

Cassandra waits her out. Dorothy rocks herself in the chair, bobbing her head to keep the momentum.

"I love this place," Elaine says. "Especially now that we farm it with the kids. You know, Brian was really inspired after he drove you up to Logan. Remember?"

"Yeah. I do. The ride, I mean. That's funny. It was snowing so hard, and he drove me all the way back, away from Hal. You were pregnant, weren't you? That seemed to be the only thing on his mind—getting back to you."

"Pregnant. Yes. I almost forgot. You must have given Brian a talking-to. By the time he came back he'd made a whole plan to learn new crops, and organic farming, and water management. My dad and brothers just about drove him off the property that next summer. Thought he was crazy. He bought books, took some extension classes. Started with small plots—grew stuff none of us had ever heard of."

"I tasted the basil. Down at the pizza place. Your granddaughter talked it up like an ambassador. She's—wow. I didn't know who she was, except she just brought back everything good I remember about the old Big Horn. I should have seen you in her."

Elaine clamps her teeth, fighting memory, then brings herself back. "It was an ugly childhood. I still don't know how to sort the good from the bad. Our father was a tyrant—there's just no other way to put it. I know he just wanted to make sure we were ready for the end-times, but then again religion can turn into a warrant for plain meanness. I want to give our children and grandchildren a real home, a place to live the true gospel in purity and prepare for the Second Coming. I hope it's not just hard work and terror for them, the way it was for me and my sisters."

Elaine represses a shudder. "Hard work is one thing. I don't mind that. We've taught all the children to work. It's the hate for everything outside and beyond the rigors of faith. He just about took a shotgun to Brian once. I told him I was marrying Brian and there wasn't a thing he could do to stop it. He told me he wasn't our kind. He arranged all my sisters' marriages, you know. End of the world came early when I chose my own husband."

Too many catch-up questions. Cassandra chooses carefully. "Second Coming?"

Elaine leans forward in the porch chair to give Cassandra a frank visual assessment. "People are imperfect. Prophecy is perfect. You've left the church, haven't you."

It's been a long time since that question meant as much as Elaine packs into it here.

"I have."

"Not just—inactive? Dormant?"

"No. I left for real. I took my name off the official records. I have a letter from the church offices, somewhere, in my file cabinet, in my own house back in St. Paul, Minnesota, telling me that the Holy Ghost has been withdrawn from my presence and I am now subject to the buffetings of Satan forever."

Dorothy stirs and settles, bobs and rocks.

Elaine enunciates, voice low. "I just don't understand that, Cassandra. I know some terrible things have happened to you, but I've seen some hard things too. Very hard. The church is filled with imperfect people. Humans are filled with darkness.

The universe is chaotic outside God's creation. But you can't let that distract you from the perfect, saving truths of the restored gospel. It's the only possible way to return to the presence of God, beyond this vale of tears. The ordinances of the temple, the vows we make, are the only—the *only*—promise we have that we will be able to live as families for eternity—safe, unthreatened forever.

"After I had children, I understood. Nothing could possibly convince me to abandon the principles of exaltation. I know my children—and grandchildren—have their own agency, and I can't make every decision for them, but I can make sure I set the right example, never wavering, and I can hope that the mercy of the atonement will allow them time to see the light and understand, beyond the trials and uncertainties of this mortal journey."

How many times has Cassandra heard something like this, in how many minimal variations? Any other speaker of it—maybe even Brian—might cause her to stand up and walk home. These same doctrines took her child from her. But Elaine is archetypal. The real thing, if there is one. Cassandra leans forward to meet Elaine's sincere, anxious gaze. Elaine is ethereal, glowing in her version of the Holy Spirit. A Madonna.

Elaine's, and Brian's, ample yard is bordered with daisies and primrose. Lavender, Russian sage, wilting daylilies, Icelandic poppies. Purple flags bloomed and faded at the beginning of high summer; Cassandra can see their tall stalks, mingled with hollyhocks, along the parking strip. Brian—or a protégée—has built a low stone and cement dike around an abundance of sand, littered with toy trucks and plastic creatures. Sandstone walkways, a clear tribute to the passion of Irene Caldwell, guide Cassandra's eyes from one section to another—driveway to front door to arched gate to rows of corn and beans to treehouse to sandbox to the prickly rows of tall raspberry bushes, glistening under the sprinkler's falling water.

"Elaine," Cassandra says. "I'm past saving, if that's your kind intention."

"It's never too late. Not in this world. I know you're a good person. I've always known that. Whatever happened to you in high school was beyond your control. I know that, too. Heavenly Father loves you, and longs for you to come home—here, and in eternity."

"We live in different visions of 'home,' I think. Is that all right with you? I mean, all right enough for me to sit here on your beautiful porch and be—I don't know—your sister-in-law? Your children's aunt? Your hometown friend? For the time being. Mortality, I mean. Before the separation."

Elaine winces as if she's warding off a blow. This woman spent the first two decades of her life in a gauntlet, in a family that made the Soelbergs look like a flock of happy quail.

Dorothy licks at the rim of her water glass like a cat.

"I don't always understand the ways of the Lord," Elaine replies. "The scriptures say God's ways are not our ways. I know he wants us to love the lost sheep, and seek after them, and bring them home. But…"

She trails off. Her face, her tightened shoulders, her legs drawn tightly together and her fingers white as they grip the armrests—Elaine Goddard never was one for easy repartee. She was the purest, kindest girl Cassandra had ever known in the rough child-world of Big Horn. Thoughtful. Otherworldly. Brutally trained to obey. Not stupid in the least. No malice in her, but, then as now, her radiant old-world countenance, one pioneer frock away from Mormon beatific, is undergirded in cast iron.

Cassandra's parents were religious freaks, too, but it's just what they were, like granite was granite. The mountains above them: the world as it was, singular, unreflecting. Elaine's folks—at least Elaine's father—another phenomenon entirely. Nephi Goddard was the kind of man Hal recognized at bone level, deferred to in conversations, uttered certain phrases and ducked his head in either respect or revulsion—synonymous sensations. Nephi Goddard was a Utah Cotton Mather, a freakishly gifted verbal imagist, magma-heat reformer. He kept his wife (wives?) and children in thrall by wielding the flaming sword of God in all places, all hours, and (apparently) every bedroom. The natural world itself a Urim and Thummim, every stone prophetic.

"But, what?"

Elaine takes care to answer truthfully. "Brian is the head of this household. He holds the keys to our family salvation. I promised when I became his wife to honor and obey him. The prophets say that even if a priesthood holder directs his wife to do the wrong thing, she will be blessed for her obedience."

Dorothy bobs, and rocks, open-eyed but elsewhere.

Elaine continues. "Brian is a good man. He saved my life, my capacity to love and trust. He's redeemed everything good about my father's dream, shut out the terrible, and he's unbelievably kind. Sometimes I still wake up, late at night, him breathing beside me, and I wonder when he's going to show me the monster inside him."

"Well, he was kind of made to be one. Elaine, he's been hit, hard, a few thousand times. But he refused it, way back. I saw it again and again."

"I know. Look at him."

Brian has taken off his boots and socks, rolled up his jeans. He stands, fully clothed, soaking wet, straddled over the waving sprinkler, catching each shrieking child who runs toward him, lifting them into flight. Little guy stands at the edge of the spray, buck naked, perfectly mimicking Brian's stance.

"Whose kid is the little boy?"

"Ours, at least for now. The state gave us custody."

"At your age?"

"He's my sister's grandson. His mother—her daughter—is addicted to meth. Was."

"Is she dead?"

"No. Locked up, for now. Went out of her mind last year, nearly died in her bedroom, forgot she had a child in the house with her. He was so malnourished when my sister and her husband broke through the window to find him…I just. I don't know. What in the world. Such a helpless child. The scriptures say, better a millstone around the neck, but I just don't know what to make of it all. That poor mother—my niece—and yet—"

"Where's the father?"

"He has other things to worry about. He has other—"

"—wives?"

Elaine clamps her jaw. Her hands reach to grasp something tangible. "Yes. He's not a particularly terrible man. But he doesn't see up-close child rearing as his responsibility. It's hard to account for plural marriage here in this world, but you know, as I do, that it's the order of heaven."

"Does Brian… ?" Cassandra can't finish the question.

"No. He says I'm plenty. He doesn't like any of that. I'm prepared to share him in the celestial kingdom as I progress in charity and faith, and if he accepts the idea. Maybe I'll be stronger there, but here, and now, I'm grateful he's not ready to enter eternal law."

"Does he believe in it, though?"

"Sometimes I wonder whether he believes in any of the gospel doctrines at all. I don't know if he even believes in God. He never says anything against the faith. He does his job, as a husband, as a father, because he loves us. He really does. I don't know where he found that, where he nurtured it, how he has enough of it, but somehow there's always more. It's not that he's been perfect. He's carrying a lot of pain and anger, and sometimes I think he just wants to give in to it all."

"What would that look like?"

"He could snap a kid in two, if he lost control. He could take me out with one swipe. He could put everything he needs in the back of his truck and disappear. He could pick off a flock of sinners and perverts, one by one by one, and never miss a shot. You know what a man like Brian could do, if he lost equilibrium, clung to one too many grievances, slipped into fever dream—and most of the people I grew up with would see it as God's sanctioned wrath."

"Would you?"

"I don't know."

"Really?"

"God's ways are not our ways. Better to be lost on earth than to be lost for eternity. Better one sinner should die than a nation dwindle in unbelief, is what my dad believed, and he had scripture to shore him up."

"I have to say, Elaine, I'm surprised you're telling me all this. I'm not—I've made it clear, haven't I? I don't want to misrepresent myself. I've tried very hard to leave this kind of thinking behind."

Elaine stands. She leans toward Dorothy. "Mother, shall we go in the house? Who knows who'll be here for dinner. I have a couple of chickens already plucked. Stay and eat."

Dorothy pats Elaine's arm, then pulls her close to whisper something in her ear. But she's already forgotten the secret. Cassandra stands, offering her hand to her mother.

"We can head back," Cassandra says. "You have your hands full already."

"Can you cook?"

"Yes. I'm good at it. And it looks to me like you have a whole farm's worth of great stuff to work with. Do you sell to small-time clients like me?"

Elaine laughs. "Stay and help, then. You know, when I was dating Brian, my mother warned me I was in for trouble. I'd told her he put hot sauce on his eggs and potatoes. She said it was an unmistakable sign of carnality, that I was after a man too sensual and devilish to fix his sights on heavenly promise."

"Well, look at him now. Your mother was right."

Brian approaches, soaked and barefoot, grinning, a squealing child flailing under each arm. He sets them down gentle on the porch. Dorothy flaps them away with her hands. The bigger kids are making their way in, giggling, blue-lipped and shivering.

"Stand right here," Elaine orders. "I'll bring towels."

Manneken Pis stands in the sideways sunbeams in all his glory, fingers in his mouth, eyeing Cassandra.

"What's his name?" she asks Brian.

"Elijah."

Elaine appears with towels, clean and dry. Brian kneels to swaddle tiny Elijah, then lifts him into Cassandra's arms.

"No. Brian. Please," she says, but takes him, and sits back down in the chair. The child leans against her, relaxing in increments like a kitten, then sinks into sleep. Brian and Elaine make eye contact, some prior significance between them.

"Come on, Mama," he says, and Dorothy rises, pleased to take the arm of a strong man. They vanish into the house, behind the screen door. Kids troop in behind them.

Elaine lingers, unfinished.

Cassandra: "What sin has Brian asked you to commit, in his patriarchal role?"

"Not a sin. Just—ambiguous. I admit I prefer clarity."

Cassandra runs her fingers through the little boy's damp hair.

Elaine lays it out: "He says we bring you back into our children's lives. Our grandchildren's. Even though you're an apostate. He says there's no god he'd worship that would keep you from us any longer."

On Elaine's porch, Cassandra has no answer to this.

Elaine finishes, pleading: "If you were an obviously bad person, I wouldn't be so afraid. But you're not. I can see that. So will they."

Elijah's breath stops in a long exhale, then jerks back into motion, resolving into its small right rhythm. Cassandra can feel his sparrow heart through the curve of his back.

"You mean, they won't understand that I'm the wrong person to emulate. That I'll make them think there are other—um—paths. James said something similar when he came to see Mom."

"I think we all travel many paths, but they have to lead us, finally, to the straight and narrow way. To the iron rod, guiding us through the mists of deception."

"And mine leads…"

"Away."

The child breathes on, peaceful in the arms of a sinner.

"I see."

"If you could just show them that you have an open heart. I mean, that you might be able to come back to the faith. Even if you never do, you know? Then—I don't know—the meaning is different. For them."

"As in, they'll think they can save me?"

"Yes."

"A lie, then."

"Well, I don't know if it's a lie. How can I know that? I believe the Lord can still touch your heart."

A lie, then.

Part Five

. . .

Reify

Chapter 36

Dorothy functions now in two settings: agitated / catatonic. This morning she's on a path toward glassy oblivion. She's washed clean, dressed in yet another pastel velour ensemble, and pleasantly scented. She put up a bit of resistance over the diaper—more of a toddler tantrum than an adult woman's appeal to dignity, but the threads of memory have subsided into speechless resignation. Cassandra intended to wash her mother's hair, lengthening and silky gray, but chose the path of least disturbance, twisting it into a neat knot at the nape of her neck. It's Relief Society helper morning. Toni Fuller has remained true to her word. One or two effusive but unreadable women appear on the doorstep every Tuesday and Thursday to sit with Dorothy, allowing Cassandra to run for groceries, take a walk, or drive toward peripheries and yearn for more.

Dorothy's moods—and worsening incontinence—might soon make it impossible to leave her with well-meaning amateurs. Cassandra recalls a scripture about sins being shouted from the rooftops. Dorothy might not be able to climb onto the roof but golly, can she holler. Vivid patches of associative memory. Dream metaphors. Unsettling glints of revelation.

Here's the doorbell.

"It's that boy," Dorothy mutters. "Don't forget. You're in control. The art of seduction is the subtle aroma of girlish helplessness under a veneer of womanly confidence."

"Mom. It's the Relief Society."

Cassandra opens the front door to her mother's feminine ideal, as if Dorothy has called forth a visual aid.

"Hello Cassandra." A tone so complex it might as well be a jazz chord. "I'm here to babytend your mom."

Cassandra backs up to let the woman in, along with a gush of dry late-autumn cold.

She moves like toothpaste squeezed into shapewear. Again with the super-embroidered jeans, Big Horn casual. Suede boots with three-inch heels. She removes a down comforter in the shape of a cropped jacket, some animal's fur at the collar.

"I'm sorry," Cassandra manages. "Are we acquainted?"

"You don't recognize me? I'd know you anywhere."

Memory shuffles like a Rolodex.

"Oh. Kendra! Kendra Price."

"Kendra *White*. It's been Kendra White for a long time now. You're still Soelberg, isn't that right? Did you not get married, or is that a feminist thing?"

"Both."

Kendra narrows her eyes by lifting the corners of her lips. "And here you are, back at your family's place. Must be so hard for you."

Cassandra stands in place.

"Ah!" Kendra fawns. "Sister Soelberg!"

Dorothy lights up as usual when she's addressed in church honorifics. Women here communicate in sublingual bird sounds.

"Remember me, Sister Soelberg?" Kendra Price White coos in Dorothy's direction.

"Well of course I do!" Dorothy responds in the ecstatic certainty of cluelessness. "You should come see me more often."

"Well, here I am," Kendra says. "I see James and Paige almost every day. Such good, *good* people. James is such a devoted counselor to my husband, Bishop White."

"Did you say James?" Dorothy asks.

Kendra raises her voice as if Dorothy had a hearing problem. "Your son James! My husband's first counselor! They built such a beautiful home close to Allan's folks. You know my husband is a developer, right? James and Paige built in one of his subdivisions."

"Oh! Yes."

What's with that? Stockholm syndrome?

Dorothy's eyes drift toward wallpaper seams.

"She can get worked up," Cassandra says. "Trying to remember things. Sometimes familiar names make her brain hurt. But she's settling this morning. She'll probably just sit quiet. You can relax and—read? Or something? Internet is 'Toto,' even though this Dorothy dislikes dogs."

"Huh?"

"I wrote the password on the whiteboard above the kitchen counter."

Kendra looks alarmed. "What if she gets worked up? What am I supposed to do?"

"Call. My cell number. On the whiteboard. Or, you know— summon the devoted counselor."

"What?"

"I'll be back by one."

She overshoots the grocery turn by a quarter mile. She can't make herself go back. She thinks about driving right on to St Paul. Sam could remain in the extra room, nibbling gummies, picking at the guitar, long as he wants.

The car, however, chooses west, showing Cassandra that what used to be sagebrush and mesquite, miles of "nothing" on approach to the west desert ranges, is now one congested intersection after another. How can this dry landscape sustain so many people, so much traffic, so much cheap franchise commerce? Where's the water coming from? Certainly not filthy

Clearlake, choked with carp and algae. She resents it all, here as she sits before another red light, burning gasoline like everyone else, going nowhere for no reason but to boil under the pressure of memory. The light turns green. The car advances another half mile before she brakes for the next red. The far side of the lake, where her father and brothers used to shoot rabbits and coyotes, is one long procession of burger chains, multi-island gas stations, big-box grocery stores. Close-packed subdivisions carpeted with iridescent lawns.

Another light, another long stop, another stream of left turns and multi-lane cattle chutes. Beyond the lake, the stoplights dissipate but subdivisions roll on. She's been driving nearly an hour. She has three more to return to Dorothy, and Kendra White, the woman Hal intended his daughter to be.

Kendra was a plain country mouse from a family so nondescript Cassandra can hardly retrieve a standout memory—at least until Kendra's mother, Marjorie, died of thyroid cancer when Kendra was twelve. Kendra's dad married another indistinguishable woman, a widow with two seriously fucked-up sons, and carried on, now with a couple of extra boys for his own to bully.

"Straightened those half-wits right up," Hal liked to say. What made men hate those boys so viscerally? Something showy and vulnerable about them, like they were asking for it. Mouth breathers. Both stepsons joined the marines the minute they were old enough to make a run for it. Came back to Big Horn wearing full dress uniforms. Everywhere. Cassandra couldn't see it in high school, but her vague, free-floating contempt for the Price family was founded on irremediable discomfort with her own. Mirror families, hometown wallboard: hardworking, shut-mouthed, outwardly bland, inwardly livid, barely middle class. Resentful communist-hating stalwarts. Mormon paranoia splashed like lamb's blood on the lintels.

People raised in Cassandra's class were raised to snipe at one another. Keep each other in place. Snideness a form of intimacy.

"Everything you do," Kendra said to Cassandra after a cupcake decorating extravaganza in the church kitchen, "is you just trying to get attention. You think you're just so talented."

"Everything you do," Cassandra retorted, believing herself clever, "is you just trying."

Once she opens a line of shitty anecdotal memories, the dominoes tip. She's left the last stoplight behind. Now she's driving in relatively open terrain—a rolling gallop between the last jagged range and the next. In college, enamored of maps, bestowed with new eyes for dry West by Professor Linhardt, she memorized evocative names of pop-up ranges stretching beyond the Wasatch Front on into Nevada: Oquirrh. Stansbury. Cedar. Toano. Pequop. Confusion. Spruce Mountain. Ruby. Pinon. Adobe...secret enclosures, lush pockets, minute ecosystems hovering above the cattle- and ORV-ravaged desert valleys.

She drives on, hoping to reach Lookout Pass in time to step out, give the desert beyond a hard hungry gaze, and return through choking traffic before Allan White's wife can accumulate grievances. She turns south on the old Tooele highway, alert to the old mail turnoff coming up on the right. A mile? Ten? She's not sure. This is old, in-the-body navigation.

It comes up quick, marked by a small sign, a cowboy on a running horse—the state signaling the Pony Express Route. She thinks about her brothers. Brian would have been a perfect rider—lean and tough, livid enough to focus on the destination, thrilled to ride. Resigned to the arrows. Matthew, too. He could have been the first woman rider.

"Your brother is a faggot," one of the older girls informed Cassandra, twelve, in the church kitchen one night. "There's something seriously wrong with him."

Cassandra didn't know what a faggot was. Later, at school, she opened the dictionary on the stand in the library. A faggot was "a bundle of sticks and branches bound together."

Funny how religion taught her the truly repulsive vocabularies of bigotry and sex. Word by word. By word.

"Tell your faggot brother to call me," the big girl said, leaning suggestively toward Cassandra, ample cleavage covered with stretchy fabric, as if the little sister might convey an impression to gorgeous Matthew.

"I don't get it," Cassandra said. "A faggot is a bundle of sticks. How is Matthew a faggot?"

The room rang with laughter. Where did girls learn things? Nowhere Cassandra dwelt. All year beyond, every gathering in the kitchen: "Cassandra, I forgot already. What does faggot mean?"

"A—um—bundle of sticks?"

To Matthew, in the bathroom, as they brushed their teeth before going to bed: "Why do those girls call you a f—"

"What girls?"

"The Mia Maids. Cindy and Connie, mostly."

"Oh. Them. Cindy wants me to be her boyfriend. I don't like her."

"Why does she say you're a—fa—"

"I'm not."

"What is it though?"

"A guy who's into guys. A gay guy."

"Oh."

"I like guys who like girls."

Oh.

She knows where boys learned things: In Boy Scout tents, up in the canyons. Out here in sage and cedar desert. Allan White himself had filled her in on the nightly magazine exchanges, tent to tent, busy hand to busy hand. Jerk circles under the stars, in tents around survival candles or lanterns, as scout leaders slept or jacked off in their own tents or RVs.

At Girls' Camp, the leaders slept near the girls they super-vised, emitting close-range rebukes when talk got suggestive, or laughter went too late or hinted of shenanigans. Sure, stolen bras and underwear went up the makeshift flagpoles. Once, Carolyn Ahlstrom streaked buck naked but for her running shoes past the leaders' campfire council, but it was dark and none of the adults understood why the "young women" were laughing in the wild distance. Cassandra recalls a few hushed but informative discussions about the actual size of a penis, once with a water-saturated tampon laid on the tent floor as reference. Karla Heplin snorted at that one.

You guys, it's way bigger than that. You have no idea.

The car hurls dust and gravel. At the base of the hills, the road pitches up into easy curves—this range is low-slung but even so the altitude alters the view. Baffles, reversals, revelations.

She parks at the graceful summit. What a thrill it must have been for a pony rider. Fifteen blessed chilly minutes to gape. Wind strikes in contoured gusts. The harsh grind of pebbled dirt under her soles is a peculiar, calming relief. Late autumn has tilted the light, a diffused intensity magnified against the fuscous ground. Midmorning shadows gesture violettamaniacally westward.

"There's no such thing as blue," a professor once bellowed over her shoulder, poking at her monochromatic canvas, bluing his fingertips. "That's the point of this assignment. Don't ever say that word in my classroom again." The guy was a straight-up ghoul, that species of pedant who attracts girl groupies as he trains sophomores how to learn from self-inflating bombast. To his dubious credit, Professor Bombast had jolted Cassandra toward a new conception of color—an irreversible impression that sensation was just shifting light and generic matter.

He had only meant (she assumed) that *blue* was an inadequate word for an infinite array of hues. The whole semester:

gridded color charts, shade by shade, tone by tone, mix by mix, gradient by gradient. "What is the name of this hue?" he'd ask, poking his thick finger at a random square on the hundredth chart, set on an easel for critique.

Cyan?

Cerulean?

Azure?

Cobalt?

"Delft. Get it right."

There's no getting it right. Out here, implacable expanse: remote, serrated, unnameable hues. Always another tint between every gradation of art class busywork. What color is a certain slant of light?

Despite the sweep and silence, the view is neither empty nor pure. Nor is it a good place to throw away used razor blades. The terrain to the northwest is reserved for top-secret military use, entry forbidden. Out there, they've been incinerating chemical weapons for decades, after concocting them for longer.

Prophets and polygamists and God-eyed ranchers and red-hat henchmen reside out there. Goshute people survive at the shoreline of the increasingly waterless Great Salt Lake. Shoshone families once foraged and ate well—plant-based gourmands in an expanse that now barely feeds the cattle that displaced them. Wild horses, ghosts of Spanish galleons, run their gorgeous legs until the helicopters swoop in.

This desert wind put Hal's mother, Velma, down to nuclear breast cancer. It took a tenth or more of the children who breathed atomic dust on alkali playgrounds in Hal's time. Maybe took Hal out, too, in another way. It likely caused Kendra Price's mother's death; her family from Cedar City chalked it up as their seventh patriotic martyrdom.

Now, Kendra Price awaits in Big Horn with her hostage.

Must go. Wish to stay, to walk in, to lose oneself among the geodes, the topaz, the distant springs teeming with native and migratory birds. The Confusions. Ruby Valley marshlands.

Cassandra returns to her car, rummages for pencil and stray paper. The phone camera would catch it quicker, but it seems important to put a hand to this (Linhardt: *Not to reproduce, but to express*). No paper but grocery receipts, crumpled in the console. A French fry sack. A crate of thick colored sidewalk chalk in the trunk, stashed for a street festival she missed for the sake of a Utah sojourn.

She carries the phone, retracing her steps to the viewpoint. She draws converging Lookout slopes, the gently undulating floor beyond and distant waves of crustal heave, in the gravelly dirt with a stick. She photographs the lines, then makes a point to back over them as she pivots toward return.

Cassandra was uniquely slow to grasp the rigid yet porous contours of paradigm. At fifth-grade camp, built over the remains of an abandoned coal town, Cassandra was a puritan among the pirates. She recalls her visceral dismay when the girls in her cabin—all Mormon, most of them Primary classmates as well as schoolmates—planned a skit for skit night about wanting to "go wee-wee."

"It's not nasty, Cassandra!" Joanna Nelson said, rolling her eyes. "It just seems like it's going to be nasty until the last minute. That's how a joke works. Don't you get it?"

She didn't. She was, in fifth grade and well beyond, an anxious literalist. Why?

Andraya's older sisters Bethany and Catherine—and maybe other sisters, too—had secured husbands by getting pregnant their senior years. Graduation ceremonies one week, weddings the next.

"How else you gonna get situated?" Andraya had expounded to a perplexed Cassandra. "You have to get in there early, or what are you going to end up with? This is the rest of our lives we're talking about. Wanna be last in line in *this* town?"

That seemed to be the marry-off-the-daughter tactic Hal had been banking on, even as he thunderously forbade his daughter to soil her purity. His most eloquent formulation, at the dinner table, poking his fork toward each of his sons, each in turn looking down at his plate (anywhere but toward their sister): "What man in his right mind would pull used gum from under the cafeteria table and put that filth in his mouth? Disgusting."

His face reddened, twisting in revulsion as it did when he was caused to address bodily functions—and to him, as far as his children could tell, bodies were nothing *but* functions. Cassandra incorporated the unequivocal rules, then painfully and gradually learned that equivocations were built into the rules. The paternal vehemence she had interpreted as righteous clarity appears to her now as rage against a power more real than reliable doctrines. Hal was a destitute, possibly banished desert fundamentalist kid trying to work, marry, and reproduce his way up the echelons of Mormon social capital. Marrying Dorothy Caldwell, a pretty girl in an idyllic Utah mountain town, was spectacular vindication of his departure from hard people, hard desert. Hal loved Dorothy—he really did—with the devotion of a man extracted from the grind of generational misery.

Scrambling to preserve her desirability amid disintegrating family reputation, Dorothy loved him back. Lander Caldwell died just dramatically enough to be sanctified by neighbors who knew damn well he was a cheap, small-town Casanova. Dead and buried just in time to miss Irene's petition for divorce, a document so appalling in Big Horn it may have driven Irene out of town, wiped her children off the chart of privilege and propriety.

The material fact of that document, however thwarted in delivery, crumbled to ash in the back-field fire barrel, kept Dorothy as beholden to Hal as he was to her. Forged from secrets, humiliations, and a whiff of mutual blackmail, her parents' marriage was so perfectly constructed it was, to their youngest child, their only daughter, the hard definition of love.

Big Horn Peak hovers in the distance at her ten o'clock. Twenty miles of free-market congestion in the foreground. It's 12:15.

Kendra stands in the front window as Cassandra pulls into the driveway. 1:09.

"You're late," Kendra accuses as she opens the front door. "Don't you think that's inconsiderate, when somebody makes the effort to help you out?"

"I'm sorry. Thank you for your kindness. I know you have places to go. Goodbye, then."

"It's just the principle."

Cassandra, still on the porch: "How was Dorothy?"

"She's fine. She slept in the chair most of the morning. I gave her the sandwich in the fridge just a few minutes ago."

"Mind if I come in?"

"It's your house."

"It's my mother's house."

"Whatever."

Kendra backs up. Cassandra enters, squinting in the altered light. Dorothy sits disheveled, nibbling.

"Did she make it to the bathroom?"

"She has a diaper, doesn't she?"

"Um. Yeah."

"I figured she was set, then."

"She can go to the bathroom if you remind her."

"How was I supposed to know that?"

Cassandra holds back a sophomoric retort, not worth the expenditure. "Kendra, I'm just making conversation."

It's Kendra's long waist, coerced into something resembling its youthful form, that would have allowed Cassandra to recognize her anywhere. A sort of family lean, S-curved—that even the stepbrothers incorporated. Cassandra glances toward the sole family portrait, taken when she was ten by an amateur ward photographer. What marks a Soelberg? Like Dorothy: submissive drop of the chin. Eyes rolled upward in compensation. Like Hal: squared, rigid shoulders. Stiff-backed. No wonder Cassandra fights migraines. Hands balled like retracted claws. Thin upper lips mismatching the lower. Shaded planes beneath arching zygomatics. A little more black point and the portrait could hang in a spook alley.

Dorothy, Matthew, and Cassandra (tightly curled hair, oversize pink collar, buckle shoes) attempting to smile. Hal, James, and Brian holding their mouths expressionless, as if posing for daguerreotype.

"What do you mean, conversation? You and I have so much to talk about there's almost no point in trying."

Wow. Kendra has acquired some presence. Cassandra almost admires it. Big Horn's take on feminism: attack-wives. But, no.

"Right? I can't express my gratitude. It would just take too long, and I know you need to get on with more important things."

Dorothy has dropped her sandwich in her lap. Asleep again. A small snore, which reawakens her. Kendra giggles, distracted, then remembers the callout. She folds her arms, plants her suede boots. "I'm glad you're here to look after your mother. It was about time. But no one needs you stirring up old stories about my husband now that you're back."

"Mom," Cassandra says. "Do you need to go to the bathroom?"

"What kind of question is that? I'm a grown woman."

"I know you are. I'm just asking. I'll go pour you some lemonade."

Kendra follows her to the kitchen. "I'm not joking, Cassandra."

Cassandra leans into the fridge. Locates the pitcher of lemonade. Wrenches ice from the tray and fills a tall plastic glass. Turns full face to the intruder. "What's to stir up, Kendra?"

"You know exactly what. Don't play games with me. You're dealing with a powerful family, and no one's interested in your sob stories."

"Congratulations on your spectacular marriage, Kendra. Hope it's going well."

"No you don't."

"Is it?"

"Is it what?"

"Going well."

Kendra snarls. Or chokes. "It's none of your business how my marriage is going. Allan is the bishop. Everyone loves him."

"Do you?"

"Of course I love him! That's why I'm here talking to you. Your big mouth just about destroyed his reputation back in high school. It's one thing to degrade yourself, Cassandra, but to drag a seventeen-year-old boy into your dirty fantasies is another."

Holy shit.

"Kendra. I didn't want to come back. But here I am, because here my mother is."

"Well, I'm just so happy for you that you have a mother to come home to."

"I'm sorry about yours. I think about her every time I drive past your old house."

"Well, don't. I don't need your pity, and neither did she."

"Don't bring her up, then."

"That's what I'm saying. Don't you bring up your pity-party stories, either. Everyone's gotten on with their lives, you know."

"I've been here since June. It's November. This is the first time we've run into each other, and you did the running in. So, how about follow your own advice and don't stir things up here in my mother's house."

"If you hadn't run to the bishop with your stories, trying to make everyone feel sorry for you after whoring around, I wouldn't have to be here talking about this with you, now would I?"

Cassandra restrains herself from lunging over her mother's Formica counter, which is weird, and weirdly imagistic, since she's never in her life imagined herself brawling it out with another woman. The blue-veined skin of Kendra's neck is blotched, cheeks and forehead at high flush. Cassandra registers hard age and accumulation, the intractable resilience of a Big Horn matriarch. No wonder these women cut their hair like porcupines.

"Kendra. You've got nothing to worry about. Go home to your prestigious husband."

"See what you're doing? So sarcastic. I know what you think about us."

"I try hard not to think about either of you."

"You harbor hate in your heart. You're jealous that I got what you desperately tried to take."

"What. Him? No."

"Oh, so now you're going to tell me I got the bad end of the deal."

"I didn't make any deal at all with you!"

"You know what I really hate about you, Cassandra? The idea of you will always just sort of be around to make me feel like I married a jerk. A hypocrite. A sex fiend."

"A what?"

"You know what I'm talking about."

"Is he?"

"No! Every family has their problems. Men do love sex, you know. It's built into them. You didn't have to blab to the bishop and pull everyone else down with you."

"Kendra, I was sixteen! I was terrified! I was *pregnant*. I got hauled down to the church in my pajamas by my furious father, pushed into the bishop's office to be interrogated for five hours of hell by a whole tribunal, your father-in-law included. They asked me unbelievably detailed questions. I learned more about sex in that meeting than I ever learned in real life since. They told me I was going to outer darkness if I didn't purge my soul. The only thing they *didn't* ask me was the name of the guy who got me pregnant."

"Then how did they know, Cassandra? Why was everyone so sure it was Allan? *How*?"

"I know less than anyone! Why was Allan's father there? Why was my father shut out? I'll bet I have more questions than you do, and I am never, *ever* going to get any answers."

Kendra blinks her magnetic lashes.

Cassandra gives the plastic pitcher a hard shake, maybe to remix the lemonade, and pours over a single cube of ice. She smacks a sippy lid to seal the rim. "Do you want a glass of lemonade, while I'm tending bar?"

"No thank you."

"Got any more questions I can't answer?"

"No. I'm sorry, but I'm just a brutally honest person. You know that. Some people have to finally say what needs to be said. I can't believe I'm explaining this to someone who was raised in the gospel, but I guess you've forgotten your training."

Cassandra feels a migraine coming on, licking at the base of her neck, running threads up her skull. "I have a few questions," she says. "While you're explaining."

"What?"

"Do you have children? Grandchildren?"

"Yeah."

"Are they all okay?"

"All?"

"How many?"

"Five. But three. Living."

Cassandra waits that out.

Kendra resets her face. "We had two little girls. Our first children. It was a long time ago. We left them with Allan's mother for an afternoon."

Cassandra retreats from the counter. Kendra continues.

She's probably told this story at a hundred church firesides. "Little angels. Such darlings. You probably remember that Allan's mom was…umm…"

"Distractible?"

"Um. Yeah. Allan was raised by her, so he couldn't really see her as—you know…"

Chronically depressed? Crazy? Chemically dependent? Out of her league?

Cassandra recalls Sister White on the night of the prom, hovering in the doorway, waving, then wrapping herself in her own arms and fading. The door closing in front of her. Allan's derisive snort.

Kendra flutters her nails on the Formica. "Anyway, Allan wanted to take a little vacation up to the condo in Park City, and he doesn't like to be distracted by kids, and I figured it was just one night…"

"Kendra. You don't have to—"

"So we come back the next afternoon, and it's sunny and pretty hot and really a beautiful day, Allan's in a really great mood, like he gets sometimes, and Allan's mom is just sitting there on the couch, staring at her hands, and then she jumps up to greet us like everything's totally fine, and she doesn't even know, I don't think, that the girls squeezed through the gate at the pool and were already…" Kendra glances out the glass door. "…drowned."

"My god. Kendra. I'm so—"

"I know what you're going to say. You're going to tell me that Allan deserved it, that this was retribution from Heavenly Father to pay for what you say he did to you, but the thing is, those were *my* little girls, and I never did anything to you or to anyone else who got carried away with the whole Me Too victim thing once you went off.

"So, yes, I find comfort in the knowledge that my sweet daughters are in the spirit world with my mother, and that she's looking after them, almost like Allan's mother sent her a gift, and someday I'll be reunited and all will be restored. But you know what? I wanted them in this life." Kendra's eyes are wide, opaque, undiscerning.

"That isn't—Kendra, that's not at all what I was going to say."

"We have three more, two boys and one last girl, but not one of them appreciates my sacrifice and loss. They just roll their eyes when I bring it up, and not a one of them has lived up to what I know those special little girls would have been."

Kendra looks about to spit bile. "I'm so sick of it all, Cassandra. I did everything I was supposed to do and I've stayed faithful to the church and the commandments, and I support my husband and his divine calling and you know what?"

What? *What?*

Is some kind of compassion—at least commiseration—in the works?

Kendra leans over the counter toward Cassandra. "I know everyone suffers. But not all of us run off and leave the church. We don't abandon our families. So, how about you just get over yourself, like the rest of us have to."

Cassandra does not know she still has it in her to be so stunned. She runs thirteen or fourteen retorts / condolences through the brainmuddle before settling on "I'm so sorry about the little girls," which only inflates the fury before her.

"I told you. I am not looking for your pity!"

"Okay then! I don't know what any of this is about, Kendra. It's like you've been arguing with some weird paper-doll image of me for forty years."

"Oh, so now you're calling me crazy? So typical!"

"Typical? Of me? Why do you think you know me?"

"Oh, right. Now you're gaslighting me. Go ahead. Deceive yourself all you want, but my source of truth is the still small voice. I see right through your kind."

"Is the still small voice telling you yet that it's time to go home? Because this is all the private space I've got right now to sit in, and be sinful, and feel sorry for myself. And you're really, really all up in it."

"I came to help you, Cassandra. I really did."

"Well, I think we have very different definitions of help."

"Nothing will really help you until you embrace the true gospel again. Let whoever has eyes to see, see."

"You know what I see here, in front of me? A woman who's been given no comfort at all. At the very least, what we have in common is lost children. If that can't help us—I mean us, specifically, you and me—find some kind of compassion for each other, then—"

"It's not the same! Not the same at all! And if you ever, *ever* try to bring that up around my husband or his family, or anyone who respects that man as bishop of this ward, let me tell you, you've got a whole load of trouble coming your way. Plenty of people have tried. Lies that got started years ago have just taken on a life of their own."

"Plenty of people have—what? Tried what?"

"Tried to claim him as their—" Kendra stops, unwilling to speak the word.

Cassandra can't find a way to help, or stop helping. "What do you mean, plenty? How many is plenty?"

Kendra picks up: "If I've got anything to say that really will help you, it's that. That whole disgusting sordid affair is in the past, and it had better—*better*—stay there. You have no idea, all that's happened since. I feel sorry for your mom and all. I am blessed with a deeply empathetic nature. But you should have stayed clear of this place once and for all. So, now you're here, stay in your lane. I mean it, Cassandra."

"Get out. Please. Now."

"I can't get out of here fast enough. Just remember what I've told you. I'm here to say it gently. You always thought you were so much smarter than everyone else. So enlightened. I went to college too, you know. You think we're just a bunch of sheep around here because we stayed true to the gospel. I know who the real sheeple are, and they're going to ruin this country. Way out of hand. People think they know things. The internet is not evidence, you know. Secular education is a conspiracy, and you know it. It's a whole lot of lies about anything anyone wants to profit from. People do not get to claim fake parents just by looking them up on the internet."

It takes Cassandra a minute to locate the actual message. "Wait. You came to 'say it gently'? Did you come to deliver a threat?"

"Go ahead and twist my words, and reject my kindness, but you'll see what happens if the lawyers step in. They're old hands at this, thanks to you."

"Thanks to me?"

"You and the pack of she-coyotes you stirred up. Fake kids who think he owes them something."

Cassandra can barely hear over the noise in her head. Who is this man? What has he put Kendra through? How many children are out there? What's Cassandra's relationship to these people—*any* of these people?

What kind of parenthood is this? It could have been her kind.

It's the Mormon kind, if Cassandra squints hard enough. One man. Many women. Other women's children, somehow, also, yours in triangulation. Constellation.

"Kendra—"

"Just go to hell, Cassandra. One bad thing happens to you and you think you can just run away from it all. I'm still here. I've been here all along, doing the Lord's work. That's why you don't have anything to look forward to in the hereafter. I haven't lost my babies. They're waiting in the spirit world with my mother and they'll be mine forever. You? One bad thing happens and you forfeit everything. It's about enduring to the end, remember?"

Cassandra can barely hear her own voice, although she might be shouting. "Get out of my—my mother's—house! She's lost children too. She doesn't need any of this bullshit near her, at all, ever again. No wonder she's spent her life cowering. This town is a spook alley. I try to tell myself otherwise, just to survive my own memories, but what a sick, ugly, predatory—"

Kendra emits a little feral scream. Her arm snakes across the counter. The plastic pitcher flies in a spray of lemonade, almost slow motion, then hits the cabinet wall, drops to the counter, and bounces to the floor.

Both women in the kitchen, opposite sides of Dorothy's mustard-yellow counter, are stunned into silence.

Dorothy is crying on the other side of the wall.

"Go to her. I'll clean this up."

"No. Please, just go. I'll take care of it."

Kendra, pale, turns and walks through the gap. Cassandra hears the front door open and close. She leaves the mess to go comfort her mother.

"Mom, how about a nice warm bubble bath."

Dorothy shudders, still crying softly. She lifts her arms like a little girl to let Cassandra remove her sweater.

"It's a cardigan, Mom. Let's do it this way." Cassandra kneels on the floor in front of Dorothy, who sits contrite and sniffling as her daughter releases each pearl-shaped button from its buttonhole. Cassandra sings her a little song as she progresses. A goddamned Primary song, every word still in her memory, intact, just like every other crazy religious detail that made her into whatever the hell she's added up to: *Jesus wants me for a sunbeam / to shine for him each day...*

Dorothy sings with her, high and thin, broken into little breathy sobs: *In every way try to please him / At school, at home,*

at play / A sunbeam, a sunbeam / Jesus wants me for a sunbeam /
A sunbeam, a sunbeam...

Dorothy cries her little cries. Cassandra sings the last line alone.

I'll be a sunbeam for him.

Chapter 37

Funny, that night, almost asleep, Cassandra awakens herself with a girls' camp memory. A Sister Number-One-Camp-Rule memory. Maybe Cassandra's mind is working to block images of dozens of petitioning children.

Campfire. Morning. Bed-head girls gathered to burn toast and cheese on sticks. Girls of every shape and size, point of development, confidence, and bewilderment sat together in the chilly pine-scented air. Voluptuous Sister Christiansen sucked in a public-speaking lungful, opened her mouth. Everyone expected another high-pitched elucidation of a new camp rule.

"So, ladies, want to know how to tell if you're a real woman?"

Gapes all around.

Sister Christiansen chortled. Cassandra caught a glimpse of something wild, unhinged, in the amplitude of amply-covered flesh. The woman stood up to pantomime.

"So, you take off your bra. You take a pencil and tuck it in under your boobs. Then you jump up and down three times. If the pencil's still there at the end, you're the real thing!"

The camp girls and their leaders watched, speechless, as Sister Christiansen laughed so hard she couldn't stand up anymore.

"Let's try it," Kendra (still flat as plywood) said, leaping to her feet.

"Kendra!" Sister Peck rejoined. "Sit down now! It's just a silly joke!"

But that night, in the tent, braless boobs under T-shirts. Pencils and pens. Quarters. Shoelaces. Wild laughter. Dead silence from the leaders' huddled tents, twenty feet away.

Chapter 38

Cassandra's returns to Big Horn slowed and then nearly stopped after her first two years of college. Small nieces and nephews induced panic. She refused to learn their names.

"No," she answered flatly, Christmas afternoon, when Paige asked Cassandra to hold a saturated blob of an infant while she ran to the car for a diaper bag.

"James!"

"Wow," James intoned. "Some people aren't made to be mothers."

"Fuck you, James," Matthew said, fully Matthew, taking the redolent child from Paige's arms. "How can you say something like that to Cassandra?"

Dorothy: "Matthew!"

James: "I'm just saying. She's got no maternal instincts. Good thing she—"

Hal, roaring out of the Cozy Room: "Say that again in my house and see where you land!"

"What I said?" Matthew inquired. "Or what James said?"

"That word. Your mother is right here. Don't you have any respect? Little children, hearing that kind of thing. Don't play stupid with me. Get out."

"I'm busy holding Paige's baby. What word, Dad? *Mother*? *Maternal*?"

"It's my baby, too," James said.

"Why aren't you holding him then?" Matthew bounced James's baby in his lean maternal arms as he swiveled to turn his back. Hal wound up like a pitcher and threw his hot chocolate mug. Everyone watched it sail over Matthew's head and shatter against the brick fireplace. James stood slack. Dorothy faded back into the kitchen.

Hal snarled, maybe to Cassandra, "Clean that mess up," and stalked back to his lair. The TV volume raised itself in fury.

Paige came in with the diaper bag, dusted with snow. "What's the matter?"

Brian opened the bathroom door, a Dickensian ghost half-obscured in steam. Hips in a towel skirt. Muscle and clean sinew. "Cassandra."

She returned to her body, in its standing place. "What."

"He's okay."

"Who?" Paige demanded. And then, "Oh."

Brian: "Want to get out of here? Get your coat. Let me get dressed."

Elaine, Brian's new wife, pregnant herself: "I'll take care of it."

"Come with us?"

"No. I'll help Dorothy with dinner until you're back."

In Brian's truck, heat on, snow falling, he said, "Almost three, isn't he?"

"Next month."

"Maybe it's snowing where he is, too."

Cassandra kept her face toward the window.

"Canyon?" Brian inquired.

"What?"

"Desert?"

"Can you maybe take me back to Logan?"

Silence.

"I know. Never mind. That's four hours for you."

"I don't mind. I'll need sandbags, I think, for Sardine."

"I'm just panicking. Really, it's okay."

"Is your car up there?"

"Yeah. I came down with friends. Grandma's Dart does not love the snow."

"Do you have your stuff packed?"

"It's in my room. Just have to zip it up."

He opened his door. "I'll be right back," and he was, Elaine beside him, smelling of chocolate. Brian set Cassandra's duffel under the camper shell, then helped Elaine heave herself up and sideways onto the bench seat.

"We'll go by Goddards for sandbags," Brian said.

"And I'm happy to go home and sleep," Elaine said. "You guys have no idea how heavy—" She faded off, remembering.

"When are you due?" Cassandra asked.

"Three more months."

"Long time still."

"How did you survive it, Cassandra? All alone like that."

Hal busted out the front door, in his slippers, waving his arms and shouting.

"Let's go," Brian said, easing the stick shift between Elaine's knees into reverse. "Bye Hal. Merry Christmas."

Pulling up to the Goddard place, Cassandra murmured, "I don't know if I did."

Chapter 39

As always, Logan was a good twenty degrees colder than Big Horn, and the snow was coming hard and sideways. The green brick of the little bungalow was coated in white.

"This is a cute place," Brian said. "I didn't picture college like this."

"I live in the basement. A little dark, but it's way better than the dorms. I took over the contract when my friend moved back to Sacramento."

"What friend?"

"Just this guy."

"What guy?"

"What are you, Hal?"

"No. I want to know something about your life here."

Even though this was Brian, Cassandra felt a certain resistance to bleeding the line between this life—increasingly *her* life, an isthmus to a future that might await—and the life that Brian's presence, in this truck, represented.

How to express it to him?

"Well, I had this huge crush on him, and he was a nice guy, but he graduated and I think he just wanted to go back to California world. You wouldn't like him. Hippie type."

"Aren't they all hippies in college?"

"No. Lots of cowboys. This is an ag school, remember?"

"Why would you go to college to learn to be a cowboy?"

"I don't know. I'm not majoring in cowboy stuff."

Brian grinned. "Maybe you should, little mustang."

Cassandra said, "Turns out cowboys can dance, though. They're wilder than the hippies. Cowboys drink. Hippies smoke weed."

"What was your hippie studying?"

"Watershed science. So he actually hung out with the ag people. Especially the rancher guys."

"What, like environmentalist bullshit?"

"Irrigation stuff, I guess. But he played the piano, too. Water and Chopin."

"Why do they even talk to each other?"

"Because they're all worried about water. People talk to each other at college, kind of."

Brian raised his eyebrows. "Yeah. Okay."

Cassandra considered, and then offered, "Want to come in? It doesn't take long to warm up."

"I'll come in with your bag. Ought to get home to Elaine."

"Will you tell Mom I'm sorry about missing Christmas dinner?"

"No. Because you shouldn't be."

She laughed.

He said, "Go get the door opened up. I'll bring your bag."

He couldn't make himself enter beyond the threshold. He stood in the doorway like a polite vampire, taking it in. The tiny kitchen. Her ten-speed bike against the wall. Easel, with a sketched-over canvas, and paint tubes and charcoal, and tomato cans holding pencils.

"You're going to live a very different life than the rest of us, Cassandra."

Brother and sister *hoverrred*, divided by a widening gulf.

Brian: "Grandma. Do her proud."

He turned, climbed the concrete stairs to ground level, and his form lost focus in the snow.

"Go safe," she called, drowned out by the weight of storm and Brian's revving engine.

Chapter 40

Classes did not begin for another week, but the painting studio was open. The winter light falling from the clerestory windows would be electric blue and wonderfully strange. The sky was vibrant above thigh-high glitter on the ground. Frigid but gorgeous walking. Books and supplies awaited at the campus store.

Cassandra layered herself like a survivalist to hike the notorious college hill. Her throat and lungs burned in the below-zero atmosphere, but she felt strong and almost optimistic, as if she were at the beginning of something. Recalling the unbearable, timeless weight and distortions of pregnancy only made her marvel. How could this be her own body, here, now—after—

Enough. Walk in this sunlight. Breathe this air (what hue? Creamy, creamy...say it: *blue*).

She turned east a block before campus proper, skirting the usual route so she could linger along the pioneer-era trees. The city cemetery just north of campus looked like a miniature gothic town, snow-capped gravestones in tiny districts under the burdened trees. It probably wasn't plowed, but she was wearing boots. She could cut through.

Beyond the gate, moving among the graves but slowing: Elodie Linhardt. Cassandra stopped, disconcerted, as if she'd chanced across her elegant and articulate professor in the underwear section of a department store. Linhardt was draped in a long black wool coat, a turquoise scarf wrapped thick around her neck, extending over her head like a medieval hood. Professor Linhardt didn't look like anyone Cassandra knew, in any part of her life. On campus she was striking but less out of place, usually camouflaged by a painter's apron, dark hair pulled back or high. Present, attentive yet reserved, and no less fascinating to her students because of it.

In the snow she looked like a softened gravestone angel. A Pre-Raphaelite Ophelia drowned in blinding white.

Cassandra reared back, intending to disappear and reroute, but instead she watched. Linhardt stopped in front of a snow-covered headstone. She leaned forward and down, graceful as a dancer, reaching her leather-gloved hands to clear the inscription. She took something from an upper pocket—small and clearly precious—and laid it on the grave.

Cassandra feared if she moved it would look like she'd been spying.

If she didn't, it would still look like she was spying.

She considered stepping forward, striding at full pace all casual and oblivious, hoping it would seem she'd just happened onto the path. Linhardt, wary in some intimate ritual, must have sensed the intention. She lifted her head as if she'd caught a scent.

"Oh. My god. You startled me. Cassandra, is that you?"

"I'm so sorry. I didn't mean to—"

"Are you heading for the studio? Me too. I'll walk with you, if that's where you're going."

Her teacher's graciousness took Cassandra off guard every time. Unmasked kindness among women confused her. Women were competitors in the world she'd inhabited. Exhibits of affection were betrayed, exploited, rebuked. One year a fanatical (and very apparently frustrated) bishop had nixed all plans for the annual girls' camp. "It's just too risky. Girls of this age have strong lesbian tendencies. They won't be getting all enamored of one another on my watch."

Which of course illuminated the most terrifying implication of woman-to-woman kindness: it was exciting, causing Cassandra to wonder whether there was something fundamentally wrong with her (although, had she thought about it more cynically, her interest had just been described, by the bishop no less, as typical). For years it had troubled her, sometimes to the point of panic, that her galvanizing memory of that horrific Sunday afternoon in the unwed mothers' home—of all things (Trudy's blood spreading across the floor, the virtually imprisoned girls, the oppressive parody of "home," the stunning incapacity of supposed caregivers; the likelihood that neither Trudy nor her child had survived), was the nearly erotic jolt of witnessing Lori Ann's solicitude, one woman leaning over another in a position of tender, heedless, urgent love.

And here, now, Professor Linhardt, with the incomprehensibly beautiful foreign name: "Call me Elodie, if you wish. Almost no one here calls me by a personal name."

She had stepped away from the headstone, regathering her professor demeanor as she addressed a familiar but intruding student.

Cassandra was surprised. "Don't you have any family here?"

Linhardt gestured toward the headstone.

Cassandra: "Oh. I'm sorry…"

"No need."

The vision of Elodie Linhardt, reaching for presence but lost in the filtered light beneath the glittering lattice of planted Utah cemetery trees, draped wool a flat negative shape against the snow, long black hair not quite contained in turquoise: overwhelming. At the threshold of her own adulthood beckoning across the bridge from her dismantled adolescence, Cassandra saw her as old. Late thirties? There were not more than fifteen years between them, but Linhardt projected an image Cassandra could not dream of resembling. This woman was not a mirror of some possible future but an exoticism, an inconceivably *other* thread of genetic making. Cassandra's Utah-bred eye for human line and stance could not absorb her, except in aesthetic associations.

Proserpine. Leda. Annabel Lee.

What does it mean to safeguard the memory of such a private, unintelligible, intense interim of desire? The image of her long-ago professor has by now been re-rendered a thousand times in Cassandra's art, a stock figure, sometimes a convenient space-filler, a reliable conduit for depicting pathos.

Memory is a running palette.

"Whoo-ee, girl," the beloved polymorphous man currently guarding her house, sleeping in her bed in a city of water and craton, said to her as he leaned in to appreciate the layered light and color and shadow on her working screen. "You got a hard-on for that lady. Who even is she?"

"What lady?"

Sam leaned in to point: one tiny figure in a landscape of cliff and canyon, an embedded ancient city of tomb-shaped dwellings, Canaletto clusters of busy dwellers going about their little days.

"That one," he grinned. "That's someone you have truly loved."

"Not that way."

"Not what way?"

Even now, she cannot answer that question. She's slept with women and with men. She's settled in and lived with some of them, most of whom she continues to love in their ways and hers.

"You don't know how to love anyone," one of them accused, years ago, cutting and final. "You think you do, but you're too damaged to understand how deficient you are."

What is love, if not simply a road taken that makes a little difference?

What is hate, then?

What.

...

Elodie Linhardt was dead before the glacier lilies signaled impossible spring. Dead a year before Cassandra graduated with Linhardt's recommendation in hand—the sealed letter that opened the mysterious portal into graduate school, opening yet another portal into a livable professional life, a community, a release into a selfness she could never have perceived nor explored, reducing the stony skylines of Big Horn to myth and vaulted memory.

A life that became her.

The life she does not know how to bring back to a world that cast her out, as if she were a devil.

Maybe when (if) Matthew DeLuca returns—the man who is not her son, but the man who stands in the absence of her son—she will ask him to drive with her to the cemetery in her college town to leave an offering (a lily? A brush? A sketch?) on a mother's grave, set beside her child's.

A personal note, handwritten, paper-clipped to the sealed recommendation Linhardt left in Cassandra's studio cubby with the meticulously graded semester portfolio:

Please do not emulate my departure. I know your grief is beyond enduring, but certainly your child lives somewhere, in this world. Live until he can return to you if that's what return requires. Your loss requires you to wait, even if he cannot arrive.

My loss requires me to wait no longer. My daughter cannot return to me. I don't believe I can go to her, but I know I can't stay here.

Cassandra, wait. And, while you wait, live.

—E.L.

Chapter 41

Dorothy has not ceased crying since Kendra White stormed out and slammed the door.

Cassandra calls Toni Fuller to cancel this morning's Relief Society relief.

"Let's just drop both visits this week," Cassandra says. "She's not doing well."

"Is she sick?"

"No. Emotional."

"Is your family helping out?"

"Brian sends his kids and grandkids over. And he comes when he can."

"How about…never mind. Will you let me come?"

"Now?"

"Ten o'clock?"

"Dorothy might cheer up a little. But I won't leave you with her."

"What can I bring for you?"

"I'm good."

"We'll see."

It's not that she's wailing. She huddles, wrapped in her own arms, and sniffles, eyes wet or spilling. She builds toward little pitches of quiet sobs, then subsides, but never stops.

"Mama, are you warm enough?"

"Who are we talking to?"

"You. I'm here, Mom, talking to you."

"Don't be ridiculous."

"I can make hot chocolate."

"I just need a good cry."

"You can cry while you sip. Want to come to the kitchen table? How about toast and scrambled eggs?"

"Hot chocolate." Dorothy looks up, beseeching. "My cup runneth over."

"I'll put a sippy lid on it. It will be fine."

"Here."

"Yes. You can sip it right here in this soft chair. I'll open the curtains so you can see the mountains. A little snow up there at the summits, thank goodness."

"We'll need the water."

"Yes."

But Dorothy does not lift her eyes unto the hills.

Toni rings the doorbell, ten o'clock.

Toni and Cassandra sit on the sofa regarding Dorothy, who holds her sippy mug and cries.

"Sister Soelberg," Toni inquires, gentle. "Is something hurting you?"

Dorothy grimaces, painlike, but does not reply. She extends her right arm, lukewarm chocolate in her hand. Cassandra takes it from her and sets it on the floor.

"Don't spill on my nice carpet," Dorothy says, toneless. Cassandra picks it up and carries it to the kitchen sink. She returns to the set. Dorothy twists a paper tissue in her hands, dabbing at her cheeks.

Toni looks tired—who knows what she carries—and flabbergasted. "Cassandra. How in the world are you holding up here?"

"I don't know. How about you? Wherever 'here' is in your life?"

"I don't know. It's a bad season for a lot of people. Ugly world."

"You."

Toni keeps her eyes fixed on Dorothy, but answers Cassandra. "My son. Not well. We checked him into the psych ward last week."

"The missionary? St. Paul boy?"

"Yes."

Cassandra sits again, close enough for a fingertip reach toward a grieving, frightened mother. Toni stiffens to fortify, then releases a long, ragged sigh.

"He tried to kill himself. Almost succeeded."

Dorothy shudders and holds.

"Toni," Cassandra says. "I'm so sorry."

"Hank doesn't want anyone to know. Doesn't want it to turn into ward business."

"I'm not the ward."

"I know. Thank you for that."

Dorothy says, "Of course, my dear. You're welcome."

Cassandra says, "Stay a little, if you can put up with the crying. I'm already in the hot chocolate business."

Dorothy resumes her cadence of choking and sniffling, quelling a dire whimper every fifth or sixth off-measure.

"It's like water torture," Cassandra mutters, and Toni erupts in a quick laughing snort of a sob.

"Lay that hot chocolate on me," she says. "I could use a stiff drink."

"I can make it stiff as you want. But you might lose your church job."

Toni rolls her eyes in mock bliss. "I'm close enough to taking you up on that, you probably shouldn't offer."

"Swiss Miss it is, then. Neat. Sippy cup, or coffee mug?"

Toni smiles, wan. "Mug. I'll try not to spill on Dorothy's nice carpet."

"Can you visit him?"

"Not yet."

"When?"

"I don't know. I'm not getting a lot of communication. He's an adult, so it's up to him."

"How old is he?"

"Twenty-three."

"You have other kids too, don't you?"

"Yes, but that doesn't make up for—"

"I know. Not why I asked. Are they doing all right?"

"Far as I know. I mean, nobody's really okay, are they? But the other ones don't seem to want to be—" Toni trails off.

"Mmmm. Yeah. Can I ask a little more?"

Toni takes a long slow sip.

Cassandra steps in further, careful. "Did you come as a Relief Society president? Or as a—you know. Friend."

Toni removes her glasses. She retrieves a tiny spray bottle and a square of soft yellow cloth from her purse. She takes a moment, almost ritualistic, to wipe the lenses clean. She puts the glasses back on. Her eyes, behind light mascara, are rimmed red. "I don't really know how to separate those things anymore. Being Relief Society president gives me a certain license—or courage, or assertiveness, or maybe it's gall—to interact with people in sort of personal ways. It's not the kind of thing I do as just myself."

"Well, that makes sense. But that also means you do all the listening, and all the fixing."

"That's easier for me than unloading. Trusting someone else. I don't see why anyone would trust me with their own confidences if I didn't have the title. I doubt I'd have it in me to take them in, if it weren't my calling—I mean, sorry, my church assignment. I've thought about that a lot. I know you aren't a believer, but it's that part of the church that appeals to me. I need structure to be a better person."

Toni reconsiders. "Maybe structure isn't the right word. I think I mean permission."

Cassandra waits Toni out. Dorothy gurgles and drips like a slow-leaking faucet.

Toni: "And now I'm waiting for permission to try to comfort my own son. To be with him. Permission from Hank and the other kids. From the bishopric. The case worker. Tanner himself."

There's nothing to say. Dorothy ups the crying.

Toni gathers herself. "Thank you," she says, and stands. "Dorothy, mind if I borrow a tissue?"

Dorothy offers the crumpled blob in her hand.

"Mom!" Cassandra reaches over her mother for the box.

"Come back," she says to Toni. "When you need more."

"Wait," Toni says. "I did come as Relief Society president. At least that was my intention. What triggered all this crying?"

"Next stage of dementia, I guess. Mostly."

Toni looks dubious. "I heard you had a visit from the bishop's wife."

"You're way too close to all that. You don't need any more of it. Neither do I."

"Apparently, neither does your mother."

"I don't know what's cause and what's effect anymore. I don't know how much she comprehends. I just think the walls are crumbling. Everything she's been holding in is leaking out. Literally."

"Poor woman."

Dorothy drops a grenade: "Oh, why don't you just go to hell, the lot of you."

Toni and Cassandra step back in surprise.

"Whoa. What's that, Mom?"

"You can eat shit for all I care."

"Me? Me personally?"

Toni busts out a laugh, then recomposes her face. "My goodness, Sister Soelberg. You really are tearing down the walls, aren't you?"

"You people come in here, take whatever you want, tell me what I can and can't do in my own house. Go ahead, take it all. I'm done with it. Just leave me alone."

"Mom—"

"Who the hell are you? Get out, or I'm calling my father. He knows damn well who you are. He owes you nothing."

Dorothy bares her teeth, pokes holes in the air with an accusing finger.

She drops her hands into her lap. Her head bobs in fatigue. She shudders, picks up the crying right where she left off, and subsides as she drops into sleep, head back, jaw sprung.

Cassandra rubs the back of her tightened neck. Toni straightens herself on the sofa.

"Wow," Cassandra says. "That's a new development."

"Well, it's not anything any one of us doesn't need to say every so often."

Cassandra titters like a delinquent, pitching into full laughter as if she's just registered the punch line of a dirty joke. And now she can't make herself stop.

In the subsiding heaves, Toni manages to say, "I know they took your baby."

Cassandra stops.

Toni says, "I might as well be direct. Secrets aren't ever really secrets around here, as I'm sure you know. Things have a way of coming up."

Cassandra speaks, cold for the sake of containment. "Did you just find out? Or have you known all along?"

"I knew you'd been sent away. I knew your brother Matthew was gone, too, but I didn't know why."

Both women glance toward Dorothy, indubitably asleep.

Cassandra: "How much do you know about Matthew?"

"Gay?"

"Not exactly."

"People say he was a cross-dresser." Toni wipes her glasses one more time. Hands Cassandra a frank stare, watching for cues. "Is it okay to be having this conversation?"

"I don't know. Am I talking to the church, here, somehow?"

Toni purses her lips. "No."

Cassandra stands up. "I do better with this kind of thing if my hands are busy. Is that all right with you?"

"Of course."

Cassandra goes to Matthew's bedroom to find paper. Clips a few sheets to Masonite. A good sharp pencil, and an X-Acto to keep it that way.

She returns to Toni, and to Dorothy, murmuring in her chair.

"Okay. At least part of Matthew is Matilda. The pregnancy, and the pretty horrible late-night taking away, maybe shook something out in him once and for all. Her. My father had to find a way to come to terms with a son who kept transforming into a daughter by blaming the real—I mean the other—daughter."

Toni sits attentive.

Cassandra asks her, "Did you know my father?"

"No. He died before we moved here. What year was it?"

"Nineteen ninety."

"He was young. How did he die?"

"He was fifty-six. They said heart failure. I never got the details. Collapsed out in his tool shed. More of a workshop, but that's what we called it. Fell against—I don't know. Something hard, or sharp. Table saw? He had a big one in there. He'd already told me a few years before to get out and never come back—the last time I came home from college to try to be a good daughter. Sister. I'd skipped Christmas, because it just never went well, but it was President's weekend, January, and there was a storm, so I couldn't leave on Monday afternoon the way I'd planned. I was worried about missing classes, and fed up with Dorothy, and mad that I was stranded with Hal—my dad—in the middle of some saga between him and my brothers.

"I couldn't follow it all because it had been going on for quite a while. But that night Matthew had some kind of psychotic breakdown and ran away into the mountains. My brother Brian went after him. The whole town pretty much mobilized, a lot of the men went up on horses, everyone excited in the drama. But they turned back in the weather and darkness. Brian kept going."

Toni looks like she's assembling fragments. "What about James?"

"Dad said, 'Let the little faggot run,' and James was too afraid to defy him. Sometimes I really resent him, Toni, but he was the oldest son, and he looked most like Hal, and he'd been berated and bullied his whole life by the man he worshiped and wanted to please. I'm tired of trying to pin blame on anyone. James is James. Brian is Brian. Matthew is Matilda."

She pauses. "And Hal was Hal. I think there's a point in everyone's life where we just stop becoming anything but what we already are. Spend the rest of our breathing time preserving that."

"So, you were pregnant at the time?"

"No. I got pregnant way before that, at the end of my junior year in high school."

Toni flushes. "Oh."

"I missed my senior year. Sent off to some Dickensian unwed mothers' home in Washington. Delivered that January."

"Boy?"

"Yes. But I never saw him."

"Cassandra…"

"You know? Not sure I can keep going on that part. So, Matilda made a run for it. Brian went after him. I didn't know until a little while ago that Brian had lost a finger—and part of another one—to frostbite. My brothers, even James, are made for the mountains. More than most men who only wish they're Jeremiah Johnson. Brian is the toughest of all of them, but Matilda outran him. Both were more or less in town clothes—Brian in cowboy boots and a fleeced jean jacket. Matilda was wearing our mother's long Sunday coat, which might have been what had set Hal off.

"I think Matilda pushed right over the summit, up near the Divide. Must have spent some nights in a snow cave. I don't know. In any case, Hal turned on me, told me never to bring my sniveling female self-pity anywhere near his house or his family again, and I went out in this old car I had from my grandmother, chugged my way back up to college in a blizzard. Went off the road near Mantua, spent a few hours wrapped up in the sleeping bag I kept in the back seat thinking it would be fine to be dead anyway, got pushed out by some tired cops after the plows went through."

Cassandra stops, abrupt, stunned at the vividness of memory, surprised she's sitting here in Dorothy's white-carpeted living room gushing to a relative stranger. A Mormon Relief Society president.

Toni sits very still.

Cassandra's story resumes in the same way it paused, without volition.

"Much as I don't want to sympathize with Dorothy, who was too spineless to stand up for herself or for us, I can look back now and see that she lost her two youngest children the same night, after a long arc of capitulation and misery."

Toni murmurs but holds position.

Cassandra's hand moves around the paper, closing in on the negative space her mother's figure defines. A hole in the universe, the shape of Dorothy Caldwell Soelberg: evacuated and compressed, dissipating yet indissoluble. Dorothy as—what?

Carapace. Den.

Empty womb.

Tomb.

"The night Hal threw me out for good," Cassandra says, tired, wishing to finish, "I gathered up whatever I could pick up from my room—a few clothes in a bivy, stuff I'd been working on for my classes. Pens and brushes. Left a whole portfolio of ink and watercolor and graphite stuff. I've never been in that room since.

"I put on my coat and boots, carried it all out in one load, shoved it all in the back seat of the car so it wouldn't get wet. It was dark, and snowing hard, and I was out there trying to clear the windows enough to get in and pull away, wondering whether I should go back in for the stuff I forgot, but then Dorothy comes bursting out of the house.

"She's wearing irrigation boots, her legs are bare, she's been fluttering about in a flowered housecoat over her temple garments all evening amidst the panic, the comings and goings after Matthew, and she's managed to put on a plastic rain bonnet in her rush to get out and reach me. She's crying, and sort of pleading for me to come in and apologize to Hal, to let it go and he'd welcome me back—but she had to know it was all over. She reached toward me, grabbed my jacket, and I shoved her away. She wobbled in those big rubber boots, backpedaled, went down in the snow. Hard."

Cassandra pauses to regard the cocooning figure in the soft living room chair, breathing softly, mouth open like death. Dorothy's eyes flicker and roll under the onionskin lids. She's wrapped tight in a knitted afghan.

Toni reaches to smooth Dorothy's hair. Dorothy's hand reaches to her own face, palm open, to pat her own cheek the way she might have once, maybe, thought to comfort a frightened toddler.

Cassandra: "Maybe that's why she's always convinced it's cold."

"Well, keep her warm."

"Hal came out. He stepped over Dorothy to get to me. He grabbed me by the arm, hauled me around to the driver's door and pushed me in. He told me he'd be waiting with a shotgun if I ever tried to pull into his driveway again. At that moment I was sure I deserved it. Maybe I still think so—pushing my mother down into the snow, on the night her boys were on the mountain, lost—it's the worst thing I've ever done. Ever. The truest sin.

"And the next day, after all that time in the car, in the canyon, wondering if I'd end up like—well, this girl who died in high school on a snowy road, down near the freeway entrance in Clearlake—I get back to my apartment, I'm shook up and wrecked maybe even more than the time I got hauled off because I was pregnant. I hated everyone and everything, and I'd lost someone I cared about up there on campus, and I was considering ways to just—just, you know, end it. And I reach into my coat pocket and there's a twenty-dollar bill in it. My mom came out in the snow to give me money, because she knew—I don't know what. She just went with the only protective impulse she had left, and I shoved that helpless, desperate, pathetic woman into the snow.

"No better than anyone else. Mean as everybody." Cassandra restrains the urge to tuck her head into her arms, to curl up embryonic, by stroking the page, blizzarding and altering the maternal form. She stands up, strides into the kitchen, pauses at the sliding glass doors to gulp in rooflines, foothills, low clouds, a little sky. Beauty and hate.

She returns to speak to Toni, or to her mother, but only from the gap between the rooms. "My brother wrapped himself in her clothing—her long coat. In his sympathy, he stepped toward her, into her. Became her. What's that line? *Greater love hath no man than this.* I spent my life making sure I never understood her at all, didn't resemble her in any way. I shoved her into the snow just as she managed to do one thing—one defiant, courageous thing—to claim me, protect me beyond the point of no return."

Cassandra can't see her mother's body from where she stands. Toni, on the sofa, wary and still, is a partial figure beyond Dorothy's chair.

Toni waits to make sure Cassandra's story is finished. She speaks, barely audible. "Well, here you are. Returned to her."

Cassandra answers, clear in her own wisdom for once. "Go to your boy. Even if you can't see him. Be near. A mother does not need permission to wait."

Dorothy's breath is ragged, but she sleeps.

Toni whispers, "Thank you." She exits quietly, so as not to awaken the diminishing figure in the encompassing chair.

Chapter 42

An email from Matthew DeLuca.

Cassandra lets it sit unclicked until late afternoon, beyond Dorothy's tearful encounter with a grilled cheese sandwich. Now Dorothy is, off schedule and de-alphabetized, settled into Hal's recliner in the Cozy Room, clean and dry, mournfully absorbing the sensations of *Camelot*.

Cassandra sets herself at the kitchen table. Opens her laptop. She hovers the pointer over DeLuca's message.

18 January 2020
Cassandra,

I hope you're doing well out there in Brigadoon. I've come back to the keyboard almost every day since I left, thinking to write to you, but I haven't been able to collect my thoughts. Today I decided to let myself send whatever words come.

Much research, a lot of correspondence, a few phone calls. A couple of days ago I had lunch with a guy who's tracking down half-siblings from a sperm-donor father. He's up to twenty-seven. It freaked me out, to tell the truth. It made me ask myself (yet again) what I think I'm up to with my own pursuit. What do I think I'm accomplishing? Why stir up answers that alter nothing? Or, maybe worse, alter everything?

I don't know what I'll end up writing. I have too much

information, and too little, for the feature piece, but I'll come up with something that satisfies the assignment. Just a weird trip to Utah seems exotic enough around here to print. Adventure amidst the Mormons. An old formula, I realize. Me and Mark Twain.

But I'm shaken up. My parents have both made it clear that they've said all they ever will about our family inception. I'm surprised that it's my dad, even more than my mother, who doesn't want me to go further. He says, what's the point in knowing who it was got a little heated up a long time ago? What's that got to do with us now? Leave the fanatics to their soul-sucking business.

It's a good question, and I'm guessing you might have some opinions on what it's got to do with anything, but hell. I can see from this distance that showing up to ask you anything at all was a barbaric intrusion. I'll understand if you just delete this message. But, Cassandra, I hope you'll answer.

I sent an inquiry. Not personalized, just a notice through a lawyer, to LDS Social Services, saying I'm willing to communicate with either of my birth parents. It's sitting now in my adoption file. Nothing so far from the mother, but I received a stern legal form letter from the paternal side forbidding speculation or contact.

Screw that guy. I've felt a little like Tantalus all along, but this adventure has never been about genetic recovery. I don't know what I'm reaching for. I don't understand what I've been wanting all this time. All my life. Does everyone fantasize about alternative lives, other possible selves, or is that just an adopted kid thing? I have a lot of questions, but when I write them out I don't understand why they matter. Do I really want to know that in some other rendition I'd be rolling coal off a lift kit pickup and wearing a MAGA hat? Or hating myself—and my poor Mormon wife—every time I get hard for a man? Is it reassuring to know that the father who raised me is a better man than the one who set me going like a nervous stopwatch?

What if I meet my birth mother and she hates everything I've become? Or that she hated me from the get-go? What if I don't like her any more than she likes me? What would that mean? I tell myself it's just intellectual curiosity, but the longer I'm away from Utah, the more afraid I am to come back.

All of this hurts more than I ever imagined it would.

Jose and I hope to raise a child, maybe two. And then we don't. On some level it seems urgent to claim a whole generational responsibility for the kids we've all, in some way or another, abandoned to a wrecked future. Then again, thanks to my own history, and learning some of yours, I'll always wonder if we're stealing, and what kind of karmic reaction might ensue.

Can I send you some questions? You can answer, or not. Pick and choose?

Here's a start: How's my girl Dorothy?

Here's the second: What are you painting?

I looked up your website. I've been tracking your work. Showed it to my mother. Do you know that everything you paint echoes the shape of the mountains? I mean the Big Horn ranges. Of course you do. I don't want to say anything cheap. My god. Do you talk about that stuff, or is it off limits?

Cassandra, I hope you're well. I wouldn't blame you if you told me to fuck off and meant it this time. But please don't. I told Jose that you're as much of an origin mother as I could ever hope to find. Whatever I'm looking for, it's not yet another.

—Matt DeLuca

Cassandra closes her laptop.

She settles Dorothy, a compliant weeping child, into bed.

This is the night. Down to the basement, to the shelves of obsolete food storage, the neglected freezer. The stuff that was supposed to usher a family on through Armageddon toward a glorified existence on the planet Jesus was coming to restore.

A Mormon conundrum: the destruction of the planet a

given. Purging the wicked in the process, prophecy. What is the role of the righteous, then, when intervention only delays God's will? Why not hurry it all forward to divine renewal? Environmentalists are foolishly postponing the inevitable, competing with the almighty. Just make sure there's meat in the freezer, mac and cheese and soup cans on the shelves, powdered milk packaged for time and all eternity. Make sure you know how to take out an elk with a submachine gun while Jesus grinds the wicked to rubble.

Alas, Armageddon has already come and gone for the Soelbergs.

By morning the shelves are clean, the archaic freezer decommissioned. Empty cans bagged for recycling. Mason jars sparkling in rows, contents slopped in a bucket for compost along with frozen corn and brittle beans.

What to do with the meat—divided, dead and frozen for twenty years?

January 19, 2020
Hi Matt,
Good to hear from you. You're right. This is all overwhelming.

Hope you survived the new 1776. Hope you've loaded your musket.

I spent the night attending to riddance, but I don't feel one bit rid.

Dorothy is foundering. Some brick in the wall of her sunny disposition has been dislodged. She cries, all the time. Even in her sleep. I don't know how much is belated expression or how much is disintegration. In any case it's heartbreaking, and, when I'm tired, infuriating. I keep thinking I should feel something more identifiable as I watch my mother slip, but I just don't know how. Everything has been so strange since I came back here, I can't feel what I feel.

Yes, I talk about my work, but also it's what I make when I don't have the words, so it's tricky. It's just a freakish gift, some funny genetic concoction. Doesn't mean I'm not grateful. It does matter to me.

I understand your point about not wanting to look for yet another mother figure. It's all exhausting, and finding just confounds the mysteries. Then again, I don't want to be the next woman to stand between you and a mother who hopes to hold something of you. I don't know how any one of us negotiates the impossibility of return, whether or not the body appears, so I can't speak for her. I don't even know how to speak for myself.

Why does it all matter? It just does. Broken threads of love and relation are all we get. The planet is brief. I was raised to yearn for eternity, and there's plenty of that closing in on us, but I sure don't think it's going to be an endless family reunion in heavenly Disneyland. Don't know why we're always trying to take that quickness away from each other.

Sometimes I wonder if I'll know him by his drawing hand. Sometimes I think it's enough to simply recognize something in every child as my own.

Give my warmest regards to your parents if they wish to hear it. Warmer, even, to Jose. I think your child, also, will somehow find you. Maybe more than one.

Cassandra

Dorothy dodders from the bedroom, hair wild and silver, mouth a red cavern.

"Mother. I'll help you get dressed. We'll make breakfast."

"It's snowing."

"Yes. For real."

"We'll need the water."

"That's right. Good remembering, Mama."

"Cold."

"Warm in here. We'll turn on the fire. Cozy."

"He has…warm coat."

"Yes. Yours. He'll be all right, Mama. He knows the mountain."

February 2, 2020

Cassandra, my god, so sorry to hear about Dorothy. Hope you're holding up. It won't go on forever. What will you do, after all this?

I've submitted an initial piece based on my trip to Utah. It's a punt, more or less. Something about arid hills and pleasant, unreadable, peculiarly violent Caucasians. Mormon temple rites that radically reinvent family while ostensibly affirming traditional values. The discombobulating sensation of shouldering an entire epic American migration, late—of existing because a boy saw an angel.

Seriously, though. I knew the Mormon church had a polygamous past. I didn't know until some explainer dude explained it that the doctrine maintains that it's an "eternal principle." I've been reading up on that. What do you think it does to Mormon men to be taught that they'll be copulating gods with innumerable wives for eternity? That sounds like a cynical rhetorical question, but I'm really asking you. Maybe the question is too awful to contend with, and if so, I'm sorry.

I never imagined I'd be consorting with prophets.

By the way, did your parents understand that they named their daughter after a pagan prophet?

Believe it or not, I'm going to drive the Mormon Trail this spring. Jose says he will come with me. We'll see. He hates camping, so we'll shower up at a few motels along the way. Meet us for some—or all—of the trip if you can? I'm writing further installments. Don't want to tell you what to draw, or paint, but can I insinuate?

You'll never guess Jose's last name. Ferrero. I'm looking to raise a child with Joseph Smith.

Is the novel virus showing itself in your part of the world? How does that square among the saints?

—Matthew

Real snow. Hard wind—brutal enough to send Cassandra back in to sleep on the sofa. Intermittent darkness, moments of blinding white light.

Dorothy either sleeps or cries. Mostly sleeps, thank gods—for her sake even more than Cassandra's. Does Dorothy comprehend, in some arrested corner of memory, why she mourns? Is grief still painful even after the cause has sunk into the brine?

Brian's people come and go; Dorothy's semi-catatonics give Cassandra a little more leeway to work, or get out for a few hours, but the muffled, kittenish, incessant crying is impossible to tune out. Cassandra has begun to fear that her own low murmurs of comfort, chiding, reassurance, will become integral. Maybe she won't be able to close that spigot when this is over. If this is, in fact, ever, over.

It's okay, Mom. I'm here. Mama, don't worry. We're all right. Don't cry, Mom. Are you hungry? Do you want a drink of water? Look, we'll just sit right here together and enjoy the warm fire. I'm here, see? Today I'm working on a set design for the ballet. Lucia di Lammermoor. *Do you know that story? That's another woman who cries all the time. It doesn't go well for anyone, Mama, let me tell you...*

James and Paige manage weekly visits, Thursday evenings, interrupting the ambient comfort of Dorothy's musicals but what does she know anymore? Relations are terse but cordial. Paige manages to ask questions about Cassandra's "interesting" life in St. Paul. Cassandra manages to answer in passably conversational tones.

Brian's grandchildren are friendly and ingenuous. Shy but curious. They're still young enough to believe they inhabit a spacious philosophy. They admire her renderings, ask her to click through the layers and drafts on the glowing screen. Jared is spellbound by the software itself. Cassandra lets him explore commands and keystrokes. Charlie, self-appointed guide to the underworld and its fascinating guardian aunt, expounds to his cousins. Sometimes Cassandra distributes paper, and pencils or pens, or brushes and watercolor. Dorothy sits among them as they draw, and the crying mitigates for a few blessed moments. The kids ask questions, but, true to her promise to Elaine, Cassandra only answers within their circumference. She shoos them out the door when their shifts are over.

She inhabits Irene, who told her plenty without telling her very much at all.

Cassandra awakens to Dorothy wailing like a poltergeist.

Cassandra touches her way down the hall to stand at the threshold of the master bedroom.

"Mama! *Mother!*" Dorothy pleads. "Mama, I had a bad dream!"

Cassandra climbs into bed with Dorothy, pulling her close. Dorothy's fragile form heaves, wracked in sobs, and then subsides, and she sleeps.

In her father's bed Cassandra dreams that she's driving her mother in a transparent amphibious vehicle across the glittering crust of the Great Salt Lake. They are looking for Dorothy's Island. "There it is," Dorothy says, young and lucid, old and mumbling, pointing toward a tiny atoll in the distance.

Cassandra can't manage to get her there. Salt bergs float by, some with bison atop, some with coyotes. Pelicans flap along nested shorelines. Jagged ranges tear muted colors across the horizon. The vehicle dips into buoyant saltwater, submerges and then bobs to the surface, paddling like a beluga. She leans and gestures, hoping it will steer itself around half-submerged train cars, weave through pylons, but every obstacle throws the course a little further off its trajectory.

"No, that way. Can't you see it? Choose the right! Turn right, sweetheart. We're nearly there."

Sweetheart?

What the hell.

She might as well get up. She has salt bergs to paint. Sunken chranes.

February 11, 2020

Well, if the virus is here, nobody's letting on. I suspect it's making the rounds, but in Big Horn, as you well know, we suppress inconvenient truths. I read that the Clearlake ER got rushed by a couple of drive-through bandits who knew exactly where the surgical masks were stored. Pulled up, jumped out, ran through the emergency doors, grabbed the whole stash and peeled out. I think that news rattled people around here more than the contagion itself.

It's coming, though.

What do I think polygamous religious fantasies do to men and boys?

I've been thinking. Because, you know, my son was likely raised with all that. You could have been. We both know that there are a million ways to make people monstrous. Mormon kids aren't the only victims of crazy philosophies, but this one has its exacerbations. Probably the worst is the sense that there's always something more, and better, and still ahead, than what you've got. Like colonizing the West, I guess. Always something further on once the trash piles too high. Always more virgin territory to claim, so no need to attend to what—who—is already close beside you.

God, I don't want to think about this right now. Too much. And here you are, consorting with Joe Smith and a one hundred percent ineffectual Trojan prophetess. Good luck with that, DeLuca.

Mormon Trail? Jesus Christ. What are you thinking?

Maybe I'll come. I drove here from St. Paul by dropping through Colorado, maybe to avoid the associations. Maybe just because I love I-70. But the high route has its attractions.
Cassandra

Late evening, well after frigid sunset, knocking.
    Snow falling beyond the threshold.
    She knows him, instantaneous.
He resembles his mother and sisters more than his father and brothers. At a casual distance, she might have mistaken him for an aging but attractive lesbian. His stomach and hips are soft but well-tailored. The bones of his face are emphatic in the minor glow of Dorothy's porch light. Feminine nose, strong jaw.
    He's wearing a suit and tie under a down ski jacket. Parted gray hair falls wet over his left eye. He brushes it back with leather-gloved fingers. "Is your mother asleep? Can I come in?"
    "Why?"
    "Well, I'm her bishop."
    "That's got nothing to do with me. Dorothy has been asleep since dusk."
    "Please."
    "No."
    He steps back, abrupt. He turns his back to face snow-covered limestone. Toward the scene of the crime. Beyond the mountain wall.
    He turns, lips pink and puckered, like a butthole, under the single bulb of the old porch socket. "Cassandra, you need to understand. I'm not the person you think you knew. It was decades ago."
    He puts a gloved hand on the jamb.
    ...When I look in your eyes, I still go crazy...
    She could slam the door on his fingers. "You have no idea what I think."
    "My wife says—"

"Your wife? Why is there not a man in this valley who can refer to a woman by her given name? Do you mean Kendra?"

"You're interrupting me."

"You're standing at my mother's door in the night, telling me what I need to understand."

He pulls his hands off the doorjamb, maybe registering the hazard. He stomps his well-cobbled feet in the cold. Breathes out blue steam. "Cassandra, I really need to talk. I know you're upset, but it hasn't been easy for me, you know. I've been through a lot. I've worked hard for everything I have here. I've dedicated my life to serving others according to my God-given talents. There's a lot at stake that you might not understand..."

She reaches to close the door.

He tapers.

Vapor fingers grope the mountain crevices behind him.

"Okay, stay there," she says, "if you want to. I'll come out."

She shuts the door. She takes her time pulling on fleece-lined jeans and warm Minnesota boots. She reaches into the coat closet for high Midwestern down, then changes her mind and selects her mother's long replacement Sunday coat. She wraps a knitted scarf around her neck and over her head.

She reopens the door with mittened hands.

He's still standing there, a dark form arrested on her parents' serviceable porch. She could render him in one high-strung gestural line.

The same line, loosened, re-stanced, beautified: the essence of Matthew DeLuca.

She shudders and hearkens, and steps into winter night. "All right, Bishop. Let's do this interview in *my* office."

"Wait. Where's your office?"

"Right here. Utah branch. Standing room only."

"Oh. Haha." Up close, he's bigger than she thought. The bulk of middle age, subsiding to gravitational heft. "It's cold."

"It is."

He blows into his gloved hands. Shivers like an icy dog. "We could sit in my car."

"Are you serious?"

"Come on. It's not like that."

"Not like what, Bishop?"

"Look, I'm not here as a bishop right now."

"Despite your announcement when I opened the door."

"So you're still resentful after all these years. I'm sorry you didn't get what you wanted, Cassandra, but I'd think you could let it go by now. I was seventeen."

Cassandra's skull inflates like a pressure tank. Her right ear pulses in a five-tone ring. She can barely hear her own voice coming out of her mouth. "What did you just say?"

"I said, I was in high school."

"We. *We* were in high school. I was sixteen."

"That's exactly my point."

"What? What, exactly, is your point, Allan White?"

"Come on, Cassandra. Stop playing games. You and your father really thought you were going to trick me into marrying you with that sad, sad pregnancy story. He went up to my dad's office in Salt Lake and begged like a coyote. Made a complete ass of himself. Pathetic."

Pain pulses down her spine, wraps her shoulders. She can't make enough sound to tell him to go. He seems to believe he's here on God's errand.

"Look. I'm sorry I'm oversexed," he offers, "but Heavenly Father made me that way. There must be a reason. My great-great-great-something-grandfather was Brigham Young. He had twenty-seven wives. Dozens of children, populating Zion, building the community of saints against the persecution of the wicked.

"The world today tries to regulate the eternal principles of procreation, but why would Heavenly Father give righteous men in the latter days so many millions of healthy sperm and expect them to limit that power to such puny limitations? Sure, I believe in obedience to the law of the land, but men like me feel the motions of the higher law at work in our very DNA. So many valiant spirits, pleading for bodies, ready to join the fight for truth and order in these latter days."

The speech, or the temperature, causes him to stomp like a bull. He looks for a dry place to seat himself but finds none. He glances toward the doorway, somehow believing he'll be invited in to sermonize on sperm counts.

She backs herself against the wall, under the light, resisting an urge to break her own head against the brick. He resumes his chain of incoherence. Does he rehearse this stuff in front of a mirror? Among his counselors and congregation?

Does he say any of this crazy shit to Kendra? Does he believe that Cassandra is an old friend, a confidante?

"Maybe it was too much for me when I was young, before I learned to channel my urges," he explains. "But that simply makes me a more compassionate leader of young men in the church. I'm better equipped to understand what they're going through. So, sorry you didn't get what you wanted. But you could have forgiven me for that by now, had you chosen to. I've come to terms with that. I forgave you a long time ago, and I'm better for it. I suffered too, but I got on with my life."

All of this disaster, all of this horror, humiliation, loss, empty reach. "Twenty minutes for you. Nine months, and then forever, for me."

"If you really had a child, you should be happy that you gave someone a life. That's a great gift, Cassandra. The gift God gave to women. You could have aborted it, but if you didn't, that's something to be proud of. And you could have had others, you know, since you claim to be so fertile. You could have remedied your loss, but you have chosen to endlessly pick at the scab of attention and self-pity."

Snow, and strange albedo light, and dark beyond.

A pickup fishtails up the unplowed street and evaporates.

A guppy sensation in the space between her hips: paisley curlicues, deep, silent, safe, oblivious in its tight bowl beneath a beating heart, among the pulsing arteries the muscle and skin, the fleece-lined jeans, Dorothy's enfolding coat, the darkness, the snow.

The mountains, sky, the galaxy.

"You think," she says, flat, almost voiceless, "that I faked a pregnancy?"

"I don't know what you faked and what you didn't. The point is, I took care of myself. My family managed a crisis of reputation instigated by you and your father. I didn't come after you, did I? You should have taken responsibility and done the same. My father even arranged for your care while you were playing out your little—"

Cassandra's heart pounds, erratic, arhythmic.

"—in fact, he paid for it," Allan says, as if he just remembered.

She hears the blood pulse against her eardrums, deafening. She hears herself say, "Get off my mother's property."

He will not be moved. His exquisite watch moves still.

"Do you ever wonder," she breathes, guttural, "whether you'd be a different person if you'd been raised in some other world? I really want to know."

The question throws him off. "What do you mean? Like, another planet?"

"No. This one. Another way of being. Another history. Other family."

"The gospel makes it clear that our souls have existed forever, and will exist forever, the way they were made by Heavenly Father. We are the most valiant of God's spirit children, chosen to inhabit this world in the violent days of its mortal demise, to remain faithful against all odds so we may usher in the Millennium. Have you forgotten?"

"'Forgotten' is not the word. What do you remember, Allan, from way back in 1978? And what have you forgotten? I don't mean doctrine."

His features shift. The fog seems authentic. "I remember we fooled around. We were teenagers, okay? That's what teenagers do. I remember that your dad was super into me. He talked to me all the time, after I brought you home. He was a pretty nice guy, actually. Nicer than my dad, until yours got all worked up with that pregnancy stuff and—you know—tried to make my dad make me marry you."

Maybe at some other time in her life, Cassandra would have…what? Fought for her reputation? Defended her "pathetic" father? Opened the shotgun safe? Fled again? Drowned herself among the lilies? What in the world would have made one iota of difference? *This* is the hand of God? The divine plan? Then what now?

Nothing.

Pregnancy stuff?

"Here's the part I remember really well," he says. "My dad came home that night after he talked to yours. He told my brothers to teach me a lesson. They were happy to do it. They took me out to the foothills in our dad's truck and beat the living shit out of me. I'm not kidding. Sent me to the hospital. Broke three ribs. Skull fracture, here at the base."

He touches the back of his head, tender. "Don't tell me lies aren't powerful."

"Why in the world would I tell you that?"

"I'm not saying I was a perfect kid. I was like Saul, you know? God sent an angel to smite Saul on the road to Tarsus. Had to be blinded to see the light. I was on a wayward path, kicking against the pricks. I was like Alma the Younger, and my father saw to it that I was chastened. It straightened me up. I went on a mission and saw many miracles. I found my own testimony of the gospel and left my yearning for sin behind. I learned to discern the higher law, the spirit over the letter, to live beyond the dogmas, because, you know, it's a fact I can't deny: my lineage is the elect of the elect. I was born with a great calling, which is why I was tested so severely in my youth."

He stands there, a desperate strange boy in very cold darkness. The porch light lines his aging features. The Confusion Range.

She wraps the scarf around her face, biblical. "What I'm asking is, are your sons made like you?"

"My sons are willful and ungrateful. My daughter too. I sowed some wild oats, but at least I was headed in the right direction. I always believed in the gospel."

His hair is wet and thin, plastered against his pink forehead. "Willful?"

A snarl. "All—woke, and stuff—"

"Do they live here?"

"Yes. On land and houses I helped them buy. Jobs they got with college degrees, paid for by the family trust."

"How nice for them."

"Tell them that. No gratitude. It's a good thing we have two sweet, perfect daughters waiting for us in the spirit world. Their exaltation in the celestial kingdom is assured. My wife—*Kendra*—and I live for the blessings of eternity among the faithful. And my calling and election is made sure. The spirit witnessed that to me during a dark time on my mission."

"So many children in this place, lost. One way or another."

"Well, it's just prophecy. Many will fall to wickedness in the latter days. I've done all I can do. I've spread my ancestral seed as I know God commands. I'm not responsible beyond my part. I wash my hands of them all."

"All? Like, how many?"

"Cassandra, men and women have different callings in regard to populating the earth. Just look at the biology. And men have their own ways of coping with grief. After the girls died, I didn't want any more children, but I didn't want to waste my vitality. I found ways to help other people while I found the courage again to bring forth my own."

Cassandra can't wrap around this. "You mean—you—"

"Not anymore. Just a few times, after the—well, before we decided to start over again. It's not cheating. I told her about it. And it was strictly a private thing, only for people who couldn't have children, who wanted to raise righteous families. Deserving. Lots of men donate, you know. Family men with a proven record, maybe they don't want more kids but they don't feel—I don't know. Finished. Plural marriage used to be the answer to this, but for a time, in this dispensation…"

"What the hell are you saying to me? Are you completely insane? Allan, what the—?"

"It's not like I went out looking for prostitutes. I didn't have an affair. And, besides—not everyone wants to just accept any baby that pops out of the Social Services pipeline. Who knows what they'll get? People want good genes. This is all paving the way for the Second Coming. It's just a part of the prophecy that the elect—"

"How about I prophesy a little? Maybe they'll come looking for you. The hearts of the children will turn to their fathers, isn't that right? And the fathers to the children. Lest the earth be smitten with a curse."

"Yeah. More than likely they'll come back with lies and accusations. I'm not having it. People have been out to get me ever since—"

He shifts, and fortifies, menacing.

"Ever since…?" she prompts.

"You know what I'm talking about. I'm not the only one with a history. I don't need to explain myself to you, of all people. You know what my dad said to me after your dad stormed off? 'Well, at least now we know you aren't a faggot.' But young men have urges. They're easily seduced by the wiles of women. But, in the final view, the Lord made me able to multiply and replenish the earth, and he knows my heart and my purposes. Even if my wife and children do not."

"Alas. How sharper than a serpent's tooth."

"What did you say?"

The wind picks up.

"I said get the fuck off my mother's property, Bishop Allan White."

"Huh?"

"Go forth into the wilderness. Preach your loony gospel."

He gapes at her, unbelieving.

He steps down and walks into dark, a cipher in the snow.

He calls back, muffled, from the dim form of his expensive car. "Wait. What do you mean, they'll come looking for me? Who?"

"All your pretty ones."

"You've never made any sense, you know that? You're full of shit, just like your father."

She retreats into her mother's house.

She sleeps on the sofa, wrapped in Dorothy's coat.

Chapter 43

She awakens to the sound of her mother's silence. The crying has ceased.

Cassandra runs, shedding the coat at the bedroom door. Dorothy sits on the bed, wide-eyed, wild flowing hair. Stark raving naked, skin pinked with fever.

"Oh, Mama…"

Cassandra opens the window. Cold air pours in. She wraps Dorothy in a floral sheet and helps her lie back on the bed. Dorothy curls like a fetus.

Cassandra calls Brian, who says he'll call James. They're on their way.

She wraps ice from the freezer in a clean dishtowel. Dorothy has thrown off the sheet. Cassandra buttons a housecoat over her mother's nakedness. Rests ice on her forehead.

"It might be that virus," she tells James, who lives closest and arrives first. Paige clings to his sleeve.

"That's a hoax," James answers. "There's no virus. That's just—"

"Whatever it is," Cassandra snaps, "it's in her. And she got it from someone. We need to check on anyone who's been here."

"You go right ahead and do that," James answers. "You'll see that nobody appreciates your lib propaganda at a time like this."

Brian is pulling in, Elaine beside him.

"Elaine is a holistic practitioner," Paige reassures. "She'll get that fever down. Once, when Jimmy fell and burned his arm and chest in a campfire—third-degree burns, we saw it—James gave him a priesthood blessing, and Elaine applied poultice after poultice of shredded carrots. Drew the burns right out of his body. Not even a scar."

Cassandra purses her lips. Bites. Bleeds.

They crowd the bedroom. Dorothy writhes in the housecoat as if it were a straitjacket.

"Why isn't she wearing her temple garments?" James demands.

"She tore everything off. I barely got her covered before you came."

"That's just plain dangerous. She needs all the protection she can get right now."

Cassandra points to Dorothy's underwear drawer. "Be my guest."

James scowls and backs away. "I brought consecrated oil. That will be enough for now. Brian, join me in administering a priesthood blessing."

Elaine sits on the side of the tousled bed. "Mother Dorothy, do you think you can sit up? James and Brian are here to give you a blessing. I'll sit right here, next to you. You can lean on me."

Dorothy doesn't understand a word. She's so hot she's probably delirious, whatever that means in an already melted brain. James and Paige, and Brian and Elaine, work together to prop Dorothy upright. Elaine sits close against the old woman, supporting her. Paige retreats beyond the circle, relieved, but stands apart from Cassandra, as if to keep the faithful circuit pure.

Brian shoots Cassandra a look. Pleading? Apology?

The brothers lay heavy hands on the madwoman's silver head. Cassandra fears the power of the priesthood will snap Dorothy's chicken neck. She raises an eyebrow toward Brian, then stares down the rather gothic portrait of Hal and Dorothy on the east wall as Brian anoints and invokes the power of the consecrated oil.

Dorothy seems comforted, as ever, by the ponderous tones of a righteous priesthood holder. This is what James does best.

"Dorothy Eliza Caldwell Soelberg, we place our hands on your head to seal the anointing of this holy oil, and to bless you by the power of the holy Melchizedek priesthood, which I hold."

Dorothy emits mewling kitten sounds, maybe because she feels safe under heavy masculine hands. Maybe because she's struggling to hold up her head.

"Dorothy," James resumes, "I am moved by the Holy Spirit to bless you with inner peace, in the latter days of your long life and the latter days of the mortal planet, verily bound for a season of terror and destruction to be followed by renewal and celestial glory at the hand of our Lord and Savior Jesus Christ, who prepares for his return with a flaming sword to strike the wicked and unbelieving. You have suffered much, and lost many of those whom you love, yet you have remained faithful and diligent to the…"

He pauses. Even Dorothy strains to grasp the next word, the flat truth of closure: "…faithful and diligent to the…end."

The word ejects like half-tasted poison. As if the truth of his mother's approaching death is plain insupportable. It occurs to Cassandra that it's been James who has loved their mother, passionately and desperately, since the beginning. Her first child. Her original hope. The fruit of his parents' fairy-tale passions, their 1950s Mormon bougie dreams. And so, of course, the reality of him—just the simple, everyday disappointments a child delivers—the end of their fragile passions, the fall to hard earth. Expulsion from Eden.

James is obtuse, but almost impossibly uncynical. A heartfelt and unwavering believer. Maybe a fool but not stupid—and as far as his sister can discern, no hypocrite. That's a thing to marvel at. Dorothy, even in fever and oblivion, yearns after his voice, and now that there's no angry husband to rebuke her love, she revels under the hands of his likeness, a man who is exactly and only what he purports to be.

Brian stands committed, yet in their parents' bedroom, the very (only possible) site of his own conception, he remains stoic and detached. Two bewildered brothers, forever seeking the mother who never found herself. Breathless Dorothy Eliza Caldwell Soelberg, forever pursuing a father. Is family just a long sequence of unsatisfactory substitutions?

Cassandra can't bring herself into the image until she envisions Matilda bumping against the ceiling like a rugged American angel, long coat transformed into ample wings.

Four grown and aging children, asymptotic astral streaks.

Wild horses driven through the same chute and released unready.

Their mother self-immolating in viral heat.

Five women (if Cassandra counts the hovering angel) vibrant, spent, pivotal, corollary. Three men (if she counts the hovering angel) charged with the powers of a perplexing and voracious god. Old Testament, New Testament, Holy Ghost.

Why, in the name of this three-personed god or any other, would yet another child of this beleaguered band wish to be battered within it?

James emits an almost Pentecostal yelp. Paige purses her collagen lips. Elaine sways in her own quiet trance. Brian holds position. Matilda grins and bobs against the ceiling in her mother's billowing coat.

Dorothy burns. Cassandra attends.

"Mother! You have lived a full and righteous mortal life, enduring to the end. You have borne the loss of children and grandchildren with the most tender grace. You have mourned the strong and faithful husband, who now awaits you with open arms in the kingdom of heaven."

Matilda glitters and floats like a soap bubble, harmless and demonic, eyes blinking from stoplight red to yellow, to green to red, red yellow green.

"Dorothy, you have been blessed in these last months of your long life with the gift of forgetting, a balm for your troubled soul, ever grieving the in trials of a righteous mother in Zion. But I bless you now to pass into a vale of new remembrance as you reunite with the generations of the faithful, those who will compensate a hundred-fold for the absence of the unrepentant, the perverse and the stubborn, those who had eyes for this world but would not see, for those who pursued earthly prestige over the riches of heaven—"

"James," Paige whispers.

Matilda purrs, a sinuous cat wrapped around the ceiling light, dangling a languid paw. A small shudder, and low cough, from Brian.

James is undeterred. "May we not falter now in the presence of thy power and truth! Lord, fortify us in the great cause of justice! Let not our hunger for mercy overwhelm our sure knowl edge that your laws are immutable, that great nature itself rolls forward in justice, deaf to the howls of delusion and self-pity, blind to the theatrics of the doomed, the unnatural, the arro gance of the sophist philosophies of the world, the latter-day Korihors, the—"

Matthew curls a lip, baring a saber fang.

Brian, low but firm: "James, wrap it up. This is a blessing, not a curse."

Paige glances up in gratitude. Elaine sways in her own post-traumatic trance.

Cassandra steps quietly out. The paper-thin door of her childhood bedroom greets her in blank reproach. She tiptoes down the hallway, turns at the kitchen threshold, passes around the table and chairs, and steps out to the balcony, into bracing winter morning air. Purple clouds crowd the horizon above the snowy foothills. She thinks of the does in the recessed folds, under the sheltering cedar and oak, sleeping amid the warmth of other bodies, heavy with fluttering fawns.

Paige opens the sliding door and steps out in her après-ski boots. No coat; only a sweater. She moves to the railing beside Cassandra.

They watch the roil of morning clouds, more storm coming, the color of bruise tinged with pink morning sun.

"Elaine is applying essential oils," Paige murmurs.

"I hope it helps."

"She's good at this kind of thing. And she's gentle. In any case, it's comforting."

A few spinning flakes herald impending storm. Cassandra fills her lungs with wet, cold, fragrant air.

Paige: "I know you think it's—"

Cassandra: "Paige, you don't have to worry about what I think."

"I'm sorry about James. It's just that he's—"

"And, truly, no need to apologize for a man who's simply being himself."

"He's a good man. Answers to his best lights."

"I know."

"His heart is so tender he sometimes struggles to do the right hard thing."

"Mmmm."

The snow comes sudden. Heavy and thick, halting the wind.

"There's a funeral coming," Cassandra says. "Will it bring your daughter home?"

James stands at the open door, neither inside nor out.

Paige shivers. "It's cold."

"Yes."

"Will you come back in?"

"In a minute."

Cassandra watches the snow fall, cloaking the remnant of her father's orchard, entombing the toolshed.

"Did you clear it out?" Cassandra asks Brian, who now stands beside her.

"No. It's all in there. Intact. No one's opened that door since the week we brought the body out. Let the police and the coroner in to take pictures. Sprayed everything clean. Locked it up."

"That must have been terrible."

"What's not terrible, in the run of things? At least it was quick."

"Grandma used to say beauty comes from ugly. I don't know. Maybe it's just all ugly."

Brian shifts weight from leg to leg. "I don't know. Look at that pretty snow. No ugly in it."

"Until you're stranded. Slid off the highway, head in the windshield."

"You're worse than I am, little sister."

"What will you do about the shed, once Mom's gone?"

"I don't know. The house is yours. You know that, right?"

...Snow falling and night falling fast, oh, fast...

"Brian..."

"Dad left James and me the land. We sold a few years ago. All those super-nice people out there got showy houses because of it. Ain't that touching? How do you think James afforded his big house up by those people he worships?"

"I've never been there. What, did you think we've been socializing?"

"It let me pay off farm debts, which gave Elaine and me a better hold on our place out there."

"What about Matthew?"

"We put up a trust fund."

"Who?"

"Me and James, of course."

"James went for that?"

"It was his idea, mostly. We heard Matilda had—has—a kid. Maybe more than one."

"Brian, how did you hear that? Who did you hear it from?"

"Missionaries. He—she—kept her name on the church rolls. Probably didn't care enough to remove it. You know how the church keeps running after its own. Any place he registered something like an address, they took note. Haven't heard anything for a good ten years, though."

Yes.

"Did you ever hear from them? Matilda, I mean. Her kids?"

"No."

"My god, Brian. How many of us are out there?"

"I don't know."

He turns to face her. "Dad left Mom the house, of course, and the acre it sits on."

Cassandra isn't following.

Brian: "And she assigned it over to you at her death. Right after we sold the orchard."

"How do you know this?"

"I signed as witness. I should have known she was too scared to let you know."

"Too *scared*?"

"Or—you know Mom—liked to think she was clever."

"Maybe she thought I'd shove her into the snowbank."

"Haha. You got her that time."

"Brian. What the hell? Do Elaine and Paige know?"

"Uh-huh."

"And nobody's brought it up?"

"We thought you knew by now. Mom put the documents in your tacky little Barbie desk. In your room."

"Nothing's ever gonna make me open that door."

"Maybe she knew that. Maybe she thought it would be the one thing to make you do it. There's a whole lot of your old artwork in there, too. I'm hoping maybe you'll let some of the kids and grandkids pick some of it? I'd help them frame what they like. Grandma. Gardens. Really beautiful angles on the mountains."

"My god. That's just batshit crazy, Brian."

"What isn't, Cassandra? Is that beauty, or ugly? Batshit sits there right between the two, right where Mama lives."

"I have no idea who that woman is. I never have."

"Are you glad you came home to her?"

"*Glad*? What a word. Sometimes I think she gave us all up at birth, just like I gave up mine."

"No. Not just like. They took yours, Cassandra."

"Maybe they took hers, too. Some point or another, comes the taking."

Twenty feet of visibility beyond the rail. No world at all beyond the encompassing snow.

"Do you want him to find you?"

"What was it you said about batshit? Beauty and ugly. Maybe he'll come for vengeance. Maybe I get Dorothy better than I pretend."

He gazed into the swirl. Groaned a little, very small in the back of his throat. She thought he was finished, about to go in.

"I think I know him, Cassandra. I've been trying to figure out how to say this to you. Trucks family produce up from Green River. I don't have proof. You should see his truck—all painted up, looks a little like your hand. I'm not kidding. I've never said anything about it to him, or anyone, but he looks just like Matthew. Not just a little. It's like a resurrection, but he's got this funny little limp, like once he broke an ankle. Every time I see him, my gut says—"

Cassandra wheels, and flees.

Chapter 44

18 March 2020

Cassandra, I need to tell you, I've lost control of the narrative in ways that might affect you. At first I thought this whole story was about parents—maybe mothers especially—and children, and of course it is, but I understand better now what will not be contained. You told me in your mother's backyard (I checked my notes) that I shouldn't let the dry grass fool me. Plenty fertile.

Well, my god. Maybe even you might be surprised how fecund your dirty Clearlake Valley really is. There's a whole group of them—us—talking to each other online. I didn't start this, I swear. It's not just White descendants tracing each other, although we're a big contingent. It was a group of the younger ones, second generation, who set the pitch. Tech kids. Not just adopted. Some disowned, some fighting addictions, some pissed off about religion, plenty queer, a whole Big Horn shadow league. Some know exactly who they came from. Some are still foggy on their exact connections, but the genetics are telling them something. They're putting their heads together. Making maps. It's like that spirit world you told me about, relatives finding each other beyond the pale. But they're no ghosts.

I don't know how much of this you want to know. You have this way of driving over people's toes. And it's kind of a secret, so please hold it close. They don't seem to be seeking parents, necessarily, which might be why I missed the phenomenon until they sent me a link. They're looking for each other. Some are Mormon, or at least raised Mormon, or started out, like me. Some had no idea they linked to Utah or the religion at all. I just got hooked in a few days ago. I don't want to be doxxed for treason, at least not this early on. But a few of your nieces and nephews—legit, named Soelberg, from Big Horn—are in on this, so someone has a pin on your trail.

I don't know how to tell you this, exactly, but I have a lot of half-siblings, from all over.

A lot, Cassandra. One group calls themselves the Hierophants. The other ones—quite a bit younger than me and your son, who I don't think is among the group—call themselves the Cups. More Cups than Hierophants.

Think, Cassandra. I don't want to spell this out.

And yes, we look like we come from the same father, if that's the word for what he is.

I have to be honest. I'm shaken up. I didn't think any of this mattered emotionally. I kind of wish I could go back to just being Frank and Carlene's happy lonely kid. I don't know who else to talk to about this, but I don't know if you're feeling up to any of it either. I'm sorry I brought any part of this mess your way.

On another track: my genetic mother died of breast cancer in Salt Lake City eleven years ago. I know her name, and I found some photos online. She was pretty, and Jose thinks I look like her. She had several more children with the man she married. Seven, I think. Way Mormon. One of them, a sister, is on the site. She's been looking for me, all these years. Don't know if the others suspect they have a gay half-brother in Boston, but I'm not in a mood to find out, at least not yet.

It's good to be here with Jose, who sends his love. Y su mama tambien.

When—if—you feel like it—thoughts? I confess I'm yearning for a desert mother figure.
—Matthew

March 18, 2020
DeLuca, not Italian, this is why I'm a visual artist. I'm good at looking at things, but I hardly ever understand what I'm looking at. You should have thought of that before you became a writer, dumbass.
Re: desert mothers. Dorothy is on the brink. I think she has that new virus, but no one in this family believes it's real. Whatever this is, it's real, but she's eighty-six and her mind is gone, and she's been weeping nonstop for weeks, and if this is what takes her it seems almost kind. Don't mean to sound clinical. I fear I'm headed for some actual emotion after this is all over. Luckily right now it's too surreal. Her fever's broken, but her breathing is ragged and strained. My sister-in-law brings woowoo essential oils, speaks gently to her, seems comforting enough, so I won't protest. Wouldn't change anything anyway.

In a way Dorothy seems more conscious, even in her sleep, than she's been since I returned. Something vivid, like a wash cycle, saturated and churning in her mind, and in that sense she's still very much alive. Her features are clear and unmasked. Her skin is tight against the bones. It's like she's traveling back in time. I see some of the girl she was. I see her sister, and mother, and even my brothers, and myself.

I draw her as she sleeps and strains to breathe. What's the efficacy in that? No better than oils and magic stones and incantations, but it means something. Sometimes I think how I've never known her—even in her presence, she's as unreachable as I have been to my son, if that's the right word for him.

There's no word for him. He's never been mine. I think of all the people I've loved, felt kinships and affinities, shared histories. They matter. They're mine. Why do I yearn for a man I've never, ever been allowed to touch, can't picture, might fear or despise? A man who likely believes I threw him away? Why have I concocted childhood anecdotes and ER visits and talents and accomplishments and disasters for him, each year of his life? Why have I set him in forests, and colored deserts, and shorelines, and strange cities? I can't go anywhere without trying to picture him. To recognize him.

Why have I cherished the shimmer of a body made by a man who gives me nightmares, who shows up on my mother's doorstep to vindicate himself, to preach his fucked up, self-serving gospel, to call me to account? A body made of angry Soelbergs? I know one reason: part of what made him, made you too, and if you'll pardon a sentimental maternal outburst here, you take my breath away.

I don't know what the body means. Except when my mother's goes dark, something already lost will be—what? Loster, I suppose.

I was raised to believe that family awaits us in an invisible dimension coexisting with ours, that fathers and mothers, grandparents generation after generation, aunts and uncles, cousins, siblings have found one another in that place, that they rejoice in eternal relation and connection. And I was told that the unworthy would be denied access—not just kept outside the celestial gates, but severed forever. Not family anymore. I've wondered how heaven could possibly be reduced to a Social Services agency, taking and reassigning, snatching other people's babies and handing them over according to people who have filled out the right forms, who got their story straight, who went under the water in the font or let someone else do it for them, who wear the right underwear.

I don't believe in any of it, at all, anymore. I can't believe I have to think about any of it again, now, here in the carapace of my childhood home, answering to the shadow of my dead, hurt, bewildered father at every turn, nursing a mother who never rose to her own power and courage. I love Dorothy, I realize, but I never had a mother. I did have a grandmother, and whatever current flows from one woman to the next to the next is about to extinguish in the body that connects us. It's just going to go out, DeLuca.

And now, Matthew of the Light, you tell me of unsanctioned encounters—feral relations within a dimension of circuits, of tiny segments of flowing energy, bright-lit familiars on flat screens. Sounds like the freaking spirit world for real, but a realm of descendants, not forebears. Living, not dead. The spectral future, not the vampire past. And you've found each other, traced connections, made your own claims. No need for divine bureaucracy.

I was told my child was not mine to hold, and it was true. Once we get you here—doesn't matter how—your lives are your own, for worse or better and both. And you're already slipping onward, and you'll soon be gone like smoke. Get ready to hand it over, DeLuca.

One April night in 1978, which was last week and also never, I took off my goddamned pantyhose on a dark mountain. Removing a miserable synthetic barrier between my own skin and home altitude brought down the wrath of the universe. The boy who had already set you going took it as a sign, as nature's call, and somehow he rose up and up, and I dropped down, and down, and hit a World, at every plunge—you know the line, Amherst boy.

Dorothy has left me her house. An acre of stolen land below the granite massif. Shoshone homeland. Mormon kingdom. Soelberg sorrow.

How could I possibly inhabit this place?

How can I depart from it?

I almost hate her for this. What the hell.

CS

Part Six

. . .

Reunion

Chapter 45

"Cassandra! Where have you gone? Come back to me!"

"I'm here, Mama."

"Cassandra, come home!"

The moon is waxing. She opens the curtain, in case Dorothy can sense the reflected light.

Cassandra climbs into the viral bed and wraps herself around the frail wheezing form. She holds her mother until she fades.

And beyond, until she hardens.

Chapter 46

Despite their doubts, Dorothy's Big Horn children and grandchildren capitulate to the possibility of plague. There will be no service in the chapel, to Cassandra's immense relief—just a graveside gathering, a few words, a dedication. March has turned lamblike and looks to hold.

Brian's boys have made an applewood box, joined with tight teeth at the corners, the lid precisely angled and peaked above Dorothy's face. Cassandra regards it with reverence. She rides with Brian to deliver it to the mortuary, where Dorothy awaits, to Cassandra's revulsion and James's relief, embalmed.

Dorothy lies nude but modestly covered with a sheet on a gurney nearly twice her length. But for the long silver hair encircling her face like a medieval halo, she looks like a peacefully sleeping child. The mortician is kind. He knows his job. He imparts a few instructions and retreats to his office. He keeps the door open in case there are questions.

James arrives with Paige and Elaine. They stand together around the holy relic. James and Brian take a walk outside while Paige uneasily but expertly applies cosmetics to Dorothy's face, cuts and curls her hair. Cassandra does not object; she knows Dorothy wishes to greet Hal as he loves her, as she envisions herself. Elaine and Cassandra lift Dorothy's head just enough to let Paige trim the long flowing hair, to give it a mild curl. Plenty of sticky spray. The scent softens the mortuary smells.

Cassandra stands back to allow her sisters-in-law to dress Dorothy in temple clothing: symbolic underwear, long white gown, a long filmy pleated something over one shoulder. A green apron, embroidered to look like oak leaves, which Cassandra kind of admires. A veil tied in a bow under the chin, then draped backward, like a bride's, over her head.

"I know this must be strange to you," Elaine murmurs.

"Death is the right time for strange," Cassandra answers. Paige and Elaine turn together. All three break into panicked laughter.

Brian and James return with the mortician and the padded box. Brian lifts their mother in his arms, and waits while James hoists the casket to the table. Brian lays her in, as if he were putting a child to bed.

Elaine opens a box of little objects: Crayon drawings on farm stationery. A plastic army man. A tiny figure made of sticks, tied with string, wearing a glued-together floral dress. A plush bunny the size of a hand grenade. Cookies in a sealed ziplock bag. Colored stones. A real silver dollar. A deck of wallet-sized photos, awkward grinning grimacing children, variations of Goddard-Soelberg collisions.

"Cassandra, help me."

"Is this now a Mormon thing? I've never seen it here."

"It's our thing."

"Yes."

They tuck the grandchildren's gifts beneath the pillow, around the edges of the box. Brian and James step forward, lay their hands on the cold flesh of the mother's forehead after anointing.

Brian speaks simply: "Be with our mother as she takes her leave."

Cassandra braces for James, but his voice is calm in summons.

"Come for her, Hal, you old son of a gun. Make this right."

He pulls the veil over Dorothy's face.

Together, they set the lid into its perfect grooves.

Cassandra seals the latches. They lift on signal, and carry Dorothy to the hearse.

Chapter 47

She has never stood at her father's grave, here in the family plot, halfway up the east side of Cemetery Hill—a three-hundred-foot knoll that gives dead people the finest views possible within the city limits.

Irene and Lander Caldwell lie side by side a few plots up, but Cassandra can only contend with one morbidity at a time.

Her parents' headstone is largely as she pictured it: gray granite, sticking up from the still brown cemetery grass, a few icy patches. A laser-etched Salt Lake temple, complete with a tiny horn-blowing Moroni atop, rising from the large SOEL-BERG arching over the two parental names: Harold Brigham, 1932–1987. Dorothy Eliza Caldwell, 1934– (still blank but about to be chiseled in).

On the back: FAMILIES ARE FOREVER. And, beneath, in smaller letters,

"OUR CHILDREN"

James Caldwell

Brian Lander

Matthew Harold

Cassandra

"What's with the quotation marks?" Cassandra asks Paige. "Am I missing the irony?"

"Huh?"

"If they were paying for quotation marks, should have hit Matthew."

Paige drifts off.

Cars arrive in an erratic procession, parking along the fence. People spill out and peer up. The hearse pulled up forty minutes ago. The applewood box hovers over a small concrete abyss, buoyed by wide fabric straps on a crankable frame. Florist bouquets adorn the lid, some with banners that say "Mother," or "Grandma," or "Eternity," or some such, most marked with small cards indicating the sender: "Big Horn Fourth Ward Relief Society"; "Condolences from the Parkington Gang"; "Our love to the Soelberg family from the—"

James interrupts the recreational reading. "Looks like there's another funeral gathering on the other side. Who else from Big Horn died this week?"

He peers more closely, looks about to wave them in this direction, as if he recognizes someone. Cassandra looks where he's looking, up toward a few cars in the north lot. People are getting out up there, too, greeting one another and milling about. James strains to discern, as if he's scoping deer. He runs a hand through his hair, puts the hand in his suit pocket, turns to look for Paige.

Cassandra is surprised that so many people are coming out for Dorothy—a death the whole ward must have been expecting, an old woman who hasn't been out much in the last few years. Of course Brian and Elaine have stocked the herd. James's children will show, won't they? At least the ones who still live in Big Horn. Probably there are Caldwell cousins, less likely a desert Soelberg or two, and a smattering of hometown stalwarts.

The bishop, of course.

Brian and Elaine's families are spilling out of cars and pickups, even a produce van. The kids are active but orderly, slicked clean and suited up. So many! Jared waves to Cassandra from the bottom of the hill, heading in her direction. Charlie zigzags among the headstones, burning exuberance as he comes. A daughter-in-law carries little Elijah, decked out in stripy engineer overalls over a soft hoodie, pulled up to cover his head against the chilly breeze. Once they're close enough, he reaches for Brian, who mounts him on his shoulders. Elijah kicks and grins.

"Don't worry." Brian winks. "He's wearing a swim diaper."

Cassandra laughs.

Toni Fuller and a big man with bushy hair and thick glasses—must be her husband—are making their way up the hill. Several Parkington sisters, a few of their kids and husbands, including Dean, with them, and—is that Eleventh? Looks just like he did when he was five, but taller. Andraya waves. Her rough laugh carries across the early spring light.

Cassandra recognizes her namesake—Brian's youngest daughter—because Jack and Rebecca each hold one of her hands. She's very pregnant. Jack, newly buzzed, ears scrubbed clean, wears a plaid sports jacket and a bowtie, clearly enamored of the dashing figure he cuts. Rebecca, in a flannel dress and bright leggings, step in boots with fringes, pulls at her mother's hand. "Mama. That's the first Cassandra. Come see her."

The younger Cassandra looks about to comply, but she's intercepted by somebody who wants to coo and pat her stomach. Jack skips on over for compliments.

"Will you draw a picture of me like this?" he asks Cassandra. "Did you bring a paper?"

"It's a little gusty for paper," Cassandra answers. "But I know something even better."

"What is it, Aunt Cassandra?"

"I left my car at the bottom of the hill. I have sidewalk chalk. I almost forgot about it. I think we have time to walk down there before the talking starts."

Jack attracts a flock of cousins and cohorts as they weave through the enlarging host. "We have to go to Aunt Cassandra's car to get some chalk," he explains to Rebecca, who finds another cousin and takes her by the hand. Two visually identifiable

Parkington kids reverse direction as Jack hails them. He expounds as they proceed. Two more are nipping at Cassandra's heels by the time the procession reaches the car. She can see Charlie speeding in their direction like the Roadrunner.

"What are you guys doing?" he asks, breathless, and Jack says, important, "Aunt Cassandra is going to draw a picture of me in my bowtie."

"Me too! Okay, Aunt Cassandra? Look at my boots," Rebecca pleads, and now the whole chorus.

"And me!"

"And me, okay?"

"How are you going to draw us?"

"She's a real artist, you guys," Charlie says. "She can draw everybody."

"We know that," Rebecca informs him. "Everybody knows Aunt Cassandra is a artist. Grandpa said already."

"Okay, Smarty Boots. Let's go see."

"Why do you have chalk in your car?"

"Because she's a artist, remember?"

"Will you draw me on a pony?"

Faces bob into the open hatch. From up at the gravesite, it must look like Aunt Cassandra will abscond with a city of children, like the Pied Piper. She glances up the hill, shuddering at the thought of the babies it has swallowed without her help. Brian waves, laughing. She reaches in for the plastic crate filled with fat sticks of brightly colored chalk.

"Okay. Charlie's in charge of the chalk until the talking is over, all right? Jack, you can be his assistant. You'll have to help everyone be patient until it's time. Rebecca, your job is to help me remember when it's time. Find me, and don't let me forget, once the praying is done."

"And the singing," Rebecca says. "The big cousins are singing after the closing prayer."

"That right, Charlie? Are you one of the singers?"

"Uh-huh."

"So you're one of the big cousins?"

"Now I am. This year."

"How'd you lose that tooth, anyway?" she asks, nudging small bodies in the direction of the hill. "Everybody out of the hatch? Back away so I can slam it closed."

"Kicked by a filly. All of 'em were loose but this is the only one came out."

"Gaaa! How did that feel?"

"Bad. Good pony, though. I ride her now."

"Bad and good, both. Help me get these kids up the hill?"

"Come on, muppets. You know what to do."

Jack takes the other side of the chalk stash. Rebecca takes Cassandra's hand. Another girl, smaller, takes the other. Cassandra holds.

"Everybody else stay in front of us so we can keep count of you," Charlie commands.

Up they troop.

Children assemble around their respective parents, who gravitate toward their own, allowing Cassandra to compile a fuzzy genealogical map. She's never met James's and Paige's clan, except maybe one of the sons when he was a baby at the wrong time. Probably he's the one who stands alongside a pleasantly generic wife, their children almost grown themselves. The daughter looks most like James, and James in a woman's form is rather striking. She stands near a dough-faced man who must be her husband, guarding a row of awkward-phase children who look either like her or like him; they're too dissimilar to combine.

Aren't there two sons? And what about the California girl? James seems to be anticipating more. He seems agitated by the other group, above them, apart.

Toni Fuller holds her husband's hand, and he seems happy for that. Cassandra hopes they can talk a little beyond the service. A report on the after-missionary.

Andraya's guffaw erupts every two or three minutes, accompanied by another deep-throated sister and the nasal chorts of the higher-pitched siblings. Their kids are indistinguishably bucktoothed and tow-headed, all Parkington charm.

And here come the bishop and his wife. Although every car but the hearse is parked on the road below, Allan White navigates his cream-colored Lexus up the narrow drive and parks almost at the gravesite itself. He opens himself out. Kendra waits for him to walk around the back of the vehicle to open her door. She steps out, lips pursed, flushed and glaring, then gets a grip, smiling graciously at the congregants. She spots Paige with wholebody gratitude and moves to her side. James shakes hands with Bishop White, conferring, affirming the order of things.

It's time. James officially clears his throat, and the crowd falls quiet. Some sit on folding chairs set up by the mortuary. Others stand among familiars on either side. Cassandra stands to the south so she can watch traveling clouds pile up against Big Horn's snowy chest and roll over the peaks.

"Brothers and sisters," James pronounces in his best ecclesiastical baritone, "we want to thank you all for coming today to honor the life of Dorothy Caldwell Soelberg, our beloved mother, grandmother, aunt, and sister in the gospel of Jesus Christ."

Cassandra's phone vibrates in her deep coat pocket. She should have remembered to turn it off. She gives the screen a quick glance as James intones.

Coming your way. We won't start anything. Here for Dorothy. And you.

DeLuca.

She tries to be subtle as she backs away from the bodies blocking her view. The other gathering does not appear to be a funeral, exactly. There's no open grave. No casket. No hearse. Just a milling group at the upper parking lot, smaller than this one but grown in the past hour. She counts eighteen visible, gravitating up toward the old pioneer section where the knoll tips steep, and crowns. Big Horn looms behind them, a guardian.

wtf where are you?

Coming from the north. We'll turn your way at the traverse path.

ALL OF YOU?

No. They're hiking on up.

Who are they?

You know.

She puts her phone in her pocket.

James has turned the time over to the bishop, who will conduct the service.

Bishop White explains the program. It's clear he likes to be in front of a crowd, but he's also jumpy, a bit erratic. He announces the opening song, "I Stand All Amazed," to be followed by memories of Dorothy's life from each of her children, at least the three who are present at this service. A few final remarks from the bishop, that is, himself. Dedication of the grave by James Soelberg, and then a song performed by Brian Soelberg's grandchildren.

Cassandra watches two men cut away from the upper herd, coming her way on the double-track traverse. She circles around and back up the other side of the huddled crowd to intercept. DeLuca, fifty feet off, points at his phone.

We'll just come stand behind you. We're your artist friends from Minnesota, come to support you in this difficult time. Okay?

An astonishing rush of gratitude and joy. She turns back to pretend she's paying attention. She keeps forgetting that this is her mother's funeral. Nothing makes sense. The song begins. Mormons, in congregation, are terrible choral singers, and the lack of accompaniment makes it all the more painful.

"I stand all amazed at the love Jeeezus offers me…"

The phone vibrates again.

Was that the hierophant?

"Ohhh it is wonderfuull…"

The lines fade like wheezing bagpipes.

She feels them heel up behind her. She reaches two open hands behind her back, drawing two otherworldly beautiful men forward to flank her. She catches peripheral glimpses of equally striking women, one on each side. Dark-haired. Dark-eyed. Moving in a certain unison. Did Ferrero bring sisters?

"You're just here for the service," she whispers to a cleaned-up, perfectly tailored Matthew DeLuca. "Right?"

"Don't worry. I know all I want to know, and more. It's not about him."

"Um. What a boyfriend."

"I know, right?"

Dean Hansen is all perked up. Andraya titters, nudging her husband with a suggestive elbow.

The song grinds to an excruciating finish. Andraya sputters and coughs, obnoxious, to catch Cassandra's eye. Cassandra smirks like a Sunday School delinquent. She stifles a rude snorting laugh as James stands to deliver memories of Dorothy.

Cassandra can't concentrate on her brother's rambling, tearful exposition. Neither can his wife, apparently; Paige is staring at DeLuca as if trying to recall how she recognizes him. Jose smells of clean, expensive cologne; the scent makes her almost high. His hands are perfect—elegant and manicured, a stunning turquoise ring on the wedding finger, a silver cuff bracelet on his wrist to match. Black lizard cowboy boots. Where does this guy come from? Cassandra wants to swivel around and face the whole apparition of him. She wants to tell these duly assembled Mormons that Jose Ferrero himself has descended from the skies to bless them.

James descends into choking sobs for his lost mother. Paige rushes to his side, offers wifely condolences, and parks him on a folding chair. Even so she won't stop jerking her head toward

DeLuca, then up the hill, then back to the mysterious men beside her sister-in-law.

A lot of people are looking at their phones. Eyes dart up the hill toward the pioneer grove, then look away. James stands up, startled; two young women (he's right, they are beautiful) approach from the higher gathering. He smiles, amazed, and waves, and strides to greet his youngest daughter as Brian makes his way to the front.

Brian clears his throat in the microphone to test the little box speaker, and the ceremony resumes. Brian looks toward the grandchildren seated on the blankets at his feet, then takes a long gander at the summits that surround them all, drawing a long nervous breath. Even so, his presence is calming.

The men beside Cassandra lean forward to attend.

"Is that your brother?" DeLuca whispers.

"Yeah."

"Hot, for an old guy."

"Gross. Stop it."

Brian goes in. "Brothers and sisters, I'm not a man of many words, but I do want to say that my mother, Dorothy Soelberg, lived her life according to her best lights, and we're here to honor that. She loved her husband. She really did. I think she took some delight in her children even though we made her nervous. She may have been made for other things, but she never got the chance to learn what they were. She loved James first and best, and that's nothing to be resentful of. It's just a beautiful thing and that's why my brother is so broken up before you now. And I see that his daughter Laura has come up from California to be with us. Laura, how good it is to see you. I know that Grandma Dorothy is happy you're here. She would be happy to know that this day has brought you home."

Paige remains seated, erect, eyes closed.

Brian comes up for air. Cassandra recalls the powerful rise of his butterfly stroke.

"Dorothy was so young when her father died, and, as a daughter will, she loved him and craved his approval. She might be the only one here among us who knew his best qualities, who—" Brian's nervous gaze stops, abrupt, at Cassandra's peculiar caucus. He has a clear view of them from where he stands—far better than her own. He squints. His eyes open wide. His lower lip curls beneath his upper teeth, as if he's parsing a story problem.

"I had no idea there was...more than one of—you. How in the world could I..." The language drains out, a small gurgle in Brian's throat.

Does he mean DeLuca and Ferrero?

Heads turn.

The women? It's time for a better look. Girls, really. Not quite dressed alike, yet identical. Twins. Dark hair, long and shining in the spring light, curling down their backs. Silver earrings, studded in turquoise. Neat skirts, white T-shirts, jean jackets. Elaborately stitched cowgirl boots. Jose reaches past Cassandra and DeLuca to pull the far one close. DeLuca puts his arm over Cassandra's shoulder.

Brian cannot recompose. Dani, the restaurant girl, stands up and crosses over to stand beside them. They seem to know each other. Jared and Charlie follow suit, understanding something Cassandra can't interpret.

Still, they all look perplexed.

"Thank you," Brian says. "That's about right."

He can't quite find his bearings, but he intends to finish. "Folks, our mother Dorothy did the best she could, but fear got the best of her at times and she suffered for it, maybe more than anyone. She saw people she loved dearly vanish from our lives. She never found the words to express her loss and sorrow, and so she had to bear it all inside herself. Something in her just couldn't fill up, and now at the end of her long life, we need to forgive our mother for being only human. And we must gather the harvest she planted but could not reap.

"Look at all of you—most of us here stand in this warm spring sunlight, too warm, in fact, below these beautiful mountains, to remember her because she's the one that gave us life. And this life is good, for all its many sorrows, and the world we stand upon is good, and she's the one worked hardest, and maybe paid the most, to give it to us."

He throws his head like a mustang. White eyes in Cassandra's direction. And he's done. "I say this in the name of Jesus Christ amen."

Brian turns once more, despite himself, to take in the perfect twins flanking Jose. He shakes his head in wonder. And then he plants himself on the ground, on the picnic blankets, among the little children.

Silence, and confusion, among the adults. Uneasy stir.

DeLuca nudges Cassandra. "Isn't it your turn?"

Her tongue is evacuated.

She steps gingerly toward the makeshift pulpit.

Suddenly she's farsighted. Every face is blurred, but the bare scrub oak on the east mountain slopes stands out in three-dimensional focus. The skyline contour cuts unnaturally clear against billowing clouds. The iced-over reservoir on the other side: an arrested crystal heart.

She believes she can hear the tick of Brian's watch.

"I don't—"

She takes a deep breath. "My mother—"

Tries again: "I don't understand—"

Andraya, Bryant, Allan, Kendra, Cassandra—the kids from church, fallen and fatigued, cynical, frightened, secretive, worn down, wary. Damned.

The body of the mother, green satin apron, in the applewood box.

Matilda flaps the wings of their mother's coat above the ancestral firs. Matilda rolls onto her back, pointing ballet toes toward the hilltop stirring with familiars.

"My grandmother," Cassandra says into the gag stick, "I mean, our grandmother, Irene, who is buried just up there behind those beautiful people who came a long way to be among us today, taught me to love the dirt that holds us here.

"Once, after a long week of fulfilling a strange assignment at school, the week before a big event, I called my folks to see if I could get a ride home. My grandma Irene came to pick me up. I was all worked up and confused about life, as only a teenager can be, and she nearly ended it for both of us by almost running into a wandering steer on the dark road, that one that runs along the mountain and drops into town the back way."

The children lean forward, wide-eyed, arms politely folded.

"I can see myself at that time, a little. My whole life was unmapped. My whole future a big sheet of blank paper, barely sketched out. I wasn't a little kid anymore, but I sure wasn't grown up."

She pauses. Except for the children, her listeners look grim and strained. Cassandra has not understood until this moment that the worst this town has taken from her may be, simply, the freedom to tell her own story. Stories. James leans forward, ready to stand and intervene. Kendra is already standing, lips pursed, arms wrapped tight around her own body.

Cassandra won't look at them. She speaks again. "This is a story about my beloved grandmother, and what she said to me that has been ever since a sort of guide. And it's a story about the woman who made our mother, and loved her, and me, and all of us, and never put conditions on that love. That's all it is. I didn't feel very important at that age and I didn't feel beautiful and I did not know whether I would find love and relationships that mattered.

"Our grandma Irene had been through plenty of hard things. She loved a few things, very fiercely. She loved her garden and she loved the mountains that surround her hometown, which is this one, here. She loved French poetry, and poems in her own language, too. And she loved her children. She loved her daughter, who became our mother and grandmother—and to some of you, Grandma Great. She knew Dorothy's heart better than any of us ever could.

"And that night, when she was driving me home, after she almost killed me in a car and cattle crash, she pulled over in front of the city park, and she made me get out and look at the stars and the mountains and she said that I was 'perfectly marvelous,' that this earth makes beautiful thing after beautiful thing and I was one of those beautiful things, and because she was the one who said it, I believed her.

"And so, let's all believe my grandmother Irene today. Dorothy, who was our mother, and grandmother, was perfectly marvelous, and she found her joys and she found love and she deserved every minute of life this planet gave her. She loved musicals. She loved bright colors and happy endings. So, let's give her one. All you kids, here at my feet, I'll remind you that your great- and your great-great-grandmothers shout from the earth you're standing on, and they say you're perfectly marvelous, too.

"And whoever stands, or sleeps, in the grove above us, milling so mysteriously? Perfectly marvelous, and they will find their way back to us. Somehow, they are ours, and if Irene could rise up from this ground, or solidify from this air for a minute and stand among us here, she would point and call and gather us closer, because she would know you   "

Cassandra turns to face the breathtaking, vivid, dark-eyed twins.

"—and speak your names and all our relations, because she knows her own, and claims us, because she was made from this hard dirt to be a mother."

The bishop's Lexus startles everyone as the engine comes to life. Eleventh stands, grinning, at the driver's window, then steps back as the car makes a six-point turn, tight on the narrow track among the headstones. The car eases toward the street. The bishop's wife sits by James, head bowed, hands clenched.

James stands and wobbles toward the microphone, wide-eyed. Paige, without looking up or behind, pats his empty seat, inviting someone to sit beside her.

No one takes her offer, but no one steps away.

James says, "Bishop White has been called away on business. Brian and I will dedicate the grave and we'll turn the time over to Brian's grandchildren for the closing song."

James murmurs the prayer of dedication so quietly no one quite understands it's begun, and then it ends, and Brian signals the singers. Dani and Jared and Charlie join their siblings and cousins up front.

Brian sidles over to stand with his sister. "It's Goddards that can sing," he whispers. "We know it ain't Soelbergs."

He gives DeLuca frank scrutiny. DeLuca gazes back, opaque. Ferrero smiles like a good prophet.

Brian whispers to the young women as if he's picking up an old conversation. "Guess you took turns driving up with your dad?"

God be with you till we meet again,
By his counsel's guide uphold you,
"Uh-huh."
With his sheep securely fold you,
God be with you till we meet again.
"Did you know who we were?"
God be with you till we meet again,
"Not 'til just barely. Of course we knew he was adopted."
When life's perils thick confound you,
"How did you find out?"
Put his loving arms around you;
"Internet. That's who's on the hill up there. Some of us. Everyone's related, some way."

God be—

"He didn't come with you?"

"Well, he's a dork."

"He's just scared."

God be with you till we meet again.

Keep love's banner floating o'er you,

Smite death's threat'ning wave before you;

Cassandra feels her coat pocket for her keys.

God be with you till we meet again.

DeLuca takes her arm, gently. "Cassandra, it's okay."

"Get away from me. I'm not going through this again. I told you a long time ago."

"It's real. They're real. Don't you even want to know their names?"

"No. I can't. And they don't have to. It's too much to put on anyone."

She's striding down the graveled road. Bolting like the jackass bishop.

DeLuca's perfect voice rises, clear. The children's voices swell to answer his:

Till we meet, till we meet,

Till we meet at Jesus' feet.

Till we meet, till we meet,

God be with you till we meet again.

She's in her car, heaving. She's packed and ready to go. Her stuff awaits in the entry of Dorothy's sparkling clean house, but she can't see to drive. She wipes her eyes clear. She breathes herself into enough composure to press the ignition. Texts boink on the screen. The phone rings through the speakers. She turns it off.

Charlie's face at the windshield, palms on the glass.

Wide Hummel eyes at the shotgun window.

Jesus Christ.

She rolls it down. Rebecca's tearful voice. Jack's big ears.

"Aunt Cassandra, you said it was my job to remind you…"
The little girl breaks into sobs.

"Please don't go," Jack says. "They sang the song. We're ready to draw the pictures. We got the whole cement, remember?"

Charlie sidles around to her side. "Can I open the door? Will you come out?"

She nods.

"Who are those guys up there?"

"People who came to honor family, just like us."

"How do you know the Mikkelson girls? We didn't even know they were twins, isn't that funny?"

"I don't."

"Sure does look like you do."

They march her up the hill like a prisoner. Many children, every size, stand at the paved flat, where the long veteran's walk circles a bedraggled monument. A ring of flags. The chalk sits ominously on the curb, laid out in a rainbow array.

"A multitude," she says. "This is gonna take all day. Somebody better find a picnic."

"It's coming," Elaine assures.

Of course it is.

"Can we get in on this?" Andraya hollers.

"Get over here, Parkingtons," Brian answers. "We need a lawyer in here, Eleventh. Fullers, you with us?"

Cassandra approaches the children, and the chalk.

DeLuca says, "I brought you some help, you know."

"Who's their mother? How are they so beautiful?"

"They look like you, stupid. And her, of course. They speak a little of her language. *Diné*. It's amazing. They're in college up here. You have plenty of time to ask questions."

She must look to him like a terrified rabbit.

"Take it easy. Right now, we're all okay."

A granddaughter (!) on either side.

Cassandra extracts two sticks of purple chalk from the bucket, an offering.

One takes a stick with her right hand. The other with her left.

Cassandra attempts to take them in. She tries to speak, but she can't comprehend her own words. "You're—you're, in school?"

One of them answers, smiling a little. "Down at the state university."

"What are you studying?"

"Art."

"Math."

"*Math*?"

They both laugh. "That's what everyone says."

"Which…?"

"Both, kind of. I'm majoring in art, minoring in math. She's majoring in math, minoring in art. We come from weavers."

"Oh my gosh. Of course. Who painted the produce truck? Brian says it's a thing to behold."

"Our dad," they answer together.

Cassandra gapes, stupid. "Is he…do you…"

They wait her out.

"Do you like him? I mean, is he good to you? Is he kind to your mother? Did he have a good life? So far?"

DeLuca touches a flat warm hand to Cassandra's shoulder. Jose gives the girls a wide grin. "You got her now," he says.

"Yeah. We like him. He works too hard. He's always worried about us."

"He had a hard childhood. Not terrible. Just—you know. Regular things. Out in the country. Farming. Religious."

"Is he, still?"

"In his own way. Not how he was raised. He says God is the desert. And mountains. His folks—our, um, grandma and grandpa—took it hard for a while. They wanted him to be some-one important in the church. But they eased up. They want us near."

"He's their only child."

"We have a brother, too. Couple years younger than us. He and Dad want to meet you, but they have to work themselves up for it. We had to talk our mom out of coming up here with us. We wanted to check things out first."

"She's easy with people. She's a teacher."

"Once we figured out the connection, we could see how much our dad looks like Brian Soelberg. We've been selling melons at his stand up here forever."

Cassandra forms her words carefully. "Brian says he looks even more like our brother Matthew, who's—not here. Brian says your dad limps a little bit. What happened to him?"

"Fell off a packhorse up in the Book Cliffs when he was seven. Broke his leg 'all to hell,' he says. Healed shorter than the other one."

Cassandra has one more question in her. "Why did everyone come here, today?"

"None of us had met in person. Just online. We did one of those genetic things a while ago. We wanted to know where our dad came from. He said it didn't matter to him, but we know it kind of does. And then we knew Matt and Jose were coming out for the funeral. So we decided—some of us—that your mother could be the reason for our first Big Horn Outcast reunion."

"And, besides, we knew you would be here. Matt told us your name, told us to look up your work. We couldn't believe it."

Cassandra holds her eyes on their stunning faces, as long as she can bear it.

"Okay, I have to stop talking about this for a little while. I'm—this—we…"

Dani waves from the background. Laura and her beauti-ful partner stand near her, chatting and pointing out Big Horn visions. Jared looks ecstatic, almost grown up among them, on the verge of his own destiny. Cassandra runs her vision on up the cemetery hill to its crest, to the milling, chattering, pulsing vitality among the old pioneer dead.

"No. Not outcasts. You are *not*. I've spent my whole life, any part of it that mattered, yearning for you." She can't pull her eyes away. "All of you."

Cartoon voices: "Aunt Cassandra!"

"Please? You promised!"

"It's time to draw the pictures!"

Cassandra jumps to. "Okay, first we draw Grandma Great, all right? Here she comes, in all her glory. If you look closely, you'll see how you each resemble her in your very own way."

The children lean together, circling, compelled.

Crazy Dorothy appears, life-sized, full bouffant, earrings, Sunday dress, lipstick, arms open wide to embrace them all. Cassandra plants Dorothy's feet in tall olive-green irrigation boots. "See? She does belong here."

"Hal too, beside the crazy lady," Brian whispers over her shoulder.

Hal comes as well, big shouldered, not smiling but looking pleased. He holds a framing hammer, as if he's about to make something.

"Now, each one of you can lie on the sidewalk, and we'll trace around you just right, and then we'll fill you in.

"We can do some ponies and dogs.

"Bikes? Sure. Orangutan? Yeah, okay. Anyone who wants to be family today, throw yourself down. Except the artists. Everybody brace for contact. We're taking our chances."

Jack and Rebecca lie on the concrete, giggling.

"You talk funny," Rebecca says.

Brian arranges a tiny engineer between them, then stretches on his back, himself, arms extended. "Me too," he says. "Elaine, come on over here. Show these snappers how it's done."

"Trace Brian twice," Cassandra says to a beautiful math (or art) major beside her. "Put your dad in there for me."

"Try not to pee, 'Lijah," Rebecca urges.

Chalk scrapes along veteran's memorial concrete.

"Watch, some cop's gonna show and bust us for graffitiing."

"We'll call it a flash mob. Performance art."

"Yeah, Big Horn goes for that."

Kendra stands with Paige, murmuring.

"You gotta take this one lying down, ladies," DeLuca says. "What's a dirty dress when you're about to be immortalized?"

"Chalk's not immortal."

"We'll take pictures."

Paige eases herself into a sitting position, then rolls back like a swimmer. Jose takes Kendra's hand to ease her down, gentle. James towers above them, then drops to his knees. "Lemme get between you two. Cassandra, make me look good."

The cousins giggle at the perfectly marvelous indignity of everything.

Elijah's wide blue eyes reflect the sky.

. . .

A gardener, writer, mother, wanderer, and heretic, Karin Anderson is the author of *Before Us Like a Land of Dreams.* Her work has appeared in *Dialogue, Quarter After Eight, Western Humanities Review, Sunstone, Saranac Review, American Literary Review,* and *Fiddleback.* A former professor of English at Utah Valley University, she has been nominated for a Pushcart Prize and holds degrees from Utah State University, Brigham Young University, and the University of Utah. She hails from the Great Basin.

Torrey House Press

Torrey House Press publishes books at the intersection of the literary arts and environmental advocacy. THP authors explore the diversity of human experiences and relationships with place. THP books create conversations about issues that concern the American West, landscape, literature, and the future of our ever-changing planet, inspiring action toward a more just world.

We believe that lively, contemporary literature is at the cutting edge of social change. We seek to inform, expand, and reshape the dialogue on environmental justice and stewardship for the natural world by elevating literary excellence from diverse voices.

Visit www.torreyhouse.org for reading group discussion guides, author interviews, and more.

As a 501(c)(3) nonprofit publisher, our work is made possible by generous donations from readers like you.

Torrey House Press is supported by Back of Beyond Books, the King's English Bookshop, Maria's Bookshop, the Jeffrey S. & Helen H. Cardon Foundation, the Sam & Diane Stewart Family Foundation, the Literary Arts Emergency Fund, the Mellon Foundation, the Barker Foundation, Diana Allison, Karin Anderson, Klaus Bielefeldt, Joe Breddan, Casady Henry, Laurie Hilyer, Susan Markley, Kitty Swenson, Shelby Tisdale, Kirtly Parker Jones, Katie Pearce, Molly Swonger, Robert Aagard & Camille Bailey Aagard, Kif Augustine Adams & Stirling Adams, Rose Chilcoat & Mark Franklin, Jerome Cooney & Laura Storjohann, Linc Cornell & Lois Cornell, Susan Cushman & Charlie Quimby, Kathleen Metcalf & Peter Metcalf, Betsy Gaines Quammen & David Quammen, the Utah Division of Arts & Museums, Utah Humanities, the National Endowment for the Humanities, the National Endowment for the Arts, the Salt Lake City Arts Council, the Utah Governor's Office of Economic Development, and Salt Lake County Zoo, Arts & Parks. Our thanks to individual donors, members, and the Torrey House Press board of directors for their valued support.

Join the Torrey House Press family and give today at www.torreyhouse.org/give.